ONE WORLD TOWER

Also by Michael Vetter

Run Before the Rain—An Antediluvian Adventure

ONE WORLD TOWER

A BABYLONIAN ADVENTURE

Michael Vetter

iUniverse LLC
Bloomington

ONE WORLD TOWER
A Babylonian Adventure

iUniverse books may be ordered through booksellers or by contacting:

iUniverse LLC
1663 Liberty Drive
Bloomington, IN 47403
www.iuniverse.com
1-800-Authors (1-800-288-4677)

Because of the dynamic nature of the Internet, any web addresses or links contained in this book may have changed since publication and may no longer be valid. The views expressed in this work are solely those of the author and do not necessarily reflect the views of the publisher, and the publisher hereby disclaims any responsibility for them.

ISBN: 978-1-4917-1835-3 (sc)
ISBN: 978-1-4917-1836-0 (e)

Printed in the United States of America.

iUniverse rev. date: 12/28/2013

To my mother
Peggy Vetter—*Girl Reporter*

Cush begot Nimrod; he began to be a mighty one on the earth.
He was a mighty hunter before the LORD; therefore it is said,
"Like Nimrod the mighty hunter before the LORD."
And the beginning of his kingdom was Babel, Erech,
Accad, and Calneh, in the land of Shinar.

Genesis 10:8-10

Now the whole earth had one language and one speech.
And it came to pass, as they journeyed from the east, that they found
a plain in the land of Shinar, and they dwelt there. Then they said to
one another, "Come, let us make bricks and bake them thoroughly."
They had brick for stone, and they had asphalt for mortar.
And they said, "Come, let us build ourselves a city, and a tower
whose top is in the heavens; let us make a name for ourselves,
lest we be scattered abroad over the face of the whole earth."
But the LORD came down to see the city and the
tower which the sons of men had built.
And the LORD said, "Indeed the people are one and they all
have one language, and this is what they begin to do; now
nothing that they propose to do will be withheld from them.
Come, let Us go down and there confuse their language, that they may not
understand one another's speech." So the LORD scattered them abroad
from there over the face of all the earth, and they ceased building the city.
Therefore its name is called Babel, because there the LORD
confused the language of all the earth; and from there the
LORD scattered them abroad over the face of all the earth.

Genesis 11:1-9

ACKNOWLEDGEMENTS

A valuable team of friends and family helped make *One World Tower–A Babylonian Adventure* an enjoyable journey for me as an author. I am indebted to many readers for offering sincere and constructive feedback about the first book. It was a wonderful learning experience.

I was excited to see how Brian Weaver would interpret *One World Tower* in his characteristic style of artwork. From his first sketches of a cover and illustrations, he captured the suspense, action, and technical character of the story. We share an interest in quirky, fun, retro images of technology. Thank you, Brian, for your talented contribution!

Thanks also to Jeremy Montano for his editorial reviews. I appreciate his insightful comments and suggestions about characters, timelines, and sub-plots in the context of Young Adult (YA) fiction. Nadine Lahan deserves special mention for reviewing the entire manuscript twice and raising many thought-provoking things that never occurred to me. Ray Toomey reviewed the story with an eye toward its use of a biblical background. We've had several discussions speculating about what revelation God gave about Himself to people between Noah's Flood and the time of Abraham. Ray's insights and teaching of the Bible continue to be a source of encouragement to me.

Several friends reviewed early manuscript versions that contained way too many of my awkward sentences, plot disconnects and inconsistencies, and arcane word usage. Don Dyer, Lori Gallo, Nancy Kraczyk, Jennifer Mitchell, and Steve Routhier patiently suggested changes that were a great help. Of course, the resulting content—with some remaining tangled sentences and esoteric technical terms—is mine alone.

I chose iUniverse as a self-publishing company because they offered a streamlined and painless way to get my work into printed and digital forms. Hope Davis led me through the submission process again and proved to be a gem of a coordinator.

My wife, Mary, is worthy of another gold medal for putting up with my bouts of solitude when particular chapters had to be captured before they were lost in the distractions of daily routine. I cannot thank her enough for allowing me the space and time to gather my thoughts and put them into writing. I promise a vacation someplace warm before the next book!

PREFACE

As a sequel, *One World Tower* benefited from many sincere critiques of *Run Before the Rain*. My writing style, plot development, and character portrayal have evolved, for the better I think, from my first work of fiction.

One World Tower is an adventure story set in the post-Flood civilization that is mentioned only briefly in the Bible. I am a proponent of the verbal, plenary inspiration of the Bible. My goal is to write nothing in this story that contradicts explicit facts or doctrines in Scripture. Bible characters such as Noah, Shem, Japheth, and others are mentioned for background purposes only. The main characters, with the exception of Nimrod, are entirely imaginary.

Little is known about Nimrod, the city of Babel, or the tower that carries its infamous name, beyond a few verses in Genesis chapters 10 and 11 which are quoted in their entirety in the Epilogue. All other information: an approaching asteroid, the triumvirate of world rulers, the giant steel tower, vapor engine technologies, and mechanical computing are all imaginary and not found in the Bible.

I needed a threatening worldwide catastrophe to draw my characters around a common, dramatic theme before the miraculous confusion of languages which they could not have anticipated. NASA's Near-earth Object (NEO) Program offered a rich, modern-day source of technical material. The probability of an asteroid or other space object hitting earth is so infinitesimal that nobody other than planetary scientists give it a second's thought. However, if NASA were to announce that a giant NEO was on a collision course with our planet, how would people react to this news? In the Gospel of Luke, Jesus ended a parable with a rhetorical question about His

Second Coming: *". . . when the Son of Man* [Jesus Christ] *comes, will He really find faith on the earth?"* (Luke 18:8)[1] The implied answer: "Probably not." When told of a certain, imminent, cataclysmic event, most people will face eternity with a response much like that in Noah's day. The Gospel of Matthew predicts that Jesus' Second Coming will find mankind in festivities up to the last minute: *"But as the days of Noah* [were] *so also will the coming of the Son of Man be."* (Matthew 24:37) Against all other influences from the world's system, a few will be encouraged by II Peter 3:7-14 and live their lives on earth in peace as they look upward for deliverance.

I am not aware of other speculative fiction aimed at a young adult (YA) audience that weaves imaginary, futuristic technologies into the context of otherwise historical, biblical events. Because I am an engineer and a student of the Bible, I find the combination to be a plausible one. I am also a young-earth creationist who believes that the Bible is literally true.

My goal in this and other books in the series is to present unusual fictional adventures from a God-honoring Christian worldview. I believe that an adventure novel can be exciting, enjoyable, intriguing, mysterious and even have dark elements of evil without being sexual, explicit, vulgar or occult. Whether you call this *science fiction, speculative, retro-futuristic, paleo-futuristic,* or *steampunk,* the juxtaposition of sometimes whimsical technologies in ancient Biblical settings grabs the young reader's attention and imagination.

---

[1]   References in parenthesis cite the book of the Bible (NKJV) and the chapter number:verse number.

PROLOGUE

In the beginning

A dark, infinite void suddenly welcomed something that never existed before. Time and space became a universe where before there was nothing to distinguish between forward or backward, up or down, yesterday or tomorrow. The Creator spoke and the vast nothingness was instantly filled with light, which was followed the next day—a "day" now held special significance—by the formation of material objects using only His spoken word.

The Creator's infinite attention, everywhere present, focused on a small, watery sphere that only a short time before did not exist. He held it suspended in the heavenly expanse of space. A sequence of equally sudden and miraculous events followed in bursts of time after the appearance of the blue sphere: places on the object were bathed in alternating periods of light and darkness as the ball rotated evenly; thin white clouds of visible water vapor partially obscured the liquid surface; between patches of white that covered the water, irregular brown features of land revealed themselves; the many-shaded terrain was soon spotted further with verdant green. Viewed from a far distance, the colorful planet spun slowly in a gentle path around its brilliant light source. A small, grey-white ball accompanied its larger neighbor in a close orbit held tightly by an invisible force. The larger globe, called Earth, was the center of the Creator's attention. He spoke often and intimately with special creatures He had placed in the garden home He created for them. He named the man *Adam* and the woman *Eve,* and they called Him *God.* With a smile, the Creator pronounced all of His creation good. Too soon thereafter, the man and woman turned from Him to seek their own independent journey that would define their offspring's sin-cursed history on the planet.

The small blue, white, brown, and green sphere was not the only substance in the infinite heavens that sprang into existence with the Creator's spoken word. There were innumerable other worlds, large and small, hot and cold, brilliant and dark that filled in space for trillions of miles around the home of God's special creatures. None of those distant places supported living beings.

The limitless Creator knew every star, planet, and spinning rock with such intimacy that He gave each a name and cared for them all without neglecting any. One small, lonely object formed from nothing on the fourth day of creation like all others began as a blob of pure, white-hot iron. Over time it cooled into a perfect sphere in the weightlessness of deep space. The silent object, billions of miles from earth, went unnoticed and forgotten—or so it appeared.

One thousand eight hundred years later

The liquid glow of the perfect iron sphere had long since cooled to darkness. Down to its core, the sphere reached the temperature of the frozen emptiness surrounding it. Its surface became slightly pitted after centuries of collisions with bits of debris, and yet the iron retained an overall mirror-like sheen in spite of those imperfections. Alone in space, it seemed purposeless.

The metal sphere was different from all others in the universe. First, it was held motionless by the Creator's invisible, omnipresent power. Like all heavenly objects, it was subject to the natural sway of gravity exerted by the nearest stars and planets, however this object was miraculously held against those forces that tried to shove it into motion. This special object, fifty miles in diameter, was the largest mass of pure iron ever created and it patiently waited for God's instructions.

Its God-given name was known only to Him. The object's human discoverer on earth would call it *Asteroid*. It was suspended in space until events, known only to the infinite mind of the Creator, reached their predetermined intersection with the arc of human life. The entire surface of earth had only recently been engulfed by water. A wide belt of bright blue, brown, and green formed around its girth, and caps of white ice and snow now covered each end of the sphere. Three centuries after Noah and his family stepped onto dry earth from a wooden ark, humankind had multiplied again in great numbers. All but a few had forgotten or ignored their Creator. It was time to remind them.

Asteroid moved imperceptibly. The metal sphere was pushed by a supernatural force that accelerated it toward a distant, empty point in space. It would take time for it to reach a speed of hundreds of miles per second. Its Creator carefully guided it through the heavens.

In time, one person on earth would notice that the shiny speck moved differently among the stars and planets in the night sky. It would take meticulous study of its motion to discover its astonishing significance. What would the inhabitants of earth, the jewel of God's creation, do when face-to-face with a test that threatened the course of all life on earth? Who would they turn to for help?

BOOK I

The Asteroid

1800 A.C. (After Creation)

*Is not God in the height of heaven? And see the highest
stars, how lofty they are! And you say, "What does God
know? Can He judge through the deep darkness?"*
Job 22:12-13

*For by [Jesus Christ] all things were created that are
in heaven and that are on earth, visible and invisible,
whether thrones or dominions or principalities or powers.
All things were created through Him and for Him.
And He is before all things, and in Him all things consist.
And He is the head of the body, the church, who is the beginning, the
firstborn from the dead, that in all things He may have the preeminence.*
Colossians 1:16-18

CHAPTER 1

New Babel, One World Tower—Luminary Ascender

The machine was safe, or so Pele said, but it had never been tested. Larger, heavier manned devices had been carrying freight for months, but they had never made it to the top non-stop. This was the passenger model—small, sleek, richly upholstered—built to carry royalty in lavish comfort to new heights. It would be the only one of its kind, therefore this machine had to be well-tested before it entered service.

The Luminary ascender capsule's first non-stop test would take it to the top of the One World Tower in a single passage, four times higher than anyone had ever ascended on a single cable of alloy. Dov had already volunteered for this test when Magus, Babel's chief magician, threatened Dov's father, Pele, with imprisonment if a member of the engineer's family did not successfully pilot the capsule to the rooftop to demonstrate its safety. By official decree, no member of the royal or priestly families would ride on the Luminary capsule unless it was proven absolutely safe.

Accidents had plagued other enclosed capsules ever since the bulky freight ascenders began carrying workers and supplies as high as the 51st Commoner level portal. The freight ascender machines were avoided by tower workers after a string of mishaps caused capsules, overloaded with freight, to plummet down their shafts and smash into the sub-basement engine room. Careful investigation of the accidents revealed that failure to obey loading instructions or operating parameters had caused those disasters. It was human nature to distrust the new vapor engines that lifted the capsules inside the sleek, modern tower in New Babel; the multiple, mile-long tempered iron cables that suspended the heavy capsules in the partially enclosed tubes were viewed as threats to everyday business. Because of his distrust, and the potential danger to Luminaries, Chief Magician Magus tightly regulated use of the ascender machines. The designers and engineers were compelled to place the lives of their own family members in any jeopardy, as test subjects, to guarantee the ascender's safety.

Dov, himself a graduate of the School of Japheth, was very familiar with capsule and vapor engine theory, but this trip was different from the others. Freight ascenders were sturdy, bulky workhorses that shuttled workers and building materials in alternating phases through the three tower portals to eventually reach the rooftop one hundred and twenty levels above the streets of New Babel. These heavy-duty ascenders carried massive loads suspended on multiple lifting strands, but they never lifted higher than forty or fifty levels at a time. Workers and materials had to be offloaded at intermediate portals, where they transferred to another ascender that lifted them to the next portal level until they reached the roof. The new Luminary passenger ascender would make the trip non-stop between the ground and the 120th level on the roof. The small capsule was suspended on one continuous strand from a drum coil in the basement that turned with power from its dedicated vapor engine, over the turning pulley on the roof, and down to the top of the lightweight passenger ascender. Technically, the single strand upon which the entire weight of the ascender depended was made of many smaller threads of tempered alloy. It was very strong, with a one hundred percent margin of safety, but it needed to be proven safe enough that the designer's life could literally depend on it.

Dov's twin sister, Yanis, was at the ground controls of the ascender located in the basement. Also a graduate of the School of Japheth, she was a mathematician who much preferred to manipulate the master controls of the ascender engines and leave the feats of daring and bravery to her brother.

"Remember to take it slow," cautioned Pele as he stood beside the controls and gave last-minute instructions to Dov and Yanis. "You've made flights before in freight capsules, but this one's much faster and lighter. You'll experience some turbulence in the ascender tube. The motion and any vibration should be manageable, if you go slowly."

Dov casually adjusted the helmet and gloves that his father insisted he wear in the event the ride was rough. He wasn't concerned about air turbulence inside the dark, enclosed tube up to the 51st level. It was between the 51st and 102nd levels, where large segments of the tower were still unfinished, that would be a problem. Partially built sections of the tower showed an exposed network of alloy girders, some already showing rust, where exterior masonry walls had not yet been built. Various levels of the interior were open to the outside and other levels were partially finished. The Luminary ascender tube was built separately from the rest of the residences and gaps still existed where the tube was only half-built and opened to the outside. This was because Magus, who controlled the One World Tower project, had decided to stop work on the tower's non-essential features to concentrate on finishing the upper Luminary floors reserved for New Babel's most elite residents.

"What if there are severe crosswinds in the open region that make the capsule hit the sides of the tube?" Dov asked. In spite of his show of optimism, the young test engineer wasn't sure what to expect. "I can only speculate," his father cautioned. "Winds around the tower, especially at great altitudes, can swirl unpredictably. Still, it's early morning and there shouldn't be strong cross currents. If you feel the capsule moving side-to-side too much you can stop and wait for gusts to diminish. If the motion is excessive, descend to the control level and we'll run the test again another day. I'll recommend that Magus authorize wind barriers in the open levels to protect the capsule before it can carry royal passengers. I doubt that he'll approve that, but he might if I told him it would make the Luminary ascender safer."

Dov and his father walked away from the control station to where the polished silver capsule was docked nearby. The Luminary ascender was decorated inside and out as a royal transport capsule. It was the size of a walk-in closet, with room for five people plus the operator in his partial enclosure. The round glass windows, of this otherwise rectangular box, were trimmed with polished gold; black and red velvet fabric—the colors of New Babel—decorated the walls. Four golden oil lamps illuminated the interior.

Dov stepped over the sand bags on the floor that simulated a full passenger load, looked over the familiar controls that he had used many times before in shorter test ascents and waved to his father and sister. He closed the protective door looking as confident as he could. As the might of the ascender's powerful vapor engine roared in the distance, Dov engaged the clutch of the speed control lever and the capsule lifted him on its journey to the top of the highest man-made structure in the world.

He leaned back against the support railing in the tight operator's enclosure and watched through a small opening in front of him for level indicators painted on the inside wall of the tube. A lamp above his head lit the numbers passing in quick succession before his eyes. His capsule sped upward at a rate of more than one level every two seconds. The vapor engine noise disappeared after the 10ᵗʰ level, and vibration was minimal. When he neared the 51ˢᵗ level he tensed for the transition out of the dark, partially enclosed tube and into the open air of parts of the unfinished Guild and Ministerial levels that were sandwiched between the nearly-finished lower Commoner and upper Luminary regions. He would not have a level indicator display in this part of the structure, but he could judge his altitude by looking outside as the levels raced by. His ears popped when he left the contained pressure of the tube.

Dov eased the clutch pressure to slow his ascent, and he felt for gusts of wind. Within seconds, he heard a deep, oscillating hum. He saw workers on the girders look at him as he rushed upward. The capsule swayed sharply to one side, and Dov heard the alloy strand hit the tower's structure and then jerk taut. The smooth upward motion changed to one that alternately slowed and accelerated as the capsule departed and reentered levels that were exposed. Dov continued to slow his speed with the clutch. Suddenly, he came to a violent stop. No sooner had he taken a breath, than he was momentarily lifted off the floor in near-weightlessness. Dov clung to his controls as he felt the ascender capsule drop in a free-fall.

When the capsule slammed to a halt after a one hundred-foot drop, Dov put his weight on the foot brake to keep from dropping further and set its locking latch. Praying that the latch would hold, he climbed onto the operator's divider bar, opened a hatch in the ceiling, and inspected the alloy cable above him as far up as he could see. It was still straining under the ascender's weight, so the problem was with the vapor engine below and probably with the take-up reel for the cable in the basement. That didn't make it any less dangerous, but it gave him a better sense that it wasn't a broken cable that caused the momentary drop. A cable break would have sent him to certain death.

He pondered what his next move would be if he had to evacuate the capsule. At least he was in the tower's partially open area and not inside the constrained ascender tube, where escape would be impossible. He waited for the engines below to resume lifting him. He grew more nervous as the minutes passed. He could climb out of the capsule and descend the girders to a freight ascender portal, as the metal and stone workers did, but that was his last resort. Only slightly more feasible was to lower the capsule manually with the floor leveler wheel but that would take all day. Ten more long minutes passed before he heard the cable strain against the foot brake. He slowly released the brake and engaged the clutch, and his ascent resumed. Whatever had happened had been corrected, and either his father or his sister had re-engaged the power to the cable.

When he left the open air and entered the enclosed shaft again at the 102nd level, the relative silence was a welcome relief from the bumping and humming noise caused by the wind buffeting his craft. He slowed the ascent to a crawl and watched the level indicator on the tube wall gradually approach the 120th level. He stopped short of the final mark and used the leveling wheel to bring the capsule even with the floor of the tower exit area. After securing the foot brake with its latch, he opened the door, walked through the roof lobby, and stepped out onto the windswept rooftop promenade. His knees were unsteady but he wouldn't admit it to anyone.

The bright sunlight and brisk wind were expected, but the view of the cities of Old and New Babel below him were surprisingly spectacular. Across the Euphrates River in Old Babel, the most prominent building on the skyline was the Ziggurat of Marduk. That old stone structure, and all the apartment and office buildings around it, were diminutive compared to the dominating height of the One World Tower, encircled by other modern buildings of New Babel and wide streets that radiated out from the tower at its center. The iconic structure was encircled by a wide plaza large enough to contain the quarter-million population of the two cities. Apart from a few hundred families who defied King Nimrod's edict against leaving the cities without his permission, this was the concentrated epicenter of earth's civilization. The One World Tower symbolized mankind's supremacy on the earth and his reach for the heavens!

Nearby construction workers stared at Dov in his strange uniform with a mixture of envy and resentment. His historic first ascent had been completed in ten minutes, not counting the delay. When all the modifications were made to the capsule mechanisms and enclosures, trips from the crowded streets of New Babel to the tower's luxury suites would take less than five minutes. Pride in this engineering marvel prevented Dov from noticing the undercurrent of resentment in the faces of workers against the privileged few who enjoyed the benefits of their positions at the expense of others.

After admiring the view, Dov navigated the capsule down at a measured pace, for he knew that the descent phase of his journey in the capsule could be more dangerous than the ascent. He tried to use the foot brake as sparingly as possible to prevent overheating. Passage through the open air sections of the tower was uneventful, and when he came to a stop in the machinery sub-basement docking area he breathed a sigh of relief.

"Congratulations!" Pele greeted him with a warm embrace and smile of relief.

"It took longer than I thought, but I have a good idea of what to expect now," Dov said as he removed his helmet. "What happened with that stop?" Dov asked his father. "I assume there was a problem with the vapor engine."

Yanis answered her brother before Pele could say a word. "It was the winding drum that slipped and unwound before I could engage the emergency brake. I tell you, my heart nearly stopped when I heard that drum spin in reverse before I could slam it to a stop."

"So I must thank your fast thinking for saving my life?"

"Of course you must," she demanded playfully.

"Then thank you, Sis," he replied with a gallant bow.

"And I expect you to return the favor at the first opportunity," she added.

Dov rolled his eyes and turned to his father. "The capsule fell about ten levels before it stopped. I didn't have time to think either. It was a rough time, but thank the Lord, and my sister, that it stopped before it gained too much speed." Dov surveyed the capsule resting on its cradle.

Pele was pleased with the test run in spite of the drum problem. "This was the last ascender milestone before the Luminary level can be finished and opened for occupancy. All of us, but especially your uncle Jengo, will be pleased when the tower project is finished and we can leave Babel. When our work on the tower is finished I've been told that there will be nothing to keep us in this wretched city."

**Dov clung to his controls as he felt the
ascender capsule drop in a free-fall.**

CHAPTER 2

Old Babel, Ziggurat of Marduk

Evina wrapped her shawl around her shoulders and walked from her bedroom in the ziggurat, along a dark marble hallway, and up a wide flight of stairs. At the end of the stairs stood the main altar of the ziggurat, where she knew her father was preparing for the noon offering to the sun-god Shamash. Evina was the only daughter of Zidon, High Priest of Marduk. This morning, Old Babel looked more crowded, noisy, and dusty than when she saw it the night before. King Nimrod's tower, which loomed in the distance, was perpetually busy with activity above the smog of the city. Having worked in her observatory all night, Evina had slept fitfully through the morning and awoke just before noon. She had to tell her father about a possible new threat to the city. He would know what to do.

Before she entered Zidon's private robing room next to the altar entrance area, she noticed her brother, Arvid, waiting impatiently in the attire of a priest in training. From the sound of voices through the doorway she could tell that attendants were dressing her father.

"You look surprised, Evina. Did you come here to see me?" Her brother's sarcasm always annoyed her; something at which he had become adept. Arvid and Evina shared their father's thin facial features with dark-rimmed eyes and, like their father, they were taller than the average Babylonian. Physical resemblance was all they had in common. He was five years older and intensely jealous of her abilities in astronomy and numerology. She meticulously studied details of the heavens, while his garrulous personality thrived in crowds among which he used his position as son of the high priest to his personal advantage. Arvid lived in his father's prominent shadow and his brilliant sister outshined him in every capacity. Unable to achieve anything through hard work or talent, he nurtured a seething ambition to replace his father one day as high priest through guile and deceit. He swore that he would do *anything* to become the next high priest.

"I came to speak with Father. I'll wait here until he's finished dressing." Evina turned her back on Arvid's smug smile and gazed at the crowds assembling for the noon ceremony. She wondered about the thousands of people gathering on the temple promenade and its surrounding terraces in anticipation of today's supposed new revelation from the sun-god Shamash. Babel's culture of all-consuming idolatry caused Evina to expel a weary sigh. The population hung on daily announcements from the priests reminding them that the planets and stars controlled their individual fates. She could feel her brother's eyes on her back but she refused to turn around and face him. What she had to say was for her father's ears only. She would gathered her thoughts while she waited for him to finish dressing.

When Zidon emerged from the preparation room, his erect, aristocratic frame was draped in golden vestments that reflected the sunlight and reinforced his authority for the daily revelation from the sun-god. His made-up face was composed of thin, fleshly lines—reddened lips that barely contained his mouth, painted eyelids and eyebrows above his grey eyes, and a narrow nose that ended in a defined point. His attendant, Vignon, carefully gripped the high priest's solid gold miter in both hands, awaiting his master's instruction to place it on his head before he stepped outside. The heavy headdress radiated a hundred gold slivers that resembled a bright, glowing sun. Zidon's erect carriage resulted from years of keeping his head and shoulders immobile under the golden helmet's weight.

"My dear, so nice to see you up this early! Did you have a productive night in the observatory?" Zidon appreciated his daughter's devotion to celestial studies that benefited him and his profession. If Arvid had half her abilities he could be confident that the family's dynasty would continue for at least another generation after his death. Zidon's two children would some day assume formal roles in the priesthood under his watchful eye. He was resigned to one day making

Arvid Priest of Nabu to honor the god of the planet closest to the sun. Tradition called for him to inherit his father's supreme title, but Zidon had other plans. His desire was that Evina, the jewel of his life, would become a priestess-in-training soon and, when the time was right, she would become High Priestess of Ishtar to fulfill a promise made to her mother, who had died two years ago. His daughter would one day lead Babel's new, modern religion and, she might even take his place in the Triad. Zidon's dreams for the family dynasty would be fulfilled, he was sure.

"Father, I must speak with you privately on an important matter." Evina knew she did not have much time before the sun reached its zenith and her father had to leave.

Zidon motioned to Vignon to set the golden headdress on its stand and wait outside. Arvid remained standing apart from them with a scowl.

"I would like to speak with you *alone*, please." Evina addressed her father respectfully while she held Arvid's eyes in a firm stare.

Zidon noticed and quickly added, "Arvid can stay. Anything you need to say to me you can share with him. Besides, it's probably time for him to begin assisting me with the Shamash ceremony, and I'll be rehearsing him in other ceremonies as well. You know, my dear, you should start training for your duties, as well."

Evina ignored his remark. She turned instead to the subject of something she had discovered in the night sky. "For weeks I've studied an object that no one has ever documented before. I believe it could be of great significance."

"A new object in the heavens! Wonderful!" Her father exclaimed. "Tell us all about it." Arvid was equally interested and edged closer.

Evina told her father about the new pinpoint object that moved against the black background of space. The countless stars stood fixed in space relative to each other. Of course, it was the earth's revolution around the sun that resulted in the perception that the stars moved across the sky. In a more complex fashion, the five observable planets moved against the starry background also. The ancients had extensively catalogued their motion, which was well known and predictable.

Evina held their full attention and paused to carefully choose her words. "I call this object an *asteroid* because, at least for now, it is a distant speck of light, like a star, when seen through my telescope. By tracking it over time I've been able to calculate its approximate path, and I fear it may come very close to earth. It's too early to tell, but it may even hit us."

"Wonderful!" Her father clapped his hands in jubilation and looked at Arvid for agreement, who returned his pleasure.

"'Wonderful'?" She replied with incredulity. "An object that comes close to earth could have terrible implications. What if it comes so close that it causes damage to the planet? What if it collides with us and kills us all?"

Her father stepped close and held both her hands in his own. His happy face revealed pride in his daughter. "Don't you see? This is a gift from the gods to secure our family dynasty even further! I will predict an impending celestial catastrophe and we, the leaders of the priesthood, will explain it to the people and cement their allegiance to us when the object appears exactly as we forecasted. This is most excellent news!"

"What if it kills us all? What then?" she asked.

"Don't worry about that. All that matters is the present. People look to the gods for their daily guidance, and to me as their supreme guide. If they think they might die, they'll look to me and the gods even more. That will benefit all of us!"

"Aren't you afraid of dying?" Evina was taken aback by her father's answer.

"I don't think about that, and I suggest you don't bother with that either. This is all we have to live for," her father said waving his hands about him. "When we die—that's the end!"

Evina masked her bewilderment. "Let me conduct more calculations before you make any public announcement about the new object. It could be some time before I can give you anything specific." Evina couldn't imagine that her father might use this information to manipulate people for his own gain. She looked up to him as her father and spiritual leader. Now he was going to use a cosmic catastrophe to advance himself. She needed time to reconsider what all this meant.

"No matter. I must go now," Zidon said. "Here is what I want you to do: use whatever temple resources you need to finish your calculations. I have three questions: When will this thing first be seen in the sky with the naked eye? How close will it come to earth? When will it make its closest approach?"

Evina had anticipated exactly what her father requested and already had a series of measurements and calculations to answer him. Now she was afraid to ponder what he would do with her answers.

"By the way," her father added while he rang for his attendant, "if you need a visualization model constructed to help your calculations, you have my full backing. You may use my personal numerologists for calculations too, if they can be of help. Be sure to give me regular updates. Now, I must go." Zidon adjusted his priestly outfit while Vignon carefully placed the heavy golden headdress on his head before the chimes rang for his grand entrance onto the altar platform.

Arvid quickly moved to block Evina's departure. "Well sister, you've finally done it. All those nights at the telescope are paying off for us." He shared his father's enthusiasm for her news and smirked with satisfaction.

"What I've done is not for you, Arvid. Please move so I can leave. Besides, you don't want to be late for Father's introduction." Evina fought to control her irritation with her brother's arrogance.

"Just make sure you keep me informed of your progress too. After all, we're partners in this now. We'll make a great team, won't we?"

"I'll tell you nothing more! If Father wants to tell you, that's his business. Now get out of my way!" Evina tried to push past him.

Arvid grabbed her arm and pulled her face close to his. "You *will* tell me when this asteroid is about to make its first appearance. I'm not going to sit in the background while you take all the credit for it. This is my chance to make a name for myself, and you're not going to ruin it. Remember that!" He released her arm and spun around to join the crowd outside.

Evina trembled as she rubbed her arm. She had to make many more observations and calculations before she could answer her father's questions. What would happen then?

CHAPTER 3

Old Babel, Nimrod's Palace

When Zidon finished his noon ritual, his attendants quickly removed his bulky ceremonial accessories so that his coach could hurry him to Nimrod's palace. He was anxious to share news of the approaching asteroid with the other members of Babel's inner leadership circle. The possibility of an impending celestial catastrophe excited him in a strange way. He urged the coach slaves to run faster while he mulled the implications of the object's detection and the One World Tower's completion happening so closely together. Could he find a way to connect the two events?

A palace page announced Zidon's entrance into King Nimrod's presence, where Chief Magician Magus was seated to the right of the king's throne. Their hushed conversation paused in mid-sentence when they saw the high priest. The king's personal sorcerer eyed Zidon warily through slits that revealed nothing about what he and the king had been discussing. Magus was small next to Zidon's tall stature and his multicolored robe with gold trim hung in folds over his diminutive frame. He practiced an intimidating sneer most of the time but could switch instantly to a false, endearing smile. Nimrod motioned for Zidon and Magus to accompany him to the secure inner room where they could speak privately. He dismissed the servants while a lone armed guard stood outside the thick door.

The bare room lacked windows or the customary trappings of royalty, for it was designed to ensure absolute privacy. In spite of that, Magus bolted the door from the inside and walked around the room, checking the smooth walls for any cracks or openings that might be used to listen in on their conversation. He did this before each meeting and, although they thought it a waste of time, the other two waited for him to finish. The spare room was never used except for their private meetings. This was where the three men discussed and formulated their strategic plans for governing the future of New Babel. Magus personally escorted servants, who cleaned the room, and he held its only key. When he was satisfied that they could not be overheard, he sat at the utilitarian table with three rough chairs.

Nimrod, Zidon, and Magus were Babel's *Triad*. They governed the city-state that was the center of human civilization. Nimrod was the warrior-king, with an instinctive thirst for power to dominate. He was tall, muscular, and physically intimidating. His reputation for hunting large wild animals, later honed by tracking and capturing men, was held in great esteem by most of the race that called Babel their home. His reputation as a hunter did not mean that he had the governing skills needed to rule the tens of thousands who multiplied in the Euphrates River valley after the Great Flood. His vanity and lust for power resulted in impulsive decisions and self-serving decrees.

When Canaan, son of Ham, devised a new mystery religion to entice people away from the God of Creation, he inaugurated a system that enslaved people in spiritual darkness. Within one generation after Canaan introduced his twisted pagan ideas and liturgies, civilization was mesmerized by visions from the "gods" and predictions of planet alignments, eclipses, and constellation patterns in the heavens. Nimrod's cousin, Zidon, fascinated his followers with secret incantations, superstitious symbols, colorful costumes, and elaborate ceremonies.

Magus added his skills of cunning and persuasion to Nimrod's power and Zidon's mysticism. Magus dazzled the population with spectacular feats of "magic," though they were nothing more than staged tricks. A gullible observer believed that Magus had supernatural abilities when, in reality, his feats were nothing but clever illusions.

The three men who composed the Triad were each essential for the success of the others. They held the population under their joint control to accomplish their ultimate goal of a central, one world civilization. They were almost there. The One World Tower marked the apex of their ascendancy.

Not all of the human race was under the Triad's direct control. Most descendants of Ham had already followed Canaan and the Triad's programs, as did many of the descendants of Shem and Japheth. A few families, however, rejected the mystery religion. They either abandoned the city of Babel entirely to disperse across the globe, as God originally commanded, or they remained in Babel for commercial reasons while refusing to participate in its ungodly rituals. Those few who lived among the population quietly practiced their trades and worshipped the One True God in peace.

"What do you have for us, Zidon?" Nimrod asked impatiently. He grabbed an apple from a bowl of fruit in the middle of the table and took a large bite before Zidon could answer. Nimrod exuded restless, animal-like energy. He could sense that the priest, emotional and flamboyant by nature, was bursting to tell them something.

"A celestial event of enormous magnitude has been handed to us by the gods!" Zidon beamed. He stood and paced the floor in excitement. "This could be the most earth-shaking thing to happen to us since the Great Flood. This could be the very cataclysm we've needed to seal our hold on the world." He looked to the other two for a reaction.

"Aren't you being overly dramatic about this 'cataclysmic event,' whatever it is?" Magus had heard predictions of impending doom from the priest before and knew they were fantasies intended to whip the public into a frenzy. He moved to a corner of the room to distance himself physically from Zidon as he watched him continue to pace back and forth on the other side of the table.

"No! This is no exaggeration. My daughter Evina, who everyone knows is the best astronomer in the land, gave me the news this morning that an object is approaching us and will come very near the planet. It might even hit us! Don't you see? This is what we've needed!"

Nimrod was uncomfortable with what Zidon was saying and waved his hand to slow the priest down. "If you will stand still for a minute, I'd like to ask you two questions." Zidon reluctantly stopped and looked directly at the king. "Have your other astronomers confirmed this? When will this supposed event happen?"

"Are you implying that my daughter is not capable?" Zidon responded defensively. "She surpassed all the court astronomers before she finished her eighteenth year, and has since put them all to shame with her new mathematics. Compared to her, the official astronomers are mere . . . stargazers."

"So we don't know *if* or *when* this is all to happen. Thank you." Nimrod was dismissive and looked to Magus for confirmation.

"We clearly have time to let this play out," the shrewd sorcerer smoothly intoned to placate the king. "Let's give Zidon time to gather more information, and then we can decide what to do. In the meantime, we can at least consider what we *might* do if the information is correct. My sense is that if it is correct—and I don't doubt his daughter's abilities—it is indeed an opportunity we cannot pass up. When will we have more information, Zidon?"

The priest calmed from his confrontation with the king and addressed Magus' question. "My daughter will gather more data and use my numerologists to compute an estimated time of visibility in the sky. Of course, I will have the results confirmed independently by my astronomers when those results are available. When I have something definitive, I will report back."

Magus appeared satisfied with the answer. He spoke cautiously for the group, "We await your report then, which I trust will be delivered shortly. If this object is rapidly approaching earth, then we will accelerate completion of the tower or at least finish the rooftop temple if there is not enough time to furnish the tower residences before it kills us all," the magician said sarcastically.

"So, I share Zidon's optimism," Magus summarized, "if not his enthusiasm, about this new opportunity that should not be wasted. It may be early, but it appears to offer us two potential advantages: it could be used to focus the energies of the people to accelerate construction of the tower; and, it could unite everyone behind us and lift us to the level of gods in their eyes. The two advantages would work well together to establish our One World system. That could cement our plans for the future of New Babel for centuries, if not millennia, to come. Is that not what we ultimately agreed to do?" Magus looked intently at the two men before him.

Both nodded in agreement. "The King of Babel must be recognized as a god if he is to rule the people forever," Nimrod declared.

"The High Priest of Marduk must speak as a god if he is to guide the hearts of the people upward to heaven," Zidon piously intoned. His eyes closed and his thin lips pursed as if in prayer.

The three men closed the meeting by agreeing that the One World Tower must be completed quickly, regardless of the future of the asteroid. Nimrod charged Magus with pressing construction forward with renewed attention, and departed their inner sanctum to resume their duties. Magus stayed behind in the silence of the closed room to think before he returned to overseeing the tower's accelerated construction.

A weak link in the high priest's announcement, he concluded, was his reliance on his daughter for further information about the asteroid. Evina was undoubtedly a gifted astronomer. What worried Magus was that he had heard Zidon express reservations about her dedication to the priesthood and its modern religion. The sly wizard would have Evina quietly watched. He then reflected with a smile on what clearly motivated the king and the priest, who were oblivious of his personal ambitions. He could easily see how one was moved by primitive, raw lust for power and the other by need for affirmation and worship. In seeking their own fulfillment they never inquired about what motivated him. That was a secret he kept to himself. One day they would realize what moved him—but by then, it would be too late. He left the room satisfied that his control of the Triad remained unchanged.

Minutes later, a fourth person in the room slowly lowered himself from the roof rafters and dropped to the floor with barely a sound. The intruder's iridescent cloak made him almost invisible in the dark roof rafters where he overheard the Triad's every word. He let himself out with his own key and disappeared into the palace hallway minutes later.

CHAPTER 4

Old Babel, Ziggurat of Marduk—Numerology Center

Five days later

Evina revised her formulary sheets, which contained detailed equations for the asteroid's motion, before she took them to her father's numerology center located three levels below the ziggurat's altar. The long sunlit hall, filled with rows of tables and benches, was occupied by more than one hundred busy numerologists, men and women, who performed the repetitive tasks of calculating the relative positions of the sun, moon, planets, and significant stars. She intended to give her formulary sheets to a few of the most skilled workers, who could produce results much more quickly than if she did the calculations herself.

The temple numerologists were organized into two groups. One group was made up of junior-level workers or *quants* who repeatedly performed standard calculations from well-known algorithms, or *algos*, for the sun, moon, planets, and stars. They also used maps of visible star clusters to make fanciful sketches of the shapes of people, animals, plants, and familiar household objects that represented the stars. The second group of numerologists was composed of people also trained as *astrologers*; they used the numbers and pictures from the quants to write daily forecasts corresponding to an individual's birth date. The most expert astrologers operated a planetary visualizer machine to verify calculations and to conduct research on unusual celestial patterns. Technically, the most expert astrologers were also astronomers, but their skills were limited to basic observation and description of the heavens. Evina was trained in astronomy, astrology, and numerology, but was also gifted with skills in complex mathematics that allowed her to predict the future positions of objects in the heavens without using the visualizer.

Hundreds of daily astrology forecasts, originating in the vivid imaginations of temple quants and astrologers, were said to be messages from the "gods" to guide readers' daily lives. People lined up each morning at kiosks across the city to purchase their daily forecasts printed on slips of paper that they kept for reference during the day. The papers contained their personal celestial picture and a message that they would use to guide their decisions that day. They bought daily forecasts for themselves and family members that corresponded to their birth date, but were unaware that hundreds of workers composed the messages to be consistent with the planet and star patterns observed overhead that night. Thinking they were receiving their own divine instructions, the people of Babel were amazed when forecasted common events happened, which they almost always did, because they were simple, everyday activities of life. When Nimrod or Zidon wished to manipulate the masses, the astrologers would insert "special instructions" into the forecasts, which readers believed and obediently followed. This method of control proved effective in keeping most of the civilization together near the cities of Old and New Babel on the plain of Shinar.

Some temple numerologists, besides being experts in their understanding of algos, were especially proficient with the large, tabletop counting device and its unique numbering system. The most skilled numerologists, of which there were only a half-dozen, were called *computers* or *algorithmists*. They performed calculations so rapidly that their hands were a blur as they fiddled beads back and forth along wires inside rectangular counting boards or *frames*. Evina enlisted a few computers to make repeated, iterative calculations from her algos to estimate the future movement of the asteroid.

She identified four who had computed for her in the past and who demonstrated speed and accuracy with her complex algos. She set her formulary sheets before them and gave each a starting list of numbers as inputs. It was not essential that they fully understand the complex meaning of the equations. These four algorithmists were familiar enough with Evina's neat handwriting simply to perform the calculations as written. After they initialized their frames for the number of significant digits required, the clatter of their counting beads was added to the background din of a hundred other numerologists in the room.

Evina rested on a couch near an open window to await their results. It could take most of the morning, but she remained available in case they had questions. She enjoyed the cool breeze wafting through the window and had almost dozed off when she subconsciously sensed a subtle change in the humming background. She opened her eyes and noticed Asef, one of her algorithmists, whispering to an astrologer from another department who stood next to him. Asef glanced up to see her looking directly at him. He rose nervously from his seat and approached her with the formulary sheet in his hand. The astrologer returned to his seat across the room.

"Excuse me, my lady. I am confused about one of your markings. I am sorry to bother you. Is this number a '2' or a '7'?" He handed her the notes she had written.

"That is a '7,' and I'm surprised that you had trouble with it, Asef. It looks exactly like all the other '7's on the sheet," she scolded. Evina was annoyed by the man's obviously false excuse for stopping his work to speak with another worker when her precise handwriting was so clear.

The experienced numerologist answered apologetically. "I am sorry to have disturbed your nap. However, I was wondering if my lady could explain the purpose of these algos. They are much more complex than any I have seen for other planetary calculations. Are they for something new?" Asef's curiosity seemed reasonable, since the algos were indeed more complex and lengthy than any she had ever given him. The appearance of new algos would naturally be of professional interest to him, although none of the others had expressed concern when she gave them their sheets.

Evina briefly explained that they were for a new astral object that she had been following and that she wanted to estimate its future path. The specific algo he had was a calculation of the object's possible proximity to earth. The numerologist seemed satisfied, thanked her for the explanation, and returned to his seat.

Computers had asked her questions about algos in the past, so his inquiry was not out of the ordinary. Besides, all the numerologists had top security clearances because their work in this part of the temple could not be revealed to the unsuspecting public.

Evina's eyes drooped again because of the numbing, monotonous background buzz of the counters. Before she drifted off, she noticed that Asef was whispering again with the same astrologer. She kept her eyes open just enough to see Asef leave the room, as if for a restroom break. She pretended to be asleep, but remained alert enough to watch the master clock at the end of the room. He returned more than thirty minutes later with a smirk on his face.

Something was wrong. Evina concluded that information about her work was being leaked outside the security of the counting room. She didn't know who was receiving her information, but she had a suspicion. This meant that the numerology center was no longer secure and none of the algorithmists or astrologers could be trusted. She pondered her alternatives and dismissed doing the calculations herself. Although she was a qualified, though slow, computer herself, she had to gather more motion data from the asteroid for new input to the algos. Doing the calculations by herself during the day would take too long. A jolt of inspiration snapped her eyes open, and the image of a mechanical device took shape in her imagination. Not only did a solution unfold before her, but she knew who could build the automated computing machine she visualized. She had to take immediate action. Evina stood abruptly and walked to the four men working on her problem.

"I thought of a possible mistake I've made," she said to Asef. "I will have to verify all of the algos again." She quickly gathered the formulary sheets and the workers' notes, thanked them for their valuable time, and instructed them to report back to their supervisor for their next assignment. She watched to be sure that they zeroed their frames. After checking that no papers were left behind, she left the room without looking back. Had she looked back, she would have seen Asef run out a side door.

CHAPTER 5

New Babel, Pele's Machine Shop

Next day

Pele was startled when he looked out the front window of his machine shop to see the daughter of the high priest descending from her coach with an elaborate entourage of transporters and bodyguards. He opened the door after the first knock. Before him stood a temple official dressed in colorful robes who announced the arrival of Evina, daughter of Zidon, High Priest of Marduk, and stepped aside. The tall, modestly dressed young astronomer stood in Pele's doorway.

"You are Pele, the Master Mechanic?" she inquired in a flat, almost detached, voice.

"I am Pele, but only a simple clockmaker, Miss. Would you care to come in and sit down?" He had received Zidon into his shop once, many years ago, to take delivery of a custom-built planetary visualizer. He was vaguely aware that Zidon had a daughter.

"Thank you." Evina turned to her hulking personal bodyguard, who stood only a few feet away. Using sign language, because he was a deaf mute, she instructed him to wait for her. *I will call you when I am ready to return to the temple.* The silent guardian wore the simple uniform of a temple servant. His ebony body rippled with so many muscles that nobody would think of harming the young woman he guarded. His glistening head was shaved except for a braided length of hair that reached his waist to indicate his status as a eunuch slave. After a respectful bow to Evina, he ducked as he entered the doorway and inspected every room of the single-story building. His departure confirmed that he was satisfied with leaving her there alone. He bowed again and closed the door to wait outside.

Evina walked hesitatingly to a chair, gave a sigh, and noticed a large dog sleeping under the table. His fur was brown and black and he had alert, pointed ears. He looked at her with lazy brown eyes. She turned her attention to her host. "I apologize for the formality when the temple official introduced me. He is responsible for my wellbeing, but I trust no one except my bodyguard, Saris." She was clearly uncomfortable and tired. "May I please have a glass of water?"

"Of course, Miss." Pele parted a curtain that led to the back room of his shop which contained a small kitchen.

Evina looked around the front room of the shop, which had the appearance of a clockmaker's showroom. Clocks of various shapes and sizes lined the walls. Some were plain day clocks that middle class families kept prominently in their living rooms. Other clocks were ornate works of art to adorn the salons of the more wealthy. Evina noticed that some were hefty chronometers suitable for a scientific laboratory. She realized that she probably had two of Pele's chronometers in her observatory which she kept synchronized to standard planetary time. Few would realize after a quick glance around his clock store that Pele was the best precision instrument maker in Babel.

He returned from the back room with a pitcher and two glasses. He filled the glasses with water and smiled at her. She drank several refreshing sips and set her glass down. "That's ice in my glass," she exclaimed. "Where did you get ice in the middle of summer?" She didn't want to sound impolite, but was momentarily taken aback by the novelty. Pele drank his cold water slowly and evaluated his guest.

"Since we are alone in my humble shop I can tell you what you have undoubtedly concluded: I am more than a simple clockmaker." Pele looked at her with genuine concern. "Why don't you make yourself comfortable and tell me what brings you to see me." He had kindly eyes and sensed that she was nervous about something.

She took another sip of the iced water, removed a sheaf of papers from her handbag, and placed them on the table. "I will begin by asking you to call me Evina. You are old enough to be my father and I am tired of all the formal pretenses. Although my reason for being here is mostly official, I prefer we discuss my problem confidentially and informally."

"I think that would be best . . . Evina. You look the same age as my twins and I would like nothing better than to help you in any way I can. How does it involve that pile of papers in front of you?" Pele leaned forward. He recognized some of the mathematical notations in her neat handwriting and was professionally intrigued.

"I'm feeling better now, thank you. I'll be glad to show them to you." She spread the papers on the table. From the corner of her eye she noticed the dog silently emerge from under the table and sit by her side.

"That's Shadow, the newest member of our family," Pele explained. "I hope you don't mind his curiosity. I can put him outside if he bothers you."

"Not at all. He seems friendly enough," she casually replied.

"Those look like algos," Pele commented as he glanced over the papers. "I assume they are yours. Can you explain them to me?"

"I'll try, but they are very complex. I don't know how much you know about infinitesimal differentials." She waited for Pele to show some indication of understanding. Receiving no reaction, she launched into a rapid fire explanation while pointing to the long notations on each page. "These algos are based on methods for rigid body motion, but involve thousands of repeated approximations. I've started to test them with a team of numerologists, but can't continue for reasons that I won't discuss. Am I making any sense so far?" Evina could see that Pele was staring at the first page with a blank expression.

"Miss . . . Evina, I'm afraid these algos are far beyond my comprehension. I have no idea what most of those neatly printed markings mean." Pele continued to stare at the papers.

"Then I'm sorry to have bothered you. I was told that you built my father's planetary visualizer and naturally assumed that you could build another machine based on newer algos." She stood abruptly and gathered her papers.

"Just because *I* don't understand your algos does not mean that a machine couldn't be built to mechanize them. If such a machine could be designed I am certain that I could build it." Pele looked at her with an inviting face that surrounded bright eyes. "I think I know some people who speak the language of your algos."

"Secrecy is of the utmost importance. Can these people be trusted?"

"If you trust me, you can trust them. I'll be gone for a little while to fetch them either from my home or the School of Japheth. Feel free to look at the planetary visualizer under the tarp there in the corner while I'm gone. It's the prototype that I never delivered to your father and you may find it . . . intriguing." Pele opened the shop door and Evina's bodyguard blocked his way. When Saris realized that the shop owner wished to leave, the bodyguard looked to Evina seated calmly inside, received her nod of approval, and stepped aside to let him pass. Pele quickly walked up the hill toward his home, assured that Evina would be safe while he was gone.

Evina's curiosity got the better of her. She went to the corner of the workshop and uncovered the planetary visualizer prototype. In spite of being draped by a tarp, the apparatus was covered with a thin film of dust from years of disuse. She brushed off the operator's seat, settled into its semi-reclined cradle and scanned the panel of switches and levers in the console before her. Evina had seen a similar, geocentric machine in the numerology center, but this version was twice its size; the tiny painted models of the sun, moon, and planets surrounded her head while she sat in their midst. The reclined angle of the contoured seat at the center of the device gave her a view of the heavens as if she were on the surface of the earth at the center of Old Babel. The positions of the sun, moon, and five known planets were accurate for selectable times and dates in the past or into the future. Within minutes she figured out how to wind the machine's spring coil, set the date for the present, and activate the mechanism. She was soon lost in the visualizer's fascinating complexity, the soft whirling sounds of gears behind the seat, and the hypnotic motions of the colorful orbs around her against a black cloth background.

When Pele returned to the shop twenty minutes later with his two children and they eased past Evina's intimidating bodyguard, he was not surprised to find her unmindful of their entrance. She was in another world as familiar celestial objects spun around her in their perfectly replicated paths at many times actual orbital speeds. The three watched the serene expression of wonder on Evina's face. If they did not interrupt her now, she would be entranced for the rest of the day.

"Excuse the interruption, but we must finish our discussion before it gets dark. Evina, I would like you to meet my son and daughter." Pele helped Evina climb out of the machine after the models stopped circling.

"This is my daughter, Yanis, who is interested in learning more about your algos." Pele's daughter was stunningly beautiful, her long golden hair was tied in a pony tail and she smiled warmly as they shook hands.

"This is my son Dov. Son, this is the astronomer lady I told you about with the algos that are beyond my comprehension." Evina extended her hand to the trim young man with short blond hair and a ruddy complexion and shook it with a firm, confident grasp. Their eyes held each other longer than necessary. She found his wide smile and rapidly blinking blue eyes disarming as he held his gaze on hers. Dov released her hand with a reluctance that only she detected.

Pele motioned them to the table in the center of the room. "You can tell that Dov and Yanis are twins, and you will soon learn that their scientific interests are equally extensive. Shall we sit down and look over your notes?"

The four gathered around the table while Evina put the pages in order along the table's length. She had hardly begun explaining the first page before Dov and Yanis each picked up a page and studied them intently. Evina stopped speaking when it was evident that they were ignoring her.

"Strange. I've never seen an acceleration term used in this way," said Dov aloud to his sister, pointing to the page in his hand. "I've never heard of a distant astronomical object moving like this. Look! This algo shows high-level, fractional exponents for both velocity and acceleration." He blinked his eyes in excitement as his finger traced the equation across the page.

His sister handed him a page from the formulary and indicated an underlined term. "This takes into account the planetary gravity factors. You wouldn't think they would have an effect at such great distances unless the object was very large or very dense. She should eventually be able to deduce its total mass from this algo."

For thirty minutes Evina and Pele sat in silent awe while brother and sister commented on, argued over, and speculated about the algos on the sheets. Papers were soon scattered randomly across the table and some had fallen to the floor. Finally, the two looked at each other, nodded, and turned to Evina.

"We can build a predictor engine to mechanize your algos," they announced in unison.

"I'm impressed! You've torn my formulary apart and put it back together again multiple times. I didn't think anyone else in Babel could do that." Evina was clearly thrilled with their conclusion, and they spoke for another half-hour about suggested changes to the algos to make them easier to mechanize. She would leave her formulary sheets with them for further study. Pele would be responsible for construction of a precision calculating engine, while Dov and Yanis would design the flow of the algos so raw numbers could be programmed into the machine.

Yanis took their young visitor aside as she prepared to leave. "I can tell that you are fearful about this approaching asteroid, but the One True God is in charge of everything that happens in His universe. Whatever this asteroid does, nothing is accidental or without purpose in His creation. My brother and I, and our family, will be praying that you find the peace of God that you are looking for." Yanis felt genuine affection for this young woman who was entangled in her family's star worship.

Choked with emotion, Evina was stunned that Yanis showed her, a relative stranger, such concern. She nodded toward Pele and Dov without speaking before she opened the door to rejoin her bodyguard and transporters and return to the temple. As she passed through the door a tower messenger arrived out of breath.

"Hurry, there has been an accident at the tower. A freight capsule has fallen again and the Chief Engineer Jengo is calling for Pele to come immediately to help him." Pele bid a hurried farewell to Evina and his twins and ran to the tower site to learn more about why his brother needed him.

CHAPTER 6

New Babel, One World Tower

Jengo was not surprised when he received a summons from Magus almost immediately after the latest freight ascender accident. As chief engineer for the tower project, Jengo was in demand around the clock from every direction. His brother, Pele, had designed the ascender system and was on call to help investigate crashes. This time a freight capsule had plunged for thirty floors, from the Commoner-Guild portal level to the vapor machine basement. The capsule occupants were killed instantly after their terrifying, fifteen-second plunge. Two others died when the impact scattered the cargo of marble statues into the nearby capsule control center. This was the fifth accident since freight ascenders became operational. Cargo capsules carrying workers and materials to finish the Commoner level had otherwise generally been safe; they had traveled up and down almost non-stop since their installation. The unfinished, metallic skeleton of the tower extending past the fifty-first floor included the framework for the Guild and Ministerial levels up to the ninetieth floor. The One World Tower, including the unfinished small ziggurat on its roof, was the tallest building on earth. It cast its shadow over the skyline of New Babel and above the Ziggurat of Marduk across the river in Old Babel.

Jengo, and engineers from the School of Japheth, designed the tower and other modern buildings in New Babel because two scientific discoveries changed the entire face of civilization. The first, and most powerful, was carbonized wood which was the product of intense water pressure and ground upheaval during the Great Flood that crushed trillions of tons of wood and vegetation underground. The heat potential of the rock-like substance, called *black rock* by its discoverers, far exceeded that of dried wood as a fuel source. The second was metallic alloys. Methuselah had experimented with formulas for alloys before the Great Flood, but when Japheth mixed a small amount of black rock powder with molten iron, and later added other rare metals, he produced new metals hundreds of times stronger than anything previously known. He didn't realize at the time that he was laying the foundation for the world's first vapor-powered industrial era.

Black smoke and stinging fumes from dozens of bloomeries and furnaces hung low like a suffocating blanket over the city. Foundries produced raw materials for taller buildings, more powerful vapor engines, and mechanical devices of every description. Consumers demanded more conveniences and appliances that factories were eager to supply. Buildings rose taller to escape the choking, acrid smog of progress.

The original buildings of Old Babel were built with stone from Accadian quarries, wood from forests of cedar and cypress, and clay bricks baked in kilns. The ancient city still favored the traditional decorative designs of the artisans, but mass-produced alloy and glass, made possible by factory vapor machines, defined the modern, progressive look of New Babel. The One World Tower was emblematic of the new alloy and vapor engine age; its bold spire declared that mankind had overcome the elements once and for all and that there was nothing it could not accomplish. The only concession to the former times was the contrasting black stone ziggurat that capped the roof of the tower in what High Priest Zidon called "stairs reaching up to heaven."

Unlike the softer iron, brass, and bronze used for small mechanisms in the previous antediluvian civilization, the new metallic alloy was strong enough to contain the heat and pressure of engines that pounded the white-hot substance into beams and twisted long braided ropes that suspended soaring freight capsules.

Magus, as chief magician, quickly grasped the usefulness of modern inventions when he envisioned a tower to reach into the sky above the city. Against Jengo's better judgment, the tower rose to a height well beyond what any prudent engineer could approve; Magus ordered it to have one hundred-twenty floors because Zidon said that this was a perfect celestial number to satisfy the gods. Jengo was already committed to building the tower when he found that it would hold a new temple to replace the Ziggurat of Marduk in Old Babel. When he resisted building a tower as part of the Triad's plans for a new world order, he and his family were threatened with death unless he finished the tower. He had no choice but to continue.

New Babel, Chief Magician's Residence

Jengo and Pele responded to the magician's latest summons after examining the accident scene at the tower. Magus looked up from the papers on his desk with a sneer. He was visibly agitated about something. Expecting a confrontation about the accident, the two engineers were on their guard.

"Where have you been? Have you forgotten that construction of the tower is my top priority?" Magus believed that he held tenuous control over Jengo and his family and so, to mask his insecurity, his contacts with the tower's chief engineer were always confrontational. His lack of technical understanding, combined with a reflexive distrust, led to bullying and explosive tantrums.

"We came as soon as we could," Jengo replied evenly. He had experience with the sorcerer's volatile temper. "The accident at the tower detained me and I felt you would want the latest explanation of its cause. I meant no disrespect in my tardiness." Jengo knew that he had to walk a thin line when dealing with Magus. His explanation must not appear to threaten the magician's authority. Still, he had to make it clear that the accident was not due to the ascender's design.

"Who is this?" Magus noticed Pele standing next to Jengo.

"This is my brother Pele. He is also an engineer, and he accompanied me to the accident site to determine its cause. We know for certain what caused the accident."

"I'm not concerned with the accident," he said with a wave of his hand. "Take care of it and ensure it is not repeated."

"Sir, I think you should be aware of the reason for the fall of the ascender. It is a safety matter that ought to concern you, for it has implications for the Luminary passenger ascender."

"Not now," Magus shouted. "I want you to make changes to the Luminary capsule and control system. You can brief me on the accident later. I'm sure my changes have nothing to do with the accident."

"Very well." Jengo wondered what Magus could have that was more important than the loss of life and damage to freight ascenders.

"I want the Luminary passenger capsule built more securely for the king and the high priest. I am aware that the capsule is the only direct route to the Luminary level and wish it to be fully under my control. This is, of course, for the protection of our leaders."

Jengo could hardly contain a smile at the thought of Magus being concerned with the safety of the other members of the Triad. He had heard about the intense rivalry among them. The safety of the ascender was no doubt more for the benefit of Magus than the protection of Nimrod or Zidon.

"You will first install a lock on the capsule so that its function can be halted independent of the control room operator. In addition, you will make it possible for the Luminary capsule to descend automatically from the rooftop to the passenger loading lobby on the first floor, and similarly ascend to the rooftop without the need of an ascender operator. This automatic operation will be initiated with the same key employed for the lockout mechanism. Both of these features will be for the Luminary capsule only."

Magus noticed Jengo open his mouth to ask a question, and snapped at him. "I'm not finished! Also, I want a second compartment built into the current capsule to carry two or three more people. Personal servants will need to accompany Luminaries, but they cannot be allowed to occupy the same cramped space as their masters or mistresses. It will be below the current capsule interior and accessible from a second door not noticeable from the main compartment. Is that understood?" Magus' glare meant that he did not want questions. Jengo pressed ahead anyway.

"Sir, these features will only complicate the already complex operation of the ascender. The added room below the capsule will increase its weight significantly and may require a total redesign of the device. A human operator is essential to align the top passenger compartment with the floor for loading and unloading at the stops. The ascenders are already prone to operator error, and allowing the

Luminary ascender to function unattended is dangerous. In fact, the already complex controls led, I believe, to the accident today." Jengo hoped that his concern for safety would persuade Magus to relent, or at least to listen to what he had to say.

"I don't care how complicated you think this is! I *demand* that you make these changes immediately. Also, the schedule for completion of the tower will be accelerated, so factor these changes into your planning." His eyes blazed like those of a madman. It was clear he was beyond logical persuasion.

Jengo decided to risk it and press him further, since none of the changes made sense to him. "May I know more about the reason for these security features? It might help in my design."

"That is of no concern to you. Just do it!" It was clear that further questions would not be tolerated.

"I will submit a design for all these changes for your approval. Is there a time schedule?" Jengo asked.

"As soon as possible. This is a top priority. I want the One World Tower declared completely functional as soon as it can be done. You will concentrate on finishing the Luminary 120th level and the rooftop ziggurat before anything else. Rooms in the new ziggurat must be ready for the high priest's occupancy as quickly as possible. I don't care about the other levels." His icy stare emphasized the urgency of his instructions. In a venomous hiss he threatened: "If you refuse to make those changes, both of your families will be in danger of execution. Need I make myself more clear?"

Jengo and Pele nodded submissively and left the room.

Magus glared at the closed door as if his look could force them to bend to his wishes.

CHAPTER 7

New Babel, Pele's Machine Shop

The two brothers walked silently through the city back to Pele's machine shop near dusk. They waited until the shop door was locked before they spoke of their meeting with Magus.

"I'm very worried about this," began Pele. "You've never trusted that weaseling wizard, and now we know he's up to something nefarious. We just don't know what it is. This isn't the first time he's threatened to kill my family!"

Jengo thought about the reason for the orders. "From my experience dealing with Magus, I'm certain that those modifications are intended to benefit him in some way. His talk about 'safety' and 'protection' was a smokescreen. When the king and high priest find out that they can ride the capsule up or down without an operator, they might use the ascender's privacy to plot against Magus. All the while he'll have someone hidden in the lower half of the capsule, listening to them. That's something he would do. I don't have much choice about the changes he wants, but I'm going to make sure I have a duplicate key made. I'll drag my feet building the extra passenger compartment for as long as I can."

The brothers spent the next two hours discussing the technical changes for unattended operation. Pele retrieved some sandwiches from the small kitchen and they continued their talk into the evening. Shadow lay on a blanket in the corner.

"By the way, when did you get a dog?" Jengo asked when he noticed that the large animal was watching him.

"A week ago he appeared out of nowhere. Yanis and Dov took a liking to him and convinced me to keep him as a watchdog. He keeps an eye on Maasi too when he's playing outside. He's become part of the family."

"You need a watchdog for your shop anyway," Jengo agreed. "Too many valuable instruments and tools are here to trust to a flimsy door."

They finished sharing ideas on ascender designs, and Jengo stood with a set of sketches in his hands for the lockout and automatic controls. Jengo worried that Magus was plotting something that would entangle them in one of his evil schemes. Their conversation had turned to their ascender crash inquiries when Dov and Yanis burst into the room.

"How can you say that she's wrong when you only saw her notes this afternoon for the first time?" Yanis prodded her brother to explain his assertion that one of Evina's calculations might be incorrect. "She's ten times smarter than you anyway!"

He took the bait instantly. "How can you be so sure they're right if you haven't studied them any more than I have? You're taking her side just because she's a girl!" He was on the losing side of the argument but wouldn't give up.

"I've studied them enough to know that they're the best algos I've ever seen," Yanis retorted. "On the other hand, you'd have a better argument if I'd said that they were the best algos because she's so pretty."

Dov stopped with his mouth open about to throw another quip. Then he broke into a grin. "She *is* pretty, isn't she? She has a nice voice too."

"See, I knew you would come around to see it my way."

They finally noticed that their uncle, Jengo, was in the room.

"You two will figure the algos out eventually so we can make a blueprint for the machine. Take a deep breath and settle down," their father advised.

"Who and what in the world are you two talking about? What algos and what machine?" Jengo became intrigued. Anything to take his mind off the accident in the tower.

After swearing his brother to secrecy, Pele explained: "The High Priest Zidon's daughter visited us today, and she commissioned me and my two algo brains here to custom-build a mechanical predictor engine for her. If they can put their sparring aside, we'll begin working on it tomorrow morning." Pele obviously relished the challenge of a new project, and preferred the hands-on construction of the large machine to helping his brother investigate an accident caused by a vapor engine-operator's error.

Dov and Yanis told their uncle about the visit from Evina and her discovery of a wayward asteroid. Without getting into the complex algos, they explained how the two would master the equations and Pele would design and build a machine to predict the object's future motion. Their enthusiasm was dampened when Jengo raised questions that none of them had considered.

"Does Magus know of this possible approaching catastrophe? What if Zidon's daughter is working for the Triad to manipulate the citizens of the city? You could be accomplices to a devious scheme she and the Triad are planning. Maybe you should reconsider working with her before you get dragged into something you'll regret later."

Pele and his two children were stunned by Jengo's suspicion of a conspiracy. Evina seemed like an innocent enough young woman; nervous and afraid, but hardly an operative for the Triad intent on mass deception.

"No," insisted Pele. "If I'm any judge of character, she wouldn't work directly for Magus or Nimrod. She believes she saw something in the heavens that it is a threat to earth. Her father could have asked her to make those predictions, and probably told the other two members of the Triad about them, but she wouldn't wittingly be part of a corrupt scheme."

Dov and Yanis agreed. Their brief interaction with Evina that afternoon resulted in an immediate, emotional bond between them. She seemed a sincere, frightened young woman.

"My intuition tells me that she's afraid," Yanis added. "I told her about the Lord of Heaven caring for her, and she was obviously comforted by that. I'll bring it up with her again when I see her in the next few days."

Dov agreed with his sister's estimation of Evina. "We'll certainly have questions as we prepare plans to mechanize the algos. I hope she's open to hearing more about the Lord again when we see her."

A soft knock at the door brought their conversation to an abrupt halt. "Who could that be at this late hour?" Pele noticed from one of his many clocks that it was almost midnight. He walked to the window to see who it was. After a momentary glance through a gap in the curtains, he opened the door.

Evina stood shaking in the cool darkness.

"Come in my dear, come in." Pele took her by the arm and led her to a chair. He looked outside and noticed that the street was deserted.

After the young woman was seated and offered something to drink or eat, which she declined, she stared at Jengo without speaking. Shadow emerged from his spot in the corner and settled comfortably at Evina's feet.

Dov realized the reason for her silence. "Evina, this is my uncle Jengo. He's a close family member who can be trusted. What brings you here at this late hour? Are you in some sort of trouble?"

Evina composed herself with a sigh and looked back and forth between Dov and Yanis. "I came here to speak with you two about a matter that I cannot contain any longer." After glancing at Pele and Jengo, she asked, "I'm sure your uncle and father can be trusted, but could I speak privately with just the two of you?"

"We withhold no secrets from our father or uncle. You can speak freely around this table," Yanis encouraged their visitor.

"It's very personal. I'd feel more comfortable speaking with you privately. Do you mind?" Evina asked again.

"It's late and I must be going," Jengo said as he stood to leave. "It was good making your acquaintance," he nodded to Evina and shook Pele's hand. "I'll see you at the tower in the morning, brother. We'll continue our investigation." He let himself out and closed the door quietly.

Pele bid his children goodnight and assured their visitor that she was welcome to stay as long as she wished. "Lock the door after I leave," he reminded them as he departed the shop for home.

Yanis locked the door and returned to their guest. She sat next to Evina, and Dov moved his chair closer. Evina spoke to Yanis in a more measured, relaxed voice. "When I was in this room earlier today you said something about the One True God that has been on my mind ever since. First, I must tell you about some things in my past."

"Evina, we're here to help you. Take your time," Yanis encouraged softly.

"You know who my father is, so you understand that I grew up in a privileged household immersed in his religion. My mother, who died when I was young, shared power with my father. They had a vision for a single world religion that all the earth would embrace. I and my brother were raised to eventually become the high priest and high priestess of what my father is calling the One World system."

"We've heard of that," remarked Dov. "Isn't that what the Triad is promoting?"

"Yes. It's supposed to be a unifying religion where the people worship many gods and eventually those in our family become gods ourselves." Evina hesitated. "When I think back to the intense indoctrination my brother and I endured as part of our grooming to be priests, I have trouble separating lies from reality. I was taught that there are thousands, maybe millions, of gods in the universe and that we are subject to them. They determine our fate, so I was told, and we had to please them so they wouldn't become angry and harm us. As a priest or priestess, we would have to appease the gods on behalf of others also. I believed those things with all sincerity because it was what I was taught by my parents. That's why what you said this afternoon about the One True God touched my heart so sharply."

"That He loves you and cares for you?" asked Yanis.

"Yes. After years of studying the heavens, I have recently come to realize that stories about the stars and planets being gods who governed our lives were fabricated from people's imaginations. My father manipulates the people of Babel to advance the family dynasty; he and my mother raised me to follow in their footsteps. Now I know that the gods care nothing for me. Since I no longer believe in them I feel an emptiness inside me without them. From studying the stars and planets through my telescope, I know that there must be a supreme God who created the complexity and order of the heavens above. Are you believers in that God?" She looked anxiously to Yanis and Dov for an answer.

"Yes, Evina, we are believers in the One True God who created all that is around us. He is a God of infinite power, but also a God of compassion and mercy toward each person. He obviously wants you to know Him too, or you wouldn't have met us this afternoon or come back to see us tonight." Yanis saw Evina's tense face and nervous hands relax slightly when she heard these words.

"I'm afraid that if I learn more of this God I'll have to turn my life over to Him, and that would cause me great problems. I love my father, but what I believe is completely opposite to his beliefs. My family situation is a very difficult one."

"I think we understand a little of what you mean," Dov responded. "You're afraid that if your father finds out that you're a believer in the One True God you'll be rejected by your family."

"It's much worse than that," Evina explained. "My father is the high priest of Marduk and, as his daughter, I'm destined to one day assume my mother's role as the high priestess of Ishtar. When my mother died, he planned for me to join my brother as a co-leader in sun and star worship. If I were to reveal my faith in the One True God, I would face unimaginable opposition and maybe even punishment. My brother, Arvid, has threatened me with harm if I do not submit to him in worship of the gods and do his bidding. I'm also afraid that he is working with Magus to take advantage of the chaos that will result from the approaching asteroid." Evina suppressed a sob before concluding. "It's all so complicated and confusing. I know what you've told me is true, but I'm afraid of what will happen to me if I tell my family."

She continued after a pause, "Besides that, I'm afraid of what will happen to us if I'm wrong about the asteroid's path and it kills us all. I'm afraid to die . . ."

For the next hour Dov and Yanis listened while Evina spoke of how she searched the heavenly bodies every night for years seeking some evidence of their family's deities, but could find none. Her observations drew her to conclude that billions of heavenly objects could not have created themselves, nor could they influence the destinies of individuals. She concluded that there must have been something, or someone, to give them their beauty and complexity; their orderly motion through the emptiness of space could be precisely described with the laws of mathematics; their origin and cause were inexplicable. The fact that she could precisely map their motions and many other observable natural processes, using fundamental laws of nature, was a puzzle that demanded a satisfactory solution. Yanis and Dov told her of God's creative work at the beginning of time; how He created the sun, moon, planets, and stars as signs and that their motion was a cosmic timepiece for the benefit of mankind. Evina gasped when they told her that God created all of this in an instant and out of nothing using only His spoken word.

The brother and sister told their visitor that this same God was a personal God who would hear her prayer to Him, forgive her sin, and would be with her at all times, even if she met opposition or hardship. She need only call upon His Name in sincere faith and He would make her His own. She would be His child forever.

Evina wept upon hearing this and relief flooded her soul. This was what she had been searching for her entire life! She had seen evidence of the One True God in the created bodies of the heavens. Now she knew why. She believed in this God with all her heart.

After drying her eyes, she looked at the clock and said, "It will be dawn in a few hours. I must return to the temple immediately. I'll be missed if the guards don't find me in my observatory. I can't thank you enough for all you've told me tonight."

Dov expressed his concern as Evina wrapped her shawl around herself to ward off the chill of the early morning. "Where's your bodyguard? Will he escort you back to the temple?"

"I left Saris back at the temple with instructions to keep my absence a secret. I came here alone."

"You can't return alone; anyone on the streets at this hour would be easy prey for the degenerates of the city."

"I'm the daughter of the high priest. Surely they wouldn't harm me, would they?"

Dov held back his laughter. "You live a very sheltered life in the temple. No, you would not be safe on the streets of Babel alone. Yanis and I will take Shadow with us and we'll escort you home. Shadow will alert us if anyone means us harm. I know he doesn't look ferocious, but he's big and highly protective of our family. From the looks of it, he's included you in his circle of friends."

They crossed the New Town bridge over the Euphrates River and hurried through the dirty streets of Old Babel toward the ziggurat. Shadow walked in a guard position two or three paces ahead of them. Dov wanted to see Evina safely home as soon as possible to avoid meeting anyone on the street at this hour. He was not afraid if they met one or two individuals; what he feared were gangs that sometimes waited in a side street to rob unsuspecting travelers or tradesmen walking to work before dawn.

Shadow suddenly stopped in the dark interval between streetlights. He looked toward an alleyway. A man's voice emerged from the darkness. "Don't be afraid. I wish to speak with you."

Dov automatically tensed and positioned himself between Yanis and Evina and the alley. "Don't come any closer. We'll walk to the next streetlight and you come out first so we can see you under the light." The voice from the dark sounded non-threatening.

"As you wish. I mean you no harm." The man behind the commanding voice waited for the three and the dog to move to where the street was better illuminated before he followed them at a distance. He stood at the edge of the pool of light. Shadow waited quietly next to Evina.

"That's far enough," exclaimed Dov. "What do you want?"

"I wish only to give Zidon's daughter a brief word of encouragement and comfort," the voice replied. They saw that the man who addressed them was of a medium height and weight. He was covered in black apparel, from his shoes to the old-fashioned, wide-brimmed hat that obscured his face. He wore a long, iridescent cape, that shifted colors from black to dark purple and back to black with his slightest movement.

"Again, I wish you no harm," he repeated in a clear, confident tone. "My message is intended to calm the young lady's fear and anxiety about trusting in the One True God."

"What?" Dov cried out. "Have you been spying on us? Who are you anyway?"

"I will answer your second question, Dov. I am a 'Watcher.' My mission is to ensure that no harm comes to you, your sister, or the daughter of Zidon. I am *not* a friend of the Triad. I too am a believer in the One True God and have unique skills to both gather information and protect those believers who choose to live in peace in the City of Babel. You will not see me unless I wish to reveal myself. Do not be afraid of me. I am at your service. With that, I bid you goodnight—for now."

Their phantom visitor turned his back on them and dissolved into the darkness. Dov ran after him but saw and heard nothing.

He returned puzzled by how their visitor could have vanished so easily. "We must get you back to the temple before he comes back."

"He won't be back," Yanis observed. "At least not tonight. I suspect we won't see him again for a while."

"I'm not afraid," commented Evina. "It's hard to explain, but it was as if Shadow knew who he was. The man came and went without a sound from your dog."

"That is strange. He's always growled or acted protectively when we walk through the city and a stranger approaches us. He was quiet when you visited us unannounced earlier tonight and now with that 'ghost' too." Dov couldn't explain what had happened.

When they arrived at the temple gates, Evina's bodyguard was relieved to see her return safely. Evina thanked her new friends for what they shared with her that night, and went to her rooms. Dov, Yanis, and Shadow returned without incident to their home.

"This has been one strange day," Dov remarked as they reached their home's front door.

"I have a feeling there will be more strange days ahead," Yanis added.

CHAPTER 8

Southern Sea, Bosrah Island—Cliff Crest

"This news from Babel is troubling," Botwa announced when he finished reading the latest encrypted message from the city. The large, dark-skinned man with the commanding presence of authority was the island's Chief Dispatcher. "The Triad is preparing to inaugurate the One World Tower soon, and this will coincide with some sort of natural catastrophe. Do you know about something called an asteroid?" he asked his assistant, Timtu.

"I haven't noticed anything in the heavens. Certainly nothing weather related is forecasted. The seasonal heavy rains and storms are still months away." Timtu was unperturbed by the news, but it was clear that something was happening in Babel that bothered the Dispatcher. Timtu was also Botwa's nephew and his eventual replacement to manage dispersion operations on the island. Their true activities on Bosrah were known to those who fled Babel to escape Nimrod's merciless grip. What began as a refuge for Shem and Japheth when they left Babel had turned into a gateway for those who sought to obey God's command to spread across the globe.

Shem and Japheth knew God's command after the Great Flood, but they hesitated to obey it. They settled along the Euphrates River and reasoned that they should raise their families first before disrupting their lives. They wanted to delay their migration plans until the antediluvian agriculture, animal husbandry, and technologies had been fully developed; they wanted to be sure that their many descendants were comfortably prepared for dispersion.

When Nimrod, the mighty warrior, became king of their growing community it became clear to Shem and Japheth that they had to leave before they became entangled in his web of corruption and violence. Sinister forces were creating a world system to rival the antediluvian world before the Great Flood. If Nimrod, a vicious and profane man, led earth's civilization, then the two sons of Noah and their families had to distance themselves from him and all that he represented. After a full confession of their sin to God they finally determined to obey Him at any cost. Sadly, many of their extended offspring chose to remain behind in Babel with Nimrod.

Shem, Japheth, and those willing to join them followed the flow of the Euphrates River to the Southern Sea where Bosrah Island became their new home. Rich soil and dense woods behind rocky cliffs above a safe harbor offered all the resources they needed to build homes for their children and their families who were safely protected from the storms that flooded the shore and marshes on the far side of the island. Wildlife in the forests and abundant fish in the shallow waters provided them with all the food they needed. When they cleared fertile lowlands, they planted crops that thrived. They were content to live on the island away from Nimrod and Babel.

Eventually they realized that they should continue with their migration to repopulate the world. Before they left Bosrah, they organized the island's agriculture and technology infrastructure to support a continuing cycle of dispersion. One condition for living on the island was that anyone who came to Bosrah had to eventually depart. A Chief Dispatcher would always be in charge of the island station to ensure its ability to promote dispersion.

Noah's two sons, approaching the seventh century of their lives, left behind an island compound which they named Cliff Crest. Bosrah became a hub from which their descendants ventured to the east and west in deep-draft, seaworthy boats. Botwa was slated to leave eventually too, at which time Timtu would assume the duties of Chief Dispatcher and help others escape from Babel, prepare boats and provisions, and dispatch families out in every direction. He had sources of intelligence in the city to help escapees. From what he had learned, Jengo, Pele, and their families were being forced to remain in the city until their duties on the tower were completed, even though he knew they wanted to leave.

"I'm worried that the Triad is planning something dramatic that will make it even more difficult for Pele, Jengo, and the others to flee Babel for good. They might not realize how much danger they face," Botwa said of recent events. "My source tells me that they are dealing with Zidon's daughter who, if she is like her mother, will snare them in the family's cults and astrologers." Botwa took a special interest in believers remaining in Babel who followed the One True God. Pele, Jengo, and their families had stayed behind to teach in the School of Japheth and build the tower structure, which originally was to be nothing more than government housing and offices. When it was finished, they planned to leave Babel. Recently, however, they had been threatened with death if they did not cooperate with Magus and finish a temple on the roof of the tower. They were apparently unaware of the full extent of the Triad's plans for the tower and the approaching disaster as a pretext for their One World system.

Timtu offered his uncle a suggestion: "Why not ask Pele and Jengo to come here for a meeting so we can get the latest news from the city, warn them in person, and make plans for their evacuation. If Pele is working on something for Zidon or one of his children he must understand the danger of dealing with that family. Even if he has no choice he must at least know what we know. If they take the *Dolphin* they can make the trip here in a few days."

"I agree. I'll send the information to Jengo right away. They could be here as soon as next week."

Botwa's message raced upstream later that day from Bosrah to Babel in a waterproof pouch strapped to the dorsal fin of a trained baiji. This white, prehistoric species of the freshwater river porpoise was often mistaken for an ocean porpoise but it could live in fresh or salt water. The mammal measured more than twenty feet in length. Japheth had trained several of these 'fish' to deliver messages between Bosrah and Babel. The brief summons would reach Jengo far faster than any boat or rider.

CHAPTER 9

New Babel, Pele's Machine Shop

Three days later

It was standard practice for either Jengo or Pele to walk to the New Town bridge each day looking for a white baiji messenger in the muddy waters below. When Jengo saw one swimming gracefully in wide circles from his high vantage point on the bridge, he descended stairs to the river's edge, walked to the end of a wooden dock, and whistled as loud as he could. Within minutes, the intelligent animal came alongside the dock and offered its dorsal fin so Jengo could open the waterproof pouch. After opening the summons from Botwa, Jengo quickly wrote a reply and sent the giant marine messenger on its way back to Bosrah. He hurried to tell Pele to prepare for a trip downriver.

"Listen to what Botwa says in his message," Jengo exclaimed when he burst into Pele's shop. "He believes we are in great danger and must come to Bosrah Island at once for a consultation."

"Does he say what the danger is?" Pele asked.

"Not in so many words. I suspect he wanted to keep that information confidential. He obviously wants to tell us in person."

"Why didn't he encipher the message? We both have the codes." Pele was still puzzled that the urgency of the meeting was not made more clear.

"I'm sure there's a good reason. Maybe he was in a hurry and couldn't take the time to explain fully. In any event, we need to leave as soon as possible."

"Where are we going?" Dov asked as he and Yanis burst into the shop from their work at school. Jengo tried to exit the room before he became drawn into a family tiff that he could sense coming. He delayed a moment too long.

"Your uncle Jengo and I are taking the *Dolphin* to Bosrah to meet with Botwa. We've been summoned there as soon as we can get ready." Pele replied.

"We'll come with you," Yanis said cheerfully.

"I don't see how you can do that. You need to stay here and work on the predictor engine design," their father insisted.

"Yanis and I have been discussing another option—one that's much faster than building a new machine." Dov had his father's attention. Jengo paused with his hand on the door latch to hear Dov's idea. "We think we can convert Evina's algos into new programs for the *Cyclone* engine that we used in school a few years ago. The machine hasn't been used in years, but it's still serviceable. We've just come back from looking at it and we think it can be made ready for programming in less than a month. Do you think that's worth a try?"

"Can you do that?" asked Pele. "It would take us a year or more to build a new predictor engine according to Evina's specifications. If you can program new frames into the *Cyclone* in less time, that's certainly a better alternative."

"I'm glad to hear that you agree, because we gave instructions to Benji, a student friend of ours, to clean, lubricate, adjust and calibrate each module of the *Cyclone*. We told him we wanted to run some experiments and he agreed to give the mechanical monster a full tune-up. Sis has plans in her head for programming the algos into new frames, so we should be ready to make trial runs shortly after the mechanism's engines are ready."

"Sounds like you have everything figured out," Jengo said in admiration of his niece and nephew.

"So can we go with you? It's been a couple years since we've seen the island."

"We all know why Dov wants to go. He likes Namasa's cooking!" Yanis said.

"No disrespect to Mom, but Namasa's desserts are in a class by themselves," Dov agreed. "Can we go then?"

"All right, I suppose that will work out," Pele conceded. "It'll have to be a quick down-and-back trip so Jengo and I can finish work on the tower ascender and controls, and so you can get those frames done. It'll take us a few hours to fuel the *Dolphin* before it's ready."

"Can Shadow come too?" Dov asked.

"I'd rather he stayed at home to protect your mother and younger brother while we're gone," their father answered. "Take him with you now to gather your personal belongings from home, and I'll be along in a few minutes to tell your mother about our plans and ask her to pack some meals. Meet me back here in two hours if we don't cross paths at home."

Shadow was listening to Pele and when he heard his name mentioned he hurried to the door. Dov and Yanis followed Shadow as he bounded into the street.

"Do you think we should tell Evina that we'll be gone?" Dov asked his sister as they hurried to match their long-legged dog's pace.

"I think that would be a good idea. You should write her a note—I'm sure she'd rather receive a letter from you than from me," Yanis said casually as they wandered through the crowded pedestrian traffic.

Dov was surprised by her suggestion and stopped suddenly. "Why would she care whether the note came from you or me? I don't want her to worry if she comes to the workshop to ask about progress on the predictor engine and finds us gone."

"Did it ever occur to you that she might want an excuse to come back to the workshop to see you and not me?"

"No. Why would she do that?"

Yanis shook her head in disbelief and tugged his arm to keep walking. "I can see that my brother is clueless. Let's pack for the trip and I'll *try* to explain things to you about women."

Dov wondered how his sister could have almost a sixth sense about things that so easily eluded him. Did he really live in such a fog? Why would Evina be interested in him, anyway?

With the dog in the lead, they arrived at their front door which was flung open by an eager nine-year old boy who, from his looks alone, was obviously Dov's and Yanis' little brother.

"You're home! You brought Shadow with you!" Maasi squealed. He threw his arms around the canine who weighed more than him.

"He's come to stay with you for a while," Yanis informed her little brother. She edged through the doorway past the boy who happily clung to the dog's neck. She called out to tell her mother about their trip to Bosrah.

"Let's get you something to eat!" Maasi said as he dragged Shadow into the house.

Euphrates River, *Dolphin* Boathouse

The four travelers harnessed a single draft horse to a wagon, loaded it with their supplies, and made the hour-long trip to where the *Dolphin* was berthed downriver inside a covered boathouse. The *Dolphin* was a watercraft built from two narrow, fifty-foot hulls of traditional fishing boats, joined by a large platform between the hulls on which a vapor engine was firmly mounted. The vapor engine boiler, black rock fuel, and small sleeping quarters were below the open top deck. Drive shafts connected two giant screws in the water between the hulls for propulsion and a tall smokestack rose above the steering pedestal on the deck. Most of the carrying capacity of the hulls was for fuel that fed the compact boiler. Since a large reserve of fuel was kept dry in a shed near the boathouse, it took them several hours to shovel enough of the dusty black material into the hulls for the round trip to Bosrah. Dov started a fire to bring the boiler pressure to a level high enough to propel the screws. When they were finished loading the fuel they washed off the black powder that covered their bodies and clothes.

Back when vapor engines were in their infancy, King Nimrod had two large, high-speed ships constructed, appropriately named *Savage* and *Defiant*, both over four hundred feet in length, which he used to explore the northern tributaries of the Euphrates and Tigris rivers in search of gold. He even searched as far south as the confluence of the Euphrates with the Southern Sea. Satisfied that he had mined all of the available gold on the surface along the rivers, his ships were converted into armed military cruisers that the warrior king used more often as his personal yachts. The two royal cruisers and the *Dolphin* were the only vapor-powered vessels on the river.

Pele surveyed their heavily laden boat that rested low in the water while the vapor engine boiler rumbled and chuffed in the background and shot black smoke and flaming cinders into the air from its exhaust stack. "We'll have to keep our speed low at the start so we don't swamp the hulls. The flow of the river will add to our speed downriver, and when we return upriver we'll be lighter and should be able to reach top speed." Pele stood before the boat's wheel and tested the rudders mounted at the ends of each hull.

Dov and Yanis pushed away from the dock and into the current of the river with long poles. When the water was deep enough, Pele engaged the main drive of the vapor engine and the six-foot screws began their slow, powerful churn. The forward screw pulled water into the space between the hulls and the aft screw pushed the water out the back. The *Dolphin* emitted a deafening roar and a trail of black smoke and sparks as they moved steadily through the water. Jengo and Dov took turns shoveling black rock into the boiler at regular intervals, while Yanis monitored the pressure gauges and Pele guided them down the middle of the meandering river.

As the *Dolphin* gained speed and fresh air blew across the planked deck, the long runabout quickly outpaced the fishermen's old-fashioned sailing dhows with their large triangular lateen-rigged sails. The four ignored the heat and roar of the boiler to enjoy the natural scenery. The fertile banks of the river were home to many large herbivore dinos feeding in the lush marshes; prehistoric crocodiles more than twenty feet in length basked in the sun on sandbars, and tens of thousands of birds, startled by the loud vapor engine, screeched in the sky ahead of them. In the distance, the river's edges tapered into an alluvial plain, rich in silt and nutrients from the mountains north of Babel that turned the river a light brown.

Five days after receiving their summons from Botwa, the craft reached the part of the river that was a mile across. Soon the river split into countless muddy tributaries of the Euphrates delta, dotted with mounds of mangrove trees tentatively gripping patches of sand to form emerald chains of islands. Some channels between the islands were covered with arched vegetation that formed dark tunnels dappled with sunlight. They kept their course on the eastern edge of the river's wide main channel for hours, eager to turn around the last headland of the Euphrates where it emptied into the sea. When the river's brown silt finally met the blue translucence that clearly defined the Southern Sea, the *Dolphin* changed its course to due east.

"I hope we have enough black rock for the return trip," Dov shouted to his father over the boiler's roar. "We'll use much more fuel returning upstream." He scanned the horizon for signs of the cliffs of Bosrah.

Pele nodded in reply. "It'll be close, but I think we have enough. We should load some wood from the island, just in case."

Hours later, Dov cried "There it is!" and pointed directly in front of them. The shining white houses that greeted them from the top of the cliffs were a welcome sight.

The *Dolphin* emitted a deafening roar and
a trail of black smoke and sparks.

CHAPTER 10

Southern Sea, Bosrah Island—Cliff Crest

The tired travelers were met at the island's stone quay by their cousin Javak, who had watched the *Dolphin* from an observation tower atop the cliff. After making sure their craft was securely tied, Javak took Yanis' backpack and led the visitors up a long flight of smooth stairs cut into the side of the stone cliff.

On the wide porch that wrapped around Cliff Crest and overlooked the harbor, they were greeted by Botwa and his wife, Namasa, who lavished them with hugs and cries of delight at how the twins had grown since they had last seen them. Javak excused himself and offered to return for their meeting later, if Botwa felt he could be of help.

"Look at you—how you have grown since I last saw you!" Namasa exclaimed when she held Dov and Yanis at arms length.

"Oh, Aunt Namasa," the twins exclaimed together. "You always say that."

"I know, but it's always so nice to see my favorite niece and nephew. I only wish you would come here to live with us." The warm welcome was something to be shared with all who came to Bosrah. Namasa was beloved by all for her gregarious friendliness and generosity. She loved nothing better than a house filled with guests as an excuse to show off her culinary skills.

"Come, everyone!" Namasa insisted with arms spread wide. "I've prepared plenty of food for you after such a long trip. You must be hungry. This will freshen you up." When they were comfortably seated, she brought plates of food from the kitchen that filled the large dining table. Botwa asked Dov if he would pray before they ate.

"Dear God, we thank you for a safe voyage here to our family. We have been blessed beyond measure by your hand, and for this food we are most thankful. Please continue to protect us in the difficult days ahead. We don't know what you have planned for our future, but we know it is for our good. May you bless our time here and use it to honor your holy name. Amen."

Platters of meats and vegetables were passed eagerly around the table, along with laughter. "Eat! Talk! Enjoy yourselves!" Namasa continued with an endless parade of new dishes until her guests jokingly begged her to stop. When it seemed that they could not eat another serving, Botwa suggested that they move to the outside verandah for a hot drink made from ground, roasted beans where they could watch the sunset and talk about the latest happenings in Babel. Dov stayed behind to heap a plate with desserts to tide him over during their talk. When he kissed his aunt he left a smear of foamed white cream on both her cheeks. Namasa beamed with happiness at his compliment.

"I know it was difficult for you to get away on short notice and make this journey to talk with us." Botwa took charge of the meeting as the acting leader of the family, a role his predecessor had given him before he left Bosrah for the last time. He would carry on the patriarch's plan to scatter over the earth.

Jengo, Pele, Dov and Yanis pulled up chairs to face Botwa, while Timtu quietly joined them. "Why don't you begin by telling us what's been going on in Babel lately? We can add our concerns as you go along." Botwa began. "Who would like to start?"

Pele cleared his throat and offered an explanation of how they had first learned about the approaching disaster. "The daughter of the High Priest Zidon came to my shop only a few weeks ago with an unusual request. As you know, I built a planetary visualizer for Zidon—just a simple machine with models of planets and moons orbiting from earth's perspective; something purely scientific and nothing that would get me involved in his false religion. Apparently, his daughter Evina is an expert astronomer, and she thought of me when she needed a predictor engine for some very complex algos. Their complexity defied the skills of her most experienced numerologists."

"Why would she need something that a planetary visualizer couldn't depict?' Timtu asked. He wasn't an engineer, but mechanical devices intrigued him.

"Her astronomical observations revealed motion of a large object in deep space that she thought could be on a near-collision course with earth, but she needed an advanced machine to perform her intricate calculations. She had pages of algos that I didn't understand, so I called Dov and Yanis to examine them and decide if a predictor engine could be built to mechanize them."

"They were the most sophisticated algos we'd ever seen," observed Dov. His sister nodded in agreement as Dov continued. "We studied them and came to the conclusion that a machine *could* be built to implement them, but that it would take a long time; it might be a year or more before one could be built. She said we didn't have that much time. The object will come close to or hit the earth in less than a year."

"That's when the twins suggested programming the *Cyclone* machine to solve the algos," Pele said proudly.

"What's a *Cyclone* machine?" asked Timtu.

Pele was glad to explain. "I built a device many years ago to perform routine mathematical calculations. At first, it was supposed to be simple functions that were repetitive and boring for manual numerologists. Then I suppose I got carried away and modified it to do multiple tasks at the same time. Eventually the mechanical thing filled a large room. Others then came along and made changes to it so that I wouldn't recognize it today. I consider it my best piece of work," Pele said proudly.

"So why is called the *Cyclone?*"

"That's because it makes an overwhelmingly loud noise when it's running," said Yanis. "When the vapor engine, air compressors, and thousands of gears and sliders harmonize, it sounds like the deafening howl of a tornado or hurricane. I think it sounds *wonderful!*" Yanis was embarrassed by her sudden enthusiasm.

"Anyway," continued Pele, "if frames could convert the written algos to machine instructions, it might be possible to calculate the arrival time and impact location of the object much sooner. When the programming is done, the calculations can be repeated with updated trajectory measurements whenever needed. The machine is being cleaned and tuned now, and there may be a few hardware modifications required, but Yanis and Dov can begin programming it as soon as we get back."

"Are you two satisfied that it won't take long to program?" Pele asked the twins.

Yanis answered for her brother, "Dov and I used it before we graduated. You're right about the difficulty of its programming. Nobody has successfully harnessed its full power since we left school. We think we can make it work. It'll still take some work to keep it operational while it calculates. Each run will take hours to complete."

Botwa leaned forward to express his concern. "I'm afraid that you're entangling yourselves with Zidon and his family. Maybe even being used, without your knowledge of course, by the Triad. Neither Zidon nor his son, Arvid, can be trusted. What about this daughter of his? Do you think she could be using this approaching object for some occult or astrological purpose?" This was Botwa's main worry, although the threat of a space object on a collision course with earth was no less disturbing.

"We think she might be a believer," Yanis replied quickly.

"What? Her father and brother are idolatrous pagan priests and her mother was the most evil priestess who ever lived. I'm told that the young lady is in line to be the next high priestess of Ishtar. No true believer could possibly come from that kind of family background." Botwa was obviously skeptical.

Yanis rose in Evina's defense. "She came to us alone late at night after her first visit, and asked us many questions about the One True God. In her study of the sun, moon, planets, and stars through her telescope, she arrived at the conclusion that they could not be gods. She told us that all evidence pointed to a Creator of the infinite universe to whom she must give an account. She says that she's a believer in the Holy One, and I believe her." Yanis realized that she was pacing back and forth in front of the group in her emotional support of Zidon's daughter. She sat down without embarrassment, having spoken from her heart.

"I agree," said Dov. "She's not only convinced that a Creator God made the universe and all that is in it, but passionate in her rejection of astrology and pagan gods. I think she's amazing!"

Botwa appreciated their opinions of Evina and turned to the approaching space object. "What exactly do you expect to learn about the object when you have the *Cyclone* fully operational?"

"We should arrive at an accurate estimate of when the object or asteroid will be visible with the unaided eye, where it will appear in the sky, when it will pass by or impact, and where that will be." Dov went on to describe briefly how the machine would make these calculations, but none other than Yanis understood his explanation. He gave up when he realized they were not interested in the details of algos.

Botwa brought the technical discussion to a close and summarized what they had covered thus far: "So, we have an approaching astral object—an asteroid as you call it—that could either pass close to earth or hit it. You estimate that this thing will arrive in the next several months and we will have more precise information when the *Cyclone* performs its calculations. You are closely involved with the high priest's daughter, but feel comfortable with her motives and trust her because she appears to be a believer. Is that about right?"

The four nodded their agreement, and the group paused as Namasa brought more refreshments and set a tray on a table at the center of the gathering. She joined the group while they sipped their hot drinks and looked silently across the calm sea at the vanishing sunset. "Our God is a gracious creator of beauty," she observed as all stared out at the evening's display.

After a few moments, Botwa resumed their discussion by asking, "What about your progress on the tower, Jengo?"

"The alloy structure itself is finished, and the lower and upper floors have been fully enclosed. The freight ascenders have operated in four stages to the rooftop for more than a year. Freight ascenders relay equipment and supplies to the middle ascenders, and then they go to the upper freight ascender where work on the Luminary interior is also nearly completed. Magus wants the Ministerial and Guild levels to remain unfinished so the royal and priestly families can inhabit their upper residences in the next few weeks. As you may know, we've had many problems with the ascenders." Jengo paused to gather his thoughts. "Dov made the first ascent to the 120th level in a single flight with the Luminary passenger ascender, and returned safely after an incident that Yanis was able to quickly fix. Since then we've had numerous more freight ascender accidents. One of them resulted in fatalities. My assessment is that operator error, whether from inattention, ignorance, or outright incompetence, is the only cause. It's not a technical problem with the freight ascenders or their drive mechanisms. Do you agree, Pele?"

"Yes. I've helped Jengo with the accident investigations and concur with his conclusion. I wouldn't ride in any ascender myself unless Jengo, Dov, or Yanis were in the control room. I'm not sure what the ultimate solution is for improving safety, but Jengo and I will try to come up with something."

"You did not mention sabotage," Botwa observed quietly.

Jengo thought before he responded. "Maybe I've been subconsciously avoiding that thought. It's possible, I suppose, that a controller intent on mischief could be doing it. If the crashes were intentional, that has much wider implications."

Botwa suggested that he not rule out a wider web of intentional subversion when it came to the Triad and the One World Tower. "I'll have my source in the city keep an eye out for signs of someone or some subversive group intent on damaging the tower."

As darkness slowly came over the small group on the porch and lamps were lit in the house, Botwa's tone turned ominous. "I've learned that the New Babel Triad intends to take advantage of the approaching asteroid, and my fear is that your helping Zidon's daughter could put you, Jengo and Pele, and your families directly into their hands as accomplices. Their ultimate goal is a one world system that will enslave the inhabitants of Babel. The tower is a key part of their strategy. We think they'll publically assert that their gods are orchestrating this impending catastrophe and that the people must follow the Triad, and Zidon's ritualistic worship of so-called gods, to avert it. The results from the *Cyclone*, when passed on to them through Zidon's daughter, will probably be manipulated to achieve their wicked ends. You must take measures to ensure that the results do not reach them."

"I don't know how that'll be possible," Dov commented boldly. "We'll have to give the results to Evina, and we don't know what she'll do after that. If her father demands the results from her, she'll be in a difficult position if she denies him. She draws the line when it comes to participating in his false religion, but she's still submissive to her father." Dov's concern was evident. "She might be able to stall him for a while until we have accurate and higher confidence results. Our first outputs will be approximations until they can be verified against Evina's latest observations. I think eventually she'll have to give her father the results."

Botwa appreciated their concern and suggested something else: "The people you must be most wary of are the Triad—Nimrod, Zidon, and Magus—and Zidon's son Arvid. I have received information that Arvid may be working for Magus on something about which his father is not aware. Maybe we can isolate Evina from them for the next few weeks to buy enough time to find out what they are planning. In any event, think about that and see if you can come up with a way to keep the results from them for as long as possible."

"Have you told them about the prediction in the Book of Adam?" Timtu asked.

Botwa brightened at the reminder. "As I recall, the Book of Adam that Japheth brought with him on the ark makes no mention of a global destruction or cataclysmic disaster in its prophetic passages between now and the coming to earth of the promised Redeemer. There *is* mention of a 'time of disobedience' after the worldwide inundation, followed by 'confusion and division,' but nothing about global destruction. To satisfy this and all future prophecies, my interpretation is that the space object will *not* impact earth and destroy us. Nor do I think it will impact the city of Babel directly and destroy it and its inhabitants, although that is possible. The Lord told Noah that He would never again destroy every creature. My personal guess is that Evina's approaching object will come close, but it will not actually impact the earth. That's only my opinion, of course."

"That's some measure of comfort, I suppose." Jengo said.

"Considering the dangerous situation with the Triad and the approaching asteroid I think you should return to Babel, gather your families, and evacuate the city as soon as possible. I realize that there are complications with that, but that's my recommendation." Botwa knew he had no authority over Jengo or Pele, but believed that any delay would be more perilous.

"I agree with you in principal," Jengo said, "but knowing when and where the asteroid might impact would be useful for civilization as a whole. That will take a couple of weeks. In the meantime, we can prepare for evacuation and figure out how to slip away from Magus' surveillance. He's said that he'll stop us from leaving by holding our wives and children hostages. Pele and I have some loose ends to tie up on the tower too. I don't want to abandon the ascender situation as it is now, or the freight capsules will continue to fall and more people will die. I can't do that in good conscience."

Pele agreed with Jengo's suggestion to depart Babel when the *Cyclone* produced final, accurate asteroid information. They didn't want to wait any longer than needed.

"So you'll come here as soon as you get final results?" Botwa asked.

"Yes." Jengo said.

"What about Evina?" Dov asked. "She can't be left behind." Yanis quickly agreed.

"What makes you think she'd choose to leave the city? You implied that she's loyal to her father, at least as far as family ties are concerned. This would complicate or delay your departure." Timtu was bothered by this new twist.

"I have a solution that would at least help Jengo and Pele speed up their work on the tower," Botwa said. "Convincing Evina to escape from Babel with your family is another matter."

Botwa explained: "You met Javak when you arrived. He is a superb engineer, and I believe he could help Jengo with his ascender difficulties. Javak's son, Ashaz, has also been trained in the technical arts. He and his cousin Kittish could help you operate the *Cyclone*. It could take them a week or more to join you in Babel because they are engaged in other commitments on the island."

"I knew Ash and Kitt at school," said Yanis. "They were a couple of years ahead of Dov and me, and are familiar with the *Cyclone's* basic operation. If they could help refurbish the machine while we program the frames, and then oversee its operation, that would speed things up."

Botwa was pleased with their acceptance of assistance and felt that they were close to being finished with their business. "That sounds admirable! I know you'll want to get an early start in the morning, so I suggest we have a time of prayer here before you get some sleep, and we will see you off shortly after dawn."

The group bowed in prayer and asked the Lord to bless their families and give them wisdom for the unknown times ahead. It was best that they didn't know what the sovereign God had planned for their future.

Next day

The four travelers boarded the *Dolphin* at an early hour after Dov fired up the boiler and brought the vapor engine to its full pressure. They loaded heaped baskets of food prepared by Namasa and cast off from the stone pier while still in the early morning shadow of the cliff. The large screws between the hulls churned the water of the harbor as they pulled out of the narrow mouth of its entrance, turned west into the open sea, and aimed for the brown waters of the river. They'd look for Javak, Ash, and Kitt to join them later. Until then, they pondered what God had prepared for them in New Babel.

CHAPTER 11

Old Babel, Ziggurat of Marduk—Evina's Observatory

Two days later

Arvid returned from another late meeting with Magus intent on obtaining his sister's latest prediction about the approaching asteroid. It was past midnight when he rounded the corner of the temple porch and startled two guards posted outside Evina's observatory entrance. They crossed their spears to prevent his entry. They returned to attention when they recognized his face in the light of a smoldering lamp. Before Arvid could utter a reprimand, one of the sentinels opened the door for the hot-tempered young noble.

"There you are!" he exclaimed as he rushed across the dimly lit chamber toward his sister, who peered intently into her telescope. "I thought I'd find you here!" Before he took a half-dozen steps across the room the hulking figure of Saris stepped into his path from the shadows. Arvid collided with the bodyguard's iron-hard torso and fell backwards, tripped on his robe and tumbled to the floor.

"You should be more careful when you rush headlong into a dark room," his sister advised calmly without looking up from her telescope's eyepiece. "I'll be with you in a moment." Evina made some notes and smiled to herself while her brother struggled awkwardly to his feet in a rage.

"I'll have you arrested for assaulting me! You worthless, dumb eunuch!" Arvid's fury was wasted as the impassive Saris stood between him and Evina with an unblinking glare as if daring him to come further.

"You know he can't hear what you're saying. Why do you waste your breath?"

"Tell him to step aside or I'll have the guards arrest him!"

Evina showed mild annoyance with her brother's bluster. She stepped forward and stood next to her bodyguard. "That won't happen. The guards know that Saris is loyal only to me, and that he'd die before anyone harmed me. I suggest you stand back where you are unlikely to accidentally bump into him again."

Saris gave a guttural growl and stepped forward to reinforce what he assumed Evina had said to her brother. Arvid flinched at his approach and backed toward the door. When he had composed himself and rearranged his cloak, he directed his attention to his sister. "I want an update on that approaching asteroid. When will it appear and how close will it come to us? Father needs to know so he can make plans for a special ceremony, and he needs to know immediately." He hoped his bluster would get him what he wanted so he could retreat from Saris' piercing glare.

"Your request is unconvincing," Evina stated calmly. "It's past midnight and I find it hard to believe that Father sent you at this hour to demand an update. I'll see him tomorrow morning and tell him of my most recent observations. Besides, I thought I told you I would report to him and not to you."

"So help me . . . you'll regret not giving me what I want. You may be able to hide behind your dumb protector now, but some day he won't be here and I'll show you who'll rule over you when Father is dead."

"Are you expecting him to die soon? Is that a threat against Father?" Evina demanded. She detected more evasion and duplicity than usual in his tone. His eyes refused to meet hers. "Your ambition and arrogance know no bounds!"

"I intend to get what I want, no matter who gets in the way—even if that includes Father!" Arvid spun around, fumbled clumsily with the door latch, and hurried from the room.

Are you all right, Miss? Saris signed with concern after the door slammed.

Evina looked at him with troubled eyes. *I am frightened by the approaching asteroid and my brother's threats. Now he is threatening harm to our father. Thank you for keeping him away from me and placing yourself in jeopardy for my sake. I will get some sleep when I have finished these calculations.*

After organizing her papers and locking them in her desk, Evina and Saris walked back to her bedroom flanked by the two temple guards who, after one look from Saris, kept their distance. They had overheard fragments of the conversation inside the observatory and, given the disdain palace guards had for the arrogant, overbearing son of the high priest, they held Saris in new regard. Saris took up his post outside Evina's bedroom door, where he would stand all night. The palace guards would remain at a deferential distance from him until their shift changed at dawn.

New Babel, Chief Magician's Residence

"She refused to give me any information!" Arvid announced petulantly when he was admitted into the chief magician's residence. He felt humiliated by his failure to accomplish the simple task given to him by Magus; his sister's refusal to do his bidding was further demeaning.

"I'm not surprised," replied Magus. "You don't understand that she's an independently minded young woman, especially when it comes to ethical matters. She has an old-fashioned sense of loyalty and honor toward her father; something that is obviously not a problem for you." Magus smiled at the morally pliable young man slumped in the chair before him.

CHAPTER 12

Euphrates River, *Dolphin* Boathouse

Five days later

A swift downstream current and a strong headwind kept the craft from making any progress towards Babel until the wind shifted, and these hindered the *Dolphin*'s progress as it headed north from Bosrah. The crew of the *Dolphin* fed the boiler of the vapor engine, took turns sleeping and watched the shoreline move steadily past them in an unending show of colorful wildlife, dense foliage, and low savannah that extended to the horizon. When the exhausted crew arrived at the boat's dock nearly a week after leaving Bosrah, they took care to securely tie up their craft inside the boathouse.

While they waited for the embers in the boiler's firebox to cool before they left for home, Jengo gathered them to review their assignments. "I've been thinking about our next steps since we left Bosrah, so tell me what you think of this: I must return to the tower and assess the situation with the ascenders and see what Magus has muddled during my absence. Pele, I think you and the twins should go to the school and check on the status of the *Cyclone* to make sure that the needed changes are being made. Then Dov and Yanis can begin coding the machine."

"I'd like to check on Evina to find out if there have been any new developments with the asteroid," Dov said.

Yanis looked at her brother with a knowing smile. "I'll go with you after we've looked at the *Cyclone*. That way we can give her an estimate of how long the programming will take and get the latest data from her observations."

"Good! So, those are our assignments. We'll meet up at the shop later tonight and discuss any new information." Jengo stood with the others to finish shutting down the boiler. They headed north toward the city, where they split up on their various missions.

New Babel, One World Tower—Capsule Control Room

What Jengo found when he entered the tower basement control room did not completely surprise him. A junior trainee was overseeing instruments for the engines that actively powered eight freight ascenders. He was dozing in his chair when Jengo entered the room and called out, "Where are the other operators?"

The trainee controller jumped to his feet and wiped his eyes. "Sir, I did not expect you today!"

"Obviously not. Where are the other operators? Young man, what's your name?"

"My name is Tulee, sir. They were here this morning and all was well with the vapor machines. Boilers are running smoothly, the black rock is feeding automatically, and I have been watching the pressures to keep them within limits. The senior shift operator stepped out for a few minutes. I'm sure he'll be back momentarily." Tulee's explanation appeared to approximate the truth, which Jengo accepted for the moment.

"How long have you been a trainee on the ascenders?"

"Two weeks, sir. This is my first job," the young man said proudly.

"How old are you?"

"Fifteen . . . sir."

Jengo groaned and looked around the control room at the empty consoles. No wonder there were problems with the ascenders. A brand new operator left in charge of the entire building! "Have there been any ascender accidents in my absence? Specifically, has the Luminary ascender been used?"

"We had one problem with that ascender, but there were no fatalities." The youngster appeared nervous. "There was some minor damage to the capsule when a brake failed during descent, but it's been repaired."

"Who was the ascender operator and who was the controller?" Jengo had an inkling about what had happened, and dreaded what else the young man might have done when left unsupervised. "Were you in the ascender at the time?"

"No, sir. I was here operating the engine."

"Who was in the capsule at its controls?"

Tulee hesitated, but he had no alternative but to answer. His eyes darted around the room before he spoke. "Nobody, sir."

"So I think I know now what happened. You were operating the Luminary ascender from here, using the clutch and brake on the vapor engine only. You misjudged its speed and when it approached the docking area you couldn't stop it in time before it hit the bottom stop. For your sake, I hope there were no Luminaries in the capsule, or both of us will lose our heads."

"Sir, the ascender capsule was empty. I . . . I wanted to see if I could control it myself from here without an operator inside. I'm sorry, sir." Tulee stood paralyzed with fright pondering the consequences of his experimenting with the Luminary ascender.

Jengo paced back and forth to rein in his temper. He resisted blaming the young operator, a teenager with only two weeks of training, who had been left by his supervisor to watch pressures for eight vapor engines running at once. He was frustrated with operators who had no sense of responsibility or awareness of how dangerous the engines could be if pressures went into the red or they "forgot" to apply the drum brakes in time. A boiler explosion in the basement could destroy the control spaces, rupture high-pressure delivery lines, and lead to many deaths. It might even compromise the integrity of the building's structure. His tower employees, hired by Magus into patronage jobs, didn't think about the destruction or loss of life that could result from their actions. No wonder the chief magician didn't want them at the controls when he was in the ascender!

CHAPTER 13

New Babel, School of Japheth—*Cyclone* Computing Center

Progress on modifications to the gigantic computing engine was far more encouraging than what Jengo encountered at the tower. The processing center was quiet when Pele finished his inspection of the hose connections and background linkages. Benji and the three remaining students in the School of Japheth proudly stood before the polished panels that fronted thirty cabinets of the *Cyclone* core.

"I'm very impressed with your accomplishments!" Pele pronounced with a wide smile. The young workers cheered noisily. Dov and Yanis joined in to compliment the workers' achievements in such a short amount of time. They shook hands with Benji, who was their team leader for the machine's hardware.

Pele raised his hands to quiet the group. "Save your partying until we've completed tests for the initial operational capability. This hunk of metal may be polished like a mirror on the outside, but now it must be powered up, tested for internal integrity, and all calculations checked before we can declare the work finished." He gave them a mock scowl and swung his arm with the motion of cracking a whip. "Now, back to work!"

Pele waved Dov and Yanis to his side as the students returned to their duties in a joyous mood.

"The hardware appears to be in good condition, but you have your work cut out for you before meaningful results can be obtained. Do you have any idea how long the programming will take?"

Dov answered for himself and his sister. "We think it will take a week or more to convert Evina's formulas to frames and make the settings on the *Cyclone* control panels. Evina's numerologists have already performed some manual computations, so we can compare the machine's results with those outputs for an initial check. If they agree, then we'll input the latest figures from Evina's observations and see what comes out."

"Excellent!" beamed Pele. "Now, I think Dov is anxious to see Evina, so why don't you two head over to Old Babel and give her an update on the state of her predictor engine?"

Before they left, Pele added, "By the way, don't mention anything to her about our conversations with Botwa or our plans to leave the city. Until we're sure that our information exchange with her is secure, I don't want anyone else to know what we're doing. I don't doubt Evina's trustworthiness, but she may unintentionally reveal something to her father or brother that puts all of us at risk. Play down our visit as a short 'vacation,' and limit your talk to her observations."

Old Babel, Ziggurat of Marduk—Evina's Observatory

Guards escorted Dov and Yanis to the temple observatory, where they approached Saris standing squarely in front of the tall double doors. Saris smiled broadly when he recognized the two. The bodyguard raised his hand to stop the escorting guards from coming further and opened one of the observatory doors himself to admit the visitors. He closed the door behind Evina's friends and looked at the guards, who by now had no trouble understanding his unspoken command: *You wait there!*

"Oh, Dov, I'm so glad to see you!" Evina gave him an unexpected hug before she turned her attention to Yanis with another hug. "I've missed you these past days! How was your trip to Bosrah?"

Yanis answered her leading question and told her of the trip on the *Dolphin*, seeing their cousins again and staying in the large family complex at Cliff Crest. They joked about Namasa's huge quantities of home cooked food and how Dov stuffed himself with desserts. When it was obvious that Evina had no suspicion of an ulterior reason for their absence, Yanis asked Evina for the latest information about the asteroid.

"The motion of the object has been steadily progressing along the same trajectory," Evina proclaimed while she shuffled through papers on her desk. She found one sheet and handed it to Dov. "You'll see that it hasn't gained speed since we first spoke. My approximate calculations still show it still moving straight at earth."

The twins shared the paper and perused her numbers. "We agree," said Yanis as her brother nodded. "I'm sure your algos are correct for these inputs. We'll check them again before we run them through the *Cyclone*."

"Is it ready to perform calculations?" Evina asked with quick excitement.

"Not yet," said Dov. "The machine is cleaned and broken parts have been replaced. The hardware will undergo power and mechanical testing for a week or so while we check these numbers and program the frames. When the machine produces simple calculations that match those your numerologists came up with, we'll be ready to do more extensive runs with updated observations. You'll be able to spend all your time at this telescope while our machine 'crunches' the numbers!"

"I'm relieved to know that. You two are my best friends, and I can't believe I've only known you for a short time," Evina sighed.

Yanis sensed that there was something more. "What's the matter? What happen to you while we were gone?" she asked as she and Dov pulled chairs next to her and waited for her to answer.

"My brother came here late one night and threatened me if I didn't give him my latest results. I refused, of course, but he continued his threats. He stated clearly that he would do *anything* to get what he wanted. I think he might even harm Father if he doesn't get his way.

"I almost gave away our plans when I alluded to the use of an engine to perform more accurate calculations. I never mentioned your names, of course, but Arvid was interested in finding out who I was dealing with. Believe me, he'll stop at nothing to intercept the results or sabotage them, if necessary." She looked at her friends with tears in her eyes. "I don't want you two hurt because of something I said."

"Please don't worry. We'll be all right." Dov stared across the room in contemplation before making a suggestion: "We must be more careful to keep the connection between you and our family a secret. It may already be known since the temple guards saw us visiting you today. They might tell your brother, and who knows what he would do then. We can't risk visiting you here. You certainly can't visit the shop or the school either."

"That's right," added Yanis. "We need a secure method for you to communicate your latest data to us and for us to send *Cyclone* results to you. We can't have direct contact with each other. How do you feel about making our exchanges in writing through Saris as a courier? As long as we know your papers won't be intercepted, we'll be confident that the danger is minimized."

"I owe Saris my life. He can be trusted with anything. It would take half of the temple guard force to extract anything from him. When he's away though, nobody will be here to protect me. What will I do then?" From her plaintive question it was obvious that Evina feared deeply for her personal safety.

"I have an idea that might solve that," Dov said suddenly. "I'll send someone to guard you when Saris is away. You can trust him as much as you trust Saris or us. He'll come to the observatory later tonight and be your protector when Saris is away."

"I'd like that. Thank you."

The two left her not knowing when they would see their friend next. Outside the observatory doors Dov motioned to Saris to go inside and see Evina. He startled the friendly eunuch by reaching out and clasping his giant hand in friendship and silently mouthed, *Take care of her.*

Saris read his lips and nodded solemnly as the temple guards escorted the two away. He hurried inside to see what she needed.

"Who in the world could possibly take Saris' place as Evina's bodyguard?" Yanis exclaimed when they left the ziggurat temple gate and crossed the bridge between Old Town and New Babel. "I can't imagine anyone else trustworthy or strong enough to protect her."

"Well Sis, we do know someone, or rather something, that can protect Evina."

"So tell me!" she insisted.

"You'll have to wait!" Pleased with himself, Dov laughed and broke into a jog into the streets of New Babel toward their father's shop. His sister hurried to keep up with him.

CHAPTER 14

New Babel, Pele's Machine Shop

Dov and Yanis burst into the shop out of breath from running. They surprised Pele and Jengo, who both sat at the worktable. They immediately assured the startled brothers that there was nothing wrong.

"We ran here as fast as we could to tell you that Evina needs protection from her brother, who wants to manipulate her observations and to intercept results from the predictor engine." Dov steadied his breath and continued. "We've set up a secure route of written communication between us through Saris, her bodyguard. He'll bring her latest asteroid observations and return *Cyclone* results for her evaluation. It was critical that we disguise any connection between us and her."

"There's more to it than that," added Yanis. "Remember Botwa's warnings of the Triad's secret plans for Babel? They'll stop at nothing to harm us if they think we have detailed information about the asteroid. The Triad is key to whatever will happen when or if the asteroid impacts earth. Like Botwa said, it's vital that we not get drawn into their plans or allow Evina to be harmed." The intensity in Yanis' face revealed a fierce determination to protect her friend.

Pele agreed, but changed the subject to what he and Jengo had been discussing before Dov and Yanis came in. "Jengo tells me that operations in the ascender control room in the tower are in shambles. You two will be stretched thin between programming the *Cyclone* and operating the Luminary ascender if travel picks up because construction of the Luminary residence levels is just about completed. Once it's ready for occupancy, we anticipate that the Luminary passenger ascender will be in high demand during the day. For now, you two will have to be on duty at the ascender station." Pele registered concern that so much depended on his children; all their time would be divided between the *Cyclone* and the tower.

"We can do it," Dov assured his father. "Benji and the students will be running tests of the primary vapor engine, compressor, and air feed lines during the next few days, but we can start setting up Evina's algos right away. The students can leave the *Cyclone's* engine idling for several days at a time before it needs to be shut down completely for maintenance. We can do all our programming between ascender shifts at the tower."

Yanis added her willingness to program the *Cyclone* and cover the ascender schedule at the same time. "I'm glad that Uncle Javak will be here soon with Kitt and Ash. If we train them on the ascender controls, then Dov and I can spend more time at the computing center." Yanis felt better that pressing details were getting resolved. They would still be working almost non-stop over the next few weeks, but it was worth it if they could thwart the plans of the Triad, ensure Evina's safety, and leave the city before the asteroid hit.

"That reminds me," Yanis added. "Evina will need protection when Saris leaves the temple to bring us updated observations of the asteroid's path. If she's left alone, there's no telling what her brother might try to do to her. Dov said he has a solution that I am dying to hear about."

Dov gave her a smug look. "Oh, I have a solution all right."

"Well, what is it?" Yanis was beside herself with curiosity.

Dov paused for dramatic effect and spoke softly. "Shadow, come here."

The large dog, upon hearing his name spoken, emerged from under the table with alert eyes fixed intently on Dov, anticipating a command.

"What? You're joking!" His sister looked at him in disbelief.

"No, I'm not joking. You saw how Shadow formed an immediate bond with Evina when she was here. Neither Arvid nor any of his henchmen would dare harm Evina with Shadow by her side."

"Are you saying that Shadow is a canine version of Saris?" Yanis quipped.

"You have an interesting way of putting words in my mouth."

"Uncanny, isn't it?"

Dov ignored his sister's attempt at humor and patted the animal by his side—his back reaching almost as high as the young man's waist. Shadow was poised for a command. He concentrated on Dov so intently that the others in the room realized that they were holding their collective breaths.

"I think you might be right," Pele finally agreed. "Shadow is a unique guard animal; someone trained him very well."

Dov outlined his plan to the others then turned to the animal by his side. "Are you ready to go, Shadow?"

The dog trotted to the door and whined to be let out.

Old Babel, Ziggurat of Marduk

When they reached the commercial buildings clustered around the gate to the old temple complex, Dov and Shadow stopped at the edge of the open buffer area that surrounded the giant structure. The temple stones were cold and moist from a passing rain shower. Dov patted his friend to calm himself. The dog stared, unfazed, at the gate in the distance. "This is where we part company for now, old boy," Dov whispered to the dog as the guards made their rounds. "You take good care of Evina for me."

The guards paced back and forth between the central gates and the far corners of the thick walls. The twenty-foot high wooden gates, bound with metal straps, were closed at night, but a small entrance door was left open on one side through which guards passed one at a time. Dov and Shadow watched the guards' walk back and forth for several rounds to ensure their regularity. It didn't take long to figure out their pattern.

Dov huddled close to Shadow and pointed to the open portal in the temple door. "Find Evina. Find Evina. Go!" he commanded, and Shadow raced for the entrance door while the guards were at the far ends of the temple, their backs turned to each other. Silent as his name, the animal flew through the narrow entrance door and disappeared just as the guards pivoted to march back to the gates.

Once inside, Shadow walked silently through corridors and up stairs, searching for Saris' scent, which he instinctively knew would lead him to Evina. His brown-black body melted easily into the dark corners. When his sensitive nose detected a few molecules that his brain registered as belonging to Saris, he broke into a run toward their source. Saris tensed when he saw a large, dark object racing like a whisper of wind down the corridor toward him. Shadow emerged from the darkness into the torch light and abruptly skidded on the marble floor and stopped a few feet in front of the bodyguard.

Saris held out his hand to show his friendliness. *So you are my new helper*, he signed to the dog, not sure if he would understand. *Come here and let me look at you.*

Shadow walked up to Saris and let him rub his ears. The temple guards looked the other way in boredom—it was only a dog. Saris stepped quietly with Evina's new protector into the observatory, where she wrote in her journal by the lamplight. She heard the door close and looked up to see Saris and Shadow standing at attention beside her.

Miss, this is your new guard. He is here to protect you in my absence.

Evina rubbed Shadow affectionately. He enjoyed the attention as only a dog can when he senses the love of an owner. His devotion to her was unconditional.

CHAPTER 15

New Babel, One World Tower

Javak arrived in New Babel with his son and nephew after their long land journey from Bosrah and they proceeded directly to Pele's machine shop as planned. After they left their belongings there, Pele accompanied them through the streets of the city to the One World Tower for a tour of the vapor engine complex. Jengo greeted them at a side entrance.

"I'm *so* glad to see you!" Jengo exclaimed with genuine relief, clasping their hands in greeting. He was weary from long nights overseeing repairs of damaged machinery and training more boiler operators and freight ascender controllers. He was in need of competent assistance to keep up with the schedule Magus had imposed on him. The sooner they could finish essential repairs and modifications to the ascenders, the sooner they could leave the city.

Jengo gave an overview of what they would see in their tour of the tower's machinery: "Before we go to the sub-basements, where it's too loud to communicate easily, I'll give you a quick overview. We'll start in the bottom 'B3' level where black rock fuel is automatically fed into the boilers and water is piped from the river into the vapor jackets. We'll then go up to the 'B2' level, which is the main engine room, where superheated vapor from the boilers is piped up to drive the cast iron reciprocating engines. High in the ceiling above the engines on B2 are the winding drums of alloy cable that hoist the ascenders. The control room and ascender maintenance are on the 'B1' level. Right now we're running a total of eight freight capsules around the clock, taking supplies and workers up fifty levels to the Commoner sector where they transfer through portals to other ascenders that go to the upper levels and the tower rooftop."

"Why eight freight ascenders?" asked Javak. "That seems like a large number."

"We need that many because they pre-position materials and workers at lower level portals so they can be lifted in stages to the next higher levels. The bottom Commoner sector was low priority, but it has fifty levels and a living capacity of almost ten thousand people. Commoners must use stairs to reach their living levels, but the freight ascenders bring supplies to them and all levels above."

Javak was still puzzled by Jengo's explanation about the freight ascenders. "Why go through multiple stages to reach the upper levels? Why not ascend directly in one trip?"

"The alloy cables aren't strong enough to lift the weight of a fully loaded freight carrier more than fifty levels. Remember, they have to lift their own weight of cable too. Also, Magus wanted the sectors completely isolated from each other. It complicated construction more than you could imagine. As it is," Jengo lamented, "the three other sectors are entirely sealed from each other except for guarded freight transfer portals at the sector interfaces."

Jengo continued his explanation. "The one passenger ascender in operation is for Luminaries and their families only. A single strand of alloy cable can support the capsule and five passengers. Most of the weight on the cable is that of the cable itself that goes up over one thousand feet. It stresses the capacity of the cable, reels, brakes, and vapor engine, but we've had only minor mishaps with the mechanical part of the system. Inattentive operators are the weak links in the whole system."

"We can help you there," said Javak. "Ash, Kitt, and I can operate the Luminary and any other ascenders. Just tell us what you need done."

Jengo escorted the three through an unmarked door and down narrow stairs to the bottom basement. Amid the roar of the engines, he used hand gestures to point out key pieces of machinery.

The boiler room was loud and hot. Black rock fuel automatically fed the hungry, red-hot flames of massive cast iron boilers. The long row of dark, filth-encrusted cylinders squatted in the haze. A layer of smoke, soot, and black rock dust obscured the high ceiling of the dimly lit room. Exhaust vents struggled to keep up with the fumes. Continuous belts carried black rock down to the sub-basement from piles outside at ground level. There, other belts distributed the fuel to bins, from which augers fed the right amount of fuel into the boilers.

Up one level, the thunder from the heavy vapor engine drives was louder, but at least the noxious odors were minimal. Instead of fuel fumes, pressurized water vapor leaked from countless pipes and gaskets to make for a sauna-like atmosphere. The vibration, humidity, and high temperature drenched the visitors within minutes. The back and forth drumming of the pistons was continuous and deafening.

Jengo led them to the far end of the room and pointed to the engine labeled "Luminary Ascender." The engine's idling piston rhythmically squirted leaking jets of water and white vapor in every direction, and rotated a hefty metal rod and flywheel that reached above to a metal clutch attached to a large drum suspended from the ceiling. The shiny cable, made from hundreds of tiny, twisted wires, wound around the drum and exited through a slot in the ceiling to the floor above. Jengo pointed to the ceiling and motioned the group to follow him up to the control room.

"That was some noise!" Kitt exclaimed when the door was closed and the sound became tolerable. The constant roar of the engines shook the floor beneath their feet.

"The two levels below us are automated except for regular monitoring and necessary maintenance. Even with ear protectors, the constant noise and vibration takes its toll on the human body." Jengo walked down an aisle between rows of tables where operators watched dials and gauges. He stopped in front of a bank of instruments labeled "Luminary Ascender Control."

Before he could describe the instruments, they heard a shout behind them.

"Who are these people?" The voice was unmistakable.

They turned as a group to see Magus approach in a visible rage. His red face and snarl quickly put them on the defensive.

"Who are these people?" he demanded again. He stopped with his face inches from Jengo's. "They aren't my people!"

Jengo stepped back and raised both hands in surrender.

"These are my relatives—all engineers—here to help me with the ascenders." He was accustomed to Magus' paranoid outbursts and accusations. Those who didn't know him were stunned by his verbal assault.

"In answer to your earlier warnings about the need for safer operation of the ascender to the Luminary levels, I've enlisted their assistance to guarantee that there are no more accidents caused by operator error. They will be under my direct supervision at all times."

This seemed to placate Magus momentarily; he looked at them suspiciously. "So these are your blood relatives?" he asked.

"They are. I can vouch for their reliability and, most importantly, for their competence."

"All right then. My earlier order that a family member must always be at the controls here and in the ascender still stands. You will be held personally responsible if there are any accidents," the magician threatened with a finger pointed at Jengo. "If there is a Luminary ascender accident, I will see that these, and your other relatives, pay with their lives!" Having intimidated them to his satisfaction, he stormed out of the room before anyone could respond.

When the door at the far end of the control room slammed to punctuate his departure, Jengo breathed a sigh. "You see what I have to deal with. We must make sure there are no accidents. He's cold-blooded enough to carry out his threat."

Javak could not believe what he had witnessed. "How can you work for that maniac? Can't we leave Babel behind and head for Bosrah tonight? Nobody should have to put up with threats like that."

Jengo looked around to see if anyone was nearby to overhear their conversation. "I wish it were that easy. Magus has Adina and our children under constant surveillance and has threatened to kill them if any of us attempt to leave the city permanently. He's done the same with Pele's family. He's forcing us to finish the tower. I wish it weren't so, but we're trapped here . . . for a little while, anyway."

"Uncle Jengo, we're here to help in the meantime. What can we do?" Kitt asked.

"I'm sorry. I've gotten so used to the pressure of that madman's threats hanging over my head and being surrounded by incompetent workers that I'd forgotten what it's like to have someone I can depend on. Here's how you can help: when Magus, Nimrod, or Zidon are transported in the capsule, I want Dov and Yanis to be at the controls—Dov in the capsule and Yanis at this console. Javak and Kitt can operate the ascender system for other Luminaries if Dov or Yanis can't make it to the control room in time. We'll sort a better schedule out as we go along."

Jengo sat at the control console's chair and motioned for the others to gather around him. "This control center has separate desks and consoles for each of the ascenders. The controls from this position require one operator for the one ascender. You can also see that there are openings in the ceiling so that their respective ascenders can be lowered into a dock on this level for maintenance."

"What do these dials indicate?" Ash asked. He pointed to the row of round, clock-like displays along the top of the slanted console.

"These instruments show flows and pressures in the boiler and vapor engine." Jengo explained the significance of the units marked around the circumference of each dial and stressed the need to keep the pointers out of the red zones.

"Those levers on the right. What are they?" Ash showed increasing curiosity about the functions on the gleaming panel.

"Manual controls allow us to balance pressures between the condenser and the output of the boiler. The most critical thing to remember is that if water flowing from the condenser into the boiler slows or stops, then the temperature in the boiler will rise quickly and there can be an explosion or a meltdown. I'll demonstrate how to balance the pressures later."

Ash had pulled a chair up to the console so he could touch the controls himself. "What are these in front?"

"The center of the console is where we operate the ascender reel and capsule movement. Gauges show the capsule's approximate position in the tower, the rate of ascent and descent, and the status of manual controls in the ascender capsule. The clutch is what controls the rate of ascent and descent. An emergency brake can halt the capsule immediately as long as it isn't moving very fast." Jengo noted that the capsule was stopped above them at the 'G' level, where Luminaries boarded the transport in privacy while shielded from other building residents or workers.

With the movement of a lever he brought the capsule down to their level, where it stopped behind them with a thud in its own dock.

By this time, Ash was so absorbed in the intricacies of ascender controls that he went ahead and stepped into the passenger capsule and stood at the operator's position where he touched each instrument and lever before him.

"When can I take this up on a flight to the rooftop?" Ash asked. Jengo explained the controls inside. Ash hung on his every word. When they finished, the young engineer reluctantly left the capsule and returned with them to the console area.

Wrapping up their orientation, Jengo gathered his relatives around him to explain their assignments. "Javak and Ash can be alternate control station operators to replace Yanis. You'll have no trouble learning the freight ascender controls too, in case I need your help there. Then, I want Kitt and Ash to learn how to operate the ascenders." Jengo said smiling at his nephew.

"Can I make a suggestion?" injected Javak. "Kitt is more familiar with the *Cyclone*; more than Ash or I. How about if Kitt went to the *Cyclone* center now where Dov and Yanis are programming? He can help with that machine's operation when the programming is finished but still be an alternate ascender operator. I think Ash and I can take care of things here."

"Good suggestion. Take all the time you need to practice and become familiar with the controls here. Make as many trips in the ascender as you need to until you're comfortable with the quirks of this particular system. You're both engineers, so I know you won't have any trouble mastering the operations."

Jengo motioned the three to gather closer. "Before I get your ascender operator uniforms, a caution to all of you, including Kitt who will be working across the city: lives depend on what we do here in the tower. How we operate these machines could effect the future of our civilization." Jengo's exaggerated caution was meant to get their attention. None of them realized at the time how prophetic it was.

CHAPTER 16

New Babel, School of Japheth—*Cyclone* Computing Center

When he arrived at the school, Kitt saw Dov and Yanis programming frames in front of one of the machinery cabinets. They were so consumed with the intricacies of translating the algos from paper to the frame language that they didn't notice him enter the room. He left them to their work to find someone who could show him the modifications made to the machine.

Kitt found Benji at the far end of the *Cyclone* Computing Center. He sat where coverings were propped open revealing the machine's densely packed interior mechanism. He too was lost in concentration.

"Benji, how's it going?" Kitt remembered him from his earlier days in school. "You're still working here on the *Cyclone*?"

"Hey, Kitt! I'm still here. Slaving away on the same air lines that leak and give this old machine fits. There isn't a part of this thing that I haven't fixed or replaced at one time or another." The young man wiped the oil from his hands and gave his school friend a warm greeting.

"Yanis said her cousin would be coming to help with machine operations, but I had no idea it would be you. Still remember how this beast runs?"

"I'm not sure. It depends on what you've done to it since I was last here. Looks like it's three or four times its original size. I hear that Dov and Yanis have taken algo programming to a new level." Kitt looked down the row of cabinets. "Care to give me a quick tour?"

"Sure. Let's go to the front, or input sections, where your cousins are working. We'll start with one of the six input machines as an example."

When they reached what Benji called the "front" of the machine, they stopped to survey a metal rack that measured six feet wide, six feet deep, and twelve feet high. Dov and Yanis continued to ignore them.

"Before I show you this new frame and data input device, let me say that the functionality of the machine you used in the 'old days' remains fundamentally unchanged. It's still powered by filtered, precisely regulated, compressed air. You can hear the vapor engine idling outside that runs the compressors. We meter out compressed air from large cast iron tanks behind that wall and distribute it to each of the cabinets through a manifold of thin copper tubes behind the cabinets and crossing the aisle overhead. Regulator valves maintain the air at a set pressure at each cabinet to drive the cogs at a finely tuned speed. From the main cogs, all the miniature belt drives, flywheels, gears, levers, and sliders inside these boxes work like a precision clock mechanism. Most of the computing machinery was Japheth's design, but Pele built the first model."

"You're right, Benji, this whole complex is much larger than I remember. Besides that, what else is different?" Kitt wanted to dive into the mechanical intricacies.

"The actual calculating engine and accumulators are faster and more precise. The system is a gigantic mechanical calculator that still makes a horrendous racket when it's running."

Benji motioned to the face of the cabinet before them. "This is a new algo input station. There are over a hundred sliders in rows across the front panel that make up one algo frame. They're like the algo frames used by temple numerologists with their sliders, only much more precise and hundreds of times faster. Yanis chains the functions together to perform complex calculations like differentials, then stores those results in the accumulators or memory devices in the next dozen cabinets, and the machine continues on to another set of calculations."

"Where do answers come out?" Kitt asked.

"At the other end of the room. The cards and output display are the most fascinating new features," Benji said proudly.

They walked past the long row of accumulators to a half-dozen racks covered with dials and more cabinets with frame sliders similar to those used for the inputs.

"Are these for input too?" asked Kitt. "I'm confused. I don't see why you would need them at this end of the process. I remember the dials, but not these sliders."

"Those are for outputs. These frame sliders are controlled from inside the machine. This is where high-precision answers come out. This is something you haven't seen," he said, pointing to another slot below the sliders. "The numbers on the sliders are also punched into a paper card by sharp pins. The pattern of holes punched on the card gives you a permanent copy of the full-precision output numbers. On top of that, the card fits neatly in your pocket!"

"That's clever. It's like a portable notepad."

"In my opinion, the real gem is the drawing engine." Benji swept away a cloth covering a small flat table at the far end of the row of cabinets. "This is what Yanis calls an 'automaton' machine. It makes a drawing of the results using the series of numbers from the output sliders—the same numbers on the card."

Kitt was still unimpressed by its simple appearance. "What does it do?"

"Let me show you results from a calibration run we made yesterday." Benji unrolled a large sheet of paper measuring three feet on its side. He spread it across the surface of the device. "For a calibration run, we should see straight lines drawn across this paper corresponding to exactly the same numbers we used for inputs. Smooth, straight lines all the way across the paper." Benji waited for his explanation to sink in.

"You mean, this thing drew those lines? Let me see if I understand this. The outputs match the calibration inputs, but this automaton drew a graph of the results without somebody reading numbers off the sliders or the cards?"

"That's right. You can use both the automaton drawing and the more precise data frame numbers on the cards to understand your results. That's the new *Cyclone*!"

"Benji, I'm impressed!"

"I hoped my cousin would be impressed," Yanis said with a cheerful smile as she greeted Kitt with a hug. She and Dov had finished their programming and were thrilled to see that Kitt had arrived from Bosrah to help them.

"So when can I see this fabulous machine in action?" Kitt asked.

"Maybe later tonight," Dov answered. He turned to Benji. "Will it be ready?"

"I'll have the air lines checked out and the air storage tank up to full pressure later this afternoon. The interior mechanisms will have to idle for at least an hour so oil has time to reach all the parts and the temperature stabilizes. Then we'll be ready for a full-scale run," Benji reported.

"Dov and I need to go to the tower now to see if Jengo needs anything, then we'll go home for dinner and come back here tonight for the first run. Will you see us at dinner?" she asked Kitt.

"Thanks, I think I will join you for dinner. Besides, I want to find out more about the algos, and you can update me on the approaching . . . ." Yanis interrupted him before he could continue. "Good!" she said hurriedly. "We'll talk then!" She and Dov left before the conversation could continue.

"What was that about? What's going on?" asked Benji when they left the room.

"What do you mean?"

"I mean about the algos. Neither of them would discuss the algos with me earlier, and when I tried to look at their notes they sent me away. The frame settings won't mean much to me, but I don't know why I'm being kept in the dark. You obviously know more than I do." Benji's unsatisfied curiosity made him more anxious. "Do you know what they're up to? Is it something illegal or dangerous? Why are they keeping this such a secret?"

"Relax, Benji, my friend. The algos have to be kept under wraps for now. No, it's nothing illegal or having to do with you. The less you know, the safer it will be for you." Kitt smiled to reassure him. He didn't want his friend in danger because of their connection to Evina or the approaching asteroid.

"I suppose so. They make it sound like it's something sinister. I'll keep my mouth shut, but still . . ." He sounded unconvinced, but was willing to go along with Kitt's caution for the time being.

"This is just one of those things that Dov and Yanis can't share with you for now. Trust me, nobody is in any danger." Kitt hoped he was right.

Later that night, the steady, low-frequency drone of the *Cyclone's* vapor engine could be heard blocks away from the school. The three engineers entered the computing machine room unnoticed. Dov found Benji working behind a cabinet and walked up behind him. "We're here!" Dov shouted above the noise. The nervous assistant jumped with a yelp.

"I know that now," Benji grumbled with nervous irritation. "Everything's ready to start the first run."

Yanis and Dov looked over the frame settings at the master input console one last time; Kitt double-checked copper air tubes and connectors for leaks and looked for any telltale oil on the spotlessly clean floor.

"Let's do it," Dov announced. "Yanis, why don't you throw the switch and get this pile of scrap metal screaming."

"*Yes!*" Yanis shouted excitedly. She and the others put in their earplugs.

She lifted a red lever and a high-pitched whine suddenly layered itself onto the steady low-pitched background of the vapor engine. The sound increased steadily in volume until it became a deafening wail. Yanis looked at Kitt and mouthed her approval: *Sounds like sweet music!*

Kitt and Benji walked behind the machine cabinets, tended to its ceaseless need for lubrication, tightened loose air connections, and monitored pressure gauges. Dov and Yanis paced in front of the bank of accumulators and output panels watching the rows of dials. They weren't sure exactly what output numbers to expect, but they watched the dials display changing numbers as digits passed from one memory accumulator rack to the next at a steady pace. None of the processes slowed or seemed out of tolerance. A unique, signature howl emitted from the innards of each cabinet. Yanis and Dov knew each subtle sound and were confident that all was going as planned.

The *Cyclone* ran for over two hours. The young engineers stood at the far end of the room to admire their handiwork from a distance. The monster radiated high-volume, rhythmic pumping, hissing, and rushing of air from a hundred manifolds; tens of thousands of winding gears, clacking levers, and spinning drums clattered in chaotic harmony; needles on dials and gauges flicked back and forth; brass rods transferred numbers between adjacent accumulator cabinets with an almost musical melody. The throbbing shrieks felt like the heartbeat of modern technology. The moving metallic parts cast a hypnotic spell on the human attendants as if it were the voice of a living creature.

Glassy-eyed, Dov awoke from his daze and noticed that Saris was waiting a short distance away. Communicating with rudimentary sign language, he conversed with the patient bodyguard amid the din.

We finish in about one hour, he advised.

I will wait here, Saris replied.

Benji watched Dov and Saris. He'd never seen the large, muscular temple servant before. The man never stopped sweeping the room with his cautious eyes. Dov communicated in sign language, which made the exotic-looking visitor's presence in the computing room even more mysterious.

When the four operators detected a tonal shift from one of the machines, they hurried to the first accumulator bank to verify that its internal mechanism was spinning to a stop. The dials were motionless, indicating that no new results were being received. They walked down the row of cabinets and observed each accumulator methodically wind down and cease operation as final numbers were forwarded to the next machine. Finally, output sliders at the far end stopped and pins punched holes in output cards. When that operation finished, the drawing automaton came alive. The mechanical pen jerked back and forth in a blur as it inked a complicated pattern of lines on the paper. The room was eerily quiet after every miniature piece inside the *Cyclone* came to a standstill. Only the smell of hot oil and the background hiss of idling air manifolds remained.

Yanis, Dov, Kitt and Benji removed their earplugs, and stared at the numbers punched in the cards and the black lines on the automaton paper. Without a word, Yanis folded the paper diagram around the cards and handed the package to Saris. The bodyguard bowed to them and left the room immediately.

Drawn, tired expressions revealed the computing team's stress. "Those outputs—what do they mean?" Benji asked.

After a long silence, Yanis answered him. "I have absolutely no idea."

Kitt found Benji at the far end of the *Cyclone* Computing Center.

CHAPTER 17

Old Babel, Ziggurat of Marduk—Evina's Bedroom

After midnight

Saris knocked on Evina's bedroom door and entered. Shadow, sleeping at the foot of her bed, raised his head to acknowledge his presence, and then laid it back down, with his eyes partially closed but ears alert to every movement in the room.

I came as quickly as I could with these papers from your friends, Saris explained with his free hand.

Evina took the materials from him with a mixture of curiosity and excitement, and sat on the edge of her bed. *Thank you. I may want to send a reply tonight.*

I am at your service, Miss. Saris left the room to wait outside.

Although Evina was not familiar with the *Cyclone's* automaton output formats, she skimmed the punched cards for familiar numbers. Noticing that one pair of results stood out from the others, she uttered a gasp and stood up. In a single motion, she stepped into her sandals, wrapped a shawl around her shoulders for warmth, and ran to the door with the papers clutched in her hand. Shadow sensed her intention immediately and was at her side.

Her exit from the room at a run caught Saris by surprise. The heavy wooden door slammed open and the startled hallway guards nearly dropped their weapons. Waving over her shoulder for Saris to follow her, she and Shadow sprinted down the corridor to her observatory.

After lighting a lamp, she unrolled the automaton drawing on her desk and spread out the cards under the light. Saris and Shadow waited while she concentrated. When she found her notes, she pored over her latest input parameters. Her mind blanked out her surroundings to focus on the numbers. The figures before her eyes were significant. Each entry was inspected, compared, evaluated, and analyzed against her understanding of celestial mechanics. She looked for any discrepancy or irregularity in the calculations. After an hour Evina looked up to notice that Shadow was asleep in his bed near her telescope. She made careful annotations next to the lines on the automaton diagram. Pages in her notebook were filled with careful handwriting. She transcribed the *Cyclone* results on the punched cards to her notebook for later reference.

The young astronomer sat back in her chair and let out a long sigh that did nothing to relieve her apprehension. Her discouragement prompted Shadow to walk to her and put his head on her lap. She stroked his head and rubbed behind his ears. He looked at her with sad, brown eyes.

Evina spoke aloud to Shadow: "Things are worse than I thought. That asteroid is accelerating and we have only a few days before it becomes visible to everyone. Then it'll be upon us. What purpose could God possibly have for annihilating us? I'm afraid of dying, and yet Dov and Yanis seem at peace with whatever God does. In the morning I must inform my father about the approaching asteroid. Whatever he has planned, I cannot be part of it. He'll try to make me a high priestess to worship the gods, but I must refuse. What will happen to me then? I wish I knew what to do."

Evina wrote a note to Dov and Yanis explaining her interpretation of the *Cyclone* results: the asteroid would become visible to everyone in two days. It was still on an uncertain course that could either pass close to earth or impact it directly. She would make final measurements when the object became visible with the naked eye and send those numbers back to them.

She opened the observatory door and handed her note to Saris but did not reveal the meaning of the results or of the message. He could tell from the tears welling in her eyes and the tremble of her hand that she was deeply shaken.

In contrast to her run down the corridor hours before, Evina walked slowly back to her bedroom to rest until dawn. She wouldn't sleep, but she could at least try to calm herself. Shadow accompanied her while Saris went off in the opposite direction on his errand. Except for a lone candle, the bedroom was dark and damp with a midnight chill. Shadow laid on the bed at her feet while she curled up under her blankets.

≈ ≈

Even in her sleep, Evina sensed that someone was in her room. She had slept fitfully for a few hours, but was now suddenly wide awake. That can't be Saris, she thought. She sat up in bed when she didn't feel Shadow sleeping at her feet.

"Shadow!" she cried out. "Where are you?" She lit the candle next to her bed.

The dog gave a whine from across the room.

"Miss, don't be afraid," a soft voice uttered from the dark of her open closet.

"Who are you? Get out of my bedroom!" Evina was about to scream for the guards but was puzzled that Shadow hadn't alerted her to the intruder.

"We've met before, Miss. In the street with Dov and Yanis when they were walking you back to the temple. Do you remember?" The man made no attempt to approach her. His form remained in the darkness across the room. "I mean you no harm."

"Yes, I remember now. You're the Watcher. Why are you here? How did you get into my bedroom without being stopped by Saris? Why didn't Shadow alert me?"

She didn't see him smile. "So many questions. Yet I can answer only a few. Yes, I am the Watcher. I've been sent to reassure you that you'll not die from an impact by the asteroid. I'm aware of the results from the *Cyclone*—don't ask me how I know—and, regardless of what the numbers may tell you, the asteroid will not impact earth. I know this because God has another plan for the people of Babel. He will prove that He is God of heaven and earth. He will perform a miracle to demonstrate that He is Almighty God, that disobedience cannot continue, and that He is in control of humankind." The Watcher looked for a reaction from Evina, but sensed none. "Continue to seek the living God and stand firm in your convictions. He is faithful and true."

Evina held up the candle. "Come closer, I want to see your face. When you met us on the street in Babel I couldn't see you clearly."

The dark figure stepped closer, and Evina saw the oval of his face floating above the black outline of his clothing. He was wrapped in a strangely colored cape that hid his entire body. Evina held the candle closer, and her visitor removed his hood.

She looked upon the bronzed, clean-shaven face of an unremarkable man whose ordinary features allowed him to walk unnoticed in public. She looked for some distinguishing characteristic about his face but found none. Then she gasped, "You're no older than I am!" She had assumed from his commanding tone that he was older.

"We're almost the same age," he replied calmly. "Does that matter?"

Evina thought briefly before replying. "I suppose not . . . how did you get into my room undetected?"

"There are people in the city, and in this temple, who wish to do you harm, but you also have many friends. 'Shadow,' as you call him, is one of us. I trained him to be my eyes and ears. He will guard you with his life, as will your faithful mute servant outside." The mysterious intruder took a step closer and bowed his head. "One of my missions is to look out for you, Miss. Please don't be afraid of me." He looked up and she was captivated by the depth of his blue eyes.

"I trust you. I don't know why, but I trust you." Evina felt comforted saying those words aloud.

"Thank you. I will try to be worthy of your trust." His determined look was even more assuring.

"Now, to answer your question about how I entered your room unnoticed," he said. "Priests of Old Babel built many secret passages into this ziggurat and I use them for my purposes. There is a hidden door in the back of your closet that I will use with discretion. Shadow will alert you to my presence in the future so you will not be startled." He pulled the hood over his head. "Good night, Miss." With a sweep of his cape he disappeared into the darkness.

Evina jumped out of bed and inspected her closet closely, but she couldn't find a secret doorway. The stone blocks fit tightly together, and she wondered how the Watcher could have come and gone without making a sound. Back in bed, she thought about what he had told her and was amazed at everything that had transpired that night: results from the *Cyclone* predicting an imminent collision by the asteroid; the Watcher appearing in her room with the contradiction that the asteroid would *not* impact the earth; his assurance that she had many protectors who cared for her. She felt Shadow at her feet again and drifted off to sleep thinking how fortunate she was to have friends looking out for her.

CHAPTER 18

Old Babel, Ziggurat of Marduk—High Priest's Residence

Zidon peacefully ate his breakfast at sunrise on the rooftop garden balcony outside his bedroom. Suddenly, he was interrupted as his son pushed through the door past the guards. Arvid beamed with obvious pleasure as he hurried to give his father some much-awaited news.

"Good news, Father!" Zidon's son dropped into a chair and poured himself a glass of juice.

"I cannot imagine what would be such good news that you felt it necessary to interrupt my peaceful breakfast. Couldn't it have waited until later?" Zidon's cold, proud annoyance was typical, and Arvid had grown accustomed to it.

"This is worth telling you about immediately. The ziggurat on the roof of the One World Tower is almost finished! I found out first thing this morning that we can move the statues, altar, and vestments there whenever we wish. Don't you see? When we sacrifice on the new temple ziggurat we'll reach higher to the gods than any man has ever reached before." Arvid waited for some indication of pleasure from his father.

"That is indeed good news. However," he added coldly, "I learned that from a Triad messenger early this morning." His comment dampened Arvid's zeal, and the young man slumped deflated into his chair.

"Cheer up." his father added. "You're right that we can begin moving into the One World Tower ziggurat. I'll give the order to do so today after the noon sacrifice. Don't look so glum. Let's go tell your sister. She'll be excited about the news too. We'll have her observatory moved there as soon as possible so she can see the stars better from a more advantageous height."

Arvid wondered why his father thought Evina would welcome the news. He was almost certain that she was not a believer in the gods—not that he considered the family religion of the stars any more valid than she did, but at least he pretended to believe in them. To him, star gazing, astrology and star worship were nothing more than a lucrative family business that he would inherit one day. It meant power, wealth, and prestige which were all that mattered to him. He had learned that from his father. Maybe he would join the Triad when his father died. Magus had all but said that would be the case.

Within minutes, Zidon was poised to enter his daughter's bedroom with the news of the tower ziggurat's completion. The high priest's entry was blocked by Saris' gigantic frame. The temple guards were shocked by his obstruction of the high priest. They immediately raised their weapons at him. Zidon raised his hand and the guards backed away.

Saris held his ground as Zidon stood inches in front of him with fury in his face. "Get out of my way!" the high priest shouted. After a split-second, the mute servant turned and knocked on the door. He waited briefly and entered the room with Zidon and Arvid on his heels. He stepped aside to reveal Evina calmly seated at her dressing table.

Zidon and Arvid brushed past the stoic bodyguard. Strangely, the high priest shifted his focus from the mute servant to his daughter as if to overlook his impertinence.

"Come in Father. I was about to order my breakfast. Would you like to join me?" Her cheerful greeting encouraged Zidon to think that she would be as excited as he was about moving into the new ziggurat atop the One World Tower.

"I have excellent news for you!" Evina's father announced while he ignored his son's presence. "We'll be moving you to the One World Tower ziggurat in the next few days, and you'll be able to continue your celestial observations from a new observatory on the rooftop."

"I look forward to that. Some of my observations have been distorted lately by smoke from all the vapor engines in the city. The tower rooftop will be an excellent vantage point." Her comment came out sounding more positive then she intended.

"My latest calculations show that the asteroid will become visible in two days, so you'll be able to see it for yourself. I still can't tell if it will pass closely or impact us." She looked at her brother. "Is that good news, brother?" Her sarcasm could not be contained.

"Yes, it is!" Zidon exclaimed. "Then you'll also have no objection to starting your priestess duties as part of the move. I'll announce your future installation as high priestess of Ishtar once you're settled. Your mother would be so proud!" Zidon's plans for his daughter had been cemented in his mind after Evina's mother died. He was oblivious to the look of shock on her face.

The young woman composed herself and addressed her father, ignoring her brother lingering in the background. "That I cannot do," she stated calmly and respectfully.

"What do you mean? You sounded excited about moving into the new rooftop temple and continuing your observations. Your ascent to your mother's rank has been planned since her death, and, with this object approaching earth, now is the perfect time to introduce you to the people. You must join your brother and me in leading the people in worship of the gods. As high priestess of Ishtar you'll be second only to me in Babel's new world religion." Zidon's slip was news to both Evina and Arvid. The young man was stunned by his father's revelation. Evina thought carefully of what to say next.

"Father, as much as I love you, I can't be a high priestess in your world religion because I don't believe in the gods. The sun, moon, planets and stars are lifeless objects. Like the approaching asteroid, they follow universal, preordained natural laws of motion decreed by their sovereign Creator. They neither have nor exert any spiritual influence on our lives. They respond to the One True God who created them." Her statements were made dispassionately but firmly.

Zidon waved his hand in dismissal. "That doesn't matter. I don't believe all that foolishness about gods either, but we must uphold appearances and preserve our family legacy. Arvid here makes an excellent show of being a true believer in the gods, and so could you. It would only take an hour or two of your time each day, and you could continue your astronomy studies without interruption. You don't actually have to believe anything to be a priestess; the pageantry and myth are what makes our religion so popular. So will you join us?" Zidon reached out for his daughter's hands in hope of persuading her to agree out of familial duty. She withdrew to her bedroom window and looked out across the river at the city of New Babel and the One World Tower gleaming in the morning sunlight. She turned to face her father and brother with determination.

"I love you, Father, but I will *not* become high priestess of Ishtar because I am a believer in the One True God. It is He who created the objects in the heavens that I have studied all my life. He created me, and you, and we are accountable to Him because He gave us life. Because I believe in Him, I cannot pretend to be part of your lies." She felt an unusual strength in proclaiming her trust in the living God. "I will *never* become a priestess of false gods. I would rather die than go against what I believe. I hope that you, above all people, would understand this."

Zidon heard his daughter's clear, open profession of faith in God but could not understand it. In one sense, he could admire her integrity and loyalty, but unlike her he had chosen a counterfeit life long ago to indulge himself in the rich material benefits of his religious system. It was too late for him to change now. He looked at Arvid. Could his son be his replacement even if he thought that their religion was hollow and lifeless? Could he, like his father, do whatever it took to continue the family legacy? Zidon thought it odd that it was Evina whom he admired and Arvid who garnered his contempt.

"So be it," Zidon announced abruptly. He stood in the doorway and pointed at his daughter. "You are confined to this room until I make other arrangements. I cannot make your decision known to others until I make other arrangements. I'll triple the number of guards at your door, and you'll tell your dumb servant that he'll be executed if he attempts to remove you from this room or interferes with the guards.

"Come, Arvid," the high priest beckoned to his son. He turned his back on Evina and strode through the door with his son on his heels. His regret was a mere whisper: *I don't know my own daughter.*

New Babel, Pele's Machine Shop

An anonymous handwritten note with news of Evina's imprisonment was on Pele's worktable when he returned from a meeting with Jengo at the tower. The hastily written message stated that Zidon had placed his daughter under house arrest and explained the reason for her confinement. Pele felt that he should inform Dov and Yanis immediately, since it could compromise their communication with her in some way. He hurried to find the twins at the School of Japheth, where they were preparing another run of the *Cyclone.*

CHAPTER 19

Old Babel, Nimrod's Palace—Secure Inner Sanctum

The Triad assembled in a hurried session to plan their roles when the asteroid became visible in two days. Their intention was that the population of Babel attribute its appearance to their influence with the gods. Each, of course, also had a personal agenda. Magus closed the heavy oak door to their meeting room and bolted it securely. He quickly checked the room and hastened to address the purpose of their meeting.

"What do you propose we do, your Excellency?" He deferred to Nimrod to begin the strategy session.

"We'll say that the city is under attack from the outside and that our only defense is to take up arms to defend ourselves." His solution to any problem was military force, even if it made no sense. "We can get the city behind us if we make this a life-or-death fight to protect our civilization from invasion."

"I'm afraid that would only work for the first day or two until it became obvious to everyone that mortal men cannot fight off an asteroid from above. When it fills half the sky it won't matter how many armed soldiers aim their weapons upward. Nothing can stop this oncoming ball of fire if it hits the city. The people will scatter in panic and we'll have lost all control. Nothing we say after that will matter." Magus weighed his next words carefully.

"I suggest that we make ourselves indispensable by calming the people instead. We will assure them that the object, whatever it looks like to them, is a friendly visitor from the gods that will fill the sky and then pass us. If we show them that we are not afraid, we can convince them to trust us and do our bidding. The asteroid will either pass us or impact and kill us all. Since we'd all be dead in the latter case, let's plan what to do if it passes by. I believe you understand what I am getting at, do you not Zidon?"

"That was my thought exactly! We've already convinced them that the sun-god Shamash and moon god Nanna-Seun are their celestial friends; so too, this is a new god coming to put a seal of approval on our One World system. It's arrival will unite us as a people, and the Triad will be exalted to the heavens. Rather than be afraid, we should rejoice in it!" Zidon warmed to his fantasy.

"We'll connect this with completion of the One World Tower as our demonstration of reaching upward to welcome the new god. As it descends to greet us, we'll reach up to embrace it. We'll receive it as gods ourselves!" Zidon's twisted imagination convinced him that the asteroid was actually a god!

Magus was receptive to the useful charade proposed by the high priest. He contemplated how he could bring Nimrod into the picture without allowing him to misdirect the people with a futile military campaign. He leaned forward in his chair to share his wisdom in a conspiratorial voice. "I propose," he intoned smoothly, "that we focus our energies, and that of the citizens of Babel, on a national day of religious celebration to coincide with the time when the asteroid is scheduled to 'visit' the planet. Several factors should guide our planning: First, we know when the object will become visible, but we must also know the exact day and time when the object will fill the sky; second, all of the people in New Babel must participate; third, the celebration must include a ceremony atop the new ziggurat that is an unprecedented, dramatic pageant, with more splendor and pomp and excitement than any ever offered to the gods; finally, the people must see the three of us as their source of guidance into the future. I cannot stress enough what this means for our individual prosperity as well."

Motioning to Zidon, he continued. "Your daughter must give us the exact time of the asteroid's passage. You are the perfect person to inspire the city's inhabitants to surround our One World Tower at the appropriate time. They must fill the plaza around the tower, look upward to the Triad on the rooftop ziggurat with the asteroid as our backdrop, and become united as one people. We are the three around whom they will unite. By force, if necessary," he said nodding toward Nimrod.

Magus continued speaking to Zidon in a measured, emphatic tone. "You will reinforce your position as high priest of the new world religion. You must introduce this new god with a new name and explain why it must be worshiped. Most importantly, you must arrange a *spectacular new sacrifice* that will be remembered by all. I know you can be counted on to come up with something dramatic, magnificent and memorable."

Nimrod looked at his chief magician with shrewd skepticism. "Magus, what will your role be in all of this? You always have a motive for yourself. How will you benefit from this world-uniting spectacle?"

"You are perceptive as always, Excellency. Yes, I have my personal interests, but they are not in conflict with yours, I assure you. My ambition is to control the world's economy. You, King Nimrod, will emerge from this transforming event with even more support for overwhelming power and prestige. You will be God-King of New Babel. Zidon, you will be the spiritual leader of a united One World religion; the hearts and minds of New Babel will look to you for spiritual guidance. My role, as you might have suspected, is to be head of the fabric of everyday life in New Babel. I will own or control every part of New Babel's growing, modern industrial economy. The Triad will thus control the military, religious, and commercial structure of a new, advanced civilization on earth. Together, we will focus people on the city where they will be subservient to the Triad in all aspects of their lives. That is my vision for New Babel. I trust that we all share that same sweeping vision."

Magus sat back and looked to the other two, anticipating their full agreement.

"That will be the Triad's plan for the foreseeable future." Nimrod's words carefully approved what Magus said but his tone was tempered by caution. "I'll make the people gather around the tower on the appointed day and at the appointed time." He turned to Zidon as the key participant in their scheme to persuade the hearts of the people.

Taking longer than necessary, Zidon pondered his words before he spoke to address Magus' request for a spectacular and unprecedented sacrifice. His face revealed a tormented, inner conflict. His conscience, repeatedly trained to ignore moral persuasions, and fueled by self-interest, finally gave in to a scheme that would stun even the other members of the Triad.

"The new object in the sky will be named *Ningizzia*, which means 'God of the Gate of Heaven.' This is appropriate since Babel means 'Gate of God.' Yes, I will do something unheard of in the history of our world . . ." The high priest hesitated before exhaling with a sharp sigh. "I will make the ceremony stunningly appropriate. I will conduct a *human sacrifice* that will leave no doubt about my commitment to our new world order." Magus saw the intent behind the high priest's veiled statement, but dismissed sympathy for the man's personal anguish.

"Excellent!" cried Nimrod with a clap of his hands. He viewed a human sacrifice with little emotion and was oblivious to Zidon's agonizing decision.

Magus sounded slightly less callous, but welcomed the priest's plans with enthusiasm. "You have made the right choice! You will be remembered forever for your bold step in the cause of our One World order."

In the stillness that followed Zidon's dramatic announcement, the Triad stood to depart. Magus reminded Zidon to ask his daughter for the exact time of the asteroid's closest proximity. He stressed the need to hold to that schedule before the three leaders went their separate ways.

Within minutes after the door was closed and locked, a murky shape descended from its perch high in the rafters and dropped to the floor in one smooth, silent movement. It moved expertly across the pitch-black room as if able to see through the darkness. After listening at the door for sounds from outside, the intruder, dressed in a palace servant's uniform, unlocked the lock from the inside, departed the room and casually slipped into the palace hallway. There was no doubt who Zidon had in mind for his horrific plan. The Watcher had to notify Pele, and especially Dov, that Evina was now in mortal danger.

CHAPTER 20

New Babel, One World Tower

The next day

Magus stood alone in his gold-trimmed green robes on the paved plaza surrounding the tower in the early morning sun, while his assistants and passersby kept a respectful distance. He craned his neck to look up at the nearly completed black ziggurat on the roof, whose top was shrouded in the haze. The One World Tower—his idea, he thought proudly—was the centerpiece of his vision for a new world government. And it would all be his when he eliminated Nimrod and Zidon!

He confidently strode into the tower's Luminary lobby with a bounce in his step. The chief magician was there to inspect the finished Luminary level and the rooftop ziggurat. When Jengo saw his boss approach him with an uncharacteristic smile, he cringed inside. He couldn't, or wouldn't, dare speculate what diabolical scheme was passing through the man's twisted mind that made him smile like that. Past inspections of the building invariably resulted in heated confrontations, changes to the design, and more senseless work for the fatigued engineer.

Magus and Jengo stepped into the lavishly decorated ascender. "Who is this ascender operator?" the magician immediately demanded—his smile disappeared. He jerked his head toward Dov who stood rigidly at attention in his blue uniform before his control station. The operator dared not look directly at the infamous magician.

His challenging gaze shifted from Jengo to Dov, who stood at the controls with his back to his passengers. "I told you I wanted a member of your family to be at the controls."

"This is my nephew," Jengo responded calmly. "He's my most experienced ascender operator. We're safe in his hands." Jengo had hoped that Magus would not take notice of Dov, but little escaped the chief magician's hooded, suspicious eyes. He didn't relish having to explain the presence of Ash or Javak, who were more distant relatives, as operators in the future.

As the ascender rose slowly through fifty of the darkened Commoner levels, the three occupants of the capsule remained silent. At the fifty-first level they broke into sunlight and saw the skyline of New Babel through the portholes, as well as the ziggurat of Old Babel across the river. They were already much higher in elevation than the old ziggurat. Magus swelled with pride. *My achievement! When my plan is completed I will rename this building the Tower of Magus.* His thoughts were interrupted when the ascender shook violently, almost knocking the two passengers off their feet. Dov was braced for the turbulence, but forgot to warn the other occupants. They clutched the railings along the wall. The disturbance ended as abruptly as it began, and their ascent continued smoothly.

"What was that?" Magus asked with a tremor in his voice.

"Sir, that was only a gust of wind. There is nothing to fear." As soon as Dov spoke those words he regretted them. If the powerful official thought he was accusing him of being a coward because of a gust of wind, he could face fatal retribution. Fortunately, Jengo quickly spoke up to distract Magus from turning on the young operator.

"The Guild and Ministerial levels are, as you know, unfinished. The open spaces from the fifty-first to the one hundred-second floors occasionally produce turbulence at these altitudes. Until the exterior walls are covered with brick and mortar, these episodes will be unavoidable. I trust that the view from this height is worth the inconvenience." This distracted Magus for the moment.

The expanding view out to the horizon through the portholes revealed hills covered with green forests and fields beyond the brown plain of Shinar that surrounded the city. The densely packed living and industrial areas in the city gave way to a lush, natural landscape that supported the city's inhabitants with agricultural products and livestock. Thanks to highly productive agricultural methods that Noah and his sons brought with them, the majority of the population could concentrate on industry, learning, and cultural pursuits while it required relatively few farmers to feed them. The result of this was a civilization that could easily ignore God's instruction to multiply and spread throughout the earth. There was no logical reason for them to disperse since they had all they needed in Babel. The majority were content to enjoy a cosmopolitan, comfortable, prosperous life in the bustling city.

When they passed the 102nd level the capsule was plunged again into near-darkness. The dim light of the ascender capsule lamps illuminated the level counter as they approached the rooftop at the 120th floor. Dov used the foot brake to slow their ascent. He watched the "120" numerals appear on his display and slowly brought their ascent to a halt. He adjusted the level by a few inches with the hand crank to bring them even with the floor before he opened the gate for his passengers. There was a stiff breeze as Magus and Jengo stepped from the portal into the bright sunlight on the promenade.

"Wait here," Jengo instructed Dov curtly. "I don't know how long we'll be."

The two began their tour of the rooftop and its ziggurat, which was a miniature black version of the giant Ziggurat of Marduk seen in the distance across the river. Many construction workers, mostly stone masons from Accad, moved hurriedly about, indicating that the rooftop temple was not completely finished.

Dov walked around the open area in front of the ascender and took in the view from the railing that ran around the edge of the roof. He turned his back on the view and looked up at the black marble ziggurat before him. Unlike the giant Temple of Marduk across the river made from muted grey and pink marble, this smaller version stood out for its dramatic obsidian marble face. Slabs of the dark marble, flaked with natural veins of gold, adorned all the surfaces of the new ziggurat. Priests dressed in their ornate gold vestments would be clearly visible from the city below against the backdrop of the black temple. A priest sacrificing at the altar on the pinnacle would be visible from the street-level city plaza as a silhouette against the bright sky.

The structure occupied almost all of the tower roof except for a wide gathering area encompassing it. The bottom level of the ziggurat had entrance doors of different sizes, bay-shaped alcoves, and ornamental designs on all four sides. Some of the next higher levels of the stepped structure had windows and balconies. Upper levels were covered with slabs of polished black stone with no visible openings. A single row of steps at the front of the ziggurat, opposite the Luminary ascender portal, led from the rooftop plaza up to the altar at its highest point. Unseen to most who visited the temple were the freight ascender portals and storage areas at the back of the structure.

Dov approached a young worker troweling mortar to ask him about the doors in the side of the ziggurat. "Excuse me. Where do those doors lead?" The mason mistook Dov's ascender operator's blue uniform with gold epaulettes and yellow piping for that of a Luminary official, and immediately bowed with his forehead to the pavement. Dov took the man's arm and pulled him to his feet. "Don't let the fancy uniform fool you. I'm just a worker like you. Don't do that, please." Dov removed his blue peaked hat to show his face clearly.

The roughly dressed worker was in awe of the clean, crisp uniform and the privilege of speaking to an ascender operator who regularly piloted wealthy Luminaries. "Sir, those are rooms for the high priest and his family when they move into the temple. Other doors lead to dressing rooms, storage for priestly materials, food storage, and other spaces."

"That's a very large space occupying the bottom level of the ziggurat. It seems much more room than is needed for the temple."

"Very perceptive of you, sir. There are some open spaces inside whose purpose I'm not supposed to reveal." The worker was glad to speak with someone his own age who was interested in what he had been working on for many years. He began to relax and spoke more freely. "I've been in some of the corridors connecting the inner chambers. You could get lost inside that temple."

"Interesting. Well, thanks for your help. I'd like to get a tour sometime, but for now I have to stick around here to take the chief magician and my uncle down when their inspection is finished." Dov appreciated the worker's information.

"Sir, before you leave maybe you can answer a question for me. Something is happening that all the workers have noticed, but can't explain."

"I'll try, but you'll have to stop calling me 'Sir.' My name is Dov, what's yours?" Dov asked the man who was his age but insisted on calling him "Sir."

"My name is Kaman." The worker enjoyed the familiarity with someone he considered a near-celebrity.

"In the past few days we've been instructed to work day and night to finish the temple. For some reason, there's a deadline and the temple must be completed immediately. Last night the telescope from the old ziggurat was hauled up here and installed at the far corner of the building. That, in itself, has caused a lot of talk. What's going on?"

"There may be something to what you see going on. I can't get into details, but when you look into the heavens in the next few days you'll see something very unusual. When you see it, remember that it isn't the gods doing it. The One True God who made heaven and earth is in control of everything. Put your trust in Him and your anxiety about the future will be replaced with peace. You'll be safe in His hands."

Thank you, sir . . . I mean, Dov. Those are comforting words indeed." The two shook hands and returned to their assignments.

Just then, Jengo rounded the corner of the ziggurat. He motioned to Dov to get into the ascender. "Magus will be here any moment. Get ready."

They waited in the ascender and Dov sensed an uncharacteristic tension in his uncle. "Is everything all right?" he asked him before the magician arrived.

Jengo expressed his concern: "Magus wants me to press the workers to finish and be off the Luminary levels as soon as possible. He knows that the asteroid is approaching and has something planned. I wish I knew what it was."

"I was speaking with a masonry worker and he confirmed that. They're worried about what will happen when their work is finished. Nobody has told them what they'll be doing when they're done here. The mason told me something interesting about the ziggurat."

Before Dov could continue, Magus rounded the far corner of the ziggurat and approached the ascender entrance at a fast pace.

"Down as fast as possible," he commanded. Dov smiled at the irony of what Magus said, and hoped the official could not see his expression as he attended to the controls with his back turned to him. Instead, he closed the door, slowly released the foot brake and engaged the drive clutch. The capsule began its descent and gradually picked up speed.

When they arrived at the bottom floor Luminary entrance, Magus exited and turned to Jengo with curt instructions. "You will maintain this ascender ready for use on a moment's notice, beginning immediately. Either you or this operator will be available for me or any of the Triad who wish to ascend. Nobody but the Triad are to be transported to the Luminary levels until further notice. No other Luminaries. Is that understood?"

"Understood. How long will it need to be kept in such a state of readiness?" Jengo inquired.

"I will ignore your impertinence because I am in a hurry. You will be ready until further notice. That is all." The magician was joined by several of his waiting attendants and they departed in their customary rush.

Jengo and Dov descended in the ascender to the basement docking station where Yanis had been monitoring the vapor engine from the master console. She sensed their consternation.

"We'll be facing some scheduling issues imposed on us by Magus," Jengo stated flatly. "Fortunately, Kitt, Ash, and Javak can fill in when you and Dov need to be somewhere else. I'm thinking that they can operate the ascender if you need to make another *Cyclone* prediction run. I only hope that Magus won't question an ascender operator he's never seen before if he makes an unannounced appearance. Tell him that you are related to me. Other members of the Triad won't take notice."

"We can do that," Dov reassured him. "I'll prepare a schedule and take it to the others. Yanis and I can be here on standby during the daytime and supervise the *Cyclone* at night. We don't need to sleep anyway," he grinned. "The next few days will be exciting enough!"

CHAPTER 21

Old Babel, Ziggurat of Marduk—Basement Cell

Late morning

The confined room where Evina spent the night was deep in the basement of the Old Babel ziggurat, where no sound penetrated the thick stone walls. Although her cell was furnished with amenities, she was alone. Saris had struggled at first with a squad of a dozen temple guards who tried to keep him from her. Only when Evina begged him to not struggle did he cease his resistance and give in to Zidon's order. This probably saved his life. Zidon assured his daughter that no harm would come to Saris if he did not resist or interfere further. Her confinement in the basement was only temporary until she and her telescope were transferred to the tower. Shadow could remain with her, but Saris would be restricted from any contact with his charge. She told him, through sign language that the others did not understand, to hurry to her observatory and ensure that her notebooks remained secured.

Evina assumed that it was early morning when servants brought food and water, although she had not heard or seen anything since the day before. She thought about her friends who would eventually learn of her imprisonment and, she hoped, attempt to contact her. She wondered when she would next see Dov. Would he try to find her? What about the Watcher? He said he would see that no harm came to her. Where was he now? These thoughts and questions were interrupted by the muted sounds of people at the door.

The door opened to admit her father, followed by a half-dozen armed guards. Even the temple guards, all of whom had the greatest respect for the young woman, were puzzled by her imprisonment. Their impassive expressions revealed nothing of their concern for the young woman. Shadow stood quietly at her side and eyed the guards.

"My dear, good morning," her father said cheerfully. "Did you sleep well last night?"

"No Father, I did not. How do you think I should feel in this dungeon?" Evina fought her urge to scream and demand her immediate release. She successfully bottled up her fury for the moment. It was clear that her father had other plans for her.

"Don't be concerned by this slight inconvenience. You'll move to the tower later today and settle into your new rooftop observatory where you can continue your work. Your new bedroom is attached to the observatory, where the height will give you a better view of the heavens. I trust you will find it an improvement in every way." Zidon's upbeat tone was unnerving to his daughter. She could not believe that he was enjoying her confinement.

"Anything would be better than this dank cell," she complained.

"Good. I'm glad to hear that you are accepting your situation graciously." He was entirely mistaken about her attitude, but Evina let it pass. He obviously had a purpose other than ensuring her happiness and comfort.

"I hope you have reconsidered your decision to not assume your mother's exalted position as high priestess of Ishtar, and your decision not to join me and your brother in the family calling. Sometimes a little quiet, with time to reflect, can change one's attitude."

Evina thought she had made her convictions clear about becoming a pagan priestess. She knew that her father could not fully understand, but she explained again her newfound faith in the living God. "You and Mother taught me that the gods would direct my path and speak to me through messages in stellar and planetary alignments. When I was a child, you told me stories about the gods and how they evolved over eons from mighty men until they became divine. We stood on the roof of the ziggurat and watched the starry host move across the sky; you taught me that they were living creatures, like the earth, and that we owed our allegiance to them. I know you meant well at the time, but all that was a lie.

124

"My study of those objects, through the telescope you gave me, revealed something that our astrologers never understood. There is infinite beauty and complex order in the heavens. I lost count of the number of stars and star clusters. Each of the stars follows a course through the sky that is unchanging. Something, or someone, had to have brought them into existence. Just as my telescope, a simple thing made from alloy, glass, and other materials, could not have fallen together by accident, so too the infinitely complex clockwork that I see in the sky could not be the product of time and chance. The only explanation that satisfies me as a scientist and astronomer is that Someone more powerful than your gods brought all of this into existence. Since coming to that conclusion, I learned from others that this Someone is the Creator-God who made the universe and all of us. I have given my life to this One True God and cannot follow another."

Her decision was final. Now her father would see that she would *never* change her mind and join him in temple worship.

"I thought I would at least give you another opportunity to recant, but apparently you are determined to follow this silly notion of yours. So be it. I will be back later to move you to the tower. Try to get some rest." Zidon spun around and left the room without further comment. The last guard to leave the room looked back at her sadly before he closed the door.

Evina was stunned by her father's absolute rejection of her faith in God. She thought he might at least have exploded in anger and argued with her. After all, he was the high priest of Marduk and claimed to have all the answers about the gods. Nobody should be better able to defend his faith, but he made no attempt to convince her that she was wrong.

"He can't refute my claims about the One True God!" she said aloud to the loyal dog who climbed on her bed next to her. She gazed at the four walls and wondered what Dov was doing at that moment.

Old Babel, Ziggurat of Marduk—Rooftop Altar

When Zidon completed the noon ceremony and the ecstatic chanting of the crowd diminished, the high priest solemnly raised his hands to speak as an oracle. He was accustomed to using the end of the noon ritual for special announcements and directives from the gods. After a theatrical pause, he lifted his strong voice to reach across the crowd.

"I have received a glorious revelation from the moon goddess Nanna-Seun! She will grace us with a new presence tonight as she gives birth to her child in the heavens. Watch tonight! It will be sublimely beautiful! Watch tonight and greet *Ningizzia*, the guardian of the gate of heaven, who will usher in a New World of prosperity and redemption!

"Another announcement! My son will become High Priest of Nabu in a few days and my daughter will be initiated as High Priestess of Ishtar. They will join me then in worship of Ningizzia to celebrate his arrival. King Nimrod has declared a day of obligation for every citizen to worship the one who will be named the god of New Babel and its One World Tower. Ningizzia will be worshipped as the Guardian of Babel—the Guardian of the Gate of Heaven!"

The faithful gathered about their priest enthusiastically chanted, *Ningizzia! Ningizzia! Ningizzia!*

Arvid watched his father in stunned disbelief while the crowd chanted louder and louder. His sister had refused to be part of worshipping the gods. Had she changed her mind? She was still imprisoned in the basement of the ziggurat. What was his father doing?

New Babel, Pele's Machine Shop

Dov and Yanis met their father in his shop after dinner to discuss developments inside the tower that day. They speculated about the reaction of the inhabitants of Babel when the asteroid became visible later that night. It would be fascinating to see the object for the first time, and they wondered what it would look like against the dark sky.

Saris had come to Dov and Yanis at the ascender control room earlier in the day to inform them that Evina was under house arrest in the basement of the ziggurat temple. Since being forcibly prevented from staying to defend her, Saris was beside himself with worry; he felt that he had abandoned her. However, she expected no harm to come from her father, and Shadow would keep her brother away from her. Dov understood enough of the bodyguard's sign language to conclude that Evina, although in forced protective custody in the temple, was not in any immediate danger, at least for now. Saris accompanied them to the machine shop in hopes that he could somehow rejoin Evina in the tower later.

Kitt entered the workshop with a paper in his hand. "Did you see this?" he asked before the others could greet him. Ash followed close behind him. "Of course they didn't. It was nailed to the door. It has to do with Evina." Dov leapt from his chair and grabbed the note from his cousin's hand.

He read it quickly and the blood drained from his face, revealing bad news. "What does it say?" Yanis asked. "Read it to us."

"It says that Evina is in great danger. She'll be moved to the One World Tower ziggurat tomorrow morning. Zidon has something dramatic planned for her on the day of the asteroid's impact."

"Who put that message on our door?" asked Pele.

"I don't know, but I can guess," Dov replied. "He called himself a 'Watcher,' didn't he?" he asked his sister.

Yanis nodded. "He said he was some kind of protector to watch out for Evina and us. Somehow the Watcher must have found out about Zidon's intentions. I wouldn't put anything past that evil priest." Yanis seethed.

Pele agreed. "Each member of the Triad qualifies as evil. The question is, what can we do to help her now?"

Everyone spoke at once with suggestions for action. Pele calmed his children and nephews, and directed the discussion in more practical directions. They concluded that they had no realistic options. Concern for the young astronomer gripped their emotions, but everything they considered would put her and them in even greater danger. They agreed that they needed to know more before they formed a plan to rescue their friend. Evina was in mortal danger and Dov threw caution aside to suggest the first idea that sprang into his mind. He blinked his eyes in excitement.

"Father, can you get me drawings of the rooftop ziggurat from Uncle Jengo? If we knew more about where her room is and the layout of the inner corridors, we might be able to find a way to reach her without being detected."

"Yes. First, I want to know the rest of your plan," Pele said.

Blinking nervously and making the details up as he went along, Dov began with how he and his sister would first contact Evina. None of the others were very enthusiastic about what Dov proposed, but for lack of anything better, they tentatively agreed to go along with his idea, shaky as it was.

"What about me? What will I be doing while you're off rescuing the beautiful girl?" asked Ash.

"Evina's observations of the asteroid's movement when it appears from behind the moon are essential so we can predict the final time and course of its passage to earth more precisely. It'll be our last chance to pinpoint the time for use in our rescue plan. Can you alert Benji and help him make sure the *Cyclone* is ready for one last run?"

"I sure can!" Ash replied. "Benji and I'll go over the mechanical monster with our oil cans and wrenches one last time so it's ready."

"Good," Dov said. "When you're done with that tune-up, return to the tower ascender control room and maybe you can help Kitt."

As the group left the workshop and dispersed to their assignments, they looked up at the moon and wondered what it would be like to see the object that until now had been abstract numbers in algos, frame sliders, and holes punched in cards. The reality of a looming cataclysm had not fully sunk in.

BOOK II

The Tower

And they said, "Come, let us build ourselves a city, and a tower whose top [is] in the heavens; let us make a name for ourselves, lest we be scattered abroad over the face of the whole earth."
But the LORD came down to see the city and the tower which the sons of men had built.
And the LORD said, "Indeed the people [are] one and they all have one language, and this is what they begin to do; now nothing that they propose to do will be withheld from them.
"Come, let Us go down and there confuse their language, that they may not understand one another's speech."

Genesis 11:1-5

CHAPTER 22

New Babel, One World Tower—Capsule Control Room

The next morning

Dov, Yanis, and Kitt waited in the ascender control room to be ready when Evina was transferred to the tower from her confinement in the ziggurat across the river. They had hashed over Dov's plan for her rescue through much of the night. Saris stood in the background trying to read the lips of the three while they debated back and forth.

Dov ached to see Evina again and encourage her to escape Babel. He wrote a note to her on a piece of paper.

> *Dear Friend,*
> *Yanis and I ask you to leave Babel with our family before the asteroid strikes. Will you? We don't have all the details of an escape plan worked out yet. Your telescope has been moved, so I ask that you make new measurements of the asteroid's path for a final run of the Cyclone. You MUST give the data to Saris for delivery to the School of Japheth. DO NOT let anyone else see or intercept this message. Compromise would prove fatal for all of us. Do not be afraid. With the help of Almighty God we will do all we can to remove you from the tower if you are willing to come with us. You have others who care for you. I am first among them.*
> *Dov*

He thought of showing the message to Yanis and decided he wouldn't. His affection for Evina might be obvious, but he didn't need his sister's prying questions right now. He'd tell her about his request for more data. She should be satisfied with that. Dov folded the note carefully and put it in his jacket pocket.

A temple guard interrupted the three and announced what they had been expecting. "Sir! The high priest of Marduk requires transportation to the Luminary level roof immediately."

Dov and Yanis checked the neatness of their uniforms and entered the ascender that was docked at their basement level. Saris followed quietly behind them into the ascender. Kitt assumed control at the console. They rose quickly and he opened the door of the capsule at the Luminary ground entrance. Zidon and Evina stood in the center of the lobby, accompanied closely by Shadow and flanked by guards. Zidon stopped at the entrance of the ascender and pointed at Saris.

"Tell this one that he will *not* ride with us," Zidon instructed his daughter. "I forbid his presence on the tower." He was clearly irritated and impatient.

Evina nodded to Saris, who had read Zidon's lips. He stood helplessly outside and watched Evina enter with Shadow at her side. He was pleased for now that her canine protector was with her.

Evina looked at Dov and Yanis standing at attention like stone statues before the operator's panel. Their eyes were fixed ahead awaiting instructions from Zidon.

"Father, Shadow can come with me for company, can't he please? He doesn't weigh very much at all." Her father muttered his agreement.

While everyone stood in silence, Dov wondered why he was not instructed to depart. Possibly they were waiting for someone else. After twenty seconds of awkward silence, Zidon spoke.

"Why is she here?"

Dov snapped out of his mental fog when he realized that the high priest was speaking.

"Sir? I mean, are you speaking to me?" Dov dared not turn around. He stood at attention. Yanis tensed and held her breath.

"Yes! Who is that girl standing next to you and why is she here?"

"Your Eminence, she is my sister, who is an operator in training. The Chief Magician Magus directed that a member of our family must operate the Luminary ascender at all times. She is here to replace me in the future, if needed." Dov dared not flinch if Zidon continued to question him, or worse, if he started to question Yanis. She had a low tolerance for stupidity and Zidon was treading on dangerous ground. Dov prayed that she would control her temper.

"Tell her to get off. I don't want a girl driving this thing when I'm in it. Let's go!"

Dov tapped his sister's hand and she stepped off the ascender without turning toward the high priest. She walked down the corridor past Saris and around the corner. Dov closed the door and engaged the clutch. He was thankful that neither Evina nor her father could see his eyes twitch uncontrollably. They gained speed up the shaft toward the roof one-hundred and twenty levels above.

Evina found her father's objection to Yanis' presence puzzling. Could he be aware of the connection between her and Evina? He had never acted this way before. She looked at Dov at his operator's station and felt reassured by his silent presence.

Yanis, on the other hand, stomped down the stairs to the control console, where she startled Kitt. "I can't believe it! He threw me off the ascender! I'm so mad I could spit."

"Who threw you off? Dov?"

"Of course not. It was Zidon. 'I don't want a girl driving this thing when I'm in it.' Oh, I'm so mad!"

"I could tell," Kitt answered carefully. "Come, sit here beside me and make sure I monitor the gauges properly. You know much more about these machines than I do." He appreciated her sharp technical mind, which not everyone did. Besides, he liked being with her.

"You understand, don't you? Most people think because I'm pretty I don't know anything. I'm a better engineer than any woman and most men." Yanis was calmer now that she sat next to Kitt. After a moment she realized that she'd rather be with him than her brother anyway.

New Babel, One World Tower—Luminary Ascender

Dov's plan was to distract Zidon by pointing out the view when they transitioned into an open section, and somehow pass his note to

Evina without her father noticing it. Zidon was not interested in the sights and spoke curtly to his daughter.

"When I have you settled in the new observatory, I want you to look at the approaching meteor, or whatever it is, and tell me in the morning *exactly* when it will impact or pass us by. You promised me that you would give me regular updates. I need to know so I can prepare for the special ceremony," Zidon insisted. "Do not disappoint me."

Evina and her father stood directly behind Dov so they couldn't see his face, nor he theirs. She stood in the far corner of the capsule and Dov couldn't turn around to see or speak with her, let alone pass her his note without being observed by her father.

He thought of using sign language, but his hands were occupied regulating their speed. If he used his left hand at his side he might get her attention enough to show that he had a message for her. Maybe she'd find a way to take the paper from him on her way out.

Passing the 75th level, Dov made an attempt to distract Zidon.

"Sir, the view from this height is magnificent and a tribute to man's wisdom and power. Do you find it breathtaking?" He turned slightly to point to buildings through the portholes and hoped that, if Zidon objected to his remark, Evina could quickly distract her father.

When he saw Zidon's silent glare out of the corner of his eye he turned his attention to the control panel and remained silent. So much for that ploy.

Zidon broke the silence by speaking to Evina again. "You will be confined to your observatory and attached quarters until further notice. If the approaching object impacts the city, then it will not matter for us anyway. In anticipation of a spectacular approach and near miss, if the gods are smiling on us, it will be heralded as a sign of my power with the heavenly forces. You will participate in our special ceremony on top of the new ziggurat. I am sorry it has come to this, but you give me no choice now."

"I cannot go against my faith in God. Even if I die I cannot join in your plans," Evina sobbed.

Oh, but you will join me, Zidon thought to himself.

As they approached the 120th level, Dov was increasingly anxious. He couldn't help it. He had run out of ideas for passing his note to Evina. He removed the paper from his pocket and held it in the palm of his hand. Maybe he could pretend that Evina dropped something and give it to her. With his other hand he used the crank to raise the capsule several inches until it was level with the floor. He turned to his passengers and opened the gate. Zidon held his daughter's arm firmly and commanded Dov to wait. He walked out the door while positioned between Dov and Evina. A brace of guards met them at the door, and the group moved into the open promenade that encircled the black temple. There was nothing Dov could do. He froze in disbelief and helplessness with the paper in his hand while Evina and her father were escorted away. Shadow brushed past him and Dov suddenly had an idea.

"Shadow, come here." The dog returned and waited for a command.

"Open!"

The dog sat upright with his jaws open wide. Dov looked to see if anyone was watching, crumpled the paper into a tight ball and popped it into the dog's mouth, which closed gently around the paper.

"Go to Evina!" Shadow departed in a run to catch up with the young woman.

When his passengers were out of sight, Dov ran toward the ziggurat where he had last seen Kaman only a day before. He had to hurry before Zidon returned. Kaman wasn't there, but he saw another Accadian mason on his knees plastering trim around a doorway. He approached the older, grey-haired man reluctantly. He didn't want to get Kaman into trouble by asking too many questions.

"Sir, can you tell me where I can find a young mason named Kaman? Is he around here today?" Dov asked hurriedly. He extended his hand to help the old man rise unsteadily to his feet. "No need to be formal with me. I'm not an official—just a friend of Kaman's. He was working here a few days ago. Do you know him?"

"Yes, I know him," the old man replied. "My name is Mico, and you must be Dov. Kaman and I are in our family's guild. He told me about you. He went to the supply area near the freight ascender. He'll be back in half an hour. Can I help you?"

Sensing that Kaman's relative with the open, friendly face could be trusted, Dov continued. "I must quickly return to my post, but could you give him a message for me? Tell him I was looking for him. Ask him to find out where the high priest's daughter is being held and if he can get me in to see her. Tell him it's a very urgent matter."

Mico's eyes twinkled. "Was that the young lady I saw walk by escorted by guards? She is beautiful. I can see why you would want to see her," the old man smiled.

"Yes, she's the one. However, it's not what you think. She's just a friend. Please give the message to Kaman as soon as you see him. I must be going." Dov turned toward the ascender but the man had more to say.

"I've seen looks like yours before, my friend. Back when I was young we would say you are in love. Someday you will tell her how you feel. I'm sure she feels the same way about you." Mico's parting prediction initially made Dov bristle, but then he couldn't deny his perceptive observation. Was it that obvious?

Dov hurried back to the ascender platform and wondered that a stranger was giving him romantic advice. He shifted his mind to his ascender operator duties and tried not to think about Evina. There was no telling what Zidon would do if he returned to the Luminary ascender and found him missing.

No sooner had he caught his breath at the ascender entrance than Zidon returned alone. He swept through the doorway and stood behind Dov in the middle of the capsule. "Go!" he grunted. Dov stared straight ahead and tended to his controls. They descended uneventfully in silence, with thoughts racing through Dov's mind about what Evina must be feeling now that she was a prisoner somewhere in the tower ziggurat.

When Dov opened the door for Zidon to step into the Luminary lobby the high priest spoke curtly as he walked by. "I will need transportation tomorrow morning after the sunrise ceremony to Shamash. Be here . . . and do not bring that girl with you." He walked off with his armed escort, while Dov stood in wonder at the man's monumental arrogance.

When he brought the ascender down one level to the control room docking station he found Yanis and Kitt laughing. They greeted him cheerfully, but soon realized that he didn't share their levity. He slumped into a chair. "We need to do something. I can't sit here while Evina is being held prisoner." He looked around the room. "Where did Saris go?"

"I haven't seen him since Zidon kicked him *and me* off the ascender," Yanis said. "He's probably looking for a way to get up to the rooftop."

Dov repeatedly insisted that Evina had to be rescued from the tower soon. He had overheard Zidon's ominous pronouncement that Evina would participate in the ceremony, whether she wanted to or not. If Kaman could tell him how to reach Evina's observatory, maybe he could make a special trip up to the rooftop and whisk her away. He still needed a layout of the tower temple interior in case a direct approach didn't work. There were too many "ifs" in any of his ideas to call them a plan, but after he observed firsthand Zidon's coldness toward his daughter, it was clear that Evina was in greater peril, and that outweighed the risks of attempting a rescue, no matter how dangerous it proved. He prayed that God would help him find Evina and bring her safely off the tower.

New Babel, One World Tower—Evina's New Observatory

When Evina was alone, Shadow nuzzled her hand and opened his mouth. "What's this?" She reached into the dog's mouth and withdrew the soggy wad of paper, carefully unwrapped it, read its contents and broke into a smile.

CHAPTER 23

New Babel, One World Tower—Evina's New Observatory

Midnight

Evina was the first human to see it without the aid of a telescope because she knew exactly where and when to look for it. She had tracked the approaching asteroid since dusk through her instrument that was firmly anchored on the balcony of the black stone ziggurat. When her target disappeared behind the bright edge of the moon, she stepped onto the porch that faced away from the main city plaza. The waxing moon high in the sky flooded the valley and its surrounding hills with a tranquil, pale glow that gave no hint of the tragedy ahead.

A cool, gentle breeze washed over her. The Euphrates River flowed silently more than one thousand feet below. She usually enjoyed the solitude of the night, but tonight was different. She was terrified of what would happen if the approaching ball hit earth or passed through its atmosphere. Her loneliness multiplied fear of the future.

The peaceful scene slowly changed with the appearance of a new light that peeked out from the bottom of the dark sliver of the moon's disk. The pinpoint of light could hardly be distinguished from a star at first, but within minutes it separated itself from the narrow, jagged line of the moon's mountains and revealed a fuller, distinctive yellow color and a larger, spherical shape. Suspended between the blackness of space and the dark slice of the moon, it looked like the moon was shedding a fiery teardrop. After staring upward for a few minutes,

Evina returned to her telescope to study the surface of the object more carefully and plot its final course.

Plain of Shinar

Shepherds wrapped themselves in blankets and drifted asleep around their smoldering fire on a grassy hillside overlooking the city while their sheep huddled in clusters on the ground for warmth and safety. The animals had eaten their fill in a nearby meadow, and their keepers dozed peacefully. The city was mostly dark, save for lights blazing in the tower ziggurat and random lamps in windows and on rooftops of buildings that encircled the tower. The otherworldly appearance of the approaching asteroid was yet to be noticed by anyone other than the young astronomer who had predicted its arrival weeks before and a handful of people who remembered Zidon's prediction about something new in the night sky and happened to look up at that moment.

Four jackals stalked the sheep from a distance downwind. They patiently edged toward their unsuspecting prey. By chance, one of the predators noticed the object first. Looking upward, he forgot about the sheep. First one, and then the others, pointed their noses into the air, sniffed, and emitted a low, eerie moan. Soon, the quartet increased in pitch and volume until dogs in the city picked up their cry and instinctively joined in the growing howl. The sheep pressed tighter together and trembled. The shepherds awoke from their sleep to the wild cacophony of howls, barks, and yelps from every canine species on the plain.

"What is that?" asked the chief shepherd to no one in particular. "Go check on the sheep. They'll be terrified by this frightful noise."

A shepherd nearby answered. "I don't know what it is. I've never heard anything like it. Something has spooked wild animals for miles around. Maybe an earthquake is about to happen. I've heard that sometimes dogs know when the earth is about to shake."

After accounting for all the sheep and assuring themselves that they were not being attacked, one of the men looked up at the moon.

"Ayiiiiii!" he screamed, pointing upward.

The shepherds looked up in unison with varying exclamations of amazement, terror, and confusion. Some threw up their hands while others covered their head and faces. All cried aloud to their gods.

"Oh, Nanna-Seun! We will all die!"

"Save us Ninsun!"

"Why is this happening? Why?"

Faced with an unprecedented heavenly vision, they called out to their celestial deities. Their gods were silent. Then they heard more screams echoing from the hills around Babel. The men's only comfort was to join their equally terrified fellow human beings in crying out at the sky. For the first time in their lives, the shepherds abandoned their sheep and ran toward the city in search of help from their priests and their gods.

Soon, inhabitants of the city on both sides of the river were roused from their beds by the primal wails of beasts and humans. When they found no explanation for the clamor, and could not silence their animals, they eventually stared upward one by one and joined in the cries of despair that engulfed the inhabitants of Babel. Their nightmare was only beginning.

Old Babel, Ziggurat of Marduk—High Priest's Residence

Loud, inhuman cries from the old city of Babel roused Zidon from an uneasy sleep. After a few moments he realized that the asteroid must be visible and that panic was building. In spite of his pronouncement at the noon ceremony the day before, he had gone to sleep without giving the asteroid much thought. Now it fell upon him to assure the faithful that they were not in any danger and should look to him and the gods for salvation. The astrologers would distribute that day's paper slips proclaiming change for the better, but words of optimism on pieces of paper held little comfort to people when the menacing object in the black sky was so real.

Zidon was far from certain that all would turn out well. Years of practice as a priest gave him the hubris to stand before people and tell them blatant lies that made them feel comfortable. He always managed to come up with clever, soothing words to address the future and life after death. Did he believe that the gods were able to save humankind? No. He believed that he would die and that would be it, or at least, that is what he hoped. Maybe it was a false hope, he thought, but at least he would put on a spectacular, theatrical display so that the last vision in people's minds would be of him splendidly dressed in his golden miter and colorful robes, raising his hands to the sky atop the One World Tower's magnificent ziggurat when the asteroid turned him and all mankind into cinders.

He was not even curious to see what the approaching object looked like. The cynical cleric turned over and fell asleep.

New Babel, Pele's Machine Shop

Dov, Yanis, and Kitt descended from the roof of the machine shop after watching the asteroid slowly trace a path across the night sky from behind the moon. They assumed that Jengo, Pele, and Javak were busy convincing tower workers to remain at their posts and keep the ascenders operating in spite of what happened outside. Many freight ascenders continued running up and down during the night. Jengo decided to shut the Luminary passenger ascender down until further notice. If any Luminaries arrived in the meantime, he would take his chances with their wrath for his decision.

The twins hoped that Ash would stay at the *Cyclone* to await new data from Evina. Their discussion centered on how they could take advantage of the chaos in the streets and in the tower to effect a rescue and then leave the city.

"Evina must be worried about being alone in the tower and far from anyone who could help her. We need a break that allows us to reach her and bring her down here where she'll be safe." Dov, more than anyone, wanted Evina out of danger.

Yanis looked like she had thought of something when she stood abruptly. "We've been talking about how to get her off the tower, and we should, but what do we do with her once she's with us? I trust that God will somehow open a door of opportunity in the next few days to reunite her with us. What do we do then? Should we hide someplace if Jengo isn't ready to leave? If we're detected and pursued by Zidon's temple guards or Nimrod's soldiers, how can we defend ourselves? We need a plan for *after* we rescue Evina, whenever or however that happens." Yanis sat down and looked at the others for answers to her litany of questions.

Nobody had answers. She had raised new dangers and complications and they were at a loss for solutions.

"We should pray for wisdom," Dov suggested. "We're not thinking clearly; at least I'm not. I admit I'm scared that Evina will die by her father's hand if I don't come up with something."

"Dov, you know what's strange?" Yanis asked.

"No, what?"

"We could all die in the next few days if the asteroid hits us."

"And you just realized that?" her brother wondered.

"I'm just saying that we could all die in the next few days and yet we're not running around in a panic like the others. Don't get me wrong. I don't want to die, but at the same time, I'm not worried about what will happen if I do. I know that we'll be together in a special place that God has prepared for those who belong to Him by faith. Then, at the end of the age, we'll be raised to be with Him forever. I'm thrilled with that assurance! I only wish I was certain that Evina had the same confidence."

"I think she does. When we were in the ascender she told her father that she would rather die than go against her faith in the One True God. To me, that's powerful evidence that God has changed her heart."

"I feel better then," Yanis replied. She put her hand on Kitt's arm. "If the asteroid hits earth at least the four of us will be together."

Kitt had been silent up to this point. "We need wisdom and deliverance. Yes, we should pray," he concluded.

CHAPTER 24

New Babel, One World Tower—Freight Storage Area

Same time

Magus had no concern for the chaos in the streets when he made his way through the mobs to the tower that night. The crowds only fed his lust for future rule over the city. He would eliminate the other two members of the Triad and ensure his rule over the human race. It was time for the next phase of his vision.

Three thuggish-looking men loitered in the tower's supply storage area, where materials destined for upper levels awaited transport on freight ascenders. They were dressed in workmen's clothes but their tight muscular physiques, calculating alertness to their surroundings, and cold, roaming eyes marked them as hardened street criminals. All three were dishonored ex-soldiers. The magician had used them for secret 'activities' in the past. He was confident of their loyalty and dependability. When Magus arrived, they stood before him and awaited his instructions.

"The noise of mobs outside only confirms the timing of what you will do for me in the next days. Tonight, I want you to survey the tower rooftop and familiarize yourselves thoroughly with the layout of the promenade area surrounding the temple, the exterior terraces of the ziggurat, and as much of the interior corridors as possible without arousing suspicion. Write notes on this drawing of the temple floor plan. Workmen on the tower will be sufficiently distracted to make your job easier. You will tell anyone who questions you that you work for Jengo the engineer and are inspecting the structure. Is that understood?" He looked at each of the three former soldiers before him. They knew that he was cold-blooded; he would not hesitate to have them executed if they double-crossed him.

"We understand perfectly," their leader responded. "What if someone becomes too curious and asks too many questions? Can we remove them? How important is it that our true purpose be undetected?" He wanted to be clear about the purpose of their reconnaissance of the rooftop and the limits of their mission.

"No killing!" Magus hissed. "If you must remove anyone, make it look like an accident. The last thing I want is to alarm other workers or officials. You'll likely be noticed and even questioned, but there must be no suspicion raised among the workmen that anything is amiss. I want security around Nimrod and Zidon to be lax or distracted when they participate in the climax of the ceremony; they must feel safe in the tower in spite of crowds on the promenade and chaos in the city plaza below."

Magus sent the men on their way to the rooftop with a cart of supplies, which they would take on slow freight ascenders and through the freight portals until they arrived at their destination by dawn. He required detailed, current information about the temple layout. He would use that to brief other teams of assassins on his plan to become the supreme ruler of New Babel.

CHAPTER 25

New Babel, One World Tower—Evina's New Observatory

Before dawn

The appearance of the asteroid from behind the moon afforded Evina her first opportunity to study its size, shape and surface details. She focused her attention on what she saw through her eyepiece and ignored the distant cries from the city. With a notebook at her side, she made careful annotations about the object that might explain its origin and significance.

First, its size could be measured more precisely when done so in relation to that of the moon. Ancient astronomers had accurately calculated the moon's diameter, and the span of this approaching ball—it was obvious to her now that it was a perfect sphere—was more than fifty miles. Even now, the unaided human eye was able to discern its shape. Evina noted that its bright, yellow color was the same color as the sun. Was it that color because it was an incandescent, sun-like source of light, or was it something else? Earth's moon was a reflective satellite whose source of light was the sun. It emitted no heat or light of its own. The moon's uneven, grey-white surface of rocks, mountains, valleys, and craters caused its reflected light to diffuse and to be much dimmer than the sun. The light of a full moon varied from dapples of white to muted hues of grey.

This new object was brighter than the moon and yet the color of the sun. Evina studied it carefully with the highest magnification of her telescope and detected no irregularities in its surface texture. She searched her mind for an explanation and arrived at only one: *it was a perfectly spherical mirror!*

She wrote down her observations and turned her attention to measuring its motion parameters more exactly than was possible when it was farther away. Its movement balanced between strong but opposing forces of gravity from the earth and the moon. As the earth's pull took over these competing forces it should be accelerating, and thus, its trajectory would change from her previous calculations. Instead of building up speed, as she expected, it had slowed! How could that be? Nothing she knew about magnetic or gravitational forces in the universe could explain it. After repeated measurements to confirm the new, slower speed of the asteroid, she concluded that only God could work such a miracle. This new information made another run of the *Cyclone* predictor engine even more imperative. A quick calculation from data in her notes also revealed something about the material composition of the shining sphere. It was denser than the moon or the earth. This finding also explained its mirror-like finish: *it was a sphere of solid metal!*

After Evina checked her telescope data one last time for the new speed of the approaching object, she transcribed it from her notebook to a sheet of paper with instructions to Dov and Yanis to program the numbers into the *Cyclone*. The desired outputs would be simple for them to understand—the date and hour of the closest approach and the distance from the tower. If the distance was zero, or very close to it, they would know that nobody in the city could survive the impact. In that event it would be pointless to try to escape. Evina's rough calculations showed that the object might miss them by a slight distance. But nothing was certain at this point.

How would she deliver the results to Dov and Yanis? Her father had banished Saris from the tower. She was alone except for Shadow. Guards outside prevented anyone from entering or leaving. She thought of wrapping her notes in a cloth with a weight inside, stitching it closed, and throwing it off the tower to the plaza below. Maybe a note on the outside could instruct the finder to deliver it to the School of Japheth. Who knew what would happen to it then? No, that would never work.

The young woman looked at Shadow across the room. The dog interpreted her look as a command and trotted over to sit at her feet.

"How do you do that?" she asked him. "You are so smart!"

Shadow remained motionless while he watched her with deep brown eyes. "I suppose there's a better chance of you making your way to the School of Japheth with this message than there is of some random person finding it on the sidewalk and delivering it," she concluded.

She carefully folded the paper until it fit neatly in the palm of her hand, wrapped it in a piece of black cloth, and rolled that cloth inside one of her brightly colored scarves before tying it around Shadow's neck like a collar. Nobody would remove the scarf from the dog unless he allowed them to do so. After checking the security of the knot on the scarf, she walked him to the door.

"Go to the *Cyclone* lab at the School of Japheth and deliver this. Go to the school!" The dog's eager face told her that he somehow understood. Evina opened the door that was flanked by guards and let him out into the open area on the side of the ziggurat. Shadow was on his own.

With a casual walk that raised no alarm from the guards, Evina's protector proceeded along the edge of the ziggurat building's outer walkway. He broke into a run toward the freight ascender portal as soon as he was out of sight of the guards. Within seconds, he stood behind boxes of construction materials and supplies stacked for transit. The trained canine waited in the shadows while he observed the chaotic transfers of people and materials whenever a freight ascender arrived. All the tower workers had seen the glowing asteroid in the sky and their reactions ranged from indifference to panic. The normally routine movement of people and supplies in the rooftop portal area had turned into mayhem since the asteroid had appeared. Shadow sensed that he could leave the rooftop for another level if he boarded an ascender. For twenty minutes he watched ascenders come and go and the noisy melee of workers and goods darted back and forth before him.

Shadow also kept an alert eye on a nearby worker. Kaman had noticed the dog sitting patiently and recognized him as the dog that accompanied Evina when he last saw her. When he came within ten feet of the dog he was stopped by a low growl.

"I know you! I saw you come out of the ascender yesterday with the high priest and that pretty girl. What are you doing out here?" Kaman was an animal lover who, out of habit, spoke to them as if they were human but never expected a reply. "Are you waiting for someone?"

Shadow walked slowly over to Kaman when he sensed his friendliness and the worker stepped back, bumped his shoulder against a large crate, and fell backwards. Shadow stood over the young man's prostrate figure and licked his face. Fear turned to surprise followed by a smile as Kaman rubbed the large dog's belly. "So you're a friendly watchdog, huh? I think you want to go down in one of those ascenders. Is that right?" Kaman walked to an ascender with Shadow at his side.

"You can't take that animal on my ascender," challenged the operator.

"How do you think he got here? He belongs to one of the Luminaries and needs to go down to the ground floor. Now don't give me a hard time." Kaman hoped that the dog really did belong to that pretty girl. He thought he'd like to meet her someday.

"I'll take him to the ground level myself, so don't get in a snit about having a dog on your filthy ascender. With all the trash you haul I wouldn't think you'd care about carrying a dog." The young mason and Shadow stood at the front of the crowded ascender. The door closed and began its slow descent. They changed ascenders at the Ministerial and Guild transit portals, and each time Kaman had to convince the freight operators to let him bring a dog in their craft. When they finally reached the ground cargo portal Kaman took the dog aside.

"I don't know who you are, but you're the smartest dog I've ever come across. You're surely no ordinary street mutt. You take care of yourself. Put in a good word for me with that pretty girl." After a blink of his brown eyes, Shadow ran out of the tower cargo area and into the crowded plaza.

New Babel, School of Japheth—*Cyclone* Computing Center

The canine courier somehow found the School of Japheth and reached the *Cyclone* lab within an hour after leaving the tower. The door to the lab was closed, but this was no impediment to him. He stood with his front paws on the door, pressed down on the latch with his long snout, and the door swung inward. He heard the hissing sound of the idling *Cyclone*. Nobody was in sight, so he began a methodical search of the large laboratory area, sniffing the air for a human scent. The smells of oil and moist vapor were confusing. Soon he came upon Benji sitting at a high workbench with a disassembled gearbox spread out before him.

Out of the corner of his eye Benji noticed the large brown and black dog sitting a few feet from him. "Yikes!" he screamed. "Keep away from me!" Benji wasn't fond of dogs, especially those whose size exceeded his.

Because this human was terrified of him but did not appear to pose a threat, Shadow had been trained to make himself appear as friendly as possible until the human calmed down. The man must eventually discover the message wrapped in his collar. Shadow hated to do this, but he condescended to lay on the floor and roll onto his back as if doing a trick. Faking a non-threatening smile, if that were possible for a dog, Shadow used this pose to make himself appear as harmless as possible to the cowering human. He held this humiliating posture for more than a minute, hoping that the young man would eventually approach him. Benji finally saw the brightly colored scarf and slowly approached the recumbent animal. He carefully felt the material, untied its secure knot, and took it to the workbench, keeping his distance from the dog. He still kept his distance from the dog. Shadow rose to his feet now that the demeaning ordeal was over.

"What's inside this thing? It smells like perfume." Benji carefully unwrapped the scarf and the outer covering of black cloth that held the paper. When he unfolded the message his eyes bulged in surprise. It was addressed to Dov and contained a list of input parameters for the *Cyclone's* frames. It also had instructions for reading outputs. Dov, Yanis, and the others were working on predicting the trajectory of an approaching space object! Besides that, a high-level Luminary named Evina was feeding them current parameters. No wonder there was so much secrecy. Benji refolded the paper and put it in his pocket. He had to find Dov.

CHAPTER 26

New Babel, One World Tower—Evina's New Observatory

Near dawn

Evina lay awake in bed listening to distant rioting crowds as they called on their gods to save them and rushed about in a panic. Thousands gathered in the predawn darkness across the river around the Ziggurat of Marduk in Old Babel to beg for help from the priests, but they found no satisfaction. She wondered if her father was making an announcement about the apparition that had silently emerged from behind the moon. He should not be surprised that the entire city was in a turmoil. Zidon's religion relied on the people's superstition that hidden meanings were behind unusual, unexplained events. This was fertile ground for confusion, fear, and ultimately, dependence on the priesthood to feed them fables.

She was so deep in thought about why she was so different from her father and brother, in spite of her upbringing in a household of idolatry, that she barely heard the soft thud from her balcony. Evina walked from her room to the balcony and looked across the river at Old Babel to see what had caused the sound. A dark figure in the shadows watched her. He did not want to speak and frighten her when she stood so close to the edge of the balcony railing. She turned toward her room and he spoke her name softly.

"Evina. Don't be afraid." His announcement startled her nonetheless.

"Who is it?" she replied in a stifled scream.

"The Watcher. Do you remember me?" By training and habit, the Watcher was dressed in black to blend into the darkness. He stood motionless where the balcony railing met the wall of the tower.

"Of course. How could I forget you?" She replied. Her heart was pounding.

"I have news that your friends are planning to rescue you."

"I don't understand," Evina said after a few seconds of thought. "Why would they risk themselves coming here? Why don't you take me with you? You seem able to go anywhere. Take me to them now," she insisted.

"I wish I could, but my mission is to observe, inform, and encourage. I lack the means to take you with me, but you are not in danger for now." The man in the shadows hoped that his explanation would be sufficient to allay her fears.

"I don't understand what is happening," the young woman replied, "but I believe you."

"You must learn to put your trust in Almighty God and not in me."

Evina stared at the shrouded figure with a mixture of wonder and nervousness that always marked their nighttime meetings. Tonight he was not enveloped in his black cape. Instead, he wore a long fitted suit with flaps or folds of black cloth from his shoulders to his feet. He surprised her at odd times and places, but always had words of encouragement when he left.

"I must leave now to attend to business in the city below. Remember, place your trust in the Lord and He will never leave you."

To Evina's astonishment, the Watcher stepped onto the balcony railing and turned his head toward her. "Don't be afraid." He lifted his arms and widened his stance on the railing so she saw the webbed material between his arms and torso and between his legs. He jumped.

She screamed and ran to the railing to see the dim plummeting shape speed between her and the twinkling lights of the city. He flew into the predawn darkness with only a whoosh of wind.

The Watcher's suit fluttered about him as he shot across the cityscape at high speed through the thick, damp air. He used his outstretched arms as wings to steer away from the side of the tower and glide in sweeping arcs between nearby buildings above the streets.

Within seconds, he found the pattern of lights for his landing site and released the trigger of his parachute. He relaxed momentarily under the billowing black canopy as the sound of rushing wind abruptly diminished. His heart rate slowed slightly. He corrected his drift several times before he planted his boots precisely and with only a muffled thud on the roof of his safe house located between the School of Japheth and Pele's machine shop. Not until he had hidden his parachute and webbed outfit did he sit on the roof with a sigh of relief and look up at the One World Tower.

The insanity of jumping from the 120th floor in an untested flying squirrel suit and then parachuting onto the roof of a small house would have paralyzed anyone else with fear. He had been a lone Watcher for less than a year but hardly thought twice about taking high risks for the sake of a mission. If he had to jump from the tower again he would do so without a second's indecision. His mind raced over a long list of things he had to do before dawn. One was to repack his parachute in case he needed it again on short notice. When it was packed and hung next to his black webbed suit in a concealed equipment room, he descended another flight of stairs to his living space, where he showered and changed into the uniform of a palace courier.

The Watcher's suit fluttered as he shot
across the cityscape at high speed.

CHAPTER 27

New Babel, Pele's Machine Shop

Morning

Nobody on the crowded street noticed when the Watcher, dressed in a palace courier's uniform, paused briefly before Pele's shop, casually slipped a note under the door, and rejoined the morning rush hour throng on the sidewalk. When Dov and his companions passed him from the opposite direction returning from their recent duty at the tower, the Watcher accidentally bumped into Dov. With hardly a glance at the anonymous palace servant, Dov continued on his way.

Yanis saw the paper on the floor when she unlocked the shop door. Thinking it was an advertisement, she put it on the table and went to the back of the shop to change out of her ascender operator's uniform. Dov and Kitt made a beeline for the kitchen to find something to eat. When they returned with drinks and sandwiches made from cold leftovers, Dov offered his sister a sandwich, which she immediately refused.

"How can you eat a cold meat sandwich for breakfast?" she asked with disgust. Dov and Kitt gave her puzzled looks.

"Why wouldn't we?" Dov retorted. "It's food, isn't it? Anyway, I like it better when it's cold and all the grease is congealed." The boys laughed and dug into their breakfasts.

Yanis returned from the kitchen eating a piece of fruit and casually unfolded the paper she had thrown on the table. She read only a few lines before she let out a gasp.

"What's the matter? Is something wrong?" Kitt asked.

Yanis looked at both sides of the paper. "It's about Evina."

"Tell me what it says! If it's about Evina, I want to know!" Dov set his sandwich on the table and tried to grab the paper from his sister's hand.

She stepped away from him. "Wait, let me finish reading it." Her hand trembled as she read the ghastly news.

When she handed the paper to Dov she could not contain herself. Tears ran down her cheeks. This news changed everything.

Dov read the note quickly. Fury built up inside him with each word. "Evina's in more danger than we could have imagined. She's refused to follow Zidon and Arvid in the family line of pagan priests. We knew that. After repeatedly rejecting her father's demands, she's been imprisoned in the tower."

"We knew that too," said Kitt. "You discovered that when you took her and her father up in the ascender. So what's changed?"

"Now we know what that monster has planned. He's imprisoned her in the tower so he can use her in a ceremony atop the ziggurat when the asteroid comes close to earth." Dov had to pause to keep from choking up. He was trembling with rage.

"When the object fills the sky, he'll . . ." Dov spoke between breaths for air. "He'll sacrifice her . . . on the altar . . . to appease the gods." Dov had to sit down to calm his spinning head. "I can't believe he would do something so horrific! It's more evil than we could have imagined." He handed the note to Kitt who read it carefully.

Kitt placed the paper on the table and tried to help his cousins by being objective and to balance their despair. He noted that this news did nothing to change their desire to rescue their friend other than add to an already high sense of urgency. They still had a few days left, more or less, before the asteroid hit. If the precise hour of the asteroid's approach were known, it would only slightly affect the timing of their rescue plans. There was still time to rescue her and escape from the city.

Though they had discussed many ideas for a rescue, all their options were too complicated. It would take weeks to coordinate a safe, foolproof plan. They needed more time, information, helpers, and materials. They had none of these. Only God could help them.

New Babel, School of Japheth—*Cyclone* Computing Center

Benji met Dov, Yanis, and Kitt at the door of the *Cyclone* lab. He waved the paper with the latest data from Evina. One look at Shadow standing next to Benji told them all they needed to know about the reason for his agitation.

"What's going on?" Benji was furious. "You've kept me in the dark about the algos running on the *Cyclone*. If I'm putting my life in danger I demand to know everything! On top of that, you're planning to leave the city!"

Dov attempted to calm his friend. "Sit down and I'll fill you in about the calculations. I'm afraid that, for your own protection, I can't go into all the details, but I can tell you what these numbers are and why this *Cyclone* run will be its last." He rehearsed some of the background of Evina's requested predictions about an approaching asteroid. At the mention of an asteroid that might hit the earth in a few days, Benji's eyes bulged.

"What asteroid is that?" Benji asked. "Does anyone else know about it?"

"You don't get out much, do you?" Kitt mused. "Have you looked up in the sky lately?"

"Not in a while. I work here most days and nights. What are you talking about?"

Dov continued. "Evidently you're not aware that a bright, celestial object appeared from behind the moon last night and that the entire city is in an uproar. Our first run of the *Cyclone* predicted the location and time of its appearance to the human eye. The data that Evina sent us today will be used to predict the exact time and location of the object's passage near earth, which will possibly be very close to Babel."

"An asteroid will impact earth? Maybe on top of us?" The computer technician waved his arms in excitement. "That would be amazing! We'll have front row seats!"

"That's not exactly how I'd phrase it, but I guarantee you that it will be 'amazing.' We don't think it'll hit us directly, but it could come very close. That's why it's critical that we complete this final *Cyclone* calculation. Do you think you can have it ready to run soon?

We'll show you the results and then you can leave town too. Kitt will supervise the calculations while Yanis and I input the final numbers."

Dov finally retrieved Evina's note from Benji's hand. After the list of numbers she had answered the question he posed in his note of warning to her: *Yes, I'll come with you. I'll be waiting.*

"She wants to come with us!" he exclaimed aloud. "Evina is waiting for us to get her!"

"That's great news," Yanis said. "Now, if we only had a way to reach her . . ."

Before they could comment further, Benji spoke up. "I'm not leaving town. I want to see this thing up close. It'll be the most spectacular astronomical show the world has ever seen!" Benji's enthusiasm for science sometimes got the better of him. The others rolled their eyes in disbelief.

Kitt took charge as the supervisor of the machine's last run. "Why don't you check the air pressure connections again while we input these numbers, and we'll give this beast its final howl? Can you do that for us?"

Benji nodded and walked behind the mechanical contraption, where hundreds of air tubes snaked from the reservoirs behind the wall to manifolds and regulators affixed to each cabinet. He turned to Kitt and asked in a soft voice, "Do you really think this thing will miss us?"

"It should. I'm not too worried about it at the moment. Neither should you be." Kitt tried to sound more confident than he felt.

Benji returned to confirm that all the tubing connections were tight, and Dov and Yanis completed their input of the new data. Kitt gathered them together for a briefing on safety procedures before the *Cyclone* was powered up. When he finished, they put their earplugs in and Benji opened all the air manifold valves. When pressure gauges showed nominal values for each module, Kitt threw the switch on the first frame program panel and numbers began to cascade through the mechanical calculation chain. Soon, unworldly screams from each calculator blended together into one raucous roar that was felt more than heard. This continued for two hours as the engineers monitored dials on their respective modules and Benji roamed among the tangle of air tubes behind the racks checking for leaks. The symphonic blast decreased slightly in volume to indicate that calculations were nearing completion.

Everyone gathered at the output end of the mechanical banks to see what results Evina's algos produced from her latest data. Dov pored over the cards again with their hundreds of numbers represented by tiny punched holes. He handed the cards to his sister. Evina had told them in her note what to look for. The automaton drawing was obvious and conclusive. It showed that the asteroid—the solid, polished metal ball fifty miles in diameter—would not hit the earth. It would race directly over New Babel at an altitude above one hundred miles and a speed of over 5,000 miles per hour. It would pass directly over them at exactly noon.

After everyone had seen the automaton drawing, they went through the checklist for shutting down the *Cyclone*, bleeding air from the lines and releasing pressure in the vapor engine before shutting it down. The stillness in the lab was unnerving. They gathered to talk over what would happen next. Except for soft hissing from the last air being purged from a distant valve, it was eerily quiet.

Benji was the first to speak. "So it will miss us. That's good news, right?"

"Maybe." Dov looked at his cousin. "Kitt, you have more training in the physical sciences; we're just mechanics. What do you think will happen when that thing flies a hundred miles over the city?"

"We won't be entirely out of danger," Kitt said cautiously. He walked to a nearby blackboard and drew a circle representing the asteroid and a curved line below it for the earth's surface. Motioning to his quick sketch, he noted that it was partially to scale. "This shows the distance from the asteroid to the earth directly beneath it. That distance is only twice the diameter of the object, so one hundred miles is a lot closer than you realize. The fact that it will pass directly over us is not good news but its relatively slow speed should be a plus. The shock wave that originates from the fringe between the atmosphere and outer space will still reach the ground to shatter windows and hurt people on the surface. The overpressure will condense humid air and then just as quickly evaporate it. It will be close enough to the edge of the atmosphere to heat the air too. Depending on how hot the object is when it arrives, it could heat the air enough to produce sustained high winds closer to the surface of the earth. When the object retreats into outer space, it could suck out some of the atmosphere with it, and that could draw debris up from the surface and high into the air. Finally, the heated ball of solid metal might have accumulated a residual electrostatic charge during its flight and this could be released in the form of bolts of lightening. In all, a 'spectacular astronomical show' as Benji has termed it."

"How long would all this last?" Dov asked.

"Hard to say. The asteroid will probably only be in view for a couple of minutes. According to the automaton drawing, it'll 'rise' in the east like the sun over the horizon, pass directly over us at noon, and 'set' behind the opposite horizon. The atmospheric effects could last for hours or even days afterward. There's no saying what would happen if it tears away a large part of the atmosphere. That could set off a global climate shift that lasts for centuries."

Yanis spoke up. "I hate to bring up another twist, because I think I know what the answer is. What about the tower? What about people on the roof when this happens?"

The awkward silence was palpable. Finally Kitt gave his estimation. "That's the last place in the world anyone should be. Jengo could explain this better, but I'd be surprised if the tower was still standing after all that. Even if the building survives structurally, anything untethered—loose construction materials, temple statues, people on the rooftop—would be swept away."

"Then maybe we should find someplace deep underground to hide." Benji concluded with a tremor in his voice. "The way you describe it, I'm not so sure I want a front row seat now. There's nothing we can do."

"We still have two days before it gets here. I'm going to rescue Evina as soon as possible and then we'll find someplace to hide. I'm not going to leave her on top of that tower." The conviction in Dov's voice had a powerful effect on the others.

"I'm with you, Brother," Yanis added.

"Me too," said Kitt as he stood closer to Yanis.

"How about you?" Dov asked Benji.

Benji hesitated. "I'll stick with you guys for now," he replied. "Seems like no matter where I go in the next few days, I'll be part of the fireworks."

"Good!" Dov smiled encouragingly. "Then let's go to the tower control room and prepare for a rescue."

They left the School of Japheth and the *Cyclone* computer for the last time.

CHAPTER 28

New Babel, One World Tower—Capsule Control Room

The four, accompanied by Shadow, arrived at the control room where Ash had been waiting all night to hear from his cousins. Jengo came by during the night with news about the asteroid's appearance from behind the moon but left soon thereafter. The other operators, who at first had appeared indifferent, now spoke of nothing else and couldn't concentrate on their work. Ash tired of their constant moaning about facing certain death, but nothing he said about turning to the Lord seemed to have any effect on them.

When they were certain that none of the other ascender operators could hear them, Dov, Yanis, their two cousins, and Benji gathered in a circle to plan Evina's rescue one more time. Shadow found a comfortable spot under the console desk.

"We must get her off the tower *today*." Dov tried to energize the discussion in his search for a plan. "There's so much we don't know. How can we come up with a plan if we don't know where she is and how many are guarding her?"

"Why not break the problem into manageable parts?" Yanis suggested to her brother. "Obviously, we'll need to go up to the rooftop in the Luminary ascender, hold it there while somebody— you, maybe others—finds Evina and checks out the surroundings. Then you can come back down and we'll plan the next step with more information."

"That's a start, I suppose, but it assumes nobody will oppose us. I doubt we'll be able innocently walk to where they're keeping her and make inquiries of the guards. Are there any other ideas?"

Kitt jumped into the discussion. "It's a long shot, but your friend up there might be able to help us. What's his name, Kaman? Didn't you ask him to find out where they're keeping Evina?"

"And what about that hulking bodyguard of hers? Where's he in all this? Surely he'd help if he knew what you had in mind." Ash added.

"We haven't seen Saris for the past couple days. He's probably in the tower somewhere by now, but who knows where," Yanis said.

"I think I have an idea," Dov announced.

"I'm all ears," his sister remarked.

"How about Yanis, Kitt, and I go up together in the Luminary ascender and survey the area while Ash stays here at the controls? We might get a break and leave with Evina!" His idea was no more or less faulty than any other they had come up. If everything worked out, they'd be down from the tower and headed out of the city in a few hours.

"What about Father, and Uncle Jengo and Uncle Javak?" Yanis asked. "We can't leave the city without them."

"Right," Dov conceded. "If we go up into the tower now and bring Evina back, there'll be plenty of time to find them, gather our families, and leave the city together." He knew that his exit strategy could unravel at any moment.

"Look, I'll be the first to admit that this scheme has holes in it. If we wait until tomorrow that means we'll have less than twenty-four hours to rescue her and leave the city. By tomorrow the tower will be jammed with Luminaries, servants, and temple guards in anticipation of the big ceremony. Tomorrow we may be tied up taking Luminaries up in the ascender. I think it's worth the risk to rescue Evina now even though the plan is full of unknowns. We can always abort the mission and come back to replan if things don't look favorable." Dov took a deep breath. "Who wants to come with me now?"

Yanis raised her hand first. "I'll go. I love Evina like a sister. We can't leave her in the tower."

"I want to go on record as saying that your plan is totally crazy," Kitt emphatically stated. "I don't give it more than a ten percent chance of success, but we need to try. Besides, if Yanis is going then I want to go too."

Yanis gave him a beaming smile. "Then it's the three of us, and Ash can be our controller."

"What about me?" Benji asked. "Can I come too?"

Dov shook his head. "More than three of us would draw too much attention. Besides, we'll be wearing official ascender operator uniforms to give us a thin excuse for being up there. I have something that you could do, but it will involve a lot of work."

"As long as I can be of some use," Benji replied.

Dov explained Benji's key part. "Oh, and I almost forgot. Take Shadow with you too."

"I don't like dogs very much," Benji objected weakly.

Shadow responded to his name with a whine and wagged his tail like a puppy. Benji left his friends, opened the door for his new canine partner, and exited toward the street.

After a chuckle at the image of Benji following Shadow as they went off to their assignment, Dov motioned to his sister and cousins. "We'll change into Luminary ascender operator uniforms here and go to the roof immediately. There's no telling what we'll find there, but pray that we can be back here with Evina in an hour or so." Dov tried to sound confident, but he knew in his heart that he was placing his sister, his cousins, and himself in more danger than they had ever faced in their lives.

CHAPTER 29

New Babel, One World Tower—Freight Ascender Rooftop Maintenance Room #2

Before dawn

Targa was a hardened, muscular mercenary who fit well into the rough, dirty clothes of a construction laborer. His eyes, like those of the others on Team Talon, were without feeling from a lifetime of inflicting pain and destruction. The leader of Magus' principal pack of assassins counted their number to be sure everyone was present before he began his final mission briefing. Mercenaries anxious for action were a difficult group to control, and this bunch was no different. There was no telling how closely they would follow his orders.

"Listen up! I'll go over this one last time. The reconnaissance team surveyed the area yesterday, so the layout of the roof and temple rooms you have is accurate. There may be a few details missing, but what you have should be enough to find your positions tomorrow morning. When the signal is given, each of you must execute his part of the plan *exactly*. Is that understood?" Targa finished his rehearsal and received muffled grunts of agreement.

"When we're finished with our mission, Teams Fang and Claw will take freight ascenders down to the plaza. Team Talon, under my command, will escort Magus to the Luminary ascender. He'll descend to the plaza at the base of the One World Tower, where he'll proclaim himself king of New Babel and Arvid will be his high priest."

Omitted in his speech was the deadly havoc that would be unleashed in the atmosphere above them by the asteroid. Magus told him that pandemonium on the roof would be the perfect background for what his team needed to do. Targa was counting on his three teams to be professionals and to not be distracted by the turmoil above and around them.

Also unspoken was the possibility—the probability—that they would not survive their mission and return to the ground safely. Then again, they *might* make it out alive. They were accustomed to such high risks. Targa inspected his teams to ensure that their clothing matched their cover as laborers. They carried boxes or bags of "supplies" in which they hid their other uniforms and weapons. Slow transfers in small anonymous groups via the freight transfer portals to the 120th level would take all night. Targa boarded a freight ascender with the last of his men.

New Babel, One World Tower—Capsule Control Room

While Targa briefed his band of thugs in the freight storage area, Dov went over plans to rescue Evina. He, Yanis, and Kitt wore crisp blue uniforms in hopes that their attire would deter anyone from questioning them too closely. They'd take their chances bluffing past the guards.

"Ash, I'll drop a message for you down the ascender shaft with an update. If we need help we'll let you know. Is there anything else we need to do before we head up?" Dov's sister and his two cousins shook their heads.

"I think that's it," said Kitt. "We might as well find out what we're up against. Remember, if we encounter obstacles we can always come back down and rethink our plan."

Dov made sure he had message pouches in his pocket, along with paper and a pencil.

They stepped into the waiting Luminary capsule and waved to Ash at the console. "See you in a little while," Yanis shouted above the control room noise as the door closed.

For several minutes they rode in silence, wrapped in their own thoughts until Kitt spoke up. "What should we do if we become separated? Is there someplace we should gather? I'm concerned that

Yanis and I have never been on the rooftop before and don't know what to expect. You're the only one who's been there, Dov."

"That's a good point. If we become separated we should meet back at the Luminary ascender entrance. A waiting, uniformed ascender operator would fit in. The alternate meeting place would be the busier freight ascender portal area. It's in that far end of the roof on the opposite side of the ziggurat." Dov pointed diagonally across the building. "There are plenty of places in the storage area to wait. Our uniforms don't match those of the freight ascender operators, but that shouldn't be a problem. If we need to hijack an ascender, they operate pretty much the same way as a passenger ascender. I hope we won't need to do that."

The remainder of the ride was quiet and uneventful. Dov brought the capsule to a stop at the 120th level and slowly opened the door. It would be dawn within a few hours. Welding torches flickered in the distance. He set the ascender lock so the door could not be closed or the capsule used until they returned. He thought of sending a message pouch down to tell Ash that they had arrived, but realized that he would already know that from the console display. He needed to think more clearly now that they'd be exposing themselves to life-threatening dangers for the next hour. Where was Kaman? Where was Evina? How would they get past the guards?

CHAPTER 30

New Babel, Chief Magician's Residence

Dawn

Chief Magician Magus had finished an early breakfast and was reclined on a couch in his luxurious quarters, pondering the events of the next two days, when a servant announced the arrival of Enos, one of his informants from the tower. The man was one of a dozen paid to keep their eyes and ears open; he reported from time to time on who came and went in the ascenders, and what Jengo and other tower engineers did. The information was mostly redundant and rarely useful, but he paid his informants pennies for the occasional valuable piece of information.

"Send him in," the magician barked. He didn't recognize the individual in the filthy clothes of a maintenance technician. The man stood speechless before the powerful magician.

"What is it? Speak up, man!" Magus yelled at the shaking informant. Magus couldn't tolerate men who cowered speechless in his presence. Of course, it never occurred to him that his threatening treatment paralyzed them with such fear that they had trouble speaking.

"Sir . . . I heard something in the control room last night . . . I thought you might want to know about it." Enos halted to wait for a reaction.

"Yes! Yes! Out with it!" Magus screamed. He leapt from his couch in frustration.

"Sir . . . it was the children of Jengo and their friends." He gulped and continued. "I overheard them last night speaking about rescuing 'Evina' from the tower. I do not know who this 'Evina' is, but three of them drove the Luminary ascender up shortly thereafter. I could see the level indicator, and they went to the rooftop. When I departed the tower a few minutes ago the ascender was parked on the 120th level."

Magus sat back on the couch to think. It was unlikely that the three youths could successfully rescue Zidon's daughter, since she was being heavily guarded. When his assassins replaced the palace guards at her prison door in the morning, they would be deterred even further from removing her from the tower. However, they posed a possible threat to his intricately timed events. If they tried something and alerted temple authorities, he would lose the element of surprise.

Enos stood before him, expecting another violent tirade. Instead, he witnessed the magician's composure settle. Magus went to his desk and wrote a lengthy message. He sealed it in an envelope and returned to the waiting technician.

"You must guard this message with your life and follow my instructions precisely." Magus appeared calm, but his tone was still chilling. He wanted no thought of betrayal to enter this informant's mind. "You will take a freight ascender to the 120th level. When you arrive there you will go to Freight Ascender Maintenance Room #2. Do you know where that is?"

"Of course, sir. I have been in it many times. It is where we keep tools and spare parts for the ascenders. Sometimes operators use it for a break room. Why . . . ?"

"Don't question my orders!" Magus shouted. He continued with his instructions. "You will slide this envelope under the door to that room and then return to your duties. You will say nothing about this to anyone. Do you understand?"

"Sir . . . yes, sir." The magician's orders made no sense.

"Good. Now go!" Magus waved him away and returned to his desk.

"Sir . . ."

"What is it? Do what I told you!" The magician turned and glared at the man who had grown more emboldened than when he'd first arrived.

"Sir. If I may . . . you have paid me in the past for my services."

Magus fumbled in a drawer of his desk and retrieved a coin. He threw it in the direction of his informant. "Now get out of here!" he screamed.

Enos quickly picked the coin from the floor and scurried out the door. The cool, heavy metal felt good in his hand. He broke into a wide grin when he realized that it was gold and not copper. Magus had thrown him a coin worth three month's pay, and he probably didn't even realize it. The foul-tempered wizard was a strange one.

It took several hours for Enos to take different freight ascenders in staggered stages to rooftop. When he arrived, he asked the ascender operator to wait for him. He would be back in less than five minutes. The technician ran to Freight Ascender Maintenance Room #2 and slipped the envelope under the door. There was no light on inside the room, but he stood silently and watched the corner of the envelope from a distance. The paper suddenly disappeared. He gasped. *Someone was inside!*

Needing no further prompting, Enos raced for the freight ascender. His heart pounded through each of the stages of his descent. When he reached the ground floor he decided to go home instead of returning to work. He'd give his wife the gold coin and explain what happened. She'd understand why he was so terrified.

New Babel, One World Tower—Freight Ascender Rooftop Maintenance Room #2

Targa took the envelope from the man by the door and scolded him in a guttural whisper. "You fool! You should have left it there. What if someone saw it disappear? We may be compromised." It was a good thing nobody could see his face twisted in fury in the dark.

Team Talon had been in the dark room for hours. They could see a dim hint of daylight through the space under the door. He would wait until it was brighter outside before lighting a lamp in the room. Then, he would read the note.

In the darkness, one of the men made a suggestion: "We could stuff some rags under the door and then light the lamp. Nobody would see the light from outside."

Targa cringed at not having thought of that himself. He ordered it done and then opened the envelope to read it in the light of a single flame. It was from Magus, and it instructed him to change his mission slightly. Team Talon was ordered to locate three intruders and eliminate them before their intentions could be exposed. Magus gave him a description of the three: two young men and one woman, probably dressed in the blue uniforms of Luminary ascender operators. It should not be difficult for Team Talon to find three people and silence them permanently. He explained this side mission to the others, who then donned their workmen clothing and dispersed to begin their search.

CHAPTER 31

New Babel, One World Tower—Rooftop Ziggurat Promenade

Dov asked a nearby worker where Kaman was and quickly found him in a workshop grinding metal railings. The worker was pleased to see his friend again, but he became nervous when he saw two others with him. More than one visitor would attract unwanted attention. The three waited for Kaman to finish work on the railing before another workman took it to be painted. After introductions, they went outside where there was less noise. Dov was concerned that they not be overheard, so Kaman showed them an alcove where they had more privacy.

"We need to find Evina and take her away from the tower immediately. Her life is in danger, Kaman. Can you help us?" Dov tried to hide the desperation in his voice.

"Sure. I know exactly where they're holding her, but you can't take her out. It's a heavily guarded area. In fact, when I went by there earlier, they had replaced the temple guards with four burly guys that look like Nimrod's special forces. You're not going to get past them." Kaman saw disappointment on the faces of the three rescuers.

"There's no other way of getting in there? Can we rope down from the roof or something? Doesn't the ziggurat have secret tunnels and stuff? Maybe we could take her out some other way?"

"It's not possible. Do you think you can pretend to be a window washer and just slide down a rope to her balcony? It's over 1,000 feet to the street below." Kaman wanted to discourage his friend from doing something foolish that would kill him in the attempt, no matter how much he wanted to rescue Evina from danger.

"So there are no secret tunnels?" Yanis asked.

"I didn't say that. Technically, tunnels are dug under the earth, while corridors are inside manmade structures. There *are* corridors inside the black ziggurat. I've worked in them, but I've been sworn to secrecy about their locations. You said that your girlfriend's life is in danger?"

"She's not my girlfriend," Dov bristled.

"Oh, stop being so silly," his sister chided. "We all know how you feel about her. It's in your puppy eyes every time you mention her name. Now, let's focus on finding a way to reach her and get out of here."

Yanis turned to Kaman to explain in stark terms why the rescue was so urgent. "Zidon will sacrifice Evina on the ziggurat's apex altar tomorrow at noon when the asteroid passes directly overhead. If you have information that can stop her from being murdered, I think that's enough justification to violate your oath about the location of secret corridors. A human life is at stake here!"

Kaman shuddered at the idea of Evina being sacrificed. He was still reluctant to go against what he had promised. "I could lose my job if anyone found out that I revealed the secret corridor network."

"If it makes any difference to you, there probably won't be any jobs on the tower after tomorrow." Dov noted the shock on Kaman's face when he said this. "When the asteroid passes directly overhead it'll sweep everything off the roof of the tower. The high winds may even bring the tower down. I guess then it wouldn't matter if you told us about the corridors or not, would it?" He was growing irritated with Kaman's hesitation to cooperate with their rescue.

This news had its desired effect on Kaman, who swallowed hard and made his decision. "I'll guide you through the corridor network to rescue Evina. Then you have to leave and never use the corridors again."

Yanis looked at the others and spoke for them. "Fair enough. All we want to do is take Evina off the tower. You should leave before tomorrow too. It won't be safe up here."

"Unfortunately, I have no choice. We'll be working on finishing the altar area right up to the time of the ceremony. I have to stay here."

"That's your choice," Dov conceded. "Now, can we get going? I've left the ascender parked, and the longer we leave it unattended and hang around here in the open, the more suspicious people will become. Wait, I just remembered: I need to drop a quick message for Ash. He's expecting to hear from us. How long do you think this'll take?"

"Not long," Kaman replied. "An entrance door to the corridor network is right behind you."

His friends spun around and looked at the blank stone wall. It was impossible to see how the stones could move to open an entrance into the ziggurat. Kitt ran his hand over the solid stones and shook his head.

Kaman smiled. "I'm sure there's another concealed entrance in the back of the room where she's being held. We'll bring her back here through the passageways and you can make a run for the ascender. Should take us ten minutes—fifteen tops."

"I'll send Ash this note in case it takes us longer." Dov wrote a short message stating that they found Kaman, knew where Evina was, and would bring her down within the hour. He ran from their alcove and was relieved to find the ascender just as he had left it. He dropped the leather pouch down the messenger tube. When Ash read his message he would make final preparations to whisk them away to Pele's workshop and then to the boathouse. They should be far from Babel by the time the asteroid wreaked havoc on the One World Tower and the people of the city.

When Dov returned, Kaman put his hand on the corner of one irregular stone at eye level and pressed it, at the same time he pushed on a smaller stone near the floor with the toe of his boot. The alternating pattern of stones shifted slightly and part of the wall swung silently inward on well-oiled hinges to reveal a black hole leading into the interior of the temple. "Built by Accadian stone masons. Best there are," he pronounced proudly.

When they had all slipped into the dark interior, and filtered sunlight illuminated the first few feet, Kaman showed them how to close the door and how to open it again from the inside. When he closed the door they were plunged into total blackness. Kaman remembered that a pitch torch was located ten feet inside the corridor and, using a sparker next to the torch holder, he lit it. There was just enough light to see the floor, ceiling, and walls immediately around them. Sharp shadows quickly blended into darkness. They followed Kaman closely one behind the other. After a series of left and right turns in the unfamiliar maze, his followers soon became disoriented and were forced to trust that he knew where he was going. They passed inky corridors that branched out at right angles from their path. Mysterious empty chambers were briefly illuminated as they passed by. Further in, they saw heavy wooden doors engraved with cryptic symbols. The warren of corridors seemed endless, but Kaman walked as steadily forward as if he were in daylight. Within a few more minutes they turned a corner and Kaman came to an abrupt halt.

"The hidden entrance to her room should be down this corridor," he observed. He lifted the torch to closely examine a brick and mortar wall blocking the way before them. He pushed at various places, but nothing moved. The solid obstruction blocked their path. "This wall was built recently—within the past few days. I'm certain that this corridor continues to her room. Accadian stone masons didn't do this work. Someone put this wall up in a hurry. I don't understand it."

"Maybe you made a wrong turn someplace and this isn't the right corridor. Are you sure this is where it's supposed to be?" Dov was skeptical that Kaman could have navigated the labyrinth of corridors so precisely.

"I'm absolutely certain of it. I worked in these corridors for months and have a map of them in my head. I know that this is the right place, but why has it been bricked up?"

Kitt voiced his practical deduction: "I think the reason is obvious. Whoever ordered Evina held prisoner knew about the inner corridors and intentionally sealed off this way to enter or leave her room. They wanted her to remain a prisoner."

"Can we break through the brick wall?" Yanis asked Kaman.

"If I had the right tools I'd have us through in ten minutes." Kaman turned to Dov. "What do you want to do?"

"We're not giving up. We'll go back to the entrance, where we'll wait for you to get tools to break through the brick wall." Once Yanis and Kitt had given their agreement, they turned back and Kaman retraced their steps.

While they walked, Kaman explained the systematic network of corridors. "It isn't that difficult to move around in the dark once you understand that each level is a square grid of passageways at right angles to each other; the number of corridors in the grid becomes smaller as you move up in levels and the ziggurat narrows. It was Jengo's design—your uncle, right?—to make each level an identical series of concentric corridors in a square pattern, except for the absence of the outer corridors where the ziggurat steps up. The recessed chambers you saw are for storage of temple materials. Chambers with doors are for temple accessories such as gold vessels and garments. I don't know what the inscriptions on the doors mean."

"How do you move up or down between levels?" Kitt asked. "There must be stairways."

"There are two stairways on each level diagonally opposite each other. Because the ziggurat is a stepped structure, the stairway for an upper level only goes down one level and obviously not up to a level above. If you want to go up, you have to go in one corridor to the opposite diagonal and find an up stairway again. Unfortunately, there is no single stairway that leads directly from the bottom to the top. Does that give you a picture of the design?"

"I think I can visualize it now. Two more questions: How do we find any other hidden doors to the outside or to occupied rooms that are along the outer perimeter corridor? Have you verified that all five levels are exactly as you described?"

"Good questions," said Kaman. "You're right about the outer corridor. There's nothing that I know of to indicate that a branch from the outer corridor is an exit to the outside or into a room. I remembered the corridor to Evina's room because I worked on that. You can activate any of them by pushing on the corner of an upper block and a small lower block at the same time, like I showed you."

Kaman turned to answer Kitt's final question at the exit door to the alcove. "I haven't been on all the levels. The top two levels were built by another crew of stone masons. I saw a drawing once and don't recall it showing anything different from the other levels. Sorry, but that's all I remember."

Before he opened the door, Yanis expressed her discomfort with the gloomy, confined passageway. "Can we wait outside while you get tools? This dark, confined place gives me the creeps."

"I suppose," Kaman said reluctantly. "The longer you wait outside though, the greater your chances of being questioned. There are stepped-up patrols in advance of the ceremony tomorrow. Your uniforms might make you conspicuous this far away from the ascender entrance. Just wait in the alcove and don't walk around. I'll be back with tools as soon as I can."

Kaman opened the stone door a crack and peered around before opening it all the way to let his friends out. He left them in the alcove, closed the door, and hurried to find the tools he needed. The three tried to look inconspicuous.

CHAPTER 32

New Babel, One World Tower—Rooftop Ziggurat Promenade

Within minutes, two temple guards passed the shallow indentation in the ziggurat's wall and eyed the three uniformed operators before continuing on. "Maybe it wasn't so bad in the dark corridor after all," Yanis lamented. "We might as well stand in plain sight holding a sign that says 'Arrest us!' What do we tell them if they come back?"

"Kaman won't be long," Kitt reassured her.

But Yanis' fear was soon confirmed when the two guards returned a minute later and blocked their exit. "What are you doing here?" the first guard demanded. "You're Luminary ascender operators. Why aren't you with your ascender?"

"We're waiting for a friend of ours to meet us here." Dov said with as much confidence as he could muster. "I'm a senior Luminary ascender operator and these two are my associates. We're not doing anything wrong, are we?"

"The tower is on alert in preparation for the ceremony tomorrow. No unauthorized personnel are supposed to be on the rooftop. Who are you waiting for?"

"We'd rather not say," Kitt spoke up. "I think we should leave now."

The guard moved closer and put his hand firmly on Kitt's chest.

"Show me an identity card or paper to prove that you're Luminary ascender operators. Maybe you're imposters dressed in those uniforms. Otherwise, you'll have to come with us to the station and answer some questions so we can sort this out." The two guards stepped closer and the three moved back against the wall. Kitt thought of opening the secret entrance and slipping into the corridors, but dismissed the idea as impossible in the tight confines of the alcove. All three of them wouldn't be able to escape fast enough. The armed guards would probably overcome him before he could open the door.

"We have no papers," said Yanis plaintively. "What are you going to do with us?"

The guards motioned them out as a group and escorted them around the corner toward the back of the temple. At the same time, Kaman returned with his tools and saw them being led away. He continued walking past pretending to ignore them and then turned to follow at a discreet distance. He caught Dov's pleading look when their eyes met, but his uniformed friend was pushed by a guard to move forward. Within a minute they were in a guard station, where two other armed men herded them through the single station entrance into a second room in the back. It contained tables, chairs, a food preparation area, and an empty rack for weapons storage. Kitt noticed that the rack was attached to the back wall, exactly where he might find a secret entrance into the inner corridors.

"The chief of security will question you further. You will remain here until we verify your identities as Luminary ascender operators and he is satisfied with your story." The guard slammed the solid door and they heard a key turn in the lock.

"Great!" exclaimed Dov. He slumped into a chair and cradled his face in his hands. Kitt and Yanis moved to inspect the back wall. The weapons rack was bolted to the wall; they explored around the rack's edges for some evidence of secret stones that would open into the inner corridors. Finding none, they joined Dov and looked around the room for another way out.

"If there are stones to trigger a secret door mechanism, they're covered by that weapons rack. We're stuck in here." Kitt sat in a chair next to Dov.

"Now what?" Yanis asked. "I don't relish the idea of being 'interrogated' by the chief of temple security. What will we tell him?"

"We'll tell him the truth. We'll say that we came up here to see Evina. I don't think we're obligated to tell him every detail of Dov's plan, shattered though it seems to be now," Kitt observed. "We're her friends and we want to make sure she's all right. Beyond that, we should keep quiet."

Dov put a damper on that suggestion. "I told them we were waiting for someone. If we give them Kaman's name then he'll get dragged into this mess too. It's all my fault that this has happened."

"Even if the chief believes us," Dov added, "it could take his men hours to check our story. We'll lose most of the day and have to come up with another approach. I was in a rush to rescue Evina with a half-baked arrangement and now someone will have to rescue us."

"No, it was my fault." Yanis bemoaned. "I wanted to wait for Kaman outside in the fresh air. If only we'd waited inside the corridor this wouldn't have happened."

"Don't feel bad, Yanis. I didn't want to wait in the dark either," Kitt said. The three dejected rescuers sat in silence thinking about how everything they tried to do had fallen apart.

They'd heard occasional muffled voices from the office outside the door, but had not seen anyone since being locked in. Then, a soft scraping sound alerted them that someone was coming and they looked anxiously at the door. Then they realized that the sound came from behind them.

The weapons rack shook and moved an inch; the base of the heavy wooden rack was catching on the uneven stone floor. The three lifted the rack slightly so it could slide unhindered on the floor. It swung open about a foot and Kaman's smiling face peered out at them from the darkness.

"Quick," he urged. "Get in here so I can close the door."

The weapons rack dragged heavily on the floor with a grinding sound when they opened it wider. Once inside, they pulled the door closed as hard as they could and hoped that the sound would not alert the guards. The door finally secured with a muffled click. They all breathed deep sighs of relief in the blackness.

"How did you find us so quickly?" Yanis asked.

"I saw the guards take you into custody and followed you. Then I entered back through the alcove. Opening the door was difficult because that rack was holding the door back. I had to take a chance that you were alone in the room. If a guard had been left in the room with you I don't know what would have happened. At least you're safe in here for now."

They spoke in total darkness as Yanis slowly became claustrophobic again. They heard shouting through the stone door. Their absence had been discovered.

"Do the guards know about the hidden corridors?" Kitt asked. "If they do, they could open that doorway and be on us in minutes."

"I'm sure only the chief of temple security knows; the regular guards are always changing and don't need to know. As soon as they tell their chief that you disappeared from the locked room, he'll know to look for you in here. We should move away from this entrance and find someplace to hide." He walked away in the darkness until Yanis pleaded softly in the echoing hallway. "Could you light a torch or something? I'm not good in dark confines like this. I feel another panic attack coming on."

"I'm right here," said Kitt as he reached out for her and held her hand. "Kaman, can you find a torch?"

"Yes. Around the next corner. Follow the sound of my voice and feel along the wall." Yanis felt better with Kitt close to her. The panic attack diminished for the moment. When Kaman lit the torch she noticed that Kitt continued to hold her hand tightly. She definitely felt better now.

"I'll take you up two levels—from this fifth, or bottom level, to the third level of the ziggurat—and find a chamber where you can hide. It's after noon now and I need to figure out a way to get you off the tower tonight without being recaptured. First, let's get you safely hidden."

Dov stopped their advance. "What about Evina? We need to get her before we leave." He was insistent. "Can't you go back and break through that brick wall?"

"I've been away from my work for too long already. Let me get you settled and then return to work for a little while. I'll have some time tonight and then I'll break through the wall and bring her to you. Even if I can do that, it's still very dangerous. Again, if there's a guard with her inside the room we'll be captured trying to rescue her. At a minimum, the alarm will be sounded and they'll search for us in here until they find us." Kaman was frustrated that he had become entangled in a rescue whose practical details were crumbling.

He led the trio along cold, damp corridors and up stairways until they reached an inner corridor deep inside the ziggurat. They found a small chamber with piled boxes at its center. Kaman mentally oriented himself to ensure that he knew which chamber they were in before he departed. He gave Kitt an unlit torch and a sparker. "I suggest that you wait in the dark behind these crates and not waste torch fuel. It will be difficult," he said, thinking of Yanis, "but if anyone uses the corridor while you're here you shouldn't be discovered unless they enter this room with torches and look behind the boxes. Work on the passageways is completed, and all the masons are busy finishing the temple's outside trim and details for the ceremony tomorrow, so it's unlikely anyone will come into this chamber for supplies. Judging from the amount of dust on the boxes, they've been untouched since the corridors were finished. Stay here, and hopefully I'll return with Evina in four or five hours. If I can't rescue her, then at least I'll try to get you off the tower before dawn." He waved and walked back into the pitch-black corridor.

New Babel, One World Tower—Rooftop Ziggurat, Inner Level 3

Yanis sat between Dov and Kitt, and tried to calm herself. She still gripped Kitt's hand and didn't want to let go. Eventually Dov became restless. He explored the crates in the chamber and found that they contained small iron chisels and wedges in addition to bags of dry mortar. He was getting hungry and that always made him nervous. He walked out of the chamber into the pitch-black corridor, guiding his hands along the walls. The hallway was narrow so he could stretch out his arms to touch each wall and easily navigate.

"Where are you going?" Yanis asked her brother plaintively. "Don't leave!"

"I'm walking a short distance down the corridor in either direction to check out other chambers. I can't get lost now that I know the layout of the grid. I'll be back in a few minutes."

"I wish he wouldn't go off like that," Yanis said softly. She held Kitt's hand tighter.

Dov was gone only a few minutes when Yanis and Kitt heard voices echoing in the distance. Male voices grew more distinct as they came closer. "This is a waste of time," one of them exclaimed in a voice that reverberated in the confined space of the corridor. "We've been at this for hours and haven't seen anyone. Let's go back."

"The stairs are around the next corner," said the other male. "We can leave when we've searched this level. The others should have finished combing the upper levels by now."

The two searchers stopped outside the chamber where Yanis and Kitt were sheltered from view behind stacked boxes. If they searched this room, Yanis and Kitt would be discovered! The searchers made no effort to lower their voices, which bounced off the walls and down the corridor.

"So Magus is worried that three ascender operators will spoil his plans. Ha! The chief magician of Babel is scared of his own servants!" The two laughed heartily. "I'll be glad when this mission's over tomorrow and we can get out of here. I don't mind taking that weasel's blood money, but I hate doing the dirty work so he reaps the benefits."

"I'm sick of these corridors," said the other. "Let's get out of here."

The light from their torch and the sound of their voices gradually disappeared. Kitt and Yanis exhaled.

"What if they find Dov?" Yanis whispered.

"I'll run to help if we hear a commotion from that direction."

Footsteps in the corridor caused them to hold their breaths again. The sound stopped outside their chamber. "It's me. They're gone."

Yanis walked toward Dov's voice. When she reached her brother in the dark she hugged him tightly, then stepped back and punched him in the chest. "Don't you *ever* leave me like that again!" she said through clenched teeth. She was glad that Dov couldn't see her tears.

Dov smiled in the dark. "I left you with Kitt. He protected you."

She pressed her hand on her brother's chest and suppressed a sob. "That's not the same. You're my brother—we're twins! Don't walk off and do stupid things like that!" She hugged him tightly. It was a moment that Dov would never forget.

He had heard the two searchers in enough time to hide in the shadows of an empty chamber. Apparently they were too tired to bother searching more thoroughly. He heard what they said about Magus and more.

"Kitt, what do you say we explore the layout of the corridors above us?" Dov was getting restless again. "I have the start of a plan in my mind. If the top level looks like I imagine, then we might be able to rescue Evina tomorrow if Kaman can't bring her out tonight."

"We need a new plan, that's for sure. You'll think of something," his sister encouraged.

"Whatever it is, we need to stay together. I'm not leaving Yanis alone." Kitt insisted.

"I agree. Do you think you could find this chamber again in the dark?"

"Probably. I have a picture of the overall grid in my head. We could leave something behind in the corridor so we can tell this chamber from the others in the dark."

"Let's do that," Dov agreed. Before they departed, Kitt propped a small iron chisel against the wall near the floor. He would search for it when they returned to the general vicinity of the chamber. With Kitt in the lead, the three left the protection of their hiding place to locate the nearest stairwell up to the next level. Still in total darkness, they felt along the wall of the corridor toward unseen stairs that would take them higher.

Kitt discovered the stairway exactly where Kaman said it would be. Dov made an observation that encouraged his thinking forward: "Do you feel that breeze? There's a flow of air up. That means that there must be an opening to the outside. I want to skip exploration of this level and go straight to the top."

When the others agreed, Dov took the lead and they continued their slow advance in the dark. The ziggurat floor footprint became smaller as they neared the top. Dov wondered if the top level would have one corridor around its perimeter and only a few inner rooms. They came across the next stairwell in its expected location in the three-dimensional grid. The breeze up the stairs had become stronger. No sooner had they reached the top than they noticed dim illumination ahead. The far ends of both corridors, to their left and right, were lit with outside light. They waited and listened before carefully walking down the corridor to their left. They proceeded cautiously in a single corridor that circled the highest level of the ziggurat. Eventually, they came across stone steps leading to a large, lattice-like cast iron grating in the ceiling. Distant voices from above prompted them back into the shadows where they continued walking around the outer corridor. In what they suspected was the middle of one side of the ziggurat, they found a passageway at right angles leading to the exact center of the structure. This was what Dov hoped to find.

Dov spoke quietly. "I was hoping we'd find stairs and an opening at the center of this level leading to the raised altar. It would make sense for there to be a way up from inside to do the mumbo jumbo rituals that the priests and sorcerers do. I'm guessing that these stairs will lead up to the altar." They stood in the middle of a large circular room with a stack of firewood.

There was another stairway, exactly as Dov had speculated. The metal grating at the top of the stairs let in the dwindling evening sun and distant voices. From the sharp angle of the sunlight they concluded that it was almost sunset. The three hid under the stairs and listened. The voices were not nearby, but they could tell from the tone of their conversation and the hammering that the sounds came from workmen finishing stonework in advance of the ceremony tomorrow. When the hammering ceased and the voices disappeared into the distance, Dov stood and crept up the stairs. Yanis and Kitt waited in the twilight.

At the top of the stairs, Dov observed that the grating was hinged on one side and that there was no lock or clasp securing it. He pushed on the grate with all his strength, and it barely moved. He motioned for Kitt to help him. The two moved it silently on its hinges until it rested against the wall above them. Dov stuck his head above the opening for a quick glimpse around. If he was noticed by anyone, he'd close the grate and they'd run for the stairway back down to hide, but nobody was in view. He rose until he was standing on a step where he was visible from his chest up. Workmen were far in the distance. Nobody took notice of him. He was at the back of the ziggurat's main altar—acolytes and religious functionaries would probably ascend from here to join in the religious ceremonies around the altar. When Dov noticed two temple guards walking up the wide stairway on the outside of the edifice, he dropped down behind the altar, then he and Kitt slowly lowered the heavy grating without dropping it. When they rejoined Yanis under the stairs, they had to catch their breath from handling the heavy grating.

"Where does that lead? Did you see anyone?" she asked.

"It opens behind the altar like I thought. There are some workmen around and one patrol."

"Imagine how easy it would be to wait until dark, casually walk down the ziggurat steps to the ascender entrance, and take the ascender down to the city. We could be home within an hour," Yanis speculated. Dov shook his head. "Go home and leave Evina here to die? Never. You and Kitt can leave, but I'm staying here to find a way to rescue her. I have the glimmer of an idea that involves waiting until tomorrow morning, and the chance of success is slim, but it's the best I can come up with if Kaman doesn't come through." Dov clenched his jaw in determination.

"Sorry. I was just trying to lighten things up. I didn't mean that I'd leave Evina here to die."

"I know, Sis."

Kitt studied Dov's profile in the gloom. "You said the chance is slim, but that means there is *some* chance, right?"

"*Some* chance, yes." Kitt and Yanis listened while Dov explained, in measured tones, what he had in mind. As the three sat under the stone stairs in the last light of what could be their final evening on earth, Dov unfolded a rescue that was bold and perilous. He didn't gloss over the risks: they could be captured or killed by guards; his speculation about the high priest's ritual before passage of the asteroid at high noon may be incorrect; they might be killed in the tower by the asteroid's shock wave; they may not be able to flee from the tower before it collapsed—the uncertainties were innumerable. After he had finished explaining all the things that could go wrong, the three stared at the wall before them in silence.

Yanis spoke first. "I'm sorry for being so selfish. Evina is like a sister to me. I love her dearly and should be willing to do anything to see her saved from her father's murderous designs. I'll stay and help you all I can. Will you stay with us too, Kitt?"

"Of course. I don't want to leave your side, Yanis. Dov, what do we do between now and tomorrow morning?"

During the last of the daylight that filtered down through the overhead gratings, the three explored all the rooms on the top level under and around the altar. They found other steps leading to the outside and several storerooms containing colorful clothing and accessories for the elaborate pagan rituals. They returned to examine the large circular room directly under the altar more closely. Above their heads, between them and the darkening sky, was a circular metal grating almost ten feet in diameter, which was the main altar. Under it was a large pile of wood, stacked in a circle six feet high, that was saturated with a flammable liquid like that used in the torches. Wires around the perimeter of the circular stack led to a dozen sparkers placed within the pile.

Dov pointed to the wires that led up into the roof. "This must be how priests ignite the fire under the altar grating to consume the sacrifice. They probably chant their incantations while an accomplice moves a lever and the saturated pile of wood magically bursts into flames. I'd hate to be in this chamber or directly above it when that happens."

When they were satisfied that they had made a thorough examination of the top level, they returned to the stairway that led down deeper into the ziggurat. After feeling their way through the maze of passageways they found their marker and the chamber on the third level where Kaman had left them. Kitt found another torch and sparker along the way, and he kept it unlit for future use. They sat in the dark and reviewed plans for the next day.

"If we sleep now we should wake up in time to implement step one. I wish I had one of Father's wrist chronometers." Dov said.

The three immediately fell asleep in the silent darkness in spite of the hard stone floor.

New Babel, One World Tower—Rooftop Freight Ascender Maintenance Room #2

"We've searched everywhere on the Luminary levels, and even inside the ziggurat, and we've found no sign of those ascender operators. Their capsule is still parked on the 120th level with the door locked. They must be here somewhere." The leader of the search parties reported back to Targa.

As he counted to make sure each member of Team Talon had returned, Targa was less concerned about the three intruders. "We've exposed our presence long enough by coming and going in daylight. Forget about them. We have a primary mission to fulfill in the morning. We'll see the start of a new world with Magus as its king. Now, everyone get some rest."

CHAPTER 33

New Babel, One World Tower—Capsule Control Room

Ash remained at his post in the control room without receiving further word from his cousins. He had found Dov's message in the leather pouch hours ago and became concerned when they didn't descend with Evina as in his written instructions. He checked regularly for more messages, but none came. Ash wasn't sure what he should do. He knew he had to remain at his post in the control room to keep the vapor engine pressure at its operating level so the ascender could return at any time. For safety reasons, all ascender vapor engines automatically reduced their fuel feed and dropped pressure over time, if left unattended, in order to prevent an explosion from over-pressure. When the pressure dropped, the ascender moved slower or not at all until the pressure returned to the operational level. Jengo had discovered that lazy controllers sometimes wedged a pencil against the pressure adjustment lever when they left their consoles unattended during breaks. This had not yet resulted in a boiler explosion, but on several occasions engine over-pressure caused a runaway ascender to drop faster than the brake could retard and lives had been lost.

Ash finally decided that he would reduce the pressure to a minimal level and leave his post in search of his father, Jengo, or Pele. Maybe they would know what to do. An hour later, he found them in another part of the tower basement complex where Jengo was repairing a freight ascender mechanism in a maintenance machine shop. He briefly explained the situation. Jengo sent Pele and Javak back to the control room with Ash while he arranged for another mechanic to finish his project. It was another hour before Jengo joined them in the control room.

They gathered before the console where Ash followed the steps for raising the ascender pressure to its operating level. Jengo had his own key to unlock the ascender but the modifications that Magus had ordered to the ascender wouldn't work remotely if the door was locked in place at the other end. The override only worked when an operator was in the capsule.

"I wish they hadn't gone off alone without telling us," Pele said. "I would have gone with them."

"I think any of us would have, but what's done is done," Jengo stated. "If you'd gone too, then we'd have to rescue four instead of three. We ought to be able to figure a way to get them off the tower tonight. If we can locate this fellow, Kaman, that Ash told us about, we should be able to figure something out. If not, we'll need the Luminary ascender to get back down. I suggest that Pele, Javak, and I go up as fast as we can using the freight ascenders. Ash can stay here and work the controls. When I've unlocked the ascender, Javak can bring it down, because by then Nimrod, Zidon, and Magus and their entourages, will need to go up in the morning to prepare for the noon ceremony. Javak will try to keep the ascender on the roof between trips as long as he can. We'll do our best to meet him there when he can bring us all down at once. I don't mind abandoning the Luminary ascender at that point. The king can ride a freight ascender like the rest of his subjects. That's the best I can come up with on short notice. Any questions?"

"What if we can't find Kaman?" asked Pele.

"I know every inch of that tower rooftop. They must be hiding or held hostage somewhere—maybe inside the ziggurat. That place is a maze of corridors. It could take hours to search every one of them, but that's where we'll look if we can't find Kaman or if he can't tell us where they are."

"I just remembered," said Pele. "Dov asked me to get a drawing of the ziggurat's inner corridors from you. That's where they must be!"

The three men left Ash at the controls and headed to the freight ascenders for the long, indirect journey to the roof through the three staging portals. When they reached the lower freight staging area they encountered hundreds of people waiting.

Jengo pushed through the crowd to speak to the ascender supervisor. "What's all the commotion about?" he demanded.

"Everyone's going to the roof for the big ceremony at noon. Nimrod issued royal orders to fill the area around the ziggurat. We're loading the ascenders with passengers only—no freight today. It'll take us the rest of the night and morning to shuttle everyone up in time."

Jengo spoke to the operator urgently. "The three of us need to go up *now*. Something has happened on the roof that needs our attention." A supervisor overheard them talking and recognized Jengo as the tower chief engineer. He gave him and his group priority on the freight ascender, which was ready to leave. In spite of that, because of the large number of people and a couple failed attempts to hoist overloaded ascenders, they did not reach the rooftop until sunrise.

New Babel, One World Tower—Luminary Ascender Portal

Dawn

Ash received notice from a breathless, anxious guard that all three members of the Triad were waiting in the lobby to be transported to the rooftop. Ash thought it best to go to the Luminary lobby himself to explain the delay. Magus would be in a rage. He feared what he or Nimrod might do to him if he said that the ascender was stuck on the roof. He steeled himself against their wrath.

Magus recognized Ash's ascender uniform. "There you are! Take us up immediately!" The magician spun away without speaking further and led Nimrod, Zidon, and Arvid toward the ascender portal doorway. He stopped abruptly when he realized that there was no capsule waiting. "Where is my ascender? Where is it?" he screeched.

His use of the term "*my* ascender" did not go unnoticed by Nimrod but he remained expressionless. Ash composed himself to speak with as much respect and conviction as possible. He was shaking inside.

"Sir . . . it will be here shortly. There was some difficulty with the ascender last night. The operator flew it to the rooftop earlier and will bring it back momentarily. This is purely routine." *I hope*, he thought, as he said a quick prayer. If his father did not descend soon he could not imagine the fury that would be unleashed in his direction. "If you would please be comfortably seated here for a few minutes longer; I must return to my station and control the descent. I do not wish there to be an accident on this special day. If you will excuse me . . ." Ash solemnly backed away from the presence of the three most powerful men in the world, who could not stand or sit still.

No sooner had he returned to the control station than he noticed with relief that the capsule was descending. A display dial showed that it was passing through the unfinished, exposed region, which meant it would arrive within minutes. Ash hoped that his father would come to the basement docking portal first, so he could warn him about the waiting Triad. When the machine thankfully slowed to a stop on his level he breathed a sigh of relief.

"Am I ever glad to see you!" Ash exclaimed when his father stepped out of the capsule. "You need to go up to the Luminary lobby right now and take the Triad to the roof. I told them you were testing it before starting morning ascender runs. What's going on up there?"

"They're looking for that fellow, Kaman, so I came down to take Luminaries up to the ceremony. I'll keep the ascender idling on the roof as long as I can between trips in case they show up. I'm off!"

Javak returned to the capsule and drove it up one level. The Triad bustled into the ascender and Javak lifted off as soon as the door closed. Nobody noticed that he was not dressed in an ascender operator uniform. For the first minute of the trip he listened stoically to Magus' tirade directed at Javak for being late until Nimrod barked, "Enough!" The king needed quiet so he could think. He was tired of the high-strung magician's constant whining. If his own scheme bore fruit, he would not have to suffer the little pest much longer.

CHAPTER 34

New Babel, One World Tower—Rooftop Ziggurat Promenade

Jengo and Pele wasted precious hours looking for Kaman. Workers had seen him around the rooftop promenade area, as well as in workshops, storage areas, and freight loading portals, but since then they hadn't seen him. Time was running out to escape from the tower before the sun reached its apex at noon, which foretold certain doom for anyone on the roof when the asteroid passed overhead. They stood in the middle of the crowd in the open expanse at the base of the black ziggurat. They had almost given up hope when a dusty stone mason walked up to them. He dried his hands on his clothes after washing off mortar from a last-minute job.

"Why are you looking for Kaman?" he inquired cautiously.

"Are you Kaman?" Pele asked.

"Who wants to know?"

"My name's Pele, father of Dov and Yanis. Do you know where my children are?" The raw desperation in his voice convinced Kaman of his sincerity. He looked both ways and spoke softly.

"I don't know *exactly* where they and their cousin Kitt are. Come away from this crowd where we can talk freely." They walked away from a cluster of worshippers vying for positions from which to get the best view of the noon ceremony which was an hour away. When they were before the familiar portico that led to the hidden entrance, he spoke quickly.

"When I last saw them we had entered the hidden corridors of the ziggurat to rescue Evina, but we found that the corridor to her room was bricked up. I left them standing where we are here while I went to get tools to break through the wall, but they were arrested by temple guards and held for interrogation. Before they could be questioned, I removed them from their detention cell through another secret doorway and concealed them in a storage chamber on the inner third level, but when I checked that room a few hours ago they weren't there! That's all I can tell you." Having brought them up to the present time, Kaman hoped they would have time to find the three.

Jengo offered the only suggestion that popped into his mind: "From drawings I saw a while back I recall the general layout of the interior maze of corridors and rooms. I've never been inside them, so I'm not as familiar with them as you are, Kaman. Would you lead us to the chamber where you left them? We'll begin our search there, and maybe come across some sign or evidence of where they went."

"I still have some masonry assignments to complete this morning. My supervisor will be mad at me if I don't do them."

"There isn't time for that," Jengo insisted. "In an hour this rooftop will be swept of anything or anyone in the open. The tower itself could be toppled if the winds are strong enough. As chief engineer of the tower project I hereby relieve you of any further responsibilities. You work for me now. Your job is to help us. Is that official enough?"

Kaman nodded with enthusiasm and turned toward the stone wall. He opened the concealed entrance, and the three quickly entered the dark passageway and slammed the door before anyone outside could notice. There were no torches handy. They followed Kaman closely as he made turn after turn in the impenetrable darkness. Shortly after they ascended to the third level, Kaman found an unused torch and sparker on the wall, which he ignited. For the first time, Jengo and Pele saw the narrow walls and the other corridors and chambers that branched out in every direction. It was a confusing maze whose right angle turns and rooms all looked alike, but now they could move more quickly in the flickering light.

"This is it." Kaman halted before the masonry storage chamber where he had last seen the three. Jengo took the torch from him and closely surveyed the room.

"This box has been opened and iron implements are in a jumble on the floor. Was it this way when you left them?" Jengo inquired.

"No. Not that I recall." Kaman replied. "It looks as if they rummaged through the tool chest looking for something."

"We'll have to assume that they found one or more tools and departed with them. Could they have found tools to break through the wall into Evina's chamber?"

"That's possible. I hadn't thought of looking for tools here."

"Look what I found!" Pele said from the doorway. "This small chisel was leaning against the wall. It looks as if it was placed here to mark the chamber entrance."

"I didn't put it there," Kaman said. "They must have used it to find their way back to this room in the dark, but where did they go?"

Jengo held up his hand while he stared at the chisel leaning against the wall. "Let's think before we run off looking through every corridor in the entire building. Above all, Dov wants to rescue Evina, so he wouldn't leave the tower without her. Yanis and Kitt are with him. Let's go to that bricked wall first and see if they were able to break through. Then, if it's untouched, or if we don't find them there, we should look for them in the next most logical place. Where would that be?" Everyone pondered his question in the stillness of the inner chamber where the only sound was that of their breath.

"You're right. Dov wouldn't give up trying to rescue Evina. He would never leave her behind." Pele knew his son's determination and devotion to a friend. Then he figured it out. "The guards will take Evina from her room to the ziggurat altar just before noon. She'll be heavily guarded during the transfer. Might Dov try to snatch her away while she's being moved?"

"Not likely," Jengo said. "He and Kitt would be no match for armed temple guards."

Kaman agreed. "The guards I saw outside her door looked like rough characters. He and Kitt wouldn't stand a chance against them."

"What if the guards tied her up and left her on the altar? Could he somehow carry her away from there?" Jengo asked.

"Yes! That's very possible." Kaman exclaimed. "Dov asked me if I knew the layout of the top level of the ziggurat. He wanted to know if the level under the altar had stairs up to the rooftop."

"Then here's what we'll do." Jengo stated. "We'll take the time to check on the bricked up wall first to eliminate that possibility. If the wall is untouched, then we'll go to the top level and see if they're there. If that's their plan, maybe we can help them. By then it may be too late to get off the tower before noon, but at least we can seek shelter from the asteroid's repercussions as deep inside the ziggurat as we can."

Team Talon was in position on the large promenade to protect Magus as soon as he appeared for the ceremony. The magician wanted to see for himself that his plans for Nimrod and Zidon were set in motion before he made a stealthy exit off the tower. He had no intention of waiting to see his adversaries' demise. While the team waited, one of the men saw Kaman, Jengo, and Pele disappear through the alcove's hidden entryway. He brought it to Targa's attention.

"Sir! I think I might have seen those three that we were warned about. We never found them last night. Didn't the chief magician want them stopped from interfering with the ceremony?"

Targa stiffened with alarm at this news. "Were they dressed in ascender uniforms?"

"No, sir. But I saw three people plotting something over there. One of them pushed on some stones, the wall swung open, and they slipped into the secret passages inside the ziggurat. That's why we never found them when we searched those corridors last night."

"*Nothing* will stop this mission!" Targa vehemently insisted. "Take the trooper who was with you last night and find them as quickly as possible. I don't care how you do it—stop them now!"

Targa looked at the rest of his team and decided that their numbers and defensive perimeter were sufficient to protect the chief magician when he emerged from the Luminary ascender. He assumed that Teams Fang and Claw were also in their positions. Now all they had to do was wait.

CHAPTER 35

New Babel, One World Tower—Rooftop Ziggurat, Inner Level 1

Thirty minutes before the sun's zenith

At the same time that Kaman, Jengo, and Pele moved slowly toward the bricked wall on the fifth level, the two armed mercenaries from Team Talon entered the darkened passageway on the opposite side of the ziggurat. Dov, Kitt and Yanis had arrived at the top level, when they heard voices. The sounds came from people in the temple rooms where they stored vestments and ceremonial accessories.

"We'll wait here in the stairwell until they leave." Dov speculated that whoever was there was preparing for the ceremony and would soon depart. He could tell from the angle of the sun through a grating at the end of the hallway that it was approaching the sun's zenith. Within a few minutes the hallway was silent and the three emerged from their hiding place into the inner corridor surrounding the altar.

Dov and Kitt hurriedly dressed in colorful robes they found hanging on pegs. Yanis dressed in a feminine-looking robe. They hoped to blend in as low-level servants or assistants and remain unnoticed until they put the final phase of their plan into action. They stepped into the room with the huge pile of firewood directly under the altar and peered up through the metal grating at the sun overhead in a cloudless sky. It was almost noon. Yanis thought the two men needed something in their hands to make them look like they had a function. She gave them each a bundle of firewood to carry on their shoulders to partially obscure their faces. As they walked out the door, Kitt returned to the room, and emerged from it again a few seconds later.

"What did you do?" Yanis asked him.

"I disconnected the sparkers in the pile of oil-saturated firewood. We wouldn't want to go up in smoke while we rescue the girl in distress."

"Where's your sense of excitement?"

"After today I'll have had enough excitement for the rest of my life!"

When they reached the base of the steps leading up to the rear of the altar, Dov set down his firewood prop to review their responsibilities. His expression betrayed unflinching resolve. "Kitt and I will stand beside the altar with our bundles of wood and try to look like religious assistants—whatever they're supposed to look like. I doubt anyone will question our presence there unless they're high-level officials who know the arrangement details. I'm hoping that the high-ranking priests will all be far enough away with Zidon at the base of the ziggurat preparing to climb the steps in a procession when it's time." He avoided saying that Evina was their intended offering.

"Kitt and I will watch the crowd as the asteroid approaches. My guess is that the display in the sky will be so spellbinding that nobody will give us a second's thought. We'll have to improvise everything once we're out in the open, but once we have Evina we'll retreat back into the corridors for protection. Meet up in our safe room on the third level if we become separated."

"I'm really glad that you two are sticking with me in this. So far, nothing has gone the way I'd planned it." Dov was truly glad to have his sister and Kitt helping him.

"No problem. I just like to show your sister some excitement. We should do this again sometime."

The three quickly prayed for safety and wisdom before Dov and Kitt climbed the stone steps into bright sunlight and brisk wind on the highest point of the One World Tower. Adrenalin overcame fear in what could be the last minutes of their lives.

New Babel, One World Tower—Rooftop Ziggurat Promenade

Simultaneous events unfolded on the crowded promenade and behind the altar. Nimrod, Magus, and Zidon made their formal entrances to trumpets and cheers of adulation by people pressing against a cordon of temple guards. Each member of the Triad would put their individual schemes into play designed to elevate himself to the sole position of power and prestige in the New World order. Each felt confident that he would succeed.

Arvid joined his father, and the two, dressed in high priestly gold adornments and followed by a train of priests, acolytes, and attendants, marched in procession to their positions at the base of the gleaming black ziggurat. Temple guards would bring Evina to them, carry her up the long flight of steps to the peak, and tie her to the altar. Zidon would move the lever to immolate his daughter in sacrifice to Ningizzia when the asteroid was directly overhead. The father and son were oblivious to the practiced movement of Team Talon nearby. The assassins waited for their signal.

Nimrod was far more alert and proactive in his movements than Zidon, for he knew that Magus intended to murder him and become the ruler of New Babel. The king didn't step all the way to the prearranged mark with his attendants and bodyguards. Instead, he gathered his entourage closely around him and moved away from Magus and Zidon to the freight ascender portal at the corner of the rooftop. Team Fang was confused by this change, and looked for instructions from Targa, who hurried to find Magus. Nimrod paused at the portal entrance and turned to face the ziggurat, as if to worship from that position. He would wait for the asteroid to appear over the horizon and then escape in a waiting freight ascender while everyone's eyes were on the ball in the sky.

Magus did not intend to wait for the asteroid to appear. His fear of being trapped in the tower prompted him to leave the Luminary ascender door open. He had ordered Javak to lock the ascender door, give him the key, and join the masses around the ziggurat for worship. Javak suspected that the cowardly magician would try to escape. He had to find his son Kitt, so he disappeared into the crowd while Magus stood impatiently and fingered the ascender key in his pocket. Nobody seemed to notice that neither he nor Nimrod flanked the high priest. All eyes were on Zidon and his son.

Deep inside the ziggurat, two groups with different objectives made their separate ways through dark corridors converging on the top level. Two assassins hurried headlong through the fifth and fourth levels with orders to kill the intruders on sight. They had just missed Kaman, Jengo, and Pele by scant minutes while they were in a stairwell. Kaman led them on the shortest route to the rooftop after finding the bricked wall that sealed off Evina's cell on the fifth level untouched.

A large stone mason with a shaved head and a single braided length of hair that reached his waist stood unnoticed in the press of the crowd on the promenade at the side of the ziggurat. Evina's mute bodyguard was dressed in rough workers clothing and carried a mason's toolbox. Normally his tall frame and hulking, muscular upper body would stand out in a crowd, but all eyes were on the religious procession, and with everyone's attention diverted, he easily melded in with thousands of anxious worshippers. Saris knew that the person under his protection was in mortal danger. He had figured out for himself the horrible intentions of Zidon and Arvid after he observed special guards in front of Evina's holding cell. He moved easily through the crush of onlookers. His bulk pushed people aside, but they didn't take much notice of him as they craned their necks to see the bright pageantry unfolding before them. He appeared to be nothing more than a muscular laborer trying to get a better view. In his toolbox were sharpened weapons to fight off any guards who tried to stop him from rescuing Evina.

Dov and Kitt watched the vast religious spectacle from their vantage point on the highest point of the tower. The priestly procession stood at the base of the ziggurat. As if on cue, two guards roughly carried Evina to her father. Her hands and feet were bound, and she fought in tears against her captors.

Zidon looked at his daughter with sad eyes, then changed his expression to stone and averted his gaze toward the east. Arvid could not resist a final taunt. He leaned down to snarl in her face. "Looks like you made the wrong choice, little sister. In a few minutes I'll rule over all these people." His eyes sparkled with evil arrogance.

Evina struggled against her captors. "You'll have to answer to the God of the universe someday. It's you who have made the wrong choice." Her rough handlers lifted her from the ground and climbed the steps of the stepped pyramid-shaped structure toward the gleaming altar in the sky. Thousands of worshippers cheered when they saw Evina, but then gasps of surprise swept through the crowd when they realized that her hands and feet were bound and her dress was torn and dirty. She was being carried to the altar against her will. The horrible prospect of a young girl—the high priest's own daughter!—being a human sacrifice sunk in, and the mood of the crowd shifted. Surprise was replaced by grim murmurs and then loud objections. The people of Babel could not believe that Zidon would offer his own daughter to the approaching god. Something inside them said that this violated all decency and humanity.

Zidon and Arvid were puzzled by the crowd's stunned silence. They expected cheering and cries of approval. The High Priest of Marduk turned to face the people, lifted his hands, and shouted, *"Ningizzia! Ningizzia! Ningizzia!"* Others in his procession took up the chant and soon the crowd reluctantly joined them. Zidon turned to face the east as the voices behind him grew in numbers and volume. After Evina's hands and feet were tied to the altar, and the guards were halfway back down the ziggurat steps, a shining golden ball accelerated upward in the east like a sunrise in fast motion. The sun beckoned directly overhead as its shining twin, many times larger in appearance, sped across the sky.

All eyes were on the polished sphere and the thundering, hypnotic chant continued. *"Ningizzia! Ningizzia! Ningizzia!"*

Dov and Kitt dropped their firewood and Kitt sawed at Evina's bonds with a small pocketknife.

Through tears of hysteria, Evina recognized the two men attempting to release her. "Dov! I prayed that God would find a way to release me!" Either from exhaustion or relief, she fainted.

"You could have brought a sharper knife," Dov said to his cousin while he worked on a knot with his fingers.

"Good thing I found this in our storage room. Otherwise we'd be using our teeth."

Yanis popped her head up from the stairs below. "You have about ten seconds to get down here. Hurry!"

Evina's feet were loosed and Kitt hacked at the rope around her hands. When the last strand parted, Dov scooped Evina's body into his arms and headed for the stairs followed by Kitt.

Saris had not taken his eyes from Evina. When he saw her being removed from the altar by two attendants, he hesitated for a brief second before he clenched a two-foot sword in each burly hand and bounded up the side of the pyramid.

When he saw his daughter being released, Zidon grabbed the lever that ignited fuel under the altar and pushed it with all his might. The ceremonial timing was wrong, but he had to begin the sacrifice before Evina was removed from the altar. Nothing happened. He pushed the lever repeatedly, but no flames emerged from below the altar grating. The high priest flung off the hindrance of his golden headdress and climbed the steps toward the altar as fast as he could, tripping on his long robe every few steps.

"Evina!" he shouted. "Oh, Evina!"

A bright signal flare in the sky was visible in the diminishing reflected light of the asteroid that was poised to eclipse the sun directly overhead. Nimrod stepped into the waiting freight ascender and urged the operator to descend immediately. Magus closed the door of the Luminary ascender and released the brake for his descent. Hired assassins intent on killing Zidon chased after him before he could reach the top of the ziggurat. Arvid was paralyzed with fear when he realized that nothing was happening as he expected.

CHAPTER 36

New Babel, One World Tower—Rooftop Ziggurat

Sun's exact zenith

Saris approached the top of the ziggurat where he recognized Dov just as he carried Evina off the altar. Dov and Kitt did not see him increase his speed to reach the stairs before the tower was engulfed in darkness. When he jumped over the altar, he found the metal grid over the stairway secured. He pulled on it with all his adrenalin fueled might. The wooden peg Yanis had put there to lock it snapped and he flung the covering aside and jumped to the floor below in one leap.

Once inside the dark, constrained corridors, the rescuers were isolated from the unfolding catastrophe outside. Kitt's speculation about the atmospheric effects from the ball that brushed past one hundred miles above the earth was correct. The shock wave, high winds, flying debris, and heat did not penetrate the ziggurat's layers of thick stone. However, the young engineer could not have anticipated another effect, for he did not know that God had created a sphere of pure iron. The asteroid, fifty miles in diameter, projected a magnetic field of such intensity that its effects were felt by alloy objects hundreds of miles away. When it was directly over the ziggurat, the maximum force of its magnetic field easily and instantly penetrated deep inside buildings with dramatic, violent effects. Loose alloy masonry tools clanged throughout the corridors as they bounced against walls and ceilings. The force tugged violently on the thin alloy mesh body armor of the two assassins and slammed them so hard against the stone ceiling that they were knocked unconscious. Knives in their belts cut them when they flew out of their scabbards. The soldiers were pinned to the ceiling dripping blood until their bodies dropped to the floor when the asteroid departed. Jengo, Pele, and Kaman were themselves tugged upward by metal buckles and objects in their pockets, but no harm was done to them. They heard Yanis' voice in the distance urging the others to hurry. Kaman called out before they rounded the corner and collided with each other.

The two groups gathered around the torch that Kaman lifted up. They hugged in welcome relief. Dov helped Evina stand on shaky legs in a daze. She was still in shock from her terrifying brush with death. They were safe from the outside turmoil, at least for now. Jengo suggested that they make their way to the masonry tool chamber deep in the third level where they had been before and decide what to do next. Before they departed, Dov let out a yelp when a hand gripped his shoulder. He turned to see Saris in the shadows smiling at Evina. Her giant bodyguard had to bend over in the confines of the corridor for his head to clear the ceiling.

He signed to her: *Are you unharmed, my lady? I was much afraid for your life and came to protect you.*

Evina embraced one of his massive arms in relief. *I will be better when we are all out of this awful place*, she replied.

Dov explained their intentions to Saris in sign language, and the group, now eight in number, moved more confidently down the corridor toward their destination. Kaman led the way with his torch as Saris followed last to protect them from any pursuers. They felt strong currents of air whistling through the corridors and stairways and their ears popped from the pressure changes. The floor and walls shuddered. The atmospheric overpressure from the asteroid was reaching its peak outside. They could only imagine what it was like on the exposed rooftop of the tower. Anyone who had not found shelter could never survive.

Everyone on the roof of the One World Tower and in the cities of New and Old Babel locked their eyes on the sphere above them. This was God's final test of world civilization. Threatened with extinction, how would humanity react? Would people turn to their Creator? Or, would they deny His existence and flee to gods of their own making, closing their hearts and minds to the One who had given them life? The answer came in shrieks of terror from those on the tower rooftop and in the city streets below. They clutched their scraps of printed slogans, pleaded with the stars for help, and panicked when they found only emptiness.

The rescuers inside the ziggurat had no time to appreciate the mathematical beauty of their mechanized predictions made days earlier. Formularies and *Cyclone* calculations had exactly calculated the movement of the asteroid. The sphere appeared on the eastern horizon at the exact time they had forecasted. Its mirror-like surface reflected the bright intensity of the sun's heat and light. At the zenith the asteroid perfectly eclipsed the sun and plunged Babel into total darkness as if a lamp had been extinguished. The terrifying darkness lasted less than a minute before a sliver of the sun reemerged and its light shined on the city once again. Within minutes, the object disappeared in the west and all returned to normal—as if such a thing were possible.

Not only had the young scientists not anticipated the magnetic characteristics of the ball of pure iron, but more dramatically, the invisible forces on the structure of the tallest building in the world were incalculable. As the giant object raced across the sky, the alloy core of the One World Tower was lifted up and bent sideways by a force that its designers could never have foreseen. The silent force peaked during the total darkness when the ball's track reached its apex over the tower. The magnetic field of the iron asteroid pulled metallic objects upward with a strength greater than the force of gravity holding them down. Like the pull of silent, invisible hands, the magnetic field spelled doom for many on the roof of the tower. Iron alloy weapons, shields, and body armor of the guards and soldiers lifted them into the air and drew them over the tower's edge like toys as the force moved from east to west. Many observers wearing small metallic objects were thrown off balance; those near the edge of the building fell over the side. As the celestial object departed, others on the west side of the roof were pulled over to their deaths.

The powerful magnetic force against the skeleton of the tower produced a noticeable sway that was so amplified on the roof that anyone who was not lifted over the edge of the roof fell to the pavement of the promenade. The tallest structure ever built by man groaned and creaked in agony. Loose materials and tools levitated from unfinished floors of the tower and fell on crowds gathered in the streets below.

Then, a massive disruption of the atmosphere rippled rapidly down to the surface of the earth. The shockwave battered buildings and people minutes after the asteroid disappeared. Many who were outside escaped death when buildings collapsed. Then, hurricane force winds swept across the plain of Shinar, flattened crops, shredded already damaged structures, produced an unprecedented dust storm, and drove people into the safety of any corner or crevice they could find.

Throughout the tower's frame and its interior partitions there was structural damage that could cause its collapse at any moment. Over one thousand feet tall, the tower had been the crowning engineering achievement of civilization and the symbol of the Triad's supremacy. Now, the tower was a mockery and the Triad was forgotten. Mankind was focused on survival. The One World Tower of Babel had become the universal symbol of folly.

CHAPTER 37

New Babel, One World Tower—Rooftop Ziggurat, Inner Level 3

Hours later

Yanis awoke in the darkness of the masonry chamber with a jolt and a stifled cry. Her eyes were wide open, but she might as well have been blind.

"I *must* get out of here," she said in a loud whisper, which echoed in the chamber and down the corridor. "I'm sorry. *I must get outside!*" she cried louder.

The others awoke one by one, and Saris lit a torch and handed it to Kaman. The eight had reclined on the cold stone floor or on bags of masonry. When the adrenaline rush from their horrifying escape drained from their bodies they had drifted to sleep in spite of their accommodations. They had no concept of the time.

Jengo offered his thoughts on what they should do: "We should see what it's like outside. The wind and devastation are probably past."

"What about Javak and Ash?" Dov asked. "Do you think they found protection from the wind and destruction? What will we do if we can't find them?"

Kitt watched with a bewildered look that seemed contorted in the flickering torch.

"Ash should be safe if he stayed in the basement control room," Pele said. "Javak knew that high winds were predicted. He would know enough to seek shelter. We'll reunite you with your father." Pele gave Kitt's arm a squeeze.

"If Javak was in the ascender that might not have made any difference," Dov said without thinking. "Sorry, Kitt."

"I'm all in favor of positive thinking." Yanis said while clinging tightly to Kitt. "Can we get out of this place so I can breath some fresh air and see some daylight? That's a positive thought, isn't it?"

Pele agreed. "Yes! Kaman, lead the way to someplace where we can exit and scout around discretely. I think everyone is ready to see daylight."

The mason stared at Pele quizzically without moving.

"Let's go," Pele motioned.

Kaman grunted a string of guttural words that sounded like he had something caught in his throat.

"What?" Dov asked. Everyone turned toward Kaman.

The young Accadian mason rattled off another barrage of odd sounds in seeming frustration. He didn't understand what the others were saying and they didn't understand him. He waved the torch around and stepped back from them. He was about to run in panic.

Evina took Kaman gently by the arm. "Sit down here," she said, while she gestured and pronounced his name distinctly. "Something's happened to you that none of us understand, but you must remain calm." She used simple sign language to emphasize her words and led him to sit on a dusty box. She took the torch from his hand and gave it to Saris. Still speaking in a calming tone, she explained to the others what she thought happened. "He doesn't understand us because he's deaf, probably because of sudden overpressure from the asteroid."

"How do you explain what he said?" Yanis asked pointedly.

"Sometimes, with people who are totally deaf, the words don't come out quite right because they can't hear themselves speaking. I'm sure that's the reason," she answered confidently.

Yanis walked around Kaman, who followed her with his eyes. When she was behind him she clapped her hands and he jumped. "So much for your deafness theory," she said. When Yanis noticed that Kitt had yet to say anything, she asked him what he thought. When he didn't answer, she repeated herself.

He mumbled some words of reply with a silly grin on his face, as if he found the whole thing amusing. He mouthed more singsong words that sounded pleasant to the ear but without meaning to the others. He couldn't restrain himself from laughing out loud. Yanis was stunned.

"Is this some kind of joke?" Dov asked. "What's going on?"

Pele held up his hands to stop everyone from speaking at once. "Clearly Kaman and Kitt have been influenced somehow by the asteroid. They don't understand us and we don't understand them."

"How could a *space object* make them speak in gibberish when it hasn't affected the rest of us? I mean, physically, it doesn't make sense." Dov was as perplexed as everyone else.

"Maybe the strong magnetic field did something to them," Pele suggested. "Anyway, we don't know exactly what's happened, so for now we need to get out of here and down on the ground. Yanis, Kitt trusts you, so you lead him along with us. You'll have to be his ears until we sort everything out. Evina, keep Kaman nearby and use your sign language to calm him. Dov, you and Saris can help too with basic gestures as if they were deaf." Pele motioned to Kaman that he should stay with Evina, while it was unnecessary to instruct Kitt since he and Yanis were inseparable now anyway. Pele took the torch from Saris and led them along the corridors toward the one exit that he knew. For five minutes they followed winding passageways to the bottom level and a familiar dead-end corridor.

Pele turned and addressed them solemnly. "Jengo and I will go outside to survey the damage. He's the tower chief engineer, so nobody will question why we're walking about. We'll return here in a few minutes." When Dov pressed on the secret stones, the door opened slightly and they felt a refreshing breeze. The sunlight blinded their sensitive eyes. Pele and Jengo stepped out and shut the door. The rest of the party impatiently waited for them to return.

"That bit of fresh air was wonderful," Evina said. She had stayed close to Dov, but the trauma of her near-death on the altar, the violent maelstrom caused by the asteroid, and their race through the dark corridors was still evident in her drawn features.

Dov gripped her hand. "We'll be out of here and safe in no time," he reassured her.

CHAPTER 38

New Babel, One World Tower—Rooftop Ziggurat Promenade

Pele opened the door into the corridor after what seemed like an hour to those waiting in the dark, but was actually only a few minutes. He was alone.

"Where's Jengo?" Dov asked as they emerged blinking into the sunlight.

"He's looking for Javak," Pele replied. He held out his arm to stop Dov and the others from going further. "Something astonishing has happened that we can't explain. You need to be prepared for bizarre things before you go further."

"That's hardly unexpected," Dov said. "The destruction here and in the city must be considerable. I want to see it for myself." Dov stepped around his father and walked out of the portico and around the corner onto the promenade.

"There's more than that," Pele said in a voice tinged with fear.

The destruction on the tower was worse than anticipated. All the ceremonial decorations were gone. Thousands had crowded the promenade for Zidon's ceremony and now the expanse was almost empty except for a few people walking aimlessly, obviously dazed by their trauma. Then Dov noticed others running back and forth shouting. Voices were indistinct, but their panic came through clearly.

"Where's my father?" Evina asked. She remembered his sorrowful face when the guards carried her to the altar. Fear had blotted out all memory when she realized what he intended to do.

Dov held her in his arms. "I'm sorry. Nobody could have survived on the rooftop. He was climbing the stairs to reach you when we were plunged into darkness."

"He was trying to reach me?" she sobbed.

"Yes. I heard him calling your name."

"Then maybe he had a change of heart at the end."

"We can only hope."

"I loved him in spite of what you might think. When my mother died he drew closer to me and my brother. Even though the Triad twisted his thinking, I'll remember the good times we had." She held Dov tighter. "Don't leave me, Dov."

"I won't," he replied.

As the group stood in the center of the promenade amazed at how deserted it looked, a crazed man in worker's clothing ran up to Kaman, grabbed his shoulders, and shook him violently. After he screamed unintelligibly and received no reply, he ran for the freight ascender.

"What did he say? I've never heard anyone speak like that before," Yanis exclaimed.

"Neither have I," replied Evina. "He's not the only one. Listen to the others."

A woman sitting on the pavement nearby rambled incoherently while pounding her fists on the stones. She spoke in a monotone, as if in a trance, repeating the same unknown words over and over. A man and woman squatted on the plaza stones nearby, clutching each other in terror. They spoke to one another through tears while they ignored everyone around them. Others, either darting erratically as if searching for a companion or family member or stumbling around in a daze, shouted into the air.

The group, led by Pele and Jengo, watched from the center of the promenade while people emerged from rooms at the base of the ziggurat, freight storage areas, and stairs leading down to other Luminary levels. The volume of shouting and crying elevated as the number of people increased. Terrified people rushed about in a panic. Their speech was a garbled mishmash of sounds that made no sense to the observers. Each person was searching for anyone who could understand them. When they found one they could understand, they embraced in tears of relief.

Pele struggled to explain what had happened. "Maybe we understand each other because we're close relatives—the family of Pele and my brother, anyway."

"What about me? You and Dov understand me." Evina said. "Why does Saris still understand my signs?"

Pele forced a laugh. "That shoots my theory. There must be a reason for this . . . this *miracle.*"

"At least from our perspective, our speech has been unchanged. Maybe everyone's speech is different, including ours, and we don't notice because it's our own. Does that make sense? I wonder if our original language is gone too." The implication of what Dov speculated seemed unimaginable.

For the first time since the creation of mankind they heard and spoke different languages. In the beginning, there was a single spoken and written language with vocabulary, structure, syntax, grammar, and pronunciation that God created in Adam and Eve and that He used to communicate directly with them. One ingrained language that parents passed on to children had united the world to speed the progress of an advanced antediluvian civilization. Noah and his family could not imagine anything other than the one language of their family and the rest of humanity. After the Flood, one common language allowed the city of Babel to unify around one monarchy, one religion, and one industrial economy. In an instant, and without rational explanation, life on earth had changed forever.

"Kitt!" They heard Kitt's name shouted above the background of voices from across the promenade. Javak ran toward them with Jengo at his side.

Father and son embraced while the group listened in anticipation. "Do you understand me, Father?" Kitt asked.

"Yes, my son! Yes!" Javak repeated joyfully.

"Well, I'm glad that's all cleared up," Dov wryly observed to Evina, as they could only speculate what had been said between father and son.

"Quit joking," his sister scolded him. "This is serious. We need to get off this rooftop while we deal with different languages among ourselves. It's going to be hard enough."

"I can't help it that I'm around people who talk funny," he continued. He then went to his cousin and uncle to hug them and tell them how glad he was that Javak was unhurt. Somehow they understood his sentiment.

When they walked as a small group to the edge of the roof they surveyed the ruins of the city spread out below them. Most buildings were damaged and many isolated fires burned out of control.

"I can see our house from here," Yanis observed. "It's still standing but all the streets are littered with debris."

Jengo assumed charge of the small group of survivors and suggested that they split up to look for ways down. He took Javak, Kitt and Yanis with him to explore the Luminary levels below them. Pele, Dov, Evina, Kaman, and Saris were sent to examine the freight ascenders to see if they offered a path for escape. They would meet back in front of the Luminary ascender entrance.

Dov first opened the Luminary ascender portal door with his key and looked down the dark shaft. The capsule was nowhere in sight. The smooth sides of the shaft and the greased cables offered nothing useful for their escape. The freight ascender area was equally hopeless. Distraught people noted their ascender uniforms and shouted at them incoherently in similar hope of finding a way down. Dov and the others shook their heads and motioned people away. They waited for the others to return.

Dov leaned against a wall in discouragement that was shared by the others. "There *must* be a way down!" he lamented. "Maybe we could fly down like the birds," he said sarcastically.

"What?" Evina asked abruptly. "What did you just say?"

"I said maybe we could fly down like birds, but I was just joking."

Evina told Dov about the night that the Watcher leapt from her balcony and flew away in his black flying suit. Before she could continue her explanation, the others returned with equally discouraging news of extensive damage to the building and to the freight ascenders. They had taken stairs to the bottom Luminary level on the 100th level, but it was sealed off, by design, from the levels below. They were trapped with no way down. The danger of their isolation at the top of the tower was further dramatized by the occasional shaking of the building. Jengo speculated that the iron alloy skeleton had been weakened by the wind and magnetic storm. What they felt might be braces and trusses snapping one at a time as stresses from the tower's weight were redistributed. It would be only a matter of time before the tower collapsed.

The group huddled together in the shade of the Luminary ascender portal overhang while Pele and Jengo left in search of food and water. They returned with a meager amount to satisfy them, but their discouragement was undiminished. Discussion turned again to the miraculous appearance of different languages.

Dov was intrigued by the phenomenon. "I find it strange that we have yet to encounter anyone that speaks as we do. Our group is distinct from all the others, as far as we know. Why is that?"

"I believe this is a miracle from God performed for some special purpose," said Evina. "My father would attribute the miracle to the asteroid or the gods, but I know that's impossible. No rock from outer space could cause this. I'm satisfied to trust that God knows what He's doing and He'll bring about some good from it."

The others were touched by her simple faith. Yanis and Dov smiled as they recalled Evina's visit to them weeks ago.

Dov voiced another comment while they sat in silence. "There's also some reason why God has chosen this group of different people to speak with the same tongue. He has a purpose for us being together and I'm certain that it's not for us to die here. I think we should ask God to show us a way of escape."

While they gathered together in prayer, accompanied by those friends and relatives who didn't understand the words of their prayers, a figure dressed in black was methodically climbing up steps in the wall of the dark Luminary ascender shaft many floors below. The Watcher grasped each unseen rung welded to the inside of the shaft wall before releasing his other hand to reach higher. He planted each foot carefully before moving up to the next step. The sides of the dark shaft disappeared into the distance below him. He balanced urgency with care in his steady climb upward. His goal was to find any of those entrusted to him who survived the asteroid's devastation. Hours before, the capsule carrying Magus had missed him by inches in its descent. He protected himself on an enclosed level while the asteroid passed and objects flew around. He had had been climbing for hours unaware of the confusion of languages outside the dark confines of the ascender shaft.

At the 100th level the crossbars welded to the side of the shaft ended. He pried the ascender doors open at that level and climbed onto the floor in exhaustion. After a few minutes he forced himself to his feet and walked unsteadily toward an interior stairway in the Luminary sector. He emerged into the sunlight on the roof and surveyed the destruction around him. The sounds of strange voices assaulted his senses and he was momentarily stunned. Then, his training to act decisively amid chaotic, conflicting situations took over, and he walked intently onto the open promenade to search for familiar faces while he tuned out the pandemonium around him. He shook off attempts by frantic strangers to hinder his progress while his eyes methodically scanned the crowds.

He finally noticed familiar figures kneeling in a tight group at the Luminary ascender entrance. They were praying. He paused before them and calmly asked, "How may I be of service?"

CHAPTER 39

New Babel, Euphrates River—Royal Navy Shipyard

When Nimrod and his decimated party of bodyguards reached the military shipyard only blocks away from the tower, he examined the damage to his two royal cruisers. His Royal Ship (*HRS*) *Defiant*, a vapor-powered battle cruiser two hundred feet in length, leaned at a precarious angle in the shallow water of its berth. Its fan-like paddles were extensively damaged; planks were ripped from its hull in various places, resulting in serious leaks; its superstructure was in shambles with broken portholes and bent railings. The king considered the *Defiant* hopelessly beyond repair. He turned to his other ship, an identical grey cruiser named the *HRS Savage*, safely afloat at its moorings, although metal parts of its superstructure were twisted and deck hardware was mangled or missing after the magnetic storm and fierce wind.

In earlier times, the sleek ships were used for fast attacks against Nimrod's enemies on the Euphrates and Tigris rivers. The *Savage* was still a beautiful war machine in spite of its damage. From its high, arched bow lifting above a gently curved deck, to twin paddles driven by powerful vapor engines, the battle cruiser was intimidating. Two cannons at the bow, called bow chasers, were deadly when fired at any target. High above the sanded wooden deck was a bridge or wheelhouse from which the captain gave orders for ship steerage and attacks. The captain and his officers in the high, enclosed area could see ahead of them for navigation; open extensions, or wing bridges, to the left and right of the bridge, gave the advantage of views to the side and behind to complete the captain's situational awareness around his ship.

Since the ship was a royal cruiser, it contained lavish accommodations for Nimrod that isolated him from the smoke, sparks, and noise that issued from the two black rock-fueled vapor engines that ran non-stop when the ship was underway. The king often took his family with him on expeditions and made full use of the staterooms that duplicated, on a smaller scale, their residence in the royal palace. Nimrod hurried to this warship for his escape from Babel.

There were few sailors on the ship when the king walked across a plank from the dock to the main deck. His first concern was the cast iron engines of the *Savage* located below the deck level. He found a junior engineer surveying the damage in the engine room. The greasy, dazed young man turned when he heard the king of Babel shouting.

"Give me a report! Nimrod ranted in the dark confines of the engine room.

The engineer had never met the king before, but he quickly figured out who he was and what he wanted, even though he didn't understand a word he was saying. What he had to report would not please the agitated king, but he gave it a try. He beckoned for the king to come with him as he pointed to destruction in the engine room. He punctuated his words with animated gestures. "Sir. Both engines were lifted off their mounts. Fortunately, there were no fires burning and no pressure in the boilers." He continued to explain how the enormous, invisible magnetic force of the asteroid lifted the engines inside the vessel and shifted them from their mountings. He showed that the shafts linking the engines to the paddles were bent. "Remounting engines and realigning drive shafts will take . . . ."

Nimrod exploded in frustration at the damage to his ship and nearly struck the engineer, who backed himself against a bank of valves. His rage was directed at everyone because he realized that the ship would not be able to leave without extensive repairs.

"I want the ship ready to leave the dockyard in twenty-four hours. Everyone get to work!" The king expected royal commands to be obeyed instantly. When the engine room crew stood immobile he shouted louder. His petrified crew was forced to anticipate his commands and he would mercilessly bully them into obedience with unmistakable gestures. They concluded that the king was furious and wanted the *Savage* to leave as soon as possible.

More sailors emerged shaken from below the deck at the sound of their king's booming voice. They didn't understand his words either, but his volcanic temperament conveyed his fury and desire to depart Babel. Using violent hand signals, punctuated by shouting and clear, brutal threats, Nimrod managed to galvanize what little crew he had. They began repairs on the engine and drive shaft to effect his escape from the doomed city. Temporarily diverted, but far from satisfied, the king left the shipyard to gather what remained of his family from the palace and pack his valued possessions for their departure.

New Babel, One World Tower

Magus was slightly more fortunate than Nimrod in his escape from the tower. He rode the Luminary ascender alone to the bottom docking level in the control room. His inexperience caused him to hit the basement floor hard enough to jam the capsule door closed. Ash was startled to find Magus dazed and alone in the capsule when he pried the door open. Magus ignored his questions and looked around for the exit from the basement. He felt the magnetic effects of the asteroid before he could leave the control room. He and Ash were thrown about the room as loose equipment was lifted and moved by the invisible force. Unhurt but dazed, they rose to their feet when the magnetic storm had passed. Magus dismissed the young control operator's concern for his welfare and ran out of the building to complete his escape.

The clever magician had planned to rally the people in the tower plaza after his escape. He would announce the deaths of Nimrod and Zidon and proclaim himself the King of New Babel. When he stood in the large plaza clogged with rubble and frantic, unintelligible screaming, he concluded that, however carefully planned his assassination plans might have been, he did not want to govern a city engulfed in such chaos. He had an alternative escape route in case he was not successful in removing Nimrod and Zidon. He threw off his magician's shining cape, gathered the folds of his tunic and ran toward the river.

Less than half a mile downriver from the royal shipyard, Magus arrived at a beach where fishermen kept their sailing dhows. Most of the small boats were damaged from the winds, but he found his escape craft mostly unharmed. The hired fishermen had abandoned it in their rush to escape the asteroid's destruction. He first checked for the gold coins secreted under the floorboards. They were still there! He would sail the boat south with his treasure to a prepared hideout. He could always return to Babel later. Magus pushed off from the beach, raised the sail, and drifted slowly into the center of the river to follow its current. It would take him days to reach his hidden sanctuary but that didn't matter now. He was secure with his gold nearby.

CHAPTER 40

New Babel, One World Tower—Rooftop Ziggurat Promenade

Late afternoon

The surprised prayer circle looked up at the figure standing before them. Their silence was broken when Evina said aloud, "Thank you God!"

The Watcher was accustomed to people's stunned looks when he appeared unexpectedly. Some in the group, like Kaman, had never seen the mysterious, black-clad stranger before, and were understandably fearful and suspicious. Evina, Dov, and Yanis, had spoken with him before. Still, their encounters were always unsettling; he knew much more about them than they did of him. He was always reassuring in their times of need.

Dov was about to introduce him to the others when the figure in the black cape held his hand up. "We must get you off the tower as quickly as possible. I realize that you have many questions, but they will have to wait."

Then the Watcher did something astounding. He turned to Javak and Kitt and spoke to them in a language that Dov and the others didn't understand. After a few brief sentences he turned and said a few words to Kaman. Javak and Kitt smiled and Kaman laughed out loud.

"How did you do that?" Evina asked. "You speak more than one language?"

"Miss, I cannot explain it. As shocking as it is for you to not understand the speech of others, I am at a loss to explain how I understand most of what others say. It must be a miracle," he stated in a matter-of-fact tone

The Watcher took Pele and Jengo aside to tell of his arrangements for them to descend down to the 52nd level—almost seventy levels below their present rooftop location—where he had prepared a way for them to reach the ground level. His scheme was daring. Pele and Jengo looked at the others with grim expressions and nodded their understanding.

The Watcher finished his detailed explanation. "Now that you know the escape route and method, I must leave you to make other arrangements on the ground for your landing. I cannot overemphasize the need for haste. Jengo knows better than anyone that the tower is unstable and could collapse at any time. Please hurry."

He touched his black hat in farewell and walked quickly to the roof parapet. To the horror of the entire group, he climbed upon the railing and dove over the side. They rushed to the edge and saw his black webbed suit fluttering in the wind as he shot across the city landscape at high speed. When he was a speck against the shapes of the buildings below, a billowing black rectangle appeared above him. Although they could not see him, he steered his parachute into the wind toward his home landing spot. They saw the canopy collapse when he landed safely on the roof of his building. He then gathered his equipment and disappeared from their sight.

"The last time he did that it was nighttime. All I saw was his shape disappear over the edge of my balcony and into the dark. It was terrifying. That man has no fear!" She exclaimed. "It must have been only a few days ago. It seems much longer." Evina paused wistfully. "He told me not to worry; that he would always protect me."

She turned to Dov with a playful smile. "I suppose back then you were still trying to figure out how to rescue me, weren't you?"

Before Dov could reply, Jengo told them that they had a lengthy and hazardous descent in front of them and needed to hurry. They would have time to talk when they safely reached the ground.

The chief engineer led them down the wide stairways of the Luminary section. They passed through eighteen levels of lavishly furnished residences and wide hallways used by royal and priestly dignitaries and their families. No expense had been spared in the luxurious spaces. Elegant workmanship in precious metals and polished stones adorned every detail. They had been turned into piles of twisted metal and broken furniture. Even the stairs connecting the levels were covered with plush carpeting. The railings were solid gold. Walls covered with shining purple fabric were now in tatters. They were astounded at the opulence that was reserved for the enjoyment of only a few.

Pele interrupted their wonderment. "Enjoy the extravagance now, because in a few minutes we'll leave it behind for dirty and harsh conditions." His reminder brought their company back to reality.

New Babel, One World Tower—Luminary Level, Ascender Shaft

On the 102nd level they reached the end of the descending Luminary stairway. As Jengo had told them days earlier, the Luminary level was sealed off from the Ministerial level below. They looked at the closed Luminary ascender doors of the 102nd level.

"Dov, do you have your ascender key? If you do, it will save us having to damage these beautifully decorated doors that lead to our departure from this luxury." Jengo hoped that his jovial tone would calm the others. Nobody seemed to notice.

Dov produced his key and opened the doors. The dark ascender shaft looked foreboding. It would take more than jokes to settle their fears now.

"Here's what we must do," explained Jengo, who understood the Watcher's instructions perfectly. He assumed Javak had received the same explanation in his language. The others would follow their lead. "We'll descend in a particular order so we can help one another. It might be best to not talk very much while we're in the ascender shaft so each of you can concentrate on the ladder rungs."

"We have to climb into that hole?" Evina balked. "That's impossible. I can't do it."

"I'm sorry, but it's our only way out. We must descend as quickly as we can, without slipping or stumbling. Maybe Dov can stay near you as you climb down."

Evina gulped and moved closer to Dov. He gave her a reassuring smile that covered his own fear. He appreciated the fact that they were on the verge of death again and wondered if she had the strength to continue. He also looked at his sister with concern. Would the need for survival overcome her fear of dark, constricted spaces?

Jengo continued, "Rely on your sense of touch in the dark. Evina, explain to Saris that I want him to descend first so he can open a maintenance access panel from the inside when he reaches it. This is our only way out of the shaft onto a tower level where we can then take the stairs down. It's approximately two hundred and fifty feet down from here. There's a square door or hatch in the side of the wall that should be evident, even in the dark. Impress on him the importance of taking his time opening the access hatch. The small door was meant to be opened from the other side, so he'll have to keep his balance and force the door open with his bare hands. He may have to do this more than once in our descent if we run into obstacles preventing us from taking the stairs. Pray that the opening is large enough for him to fit through."

Evina explained this to Saris using sign language and he nodded in agreement.

I will do as he said. Saris gave Jengo a nod.

Jengo pointed to where the rungs began along the side of the dirty ascender shaft and watched Saris back down slowly into the darkness. Javak, Kitt, and Yanis followed after him, allowing space between them and Saris. Jengo motioned for Evina to follow closely after Dov. Pele came next in the slow-moving procession. Kaman and then Jengo followed in the rear.

Inside the dark shaft the only sounds were steady, forced breathing and the scrape of feet on the rungs. It smelled like oil, masonry dust, and rust. Progress was slow but methodical as each individual concentrated on the rungs before them and not the plunge to death if they fell. After about twenty minutes, Javak shouted a word that reverberated loudly in the confined tube and had the desired effect. Everyone stopped to grip their handholds tightly. Saris had reached the maintenance door. He opened the door with his bare hands while everyone clutched their nearest hold and waited. Ten minutes later they heard Yanis say jubilantly, "He's through!"

The group descended with more confidence knowing that they could rest and not have to climb back into the ascender shaft. When Jengo folded his body through the small maintenance opening that exited into the open space of the Ministerial section on the 95th level, he found the others sitting or laying on the floor favoring their scraped hands and rubbing exhausted limbs. The unfinished Ministerial section was open to the outside and the breeze was refreshing. It felt good after the stuffy confines of the shaft. It was night and the ghostly alloy skeleton around them was illuminated by light from fires burning across the city.

"That was some workout," said Dov tiredly. "How many times do we have to do that again before we reach the bottom?"

"I'm not certain," replied Jengo. "There's supposed to be a maintenance door into the ascender shaft about every hundred feet, or at least in every section. If we can take the stairs within a sealed section, that'll be to our advantage. I'll see how far we can descend in this section using stairs. Meanwhile, Pele, I want you to take Kaman and search this level, and other levels if necessary, for a crowbar or any other tool that didn't fly away that Saris can use to pry open the doors. I should have thought of that before we started. Judging from the blood on this bent door, he had a rough time of it. The rest of you wait here and regain your strength."

Pele motioned for Kaman to come with him and, as they walked away, Jengo called out: "If you come across food or water, we could use any you find." Pele nodded his agreement and disappeared into the dark, attempting to explain their mission to the young mason using hand gestures.

Evina tore strips of cloth from her embroidered ceremonial robe that was now stained with grease and dirt and tenderly wrapped Saris' bloody hands. She used the cleaner pieces from her clothing without hesitation. It was the only way she could return loving care to her bodyguard for his selfless loyalty to her. With her sensitive touch, she gently cleaned his wounds as best she could. Saris' eyes remained on Evina while she wrapped each of his bloody fingers.

When we get water I will wash the dirt from your cuts, she signed to the hulking man who kneeled before her. *This is the best I can do for now. I wish I could do more for you.* He tried to sign back to her, but she held both his hands in hers.

Later, when Dov thought back to this tender moment between Evina and her servant, he realized that he was in love with this wonderful young lady who had burst into his life only a few weeks before. Now, he didn't want her out of his sight.

Yanis and Kitt sat ten feet away in quiet conversation without thought or care for anyone else. "I don't want to go back into that ascender shaft," Yanis told Kitt, in a low voice so her brother wouldn't hear her. "The dark corridors of the ziggurat were bearable because we could stop and rest. I would have become hysterical with panic if you hadn't been with me, Kitt."

It was as if the two communicated between their hearts without understanding their spoken words. "I'm with you now, aren't I?" he responded. "I'll be only a few feet away when we climb down again—one ladder rung at a time. Think about this: When we reach the ground, we'll go to your father's shop and pick up provisions for the trip. Then we'll go to the boathouse where your family is waiting. After loading the *Dolphin* and casting off for Bosrah, we'll spend the next five or six days together. Think of it as a vacation cruise after weeks of hard work programming the *Cyclone*, running for our lives through that temple labyrinth, and doing some climbing. We can relax on the deck of the boat and you can point out your favorite animals and flowers along the shore. When we reach Bosrah, we can spend as much time together as you want. You'll probably be tired of me by then."

"I don't think I'll ever become tired of you." she replied emotionally. "You've given me some nice things to think about. Promise me that you'll think about us while we climb down in the dark?"

"I promise," Kitt replied softly.

Each understood the sentiments that were exchanged without the need for words. The fact that their hearts were so open to each other was a sign that even the language miracle had not changed how they felt.

When Jengo rejoined the group he had bad news. There were no more access panels in the Ministerial section, which extended down for only ten levels before the barrier with the Guild level. As he suspected, they would have to return to the shaft and climb down once again until they found the next access panel. He hoped that it would be no more than one hundred feet, but he couldn't be certain. Their climb would take them into the Guild section, where they should be able to take stairs the remaining distance to the 52nd level where the Watcher had another method of descent waiting for them.

Pele and Kaman returned with better news. They found a crowbar which they used to break the lock of a tool chest that was bolted to the floor. Besides other tools, they found a jug of water inside. Everyone felt more refreshed after they passed the jug around.

Jengo acknowledged the emotional demands on the group of having to return to the ascender shaft. The distance they would have to cover would probably be more than that of their first trek. He also knew what the Watcher had planned for their descent to the ground from the 52nd level. He thought it best to not tell the others about it until it was time. Some of them might refuse to go further if they knew that even greater danger was involved.

Saris opened the door with his bare hands while
everyone held tightly to the shaft's rungs.

CHAPTER 41

New Babel, One World Tower—Ministerial Level, Ascender Shaft

Before dawn

The descent party prepared itself mentally for another tedious, draining climb down the narrow shaft. Saris was armed with a crowbar, which Pele tied to his waist so he wouldn't drop it. The servant's hands could not withstand opening another access panel without it, although no one doubted his willingness to do so. Kitt whispered reassuring words to Yanis before they climbed back into the dark hole. Dov and Evina were in a hurry to put their arduous climbing behind them. The others followed in resolute silence.

The train of nine climbers lost track of time in the dark tube as the monotony of slowly moving hand over hand caused more exhaustion than expected; the tension and sense of peril never left them. When one paused to rest or catch their breath, the others were forced to wait in the dark and feel the vibrations of the creaking, groaning building. When they caught a glimpse of dawn in a half-finished segment, they realized that they had plodded through much of the night. Progress was slow as they paced every movement of hand and foot. When Javak's disembodied voice brought them to a halt again it was hoarse from fatigue. The single "Snap!" of the access door meant that Saris had easily opened their exit and they were only minutes away from lying on the floor to rest.

The marking beside the panel told them that this was the 77th level. Everyone collapsed on the cool floor.

"Promise me we won't do that again anytime soon," Yanis said to nobody in particular. Every muscle in her hands, arms, back, and legs was screaming from hours of steady exertion.

Jengo's reply was more welcome than a drink of water. "No more climbing, I promise. Now we can walk down twenty-five flights of stairs. How does that sound?"

"Like a blessing!" Evina exclaimed with a short laugh of relief. The others joined in.

Jengo waited for someone to do the math and figure out that their ordeal was far from over. Hearing nothing, he gathered his strength.

"We need to get going. The tower is still shaking and I don't like that. We'll look for more water as we descend. It's getting lighter so we can see where we're going. Are you feeling better now, Yanis."

"Oh, Yes!"

"Sis likes the wide open spaces," Dov said.

"River cruise, here we come!" she announced.

Her uncle was proud of her fortitude. He knew how much she dreaded the confines of the ziggurat corridors; the climb in the dark tube encrusted with dirt, grease, and rust was even more claustrophobic. He only hoped that she and the others would be up to the challenge that awaited them on the 52nd level.

Kaman found another water jug during their descent in the stairwell. It quenched their thirst somewhat, but did nothing to relieve their hunger. Stomachs were growling after almost two days without food and a grueling night of climbing. They needed to reach the ground soon.

When they stepped onto the 52nd level, Jengo led the group toward the side of the tower facing the Euphrates River. The end of a thick wire cable was firmly bolted to a giant girder and curved down and out toward the ground in the far distance. A nearby locker held equipment that the Watcher had left for them. It was time for Jengo to explain the final leg of their escape. It was important that each person understand how the wire slide and braking mechanism worked so they would release their grip at the right time. Too late and they would land in shallow water, or worse, hit the distant shore. Too early and they would fall into the river from a height that would kill them.

The Watcher had tested this method of escape from the tower only once. It offered the benefit of speed but posed fatal risks. He had taken Pele and Jengo aside on the roof to assure them that they had no other options because the tower could collapse at any moment. Jengo agreed that it was only a matter of time before the weakened tower crumpled inward upon itself. They had to reach the ground as fast as possible, and the wire slide was their last hope.

Jengo's exhausted audience listened to his instructions in stunned disbelief. Yanis gripped Kitt's hand even tighter. "I think I've found something I hate worse than climbing inside a dark pipe," she groaned.

When Kaman grasped what they had to do to reach the bottom of the tower he resisted. "This is insane," he grumbled in his language. "Why can't we continue down in the ascender shaft? I'd rather climb back down in the shaft to the Commoner section and then take the stairs to the ground level." He made it clear from shaking his head and backing away that he would not slide from a height of five hundred feet into the river a quarter of a mile away.

"We can't stop Kaman from taking an alternative route back into the ascender tube, but it will take much longer and the building is even more dangerous at these lower levels. Girders in the open areas are loose and could buckle at any time from the uneven weight above. Fortunately, nothing structural had fallen down the ascender shaft. If it had, anyone in the shaft would have been killed instantly."

"I'm glad you didn't share that possibility with us while we were still climbing," Dov said. "We were terrified enough contemplating a long fall into the basement."

The strain showed even on Jengo's face as he tried to be realistic. "The longer we stay in the tower the more chance we have of being killed *when*, not *if*, this damaged building collapses. The longer we stand here talking, the more time we're wasting. We need to get off the tower *now*. I'm sorry, but this is the only way."

"Show us how to work the Watcher's braking mechanism so we can go." Dov gestured and handed one of the mechanisms to Kaman, who shook his head and refused to touch it. He wouldn't be coming with them. He quickly shook Dov's hand and mouthed words of well wishes to the others. His grim smile as he lowered himself into the ascender shaft was the last they saw of their friend.

Jengo placed six braking devices from the locker in a line on the floor. With six devices for eight people, they would have to pair up and hope that their combined weight would not make the brake ineffective. Jengo and Pele each turned one over in their hands.

"This device seems simple enough. What do you think, Pele?"

"It's functional. In spite of its simplicity and light weight, it'll hold two people for that short distance. We'll be going down at a steep angle close to the building, so it won't be stressed with our full weight until the curve flattens out over the river, where it could bounce up and down with the load of our weights. I'm not sure what'll happen when several of us descend on the wire close together."

"That's what I think too," replied Jengo. "Now, you'll need to judge for yourselves when to release the brake and drop into the river. You'll have a split second to make that decision. Too late and you might hit the river bank; too early and you'll have a long drop in a free fall."

"Some choice," Yanis remarked.

"Just think of the wide open space while you fly over the river," her brother reminded her.

"I need to make sure Kitt understands the instructions," she replied. Yanis took Kitt aside and explained the braking mechanism and its use as thoroughly as she could.

"Saris should go down the slide alone first, if he's willing. Then he can help those who follow if they need help in the water. I assume he can swim?" Jengo asked Evina.

"Yes. I'll explain everything to him."

"Good. Then I want you to go with Dov and Kitt will go with Yanis. If I'm not mistaken, you wouldn't have it any other way." He smiled at the two couples.

"Finally, Pele and Javak will each use their own sliding mechanism. I'll go last. Any questions?"

"Yes," Dov said. "What do we do when we're in the river? Where do we go?"

"The Watcher will be waiting for us under the bridge on the New Babel side of the river. Make your way there and he'll escort us as a group through the city to our homes. We'll rejoin our families and prepare to leave the city."

Evina explained the final phase of their escape to Saris and he readily agreed to do as instructed. She inspected his hands wrapped in bloody bandages.

Can you hold the brake long enough? she asked. He nodded and picked up the mechanism. After attaching it to the wire cable, he stepped to the edge of the 52nd level. The cable was two inches in diameter and more than strong enough to hold his weight, which was equal to that of two normal adults. The thick twisted wire descended over the river in a gentle arc and disappeared into the distance. He looked back at the group and Jengo nodded. Saris stepped from the floor's edge. The wire cable sagged only slightly under his heavy bulk as he was whisked along with hardly a sound. The oiled wheels of the braking mechanism emitted a brief whine that was lost in the breeze. Everyone watched him become a small speck in the distance within seconds. When he was over the river he released his hold on the brake, separated himself from the wire, and dropped while his momentum continued to carry him forward. They saw his splash, but he was too far away to see in the water.

"We'll have to assume that he made it alright. Now, we can't stand here waiting for each person to be in the water before the next leaves. I'll wait ten seconds and send the next person or pair down the wire. Is everyone ready?"

"As ready as ever," Evina said. Dov hooked the brake to the cable and walked toward the edge of the floor. Evina stood behind him and put her arms around his neck.

"You'll choke me that way," he commented. "Climb on my back as if I'm giving you a piggyback ride. You can grip me with your arms and legs that way. When we start dropping from the cable into the river you can let go."

Evina did as he suggested. Dov carried her to the edge and looked down. "Hold tight," he said as he stepped over the edge. Kitt and Yanis were ready to follow. They stood at the edge, waiting for Jengo to give Kitt's arm a slap. As soon as he did, Kitt and Yanis slid down the wire.

The wind was fierce as they picked up speed. It felt as if they were dropping straight down. The two couples saw the city pass in a blur below them. Kitt looked at Dov and Evina racing ahead of them. He concentrated on estimating when to release his frozen grip on the handles. Behind him, Yanis was quiet but held on to him with all her might. Whether from her hold on him or from sheer terror, he could barely breathe. He pressed the brake as they passed over the edge of the river to slow their descent. Immediately the mechanism emitted a shrill shriek of protest. He felt the heat on his hands but dared not look up. From what he saw of the couple ahead of him, he assumed that the metal-on-metal friction was showering sparks and charred wood from the brake. The thought that sparks might catch Yanis' hair on fire broke his concentration. He saw Dov release his hold. He must have held on slightly longer with one hand, because the two spun in midair as they plummeted to the river's surface. Kitt would release at the same spot, but try to let go with both hands at the same time. Then a stray thought entered his mind while he was timing his drop. What if he landed on top of them? He released his grip as soon as he realized that they would all be hurt if he and Yanis fell on top of the other pair.

Fortunately for all of them, they did not collide, but Kitt's release was sooner than it should have been. They fell from the cable from a height of more than sixty feet and slammed hard into the surface of the water. Saris was helping Dov and Evina swim to shore when he saw the second couple fall. Evina signaled for Saris to help them.

When Saris reached the spot where Kitt and Yanis hit the water, he found nothing but a pool of foaming water. He dove underwater and surfaced within seconds holding Kitt.

Meanwhile, the others were dropping into the river around them. The Watcher stood under the bridge waving to them.

Dov swam to Saris, who was holding Kitt while he coughed up water. He had had the breath knocked out of him from the impact.

"Yanis!" shouted Dov. "Yanis!" His sister was still underwater. He and Saris dove down to look for her, but they came up gasping for air. "Yanis!" Kitt called out between coughs of river water.

Dov, Pele, and Saris searched for her while Kitt treaded water and caught his breath. They realized that they were drifting downstream and had lost track of where they had last seen her.

A deep whoosh of air and a cough startled them. They turned to see Yanis lifted out of the water by a giant white porpoise. The baiji gently balanced Yanis on his back. Dov took her in his arms and checked her breathing. She was alive!

"Don't ever do that to me again, Sis." Her brother said through his tears.

Yanis blinked in the sunlight and coughed up water. "I promise," she croaked.

They took turns towing Yanis to shore against the current while she floated on her back. The baiji had disappeared. When they arrived under the bridge the others picked her up and rested her on the ground. The Watcher covered her shaking form with his iridescent cloak.

"You're safe here for now. I have food and water and you should rest until you're ready to walk across the city to your homes. There's mass chaos, looting, and destruction everywhere. We'll need to be careful since the confusion of languages has turned people into violent mobs. It seems that those who speak differently, no matter their need of medical assistance or helplessness, are attacked or robbed. We must stay together when we're on the move." Those who had met the Watcher before noted that his self-confidence and optimism were shaken.

"It's a miracle that the baiji was there just when Yanis needed him," Dov commented.

"I wouldn't call it a supernatural miracle," the Watcher said. "I instructed him and his two sisters to be watching for anyone in need. I trained them myself for rescue, and . . . other things." His enigmatic allusion went unnoticed. He changed the subject.

"For now, rest and gather your strength. We have a journey across the city ahead of us. Then you must leave for the *Dolphin* as soon as is practical. You cannot remain in Old or New Babel any longer," he insisted.

CHAPTER 42

Old Town Bridge Between New and Old Babel

The eight survivors from the crippled One World Tower were anxious to find Ash, join their families, and leave the city. They were tired from their arduous climb down the dark ascender shaft, the heart-stopping quarter-mile descent on the wire slide, a long drop into the Euphrates River and near drowning, and the swim to shore. They had to put their ordeal behind them now. They were still in danger as long as gangs of looters roamed the city plundering homes and businesses. The Watcher left their company with the assurance that he would see them again. He urged them to go to their homes and Pele's machine shop to retrieve any last articles as quickly as possible. They would find Ash there waiting for them. They should waste no time gathering only those essential supplies they could carry on the long walk to the boathouse where their families had gathered. He noted that the river voyage to Bosrah would be one-way—they would never see Babel again. Nobody raised objections to that.

When the group departed their safe haven under the bridge they could not believe the destruction across the city. Looming high above them, the tattered One World Tower was a silent reflection of the mayhem that clogged the streets. Staying close together, they shook their heads at the frantic questions posed to them by those they encountered along the way. The unintelligible questions were aimed at finding out if they were understood. Those who spoke the same language were forming into clans. They clutched looted supplies and valuables in their rush from the city. Others, alone or couples, were distraught to the point of madness when they could find no one else who understood them.

"Is this what we've come to as a civilization?" Evina questioned.

Nobody ventured an answer until Jengo spoke as they continued to walk. "We should have seen this coming. God's command to spread out and populate the earth was disobeyed almost from the time our forefathers stepped off the ark. We're no exception," he said, referring to their little group. "When the Triad persuaded people to stay here and build a unified city they even convinced us that it served the higher good of mankind. Some, speaking for myself anyway, thought that God's command could be taken lightly or postponed while we followed our own interests. I should have refused when Magus first demanded that I help the Triad build a tower."

"All believers who decided to stay in Babel can agree with you now, brother." Pele included himself and his family in Jengo's admission. "Now, here we are. Somehow, God has exempted us from this madness of confusing languages. We've held together amicably even though some of us speak different languages. I can only conclude that He has a purpose for us." Pele looked at Javak. "My prayer is that Ash is safe and that he'll join us momentarily."

A block from Pele's machine shop they noticed that the building was only slightly damaged. Windows were broken and roof tiles were missing, but it seemed that the structure was generally intact. The same could not be said for many of the buildings on their block. Multi-level apartments, built with brick and mortar but without an alloy framework, had toppled from the high wind. Ash stood in the doorway guarding the shop with a thick wooden staff. When he saw them he waved his crude weapon with a broad smile on his face. Shadow stood on alert next to him. Javak ran and embraced his nephew.

"Ashaz, are you all right?" Javak did not expect him to understand but hoped he would sense his concern.

"Yes, Uncle Javak! I'm well. I understand you perfectly!"

Javak, Kitt, and Ash laughed heartily in the face of all that had happened, happy to find one more person who spoke their language. This alone bound them together as much as their common blood.

Ash tried to explain to Pele that his wife and young son were safe. He gestured toward the river and made motions indicating that they had escaped to the *Dolphin's* boathouse. Pele prayed that Kerin and Maasi would share his language too since that seemed to be God's miraculous pattern among families.

Turning to his uncle Javak, who understood his language, Ash told him what he had accomplished. "I helped Benji gather Pele and Jengo's families and a few of their belongings and sent them with food supplies to the *Dolphin* before I realized that the city had erupted into so much violence. The animals and carts were intact, so I thought it best that they carry all the food that they could for our trip to Bosrah. Dov had talked earlier of going to Bosrah after he rescued Evina so I figured that's what I should do. I hoped that all of you would somehow return and we could leave together tonight on the *Dolphin*. The destruction from the asteroid and the pandemonium in the city only confirmed my decision. Shadow and I have been here repelling looters ever since." The young man brandished the stave in mock defense. Shadow was bored.

"You did the right thing, son. I'm proud of you," his uncle pronounced. "Now we must gather our things and join our families at the boathouse!"

No sooner had Javak spoken than a series of deep, muffled blasts echoed across the city from the direction of the tower.

"What was that?" Dov asked.

Thump! Thump! Thump! The sound resonated in the air.

Pele was the first to speculate. "Sounds like explosions. My guess is that the boilers in the tower are bursting."

"Very possible," Jengo replied. "If the boilers were left unattended and the automatic feeding mechanisms were damaged, then anything could happen. Ash would know best, but I'm guessing that the disruptive repercussions of the asteroid's brush with the atmosphere on the basement machinery rooms and the tower structure probably drove everyone out of the building. All those giant machines, some fatally damaged, have been spinning out of control."

As if in answer to his comment, one big explosion, louder this time, resounded across the city. All eyes were on the black smoke and white vapor that billowed from behind low buildings between them and the base of the tower. The tower itself, shining in the sunlight, stood out against a deep blue sky. A single, enormous burst of smoke and vapor, followed by a lingering rumble, signaled the death of the One World Tower. The once-great icon of engineering had become a battered, stricken shell. Bricks and mortar fell from the exterior finish; gaping holes checkered each flat surface of the finished walls. They saw girders slowly bend in the mid-levels as the top-heavy stone ziggurat slowly pulled the top over. Weakened foundation supports buckled under the weight of the unbalanced structure to bend its one hundred-twenty levels in a slow, almost graceful, death descent. From their vantage point halfway across the city, the onlookers watched the mighty structure collapse into the city streets. Then the roar of thousands of tons of twisted alloy, glass, stone, and brick swept over them. The sound was followed a minute later by a blast of wind and dust that pushed them against the wall of the house. A column of smoke and dust rose into the sky where mankind's proud creation once dominated the skyline. The breeze dispersed all that remained of the tower while the group stood speechless. Like the city of Babel and the Triad, the One World Tower instantly had become a relic of the past.

One by one they walked slowly to the machine shop to gather clothing and essentials for their escape from the city. Pele stood before the planetary visualizer for a final, sentimental look at one of his technical masterpieces.

"It seems like ages ago that I visited this shop and sat in that machine," Evina said softly to Dov. "Somehow the things that held my interest back then don't seem as important now. Will I ever be the same?" she wondered.

"Would you want to be the same?" Pele asked.

"God changed my life because of you, Dov and Yanis. I'll never be the same. Now I'm ready to start a new life. Do you think that's possible?" Evina fought back tears.

"I knew you would join us the day you stepped through that door." Pele felt himself overcome with emotion. "You, once the future high priestess of Ishtar, speak the same language as our family, that should say something about God's purpose, don't you think?" He led Evina outside where the rest of the refugees waited with bundles over their shoulders. Yanis found a change of clothing for Evina so she could dress in rough clothes like the others. Pele gave Evina's hand to Dov and stepped back into his shop. Shadow angled for attention by squeezing between Dov and Evina. After a brief glance around the room, Pele closed the door, turned his back on the city of Babel, and the ragged band began their trek to the *Dolphin* where the clockmaker hoped they would finally find safety.

CHAPTER 43

Euphrates River, *Dolphin* Boathouse

When the bedraggled survivors of the tower finally reached the riverside boathouse after a two-hour walk, they should not have been surprised by the damage they saw to the sheds and surrounding forest from by the asteroid's shock wave and wind. From what they could tell, the boathouse sustained minor damage and the *Dolphin* seemed unharmed. However, the area was deserted. Where were Pele's wife, Kerin, and their son, Maasi? Where was Jengo's family? Where was Benji?

Soon a half-dozen small children ran from behind a dilapidated storage shed toward Pele and Jengo. "Papa! Papa!" they shouted. Benji stepped around the corner of the shed to greet the new arrivals.

The tearful families clung together as they walked to the *Dolphin's* boathouse. Pele wanted to see if the watercraft had sustained any damage. The flat roof of the boathouse had not collapsed, which was a relief. Unfortunately, however, the magnetic storm might have caused internal damage to the vapor engine boiler and drive mechanism. If it required extensive repairs, they might not be able to leave for days, if not weeks.

Pele noticed that Benji held back from the rest of the party, who were playing with the children or exploring other sheds. "Come with me, Benji. Show me what you've done since you've been here. We must see if the *Dolphin* needs repairs." Pele had forgotten about the confusion of languages.

Benji stood motionless and pointed to his ear, and then to his mouth. His forlorn face showed a combination of fear and sadness. He had seen the hatred in passersby when he could not understand them or they him. He was afraid that Pele, in spite of being the father of his friends Dov and Yanis, would not allow him to join them on the *Dolphin* because of the language divide.

Pele walked to Benji and gently placed a hand on his shoulder. "You cannot understand me, but that doesn't matter. Thank you for protecting my family. Now, come with us," he took the young mechanic by the arm. Pele's kindly tone was unmistakable. Benji broke into a smile of relief. The two entered the boathouse together to inspect the twin-hulled craft riding evenly in the water. From their initial inspection as they walked along the dock, Pele saw no visible damage to the *Dolphin's* hulls or upper deck. A few rafters had fallen on the smoke stack, and the small crane on the deck used to lift cargo was broken, but fixable. Pele's concern turned to the more intricate metal mechanisms: the vapor boiler or engine might have been shaken loose from their mountings; internal tubing could be bent or cracked; metal objects could have been twisted or controls damaged.

Mechanical components were Benji's specialty. He led Pele to the main firebox and boiler, where he pointed out their large mounting bolts, which remained solidly intact. A smile and a thumbs up told Pele that this was a major obstacle averted. Benji wordlessly pointing out repairs he'd made to the boiler tubing that carried high-pressure vapor to the pistons and then returned low-pressure condensed water back to the boiler. Cracks were now firmly welded where the machinery had lifted and twisted from the magnetic forces of the iron asteroid. Finally, he showed Pele that the heavy connecting rods between the piston and the paddles were unharmed. Benji could not express it in words, but he convinced Pele that the vessel's essential machinery was ready to be powered up. He would have to test pressures before they could depart, but Benji hoped that it was only a matter of an hour or two once he received the go-ahead. He was as anxious as anyone to leave Babel behind.

Pele expressed his satisfaction with a broad smile and a handshake. He was pleased at the work Benji had done. He was a fine vapor mechanic. So far, language was not a problem, since the mechanical background of the two was so similar.

Pele pointed to the boiler firebox, mimicked flames with his hands, and Benji nodded enthusiastically before stepping down into the below-deck boiler compartment to prepare the fire and attend to a few minor repairs that could be done while the engine heated.

Jengo had been the group's logical leader when they were in the tower. As its chief engineer, he was the most knowledgeable about its construction and layout. Now, in the nautical element of the *Dolphin* and its small vapor engine, Pele assumed charge of the group as the vessel's captain. He was confident that they could reach Bosrah in a matter of five or six days. He anticipated no further problems if the machinery operated properly. He called everyone together while Benji worked on the boiler.

"We have much to do before we can depart; there are only five hours until darkness settles in. I want to push away from the dock before dark so we will distance ourselves from the city and be several miles down the river when we have to anchor for the night. I'll assign each of you—including the children—important duties. I wish to leave as soon as Benji has the boiler running and pressurized. Before I give you your assignments and turn you loose, does anyone have any questions?"

"Will Benji be coming with us?" Yanis asked. "We've known him from school for years and he helped us greatly with the *Cyclone*. He has no family that I know of. Can I ask him to come with us, if he wants to?"

"By all means," Pele responded enthusiastically. "It's difficult to communicate with him about non-mechanical things, but he seems eager to help us. He'll be part of our family, if he wishes to come."

"Why can't we communicate with him by writing?" asked Maasi.

Pele was glad to hear that his eight-year old was thinking. "That's a good question. I had assumed that the miracle of languages effected written as well as spoken communication. Why don't you write something and see if he can read it?"

Maasi ran off in search of writing materials.

The group who understood his speech listened to Pele's instructions about preparing their expedition to Bosrah. Those who understood would do their best to explain themselves to the others through pantomime gestures. There were too many people and supplies for the *Dolphin's* limited carrying capacity if they included enough black rock fuel to take them to Bosrah. He pointed out a barge that was towed behind them when they made long expeditions. The vessel was a rectangular, flat box, the same length as the *Dolphin*, divided into forward and aft compartments. Fully loaded, it rode low in the water and slowed their progress significantly. Its forward compartment had to be emptied of black rock and washed out so it could carry perishables and other supplies. A canvas tarpaulin protected supplies from sun and rain. The *Dolphin* itself would be loaded with as much fuel as safely practical. Pele didn't want to stop along the Euphrates to cut firewood, so he would deal with any need for more fuel once they arrived in Bosrah. When they stopped for the night they would make eating and sleeping arrangements, offload more fuel from the barge to the *Dolphin* for the next day, and shift crew duties.

Maasi returned before the group broke up in its different directions. "Nope," he said glumly. "He can't read anything." He held up a child's book. "I can't read this either."

"That explains something else then." Dov said. "I suspected that if our own original spoken language had changed, then our written language would have changed too. Since the world's original language is gone forever, every book written since the Great Flood is worthless!"

"Including the Book of Adam?" Maasi asked.

"I'm afraid so," Dov replied.

The significance of this hung in the air, but they didn't have time to dwell on it now. Pele motioned for everyone to go about their duties. They went in different directions to prepare for departure.

Yanis and Dov left to find Benji and persuade him to stay with them. Meanwhile, everyone worked to load the barge with all available supplies before sunset. Pele was satisfied with the boiler's operation after he backed the craft out of the boathouse and turned it around in the river. A strong cable attached the barge to the *Dolphin's* stern and they pulled away from the shore as the sun set. They were not sorry to see the city of Babel disappear behind them forever.

CHAPTER 44

New Babel, Euphrates River—Royal Navy Shipyard

Three days after the Dolphin's departure

When Pele's *Dolphin* eased into the Euphrates River it was a joyous family affair; Nimrod's departure from Babel on the *HRS Savage* was quite the opposite.

Nimrod still considered himself not only master of his ship and its crew, but also king over everyone and everything on earth. The crew were his "subjects" and he lorded over them; he knew no other way to rule than by brute force. He screamed commands to the crew who understood nothing that he said but nonetheless scurried about, forced to guess what he meant and comply instantly. The normal crew's complement was close to one hundred sailors. Less than forty remained aboard after the collapse of the tower and evacuation of the city. When Nimrod coldly executed two deck hands for standing dumfounded when he issued a command that they didn't understand, the message to the rest of the crew was clear: action—any action—was better than paralysis. An unfortunate soul who attempted to desert the ship received a similar punishment. Nimrod was king of his ship and ruled with an iron fist. It mattered not that, when he screamed maniacally, none of his crew understood him. They were obligated, under pain of death, to anticipate and comply with his every directive.

The royal cruiser was eventually loaded with wealth and provisions from the palace to bolster Nimrod's position as king. Although his family occupied luxurious staterooms below deck and were oblivious to what happened above, the *HRS Savage* was still run as a royal warship. Its two bow chaser cannons were capable of firing projectiles almost half a mile. Nimrod loved gunpowder, invented by one of his royal metallurgists, as a powerful offensive resource whose formula he reserved for himself. With it, he had the ability to destroy anyone or anything in his path.

The king himself charted a course down the Euphrates River to the island of Bosrah and showed it to Captain Ghamal. The cautious master of the ship followed Nimrod's gestures with agreeable nods of his head. He clearly grasped their destination but could only speculate what Nimrod intended to do when he reached it. Of course, he said nothing verbally for fear that Nimrod would think he objected and end his life. Like all the others on the ship, he had been intimidated into submission. He would agree with anything that Nimrod said or did, but would still attempt to not endanger the ship or the lives of others in the process.

Under Ghamal's supervision, the *HRS Savage* pulled away from the naval base before sunset. In spite of the crew's mistreatment by Nimrod, those who remained were professional sailors in the king's small navy. They observed proper naval courtesy by raising the king's blue streaming pendant as a dozen deck crewmen lined the railing in full uniform. The fact that nobody on shore paid them any attention didn't matter—navy ritual and custom were not to be neglected. The officer of the deck, a young lieutenant, rendered the proper salute to a gap in the skyline where the iconic One World Tower used to stand while the ship's propellers churned the muddy bottom and the grey warship chugged noisily south trailing a dense, black cloud of soot and burning sparks from the vapor engine's twin boilers. As he guided the ship into the center of the river, Captain Ghamal wondered how he would convince Nimrod that he must moor the *Savage* for the night less than one hour after leaving the dock. He braced himself for another life or death confrontation with the mercurial tyrant.

BOOK III

The Dispersion

"So the LORD scattered them abroad from there over the face of all the earth, and they ceased building the city. Therefore its name is called Babel, because there the LORD confused the language of all the earth; and from there the LORD scattered them abroad over the face of all the earth."
Genesis 11:8-9

CHAPTER 45

Euphrates River, Pele's *Dolphin*

The crew manning the *Dolphin* that day were Pele, Benji, Jengo, and Javak. Pele wanted as much engineering help as possible, at least on the first watch, in the event the vapor boiler or other engine parts needed adjustment or repair. As it turned out, Benji had done splendid repair work, and the ship moved easily all day through the deep channel in the middle of the Euphrates. The barge did slow them to half their maximum speed, but the strain on the engine and propellers was tolerable.

The expedition was blessed with good weather. That evening, women prepared dinner on a makeshift black rock stove next to the smoke stack on the *Dolphin's* deck. Saris and Ash had piled boxes of supplies to form separate sleeping areas. Evina and Yanis helped with the meal, but Evina's ineptitude at food preparation was evident given her upbringing as daughter of the temple high priest. She had no idea where food came from or what was done to it before it arrived on a golden platter and was offered to her by a servant. Kerin and Jengo's wife, Adina, reassured her that she would learn in due time. What a relief that she spoke the same language as Pele's and Jengo's families. To her it was a miracle of God that she, an outsider of aristocratic, pagan ancestry, was so accepted by them. When she commented on this to Kerin and Adina, the two women surprised her. They had been praying for her since Dov and Yanis first met with her weeks ago and learned of her interest in the Living God of the universe. They called her "sister," and she could hardly refrain from welling with tears at such a demonstration of love for her.

Later, she and Dov stood at the boat's railing and watched the sunset. "Why haven't we seen the asteroid since it passed?" Evina asked. "From what I remember of its path, it should have been visible again even though it departed earth's orbit. Have you see it, Dov?"

"Like you, I was concentrating on other things," he replied. "Things like climbing inside a dirty, dark tube, holding on to a slide for dear life, crashing into a river, not drowning, fishing my sister out of the water, dodging mobs of crazy people. No, I hadn't noticed an asteroid," he joked.

"You're making fun of me!"

"I'm not even thinking of that asteroid now. I'm admiring how nice you look with your hair blowing in your face and dressed in my sister's clothes. You're prettier than the sunset."

Evina smiled at Dov, then huffed, "Well. I'm still an astronomer and I hope we see *my* asteroid again." She warmed when Dov put his arm around her and they watched stars appear in the darkening western sky. "Will you build me a telescope someday?"

"I'll do anything for you, Evina," Dov said softly.

Yanis and Kitt watched the couple from the other side of the deck. They could only guess what was being said as they continued their own quiet conversation through sign language and simple phrases they taught each other.

The *Dolphin* anchored for the night in the middle of the river, where they would be safe from possible intruders, human or animal. After dinner, Pele assigned a watch in case other boats came upon them during the night. The extended family, including Shadow, who had settled into a dog's routine on the boat, turned in after a welcomed day of fresh air and sunshine.

Euphrates River, Chief Magician's Fishing Boat

The fishing vessel carrying Magus slowed when the wind died at sunset. Although he wanted to drift during the night, the boat had already run aground near the shore several times because of the weight of the gold secreted in its hull. The chief magician was not used to being frustrated by things outside his control like random shifts of wind or current. He demanded instant compliance with his every wish. His will had been thwarted by the sailboat's equipment and the river's currents since beginning his voyage. His lofty title of "Chief Magician" meant nothing and he would have to get used to it, at least for now; he was an ordinary man alone in a fishing boat. Still, he thought, when he eventually reached his outpost downstream, his servants would have food and clothing ready for him. He would rest from his ordeal and make plans for a conquest that would propel him back to fame and fortune.

He drew comfort from the knowledge that a fortune in gold coins rested under his feet. He lifted a floorboard to once again admire the rows of bright coins that extended the length of the vessel. The sailboat was so low in the water that moderate ripples sometimes splashed water over the sides onto his feet. The craft was difficult to maneuver, but he didn't care. He had enough wealth to begin another civilization even if his subjects did not speak his language. Everyone understood the language of gold!

He pulled his boat onto a sandbar for the night where he ate hungrily from his meager provisions. He curled his sunburned frame on the bottom of the boat covered only by a thin cloak. He pressed his palm against the thin slab of wood that laid between him and his treasure.

CHAPTER 46

Euphrates River, Pele's *Dolphin*

The twin hulls of the *Dolphin* cut smoothly through the deep muddy water of the Euphrates' main channel. The breeze from their movement was refreshing for those who were still recovering from their nightmare in the tower and escape from Babel. None of them missed life in the busy city. They looked forward to whatever God had for them in Bosrah or wherever He led them. The boat forged ahead at its best speed towing the barge. The vapor engine performed flawlessly.

While Evina changed bandages on her bodyguard's injured hands during the day, an idea occurred to her. "Dov, what do you think of my asking Saris to teach sign language to Benji? Do you think it would help?"

"That's a great idea! Saris is still not well enough to shovel fuel into the boiler, so he has the time, and Benji is off his shift now. Why don't you get them together?" Evina brought Benji over to where Saris sat in the shade. She gestured for Benji to sit down and she signed to her faithful bodyguard.

Can you teach Benji your signs?

I will try, Miss. Is he deaf and mute also? I watch his lips, but their movement does not make sense as it does when I watch yours and some others.

Evina was puzzled when she realized that Saris also understood the common language of Pele, Jengo, and their clan, even though he could not speak it. The purpose of the differences of languages was mystifying. That's why it's called a miracle, she concluded.

He hears and speaks, Evina signed, *but he uses a different . . . tongue.* She realized that there was no word for "language" in signing or hand gestures. She continued, *He must learn to sign as if he were a little child. If he is willing, can you do that?*

I will do my best, Miss. I believe he is already interested in how we speak with our hands.

Evina was satisfied that the young mechanic and her hulking bodyguard could work out something. By now she was not surprised to see Shadow carefully watching their hands move in sign language almost as if he was learning too. She left them and joined Dov, who had watched from a distance.

"Why did God change us from one common language to many languages?" Evina asked. This had been bothering her since they were confronted with the miracle on the roof of the tower.

"One universal language was so convenient and efficient," she continued. "Now everything is complicated and confusing. It'll be more difficult for people to get along now that we can't interact freely and share our ideas and feelings." The young astronomer's analytical mind was attempting to find a logical explanation for the myriad of languages that now divided mankind.

"The asteroid's gone. I've been looking for it. It's completely disappeared, which violates all my knowledge of gravity and orbital mechanics. Then there's the chaos caused by the languages. I thought all family units spoke the same language, but obviously that's not always the case. Why do you and I understand each other even though we're not related? Saris can read your lips and understand you, but not Benji or Kitt. Why? How?"

Dov had his theory, but it wasn't thought through completely. "I'm puzzled too about why and how all this happened. Here's my best guess: the asteroid came out of nowhere; I assume it was guided by God to pass precisely overhead at an exact time. It completely obscured the sun at exactly noon. That thing must have been guided by God to teach us something—maybe to turn our attention to Him."

"How could an iron sphere cause this jumble of languages?"

"Oh, the asteroid wasn't the *cause* of the languages. Suppose God wanted civilization to turn to Him for salvation from annihilation and to not trust the cults and Babel's so-called gods. He certainly demonstrated to everyone that the gods have no power compared to His omnipotence. What happened on the tower ziggurat and throughout the city was final proof that civilization had digressed to where it was before the Great Flood. God had to do something about it. He didn't cause another worldwide flood—He promised that He'd never destroy mankind that way again."

"Why use a miracle like confusing languages instead of some other worldwide destructive event? The asteroid could have destroyed all but a handful of people who could start over again like Noah and his family."

Dov warmed to her speculation. "I'm guessing that He used this unique worldwide miracle to force people apart. Remember, we saw the divisive results on the rooftop and when we walked through the city. People ran away from each other and away from the city as fast as they could in every direction. Instead of remaining together as one government, one economy, one religion, they were finally doing what God commanded them to do after the Flood."

"Why didn't more people die? You carried me inside the black ziggurat just in time. My father and brother died but I didn't. We could have all been climbing down inside the tower when it collapsed." Evina struggled to understand why some perished and others were spared.

"The fact that we were not consumed is because of God's mercy and longsuffering. We didn't deserve to be shown the Watcher's way of escape but God chose to do so. I don't understand why some were not hurt and others suffered. I know this: God is a righteous judge and His ways are always perfect."

Dov paused to catch his breath, and then continued. "A second purpose comes to my mind, which we have already seen. The world was moving toward your father's ideal of a one world religion. God may have foreseen that those of us who trust in Him would gradually be influenced by a manmade, global, false religion. We were already feeling its effects by being surrounded by Babel's pagan culture. I think, and this is just speculation, that God acted to protect His children from the powerful attraction of a one world religious system that He knew would draw us away from Him."

"If that's the case," Evina observed, "then I'm thankful to God for loving us so much that He would protect us from that influence."

"The confusion of languages, combined with the destruction in the city and the scattering of the population, should put an end to the one world religion. When we get to Bosrah I hope we'll find unity around the One True God that transcends our different languages." Dov put his arm around Evina's shoulders. "I'm glad that you're now part of our family, which explains why we're of the same language. That's a miracle in itself, don't you think?"

"Yes. What you've said may be speculative, but it makes sense to me." Evina thought she could see why everything had happened to them. "When I studied the heavens, I knew God had to be the Creator of everything. You and Yanis helped me to grow in my understanding of God and to see my need to trust Him with my life. I was still strongly influenced by my father and his beliefs. If the asteroid and confusion of languages hadn't happened, I don't know how I would have been able to resist him and my brother. I might have found it easier to join them than stand for what I knew to be true."

The couple watched the river and landscape of the shore slide by as Pele prepared to anchor for the night.

While they shoveled black rock from the barge to the *Dolphin* after dinner, Dov debated in his mind what he had seen earlier in the day. It was dark by the time Pele turned the boiler down for the night and they washed the soot off. Rather than trouble the family with his concern, he asked his father if they could talk privately. The *Dolphin* was tied alongside the barge, so they climbed over the railings and walked to the bow away from the others to check the anchor chain.

"I saw something today that's been bothering me. Rather than alarm anyone over nothing, I thought I'd at least mention it to you." Dov wondered if he had imagined things.

"Go ahead, son. It sounds serious, but whatever it is, the Lord's in control of everything."

"Before I started my shift this afternoon I thought I saw a column of black smoke on the horizon. At first I though it might have been from fires in Babel but we're too far away. It looked like black rock smoke from a ship's vapor engine. Could that be possible?"

Pele's forehead wrinkled. He peered into the darkness along the riverbank. "If it's a black rock smoke column," he said slowly, "then there's only one explanation—one of Nimrod's battle cruisers." His frown creased further. "You saw only one column of smoke?" he asked his son.

"Yes, I think so. It was very far away. I can't be absolutely certain. Why would a battle cruiser be on the river? Where would it be going? Unless . . ."

"I can't say for certain. If it's a battle cruiser, it'll eventually catch up with us. I'm familiar with the two ships in the royal fleet and both are fast, with formidable military weapons. Whether Nimrod is on board, or else sailors from Babel have commandeered it, we're very vulnerable. For now we won't mention any of this to the others. I'll climb up the smoke stack first thing in the morning before the boiler is lit to see if I can spot anything. Unfortunately, if we see their black rock smoke, then they'll see ours. If they haven't seen us yet, they might not be running at their full speed and we'll have time to maintain our distance and figure something out. If they make a determined effort to dash for us at maximum speed, then they could catch us tomorrow night or the next day. Get some rest tonight and we'll check at first light."

Pele walked wearily toward the men's sleeping area followed by his son. Dov's father looked like he had aged ten years in the past week.

≈ ≈

When Pele scanned the northern horizon at dawn the next morning, he saw puffs of black smoke rising above the trees in the far distance. Now he was certain that it was one of Nimrod's vapor-powered cruisers. Like the *Dolphin*, the cruiser had probably anchored for the night rather than hazard unseen sandbars and other river obstructions in the dark. Pele's estimate was that they had two days, three at the most, before they were overtaken. He hoped that tall cypress trees along the shore would obscure their smoke for now. When they entered the Euphrates delta, with its low mangrove trees and vast expanse of grass, their black smoke would be impossible to miss.

CHAPTER 47

Euphrates River, Pele's *Dolphin*

Afternoon

Javak noticed the dark plume of smoke on the horizon. Pele and Dov had been looking behind the *Dolphin* as it made progress downstream toward its destination, which was still three days away. While it was Pele's desire to not worry the other passengers, Javak shouted and pointed at the smoke, more distinct above distant trees, and this drew everyone's attention and heightened their anxiety in three languages. Javak and Kitt apparently debated about the source of the smoke, but could not fully comprehend what Pele told them.

Finally, Dov got the attention of the adults and gathered them around to draw pictograms to explain what the smoke meant. He asked Jengo to sketch a picture of Nimrod's battle cruiser. Then, Dov spread out a chart of the Euphrates River. He showed them the *Dolphin's* position and the probable course of Nimrod's ship. The chart of the ever-changing delta was far from exact, but its labyrinth of channels contained the solution to their predicament. Using a pencil, he sketched on the chart a plan to stop the approaching cruiser.

Each year the Euphrates and Tigris rivers flooded with water from the rain and snow in mountains a thousand miles to the north. Their banks were especially prone to being eroded and replaced with sandbars, sunken debris, and new islands every year. After the Tigris joined the Euphrates to form one massive river more than one mile across in some places, its banks broadened into a wide, flat alluvial plain. Before meeting the Southern Sea, the Euphrates River transformed itself into countless meandering channels dotted with islands and edged by mangrove, cypress, and other trees whose loose roots lived partly in soil and partly in water. The river delta grew larger each year by depositing shifting silt and debris that defied precise mapping. Pele's chart showed vague channels with dotted markings to illustrate a maze of shallow, twisting canals. When the river reached the Southern Sea, the delta turned into a shallow tidal expanse of mud and silt divided by a single main channel.

Dov's drawing on the chart was enough to satisfy Javak, Kitt, and Ash for the moment. They still felt helpless by their inability to communicate precisely, but they also knew Pele, Jengo, and Dov. Satisfied that Dov would come up with a clever plan, they returned to their crew duties of feeding fuel into the boiler while keeping a careful eye on the distant threat. Pele gradually increased the speed of the *Dolphin* as much as he felt he could to delay their encounter with the ship that he was sure was their enemy.

Later that day, Dov explained what they needed to do in more detail to his father. When he and his father found the type of side channel he had in mind they would bait the trap.

Euphrates River, Royal Battle Cruiser *HRS Savage*

Captain Ghamal guided Nimrod's battle cruiser through what he thought was the main channel of the river. The captain knew that his life depended on keeping the ship moving steadily through the water toward Bosrah without running aground. He had spent many frustrating hours trying to convince the king that he could not run the *Savage* at top speed in a straight line down the middle of the river. The seasoned captain knew from experience that sandbars and sunken trees lurked everywhere just below the water's surface. He divided his attention between looking for telltale ripples and shades of brown on the river's surface that indicated obstacles and thinking about what he would tell Nimrod when the tiny smudge of smoke on the horizon ahead of them became more noticeable. He had watched it for the last few hours, and come to his own logical conclusion: it had to be Pele's boat, and they too must be heading toward Bosrah. It made sense that he would depart Babel for his family's island in the Southern Sea. He estimated that, at their current speed, they would overtake the boat in about two days. Captain Ghamal cringed in anticipation of what Nimrod would do when he figured out that Pele was on the river ahead of him. He did not have to wait very long.

He felt rather than heard the warrior king stomp up the stairs and enter the ship's bridge. "What's that ahead?" he demanded. "Why was I not informed that another ship was on the river ahead of us?"

Of course, Ghamal didn't understand his exact words, but he didn't need to. Nimrod literally jumped up and down pointing to the smoke in the distance. Having thought of his response ahead of time, he slowed the ship and turned the helm over to Banerjee, the nervous midshipman who had been on the bridge every day learning the captain's steering techniques. The captain drew a picture of the *Dolphin* and shrugged to demonstrate his further ignorance or uncertainty. He tried to give the impression that this was of little concern to him. Nimrod exploded in anger.

"That traitor! He must be escaping to his family's fortress in Bosrah! I must catch him before he warns them of my approach. Full speed ahead!" Nimrod pushed the young helmsman aside and advanced the throttles to their maximum limits. Nothing happened at first because the engine room was momentarily stunned by the sudden demand for full power. The captain blanched in terror and did what he felt he must. He countermanded the king's order, pulled the throttles back, and waved his arms in an attempt to show the danger of running aground. Nimrod reached for his dagger, but brought his volcanic temper under control before the weapon was fully drawn. He rushed from the bridge to vent his fury outside. Midshipman Banerjee stared ahead and shuddered. Nimrod's violent aggression would be their downfall, he thought to himself. He gladly stepped aside when the captain offered to take the wheel.

CHAPTER 48

Euphrates River, Pele's *Dolphin*

"They *must* not get any closer to see what we're planning," Dov confided to Evina as they, Kitt, and Yanis watched the ever-nearing smoke plume. "We'll be working through the night to prepare things for when we meet. If that warship were to come upon us before tomorrow morning I'm afraid we'd be no match for it. Last night Jengo drew a detailed picture of what the ship's structure looks like, and it has two large guns pointing forward. We have nothing to fight back with. So my plan better work."

"How sure are you about your idea?" Evina asked.

"I'm still working on it."

"I'm sure it'll work out," she assured him. He had taken the responsibility for stopping the battle cruiser upon himself. Not by choice but by default. Nobody could think of any other way to avoid or stop the approaching attack. Dov opened his distance magnifier tube to check on the smoke and then snapped the instrument closed. He repeated the sequence every thirty seconds out of nervous impatience and frustration. He looked at the source of smoke in the distance in the hope of learning something more about their adversary. Dov finally handed the tube to Kitt, who peered at it for many long minutes before handing it back with a shrug and a shake of his head. The defensive maneuver that Dov proposed, and the crew embraced, was based on a string of assumptions and conjecture about what their pursuer would do when handed an opportunity to pounce on the *Dolphin*. Would the captain of the ship act like a logical, practical sailor and attempt to commandeer their vessel intact, capture its occupants, and take their remaining food and supplies? Or, if King Nimrod was in charge, which was likely, would his unrestrained lust for violence drive him to destroy the *Dolphin* without considering the cost?

The *Dolphin* steamed south as fast as Pele could prudently stoke the boiler and steer through the contorted bends in the river, but their pursuer was clearly closing in on them in spite of the *Dolphin's* increased speed. Whoever was in command of the cruiser was intent on catching them. The *Savage* ran at top speed in the straight stretches of the river and only slowed when forced to do so by sharp turns in the channel or piles of debris that threatened to put a hole in the fast-moving ship's hull. There were few long, unobstructed parts of the river as the two ships entered the shallower delta region. Dov prayed that their pursuer would not see their boat until the next day. His strategy would progress rapidly and inevitably to its conclusion when the captain of the battle cruiser finally caught sight of his helpless prey.

Some of the crew and the family passengers had transferred to the barge at dawn to clear the deck of the *Dolphin*. They heard a shout from the *Dolphin* over the roar of the vapor engine: "Sail ahead!" Pele yelled in his loudest voice to alert the others. Dov tapped Kitt on the shoulder, and they ran to see what it was. They had not seen any evidence of human activity on the river since leaving Babel, aside from their pursuer. A fishing boat drifted in the middle of the river directly ahead of them. Pele slowed his progress as they came close to the small vessel. The boat's sole occupant watched them warily from under a makeshift awning.

Within minutes, Magus surmised that the approaching vessel that belched black smoke and sparks into the air was probably an ingenious contraption created by the engineer Jengo or one of his family. Jengo gasped in disbelief from his perch halfway up the smoke stack when he recognized the figure in the boat.

Ever the wily opportunist, Magus broke into a broad smile and waved for the *Dolphin* to come toward him. He hailed them enthusiastically, but of course, his speech was unintelligible and couldn't be heard over the sound of the boiler. Pele slowed and drew closer to the fishing boat. "What is that rascal doing out here in a boat by himself?" Pele muttered. As if he understood what Pele said,

Jengo offered his own observation in his language. Shadow stared at the waving figure and emitted a low growl. Jengo motioned for Pele to keep their boat away from the devious magician. Dov called out to his father from the bow. "Don't stop!" Pele had no intention of doing so.

The two craft passed within fifty feet of each other. As the bow wave from the *Dolphin* rocked the smaller sailboat, the broad smile on Magus' face changed to a snarl. They were not stopping for him! He shouted what they supposed were blasphemous curses as they left him bobbing in their wake.

"Why is he out here in a sailboat?" Dov asked Evina after they lost sight of the boat around a bend in the river. The secretive member of the Triad was shouting and gesturing wildly when he disappeared from their sight.

"I can't imagine anyone helping him after all that's happened in Babel. His high position must have evaporated when his subjects scattered in the confusion of languages. He manipulated my father and brother for his own advancement; I hope we never see him again," Evina exclaimed.

"Wherever he goes, he'll be just another hungry human being trying to scratch out a living in the jungle." Dov speculated. He was eager to put the evil magician out of his thoughts.

"Still, what do you think will happen to him? Will he ever be a problem to us, or the rest of civilization? We don't need people like him in authority again," Evina lamented.

"He's a shrewd one alright, but I doubt he'll be able to survive if he isn't able to trick people into serving him. Wait, I just thought of something . . ." Dov looked back at the smoke of the distant battle cruiser. "Maybe Magus will be in for an even bigger surprise before the day is over."

CHAPTER 49

Euphrates River, Royal Battle Cruiser *HRS Savage*

A lookout clinging to a pole ten feet above the roof of the *Savage's* bridge noticed the fishing boat far in the distance and wondered if he should mention it to the helmsman. From his shaky perch above the ship's highest structure and ahead of the smoking stacks, his job was to shout and point to sandbars or tree trunks in their path so the helmsman could avoid them. A breeze had pushed the fishing boat toward the eastern edge of the river's main channel, where it posed no obstacle for the battle cruiser navigating on its present course. The image in his distance magnifier tube looked like a typical Babylonian fishing dhow low in the water, with a tall lateen sail slatting in the weak wind. He saw nobody on board. Lowering the cylinder from his eye, the lookout wondered what a fishing boat was doing this far from Babel, but decided not to mention it, since its presence would soon be obvious to the midshipman at the helm and it posed no evident danger to the ship.

Magus could not believe his luck that he had sighted two vapor-powered vessels in the space of a few hours. There was enough gold under the wooden deck of his fishing boat to buy the approaching ship and its crew. This was almost too good to be true! He could use the large vessel as a base of operations instead of starting from nothing in the jungle. He wondered if a favorable planetary alignment guided his fate after being snubbed by Pele and Jengo. He emerged from under his awning with a friendly smile to greet the approaching ship.

Banerjee easily saw the fishing boat at the edge of the river and concluded, as had the lookout, that it was not an obstacle in the ship's path. He continued on his course. The last thing he wanted to do was needlessly alert Nimrod or the captain so that they could argue again about what to do. He was enjoying the quiet on the bridge.

When Magus realized that the approaching ship was a royal battle cruiser, his smile dissolved. The massive wood and alloy vessel was an ominous sight. Its sharp bow cut smoothly through the water and pushed ripples of brown river foam ahead of it. Small waves marched in rows along the sides of the long grey hull. The ship's tall superstructure and trailing plume of fiery black smoke from twin black rock boilers created the illusion that the solid mass was aimed directly at him. Magus sighed with relief when the ship slowly turned to hold to the center of the river and pass by. He waved energetically at a few sailors watching him from the ship's starboard railing. He hoped that someone would give the command to stop and pick him up. He watched helplessly as the ship continued on its course without slowing.

At that moment Nimrod glanced out an open port of his royal stateroom and noticed the boat pass through his field of view. With an incredulous roar he recognized Magus smiling and gesturing cheerfully at his ship. The enraged king raced up to the bridge and screamed at the young helmsman, who stood paralyzed with fright at the ship's wheel. When Nimrod grabbed the wheel from him and spun it violently, the *Savage* made a sudden sharp turn that threw the crew off their feet. The fact that he initiated the turn that resulted in slamming himself against a bulkhead only further infuriated the king. The midshipman recovered his balance first and grabbed the ship's spinning wheel, regained control of the ship, and completed the course reversal more smoothly, which he assumed was the king's intention. He slowed their speed and steered around toward the fishing vessel.

When Magus saw the battle cruiser turn around he was overjoyed. He realized that he was in shallow water where the ship could not go, so he adjusted the sail to guide his craft into deeper water in mid-river. When the ship stopped to pick him up he would bribe the crew to safely transfer his bags of cargo below the floorboards of the ship. He beamed with self-satisfaction as the boat slowly approached him.

At that moment, Nimrod recovered from his fall and stood up in the middle of the bridge. He noticed that the ship had reversed direction back toward the boat carrying Magus. That charlatan was the last person he wanted on his ship! Nimrod screamed, "No!" at the helmsman and flung the young officer against an instrument panel, where he fell stunned in a heap. At that moment Captain Ghamal entered the bridge area from the vapor engine room below deck, nursing an arm burned when the *Savage* made its violent turn. He saw Banerjee crumpled on the deck and Nimrod at the helm; he feared for his life and the safety of his ship and crew. He watched incredulously as Nimrod jammed both engine throttles to their maximum "Battle Speed" positions. Nimrod had become an rabid beast. His uniform was drenched in sweat. Rage shook his body with such intensity that his massive hands could barely grasp the ship's wheel. A primeval growl emerged from his throat and saliva dripped from his lips. His eyes protruded unnaturally from their sockets as he aimed the *Savage* directly at Magus.

In a single instant, from a distance of one hundred yards, Magus recognized Nimrod at the wheel of the speeding battle cruiser and realized that the king was intent on killing him. The magician jerked his boat's tiller back and forth and paddled with his hands in a futile attempt to move out of the way, but a collision was inevitable.

Nimrod's target disappeared from his sight when the cruiser's high bow loomed over the small boat. The sharp bow of the *Savage* sliced the small wooden boat in half. Those on the bridge felt only a mild shudder under their feet. Had they been able to view the actual impact at the water's surface, they would have seen a golden spray of coins shimmer in the bright sunlight before they splashed into the muddy river. The king released the ship's wheel to look for the magician's body from the flying bridge or bridge wing, an open platform that extended out from both sides of the enclosed bridge for an unobstructed view.

Captain Ghamal reduced the throttles from "Battle Speed" to "Stop" and stepped back in anticipation of Nimrod's wrath. The king's thirst for blood dissipated as quickly as it arose. He remained on the bridge wing examining the wreckage in their wake. With the *Savage's* momentum under control, the captain turned the ship around and advanced to "Slow Ahead" in hopes of continuing their progress down the river. He assumed that Nimrod would not want to recover a survivor, if there was one. When he heard Nimrod shout and descend to the main deck he returned the vapor engines to "Stop" and held the ship in mid-river. What would Nimrod do next?

Magus' fishing boat was gone, but Nimrod noticed a swimmer struggling in the current to reach the distant riverbank. By this time the *Savage* was adrift in the middle of the river. The warrior king glared at the crew manning the starboard bow chaser on the main deck, and they fled to the opposite side of the deck. Nimrod hoped that the gun was primed and loaded with shot. He used a nearby pike to manhandle the gun platform slightly so that it aimed directly at his target. When he jerked the firing cord, a loud explosion and blinding flash burst from the weapon and hurled a small iron ball in an arc that was perfectly aligned with the swimmer a thousand feet away. When a fountain of water erupted into the air, the crew watching from the ship's railing burst into cheers in a dozen dialects. A convincing hit was cause for celebration in any language.

What passed for a grim smile creased Nimrod's face as he stomped triumphantly back to his stateroom. His next target would be the *Dolphin*.

Euphrates River, Pele's *Dolphin*

Dov and Kitt both heard the single, muffled sound of a cannon shot, and smiled at each other. Not only had Magus met his fate, but now they also knew that they were facing Nimrod and his cruiser. Dov was more confident that they could count on the king's vicious insanity to lure him into a trap that was too tempting to resist.

Euphrates River, Jungle Swamp

Magus' ears were still ringing from the concussion of the cannonball's near-miss when he opened his eyes in the dusky moisture of a swamp. He was vaguely aware that he was near the river as he surveyed through his blurred vision the low mangrove trees and scrub brush rooted in black, decaying muck around him. He had no idea where he was. His fortune of gold coins was scattered somewhere out there on the river bottom. His once-elegant robes were torn, soggy, filthy rags. He had nothing. Nobody would ever come to rescue him now. He curled up in a small jungle clearing and cried in despair.

The sharp bow of the *Savage* bore down on Magus' small boat.

CHAPTER 50

Euphrates River, Pele's *Dolphin*

Early evening

Naval encounters between ships in deltas, bayous, swamps, and muddy backwaters used unique tactics suitable for close-in confrontations that sailors in the future would call riverine warfare. Those methods differ markedly from deep-water, open-ocean battles between large ships and navies. What Dov envisioned was a ploy that would use the advantages of the smaller, more maneuverable *Dolphin* over the deeper draft and sluggish turning capabilities of the *Savage* to incapacitate the attacker and, he hoped, allow them to escape unharmed.

He combined surprise, deception, agility, and maneuverability into a ruse to lure Nimrod to them. The heavy cruiser's size, speed and firepower gave the bloodthirsty king no advantage in the narrow mangrove channels of the Euphrates delta. The king's impulsive aggression would draw him to his own destruction. All this should play out in the morning when the *Dolphin* and the *Savage* came face-to-face in the serpentine backwaters at a time and location of Dov's choosing.

Dov and his father piloted their boat away from the main flow of the river in the dwindling daylight to search for a channel covered by taller trees that was suitable for hiding the barge and their families.

By nightfall they disconnected the barge from the *Dolphin* and pushed it into a tributary "thumb" in shallow water covered by arching trees. When the barge was secure and invisible from the nearby channel, they offloaded black rock, supplies and equipment from the

Dolphin to make it as light as possible. They retained enough fuel to give them power for what they had in mind. Any more would deepen their draft too much and slow them.

Pele gathered everyone around before they departed and left the barge in the jungle. "I know that not everyone can understand me, but for those who can, here's how we'll divide up: our wives, the children, Yanis, and Evina will all stay here on the barge. Shadow will be with you for added protection." Yanis stiffened in objection. "Hear me out," Pele continued. "The next few hours will be decisive, and it's important that we split the family up so you have a chance of survival if the *Dolphin* is captured or destroyed. If we don't return, I'm counting on the rest of you to come up with a way for survivors to reach Bosrah. It's still several days away. You could reach it by barge if you pushed with long poles. You have food and tools with you to devise something. That's all I can advise. I'm trusting that the Lord will provide you with a means of escape if we fail."

"I am more confident than ever that we can stop Nimrod's attack," Dov said. He could see the strain on the faces of Evina and his family as Pele painted a dim picture of the future. "I ask that you pray for us while we're apart. By God's grace, we'll be back with you tomorrow, and we'll be in Bosrah in a few days to join the rest of our family."

As the group gathered to pray in three different languages, their petitions went up to heaven like sweet incense. Their need for help from God could not have been greater. All that remained was for the men on the *Dolphin* to work through the night, preparing for their encounter with Nimrod. They said their goodbyes and pushed the *Dolphin* back to the wider side channel where the *Savage* would "find" them in the morning.

The crew was exhausted from their all-night activities illuminated by dwindling moonlight. Not wanting to become entangled in the jungle along the banks or hung up on a sandbar or underwater obstacle, they had slowly pushed and pulled their craft through shallow water to a place where they would be visible to Nimrod at dawn when he rounded a turn in the river. During the night Pele remained aboard while Saris, Jengo, and Javak waded in water up to their chests, straining on ropes that moved them silently ahead. Behind them, Dov, Kitt, and Ash swam to locations on each bank of a side channel selected earlier. They made mounds of driftwood from debris on sandbars. They piled large quantities of dry, sun-bleached branches into pyramids. Satisfied with their handwork, they swam to a channel intersecting the main river and rejoined the *Dolphin*. When Pele and the others pulled them aboard, they were panting from their swim.

"I hope all this works," Dov said between heaving breaths. He lay on the deck with his cousins and looked up at the starlit sky. Soon the horizon would brighten with a new day. He prayed that God would deliver them from Nimrod's attack in the next few hours. They had stepped out in faith to do what they could. Now it was time to wait and pray that God would spare them, if He willed.

For the remaining time before dawn, Dov watched the surrounding jungle and the confluence of their side channel and the main river. In the silver moonlight, he thought he saw movement on the river. He reached for his magnifier tube with little expectation that it would reveal anything more in the dark than his unaided eye could see. He scanned in the direction of the movement, thinking that it was a branch floating downstream. His sudden start caught his father's attention.

"What is it?" Pele asked. "Did you see something?"

"I thought I saw something move out there," Dov hesitated. "My eyes must be playing tricks on me."

"It'll do that in the moonlight. Especially on the river. Probably just a bird or a large fish feeding on night insects."

"That's not what I thought I saw." Dov shook his head and laughed. "It looked like somebody, a dark shape only, standing in the middle of the river. That's not possible!"

"Get some rest. You're all keyed up for the attack in a few hours." Pele handed his son a blanket to ward off the damp chill of the river.

When dawn peeked through the surrounding mangroves, the crew of the *Dolphin* added black rock to the glowing embers in the boiler to bring it up to operating pressure. The more smoke that belched from the funnel the better. A glance toward the main river showed that the *Savage* had also fired up its boiler. They were less than a mile apart.

CHAPTER 51

Euphrates River, Royal Battle Cruiser *HRS Savage*

Dawn

Nimrod stood on the bridge of the *Savage,* scanning the horizon for the expected telltale smoke of his target. In his twisted thinking, anyone who dared to hinder his plans was his enemy and had to be destroyed. If the ship ahead of him belonged to Jengo or Pele, then they were traitors to Babel and headed for Bosrah Island ahead of him. If they escaped his grasp and warned the island's inhabitants, he would lose the advantage of surprise. His ambition demanded rebuilding and expanding another Babel before others could take over. He would easily destroy the small ship in his path and move on to conquer Bosrah.

Black smoke from the *Dolphin* contrasted against the clear sky. Nimrod grunted and motioned for Ghamal to raise the anchor and proceed onward. The exhausted captain assumed that the king intended a frontal attack. The small craft would be annihilated like the fishing boat was yesterday. He felt powerless to prevent bloodshed without being killed himself. With his right arm bandaged and in a sling, he used his free hand to give hand signals to Midshipman Banerjee to increase their speed to "Slow Ahead" and proceed downriver. Soon the *Savage* was in deeper water and the helmsman moved the settings to "Half Ahead," leaving a cloud of river mud swirling behind them. For now Banerjee was able to maintain a reasonable speed and oversee the ship's course. The young midshipman probably had a concussion from being thrown against the bridge instruments the previous day, but he was the only other member of the crew competent to steer the craft besides the captain. He was also the only one that the captain could count on to comprehend and follow his hand signals. The captain's job was to ensure safe navigation and movement of his ship. It required that he preserve the ship and the lives of its crew as best he could, even if Nimrod took over the controls.

The king was able to control his subjects by being suspicious of everyone. Anticipating that Captain Ghamal might countermand his orders again, he had been in the engine room earlier and threatened the boiler engineer and his mates with death if they did not respond instantly when told to extract maximum speed from their thundering vapor machines.

Minutes after getting underway, the lookout above the bridge gave a shout that swiftly brought Nimrod's magnifier tube up. The king saw the *Dolphin* disappear around a bend in the river a half-mile ahead! Sadistic pleasure swept through him when he thought of blasting the small boat and its occupants to pieces. The little boat would be helpless against the overwhelming firepower of his battle cruiser. Ghamal gave his helmsman a worried look which Banerjee interpreted correctly and placed his hand on the throttles ready to slow the ship immediately if he saw underwater obstructions or shallow water. Sweat covered the young midshipman's face in spite of the morning breeze.

When their ship rounded the next turn, the captain was surprised to see that the smaller craft was closer than he expected. In fact, it was at the maximum range of the bow chaser cannon. He wondered if Nimrod noticed this too. He got his answer when the king leaned over the railing of the bridge wing and shouted to the gun crew on the deck below. His gesticulation could not be mistaken, and the crews of both starboard and port bow chasers adjusted elevation for maximum range and waited for the ship to align with the target. When the starboard gun mate saw the *Dolphin* in his sights he pulled the firing cord and the heavy carriage recoiled against its restraints with a deafening blast. The captain looked downrange while the crew reloaded. The ball fell short of the target and created a towering splash of muddy water. They would be within range in a minute at this speed. The port gun mate looked at his starboard counterpart and said something that sounded like a challenge. Each wanted their gun crew to be the first to destroy the vessel in their first real battle.

Pele pushed the throttle of the *Dolphin* to three quarters of its maximum speed and turned into a winding tributary off the main river and again disappeared from view of the *Savage*. He needed enough speed to entice the *Savage* to chase them into the maze of shallow channels without being hit by a cannonball! The king was being drawn into a reckless chase after their slower, helpless vessel; he would be so intent on destroying his foe that he would disregard the safety of his own ship.

Nimrod emitted animal-like sounds when he saw the *Dolphin* again. The gun crew was unable to fire while the heavy cruiser turned back and forth to stay in the middle of the winding tributary.

Banerjee reduced the throttles to "Slow Ahead" when the captain motioned to him. The helmsman tensed as he and Ghamal eyed the mangroves banks on either side of them. Nimrod, on the other hand, was so focused on the prey ahead of him that he shut out all else. He screamed at the gun's crew, who had fired only once more, a wide miss, since their first salvo. They fired again as the *Dolphin* crossed their field of fire, but the quick maneuvers of the smaller boat caused their projectiles to fall harmlessly into the jungle. Those that aimed true fell short but skipped along the water, lost their energy, and appeared to hit the hull and cause minimal damage. None of the shots was a direct hit. Nimrod was a raging madman. Each time the cannon fired and missed, he brought his cutlass down on the bridge railing. Splinters flew in all directions. When Ghamal moved the throttles to their "Stop" position Nimrod instantly whirled on the two men. With a wild swipe of his cutlass he barely missed the captain's head and tore a large hunk of wood from the ship's instrument panel. Sensing that Nimrod had lost all reason, and realizing that he was intent on destroying the *Dolphin* at any cost, Captain Ghamal hurried to the opposite side of the bridge, climbed over the railing, grabbed a life preserver with his uninjured arm, and jumped into the river as far away from the ship as possible. The terrified midshipman followed his example and flung himself over the other railing into the water. In a swift movement that belied the massive bulk of the ship, Nimrod jammed the cruiser's throttles from "Stop" to "Battle Speed" in a single motion that bent the control arms. The engineering crew waiting below was still startled by this sudden change, but engaged the twin drive propellers out of fear that the king would have their heads if they hesitated. As it was, the ship took more than thirty seconds to reach its maximum speed. Nimrod aimed the *Savage* at the *Dolphin* as if his cruiser were a giant javelin.

On the *Dolphin*, the crew passed the heaps of driftwood built up during the night on each side of the channel and threw flaming brands into the piles. The dry wood immediately burst into flames. The smoke quickly spread in the dawn stillness and settled above the surface of the water. Soon, patches of smoke obscured parts of the river while sunlight illuminated others. They turned five hundred yards beyond the smoke and stopped carefully in the precise spot they had marked the night before.

Aiming his massive cruiser at full speed, Nimrod weaved the ship down the tributary in such sharp turns that the crew were violently thrown from side to side across the deck. They clutched any solid object within their grasp. Speeding the massive warship in such narrow confines was total insanity! The ship's large paddles dug furrows in the muddy bottom of the channel but their momentum propelled them forward. The smoke ahead of his careening ship caused Nimrod to wonder if he had lost the *Dolphin*, but then he saw it straight ahead through breaks in the haze and howled with delight. He was on a collision course with the enemy! He pushed against the throttles harder, hoping to gain more speed while with his other hand he kept the bow pointed at the middle of the *Dolphin*.

For a split second the king was perplexed by the apparent calm of the men who watched motionless on the *Dolphin* as he sped directly at them. In seconds he would slice them in half with his warship and yet they stood looking at him. When that puzzling thought finished passing through his brain, the bow of the *Savage* hit the sandbar covered by a foot of water and masked by smoke. One hundred tons of wood and metal lifted its bow into the air and ground to a sudden stop.

The *Savage's* terrifying, abrupt collision with the sandbar ended the life of the most powerful military machine on earth. To those on the battle cruiser, the episode was over in an instant. Nimrod's face went through the glass and metal of the bridge window; the rest of his body followed through the opening and thudded onto the roof of the first level below. Most of the crew had braced themselves when they saw or sensed that the ship's speed was suicidal. The crew in the engine room were already on their way up to the main deck when they were slammed against immovable bulkheads or inner partitions. The back half of the hull split along a seam and water rushed into the engine compartment and flooded the boilers, preventing their explosion. Compressed vapor billowed topside through hundreds of ruptured pipes. It was a miracle that there were no deaths amid the churning chaos. The hissing, motionless hulk wallowed in the brown water and sank by its stern.

To those on the *Dolphin* watching the menacing bow speed directly at them, and to Captain Ghamal and Midshipman Banerjee treading water and watching their warship speed away from them, the *Savage* died a slow death. They foresaw the inevitable. When the bow rose into the air on the bar it was as if time slowed in a dream. The vapor engines drummed and the paddles spun forward, but the ship stopped moving forward. A buzzing *rrrrrrrip* of the hull's seam parting down half the length of the vessel overpowered all other noises from the ship. It was then replaced by the sound of river water surging onto the twin boilers and the blast of a vapor cloud expanding high into the morning sky.

"Should we recover survivors?" Dov asked his father when he finally realized that they had succeeded. Nobody had thought about this dilemma.

"I suppose it's the right thing to do," Pele replied. "I don't think the crew meant us any harm. It was that maniac who was after us. Besides, after that ordeal, I suspect any fight that was in the crew will be redirected toward their survival."

As their boat's captain, it fell to Pele to decide how much mercy could prudently be extended to survivors without risking their own lives. He turned the wheel of the *Dolphin* around and they emerged from behind the hidden sandbar and approached the stricken, steaming hulk to search for people in the water. As expected, they pulled three grateful men from the water who caused them no problems.

When they were alongside the forward section of the *Savage*, they faced a different reception. Sailors on the deck, some evidently injured, were surprisingly hostile. They threw objects at the boat and shouted what could only be interpreted as threats and curses. Bow chasers were pushed to aim in their direction but remained silent. Nimrod was nowhere to be seen.

"Why are they so angry with us?" Dov wondered aloud. "We're trying to help them?"

"We're the ones who tricked their king into attacking us. They probably blame us for the shipwreck and for being stranded in the river. Rather than being victims of Nimrod's venomous hatred, we're the bad guys." Pele shook his head. "I can't bring them aboard. There's no telling what they might do to us. I don't want Nimrod near us either." The crew of the *Dolphin* watched as their captain reluctantly turned the boat away from the wreck.

When they saw Captain Ghamal and Midshipman Banerjee waving from shallow water a short distance upriver, they took them aboard also. Out of forty crew members, they recovered only five survivors in the water who appreciated their generosity.

Later in the day, the crew of the *Dolphin* was joyfully reunited with their families. Evina rushed to hug Dov, who blushed in embarrassment. Kitt and Yanis were less demonstrative, but just as glad to see each other. Pele and Jengo embraced wives and smaller children with relief. The rescued sailors were given food and clothing and responded appreciatively to the unexpected kindness.

With the contest with Nimrod over, a quiet calm came over those on the barge and the crew of the boat towing them to their next destination. Dov and his father discussed the possibility that some or all of their relatives on the island might not speak their language. In spite of this possibility, they were certain that their own flesh and blood would still be supportive of their decision to resupply the *Dolphin* and continue on their voyage to spread across the world as God originally commanded.

CHAPTER 52

Euphrates River, Royal Battle Cruiser *HRS Defiant*

Same time

Thanks to round-the-clock work by the Babel shipyard workers, the *HRS Defiant* had been marginally repaired and set sail from the destroyed city two days after the *Savage's* departure. Determined welders, carpenters, machinists, and divers mended the most serious structural and underwater damage inflicted by tortuous winds and wrenching magnetic forces. While the *Defiant* was moored alongside the pier in Babel, the repair workers brought their families aboard in droves. Militia carrying weapons and holding allegiance to no one also joined those on the ship until the vessel was so low in the water that Captain Okan had to keep any more people away. Out of concern for the safety of his ship, the captain stationed armed guards and soldiers with orders to stop any more from boarding.

Captain Okan looked over the crowded deck from the bridge high above the water. For the past twenty-four hours he had been at his post where he supervised sailors under his command and maintained order on the crowded deck as best he could without a common language. He would stay on the bridge until he could navigate the ship into the deeper waters of the Euphrates River and guide it south to the sea. The *Defiant* was sister ship to the *Savage*, which had departed earlier when Nimrod forced Captain Ghamal, Okan's counterpart on the *Savage*, to take her down the river without the benefit of surveying or repairing the vessel for a lengthy voyage. Okan was more than happy to see

Nimrod disappear down the river. The generous captain had taken as many refugees as he safely could with him to start a new city in a distant land.

Okan reflected on his more than fifty years as an officer in Nimrod's navy and how the *Defiant* and *Savage* had come into service. Trained for river duty, Nimrod's royal navy had never seen military action because there were no enemies to fight. Each time Nimrod went after rebellious factions who escaped from Babel to start their own colonies along the river, the mere presence of the *Savage* or *Defiant* with their cannons was enough to convince them to surrender without resistance. When they surrendered, they were executed to send a clear message to the king's subjects: any unauthorized departure from Babel's city limits would result in death. Recent concessions to live outside of Babel in the authorized colonies of Erech, Accad, and Calneh. Nimrod insisted that any structure in the colonies had to be aligned so that the skyscrapers of Babel were always in view as a reminder that he held ultimate power.

The rebel settlement on Bosrah Island was an embarrassing exception to the official colonies. It was an irritant that he tolerated until he could mount an overwhelming attack to destroy them. Nimrod smirked when he thought that the vapor machines invented by Japheth and his kind more than a century ago were the very technology that would spell the downfall of Bosrah. When Pele demonstrated the vapor-powered *Dolphin* to the public, Nimrod commissioned his artisans to fashion a craft from alloy and wood that would dwarf the runabout that annoyed him racing back and forth on the Euphrates. Royal engineers produced a boat that terrified Nimrod's senior mariners who were accustomed to adapted fishing boats as a navy. This confirmed to him that this was the ultimate weapon he had been looking for to dominate the Euphrates and Tigris Rivers.

The HRS *Defiant* was the first of Nimrod's navy commissioned in an elaborate ceremony at the shipyard by the bridge that connected Old Babel and New Babel. Nimrod smiled with grim satisfaction when he saw Pele in the crowd silently watching as the finished ship slid down the rails into the river and pushed a giant wave ahead of it that swamped fishing boats on the opposite shore. Its "battle cruiser" designation amplified its intended purpose. More than twenty times bigger than any fishing boat, the *Defiant* was an imposing vessel that dominated anything else mankind had ever seen. Its bow and sides were two-foot thick oak reinforced with alloy ribs that could withstand ramming into other craft and deflect any known projectile thrown against it. The foredeck sloped upward to a high prow, two large cannons protruded from open ports on each side to fire at targets immediately ahead or to the sides, and a blue royal ensign flew from a single staff on the bow. The ship's razor-sharp bow could cut through any obstacle at its waterline.

Moving back from the bow, the bridge was the tallest structure on the ship. It was located in the middle of the vessel atop three decks where the crew worked and lived. A small platform and mast on the roof of the bridge allowed a lookout to perch high above the water and watch for river obstructions that came into view before they could be seen from the bridge.

The most visually prominent structure on the ship was the pair of tall stacks or funnels behind the deckhouse that carried black rock smoke and flaming cinders up from the large vapor engine fireboxes that glowed in the bowels of the ship. A deafening roar and dark fumes interspersed with flaming sparks spewed from the stacks and drifted away in a murky tail when the ship moved through the water. When the ship was stationary, or if there was no breeze to carry the smoke away, soot and flaming embers covered the smoothly sanded wooden deck and grey deckhouse. Sailors hosed the decks and structure to extinguish any potential fires.

The king personally chose Ghamal and Okan to be captains of his new battle cruisers. He needed their naval skill and military ambition to set the pattern for others in his new navy. Most of all, he insisted on their absolute loyalty to him, the kingdom of Babel, and his new world order. That was fifty years ago. Today it was a different world.

Enough reminiscing about the past, the captain thought to himself. It was now three days after his overloaded ship had left Babel behind and Okan was slowing to pick up a new passenger. His youngest son, Jelani, was at the lookout position and had called out: "Castaway, dead ahead!" His magnifier tube presented the strange sight of a thin, ragged, sunburned man waving frantically from a sandbar in the middle of the river. His speech was unintelligible—normal in this new world. Okan gave the helmsman, his eldest son, Bharata, instructions to slow and stop a hundred yards from the sandbar. A ship's boat brought the man to the side, where he climbed slowly to the deck. The crew gave him water and a shirt to cover his sunburned back. A woman in the crowd understood some of his speech and stepped forward to help him. After a lengthy exchange, she brought him to the captain. She introduced herself as Toliara and explained the man's story using words mixed with sign language. It was a wholly inadequate form of communication among the confusion as various others crowded onto the bridge and tried to join in. After a lengthy time of frustrated shouting and gesticulating, the man's sorry tale finally emerged. He claimed to be a fisherman named Fibbian who had fallen into the river when a great wind capsized his boat many days ago. He could not swim and was stranded on the sandbar without shelter or food. He smiled and laughed as he gave thanks to the captain for rescuing him. Okan shook his hand and welcomed him aboard. He then dismissed him and the others, who had pushed their way onto the bridge, so he could return to his duties. When the thin man and Toliara finally departed the bridge Okan watched them descend the ladder to the crowded deck below. Something wasn't right about his story.

That man was no fisherman! His hand felt like he had never pulled a line, mended a sail, or thrown a fishing net in his life. Though Okan didn't understand his actual words, his diction and tone of speech seemed that of a proud, educated man accustomed to giving orders and having them obeyed. A fisherman's back would be dark brown from the sun and not sunburned. No, his name wasn't Fibbian and he was no fisherman. What was he hiding that made him need to lie about his identity?

Captain Okan called Hidush, his middle son, to the bridge. "I want you to keep an eye on that man we picked up. I have a bad feeling about him. The last thing we need on this crowded ship is more trouble. Let me know what he does and who he talks with." Hidush left the bridge to find "Fibbian" and Toliara.

While Toliara showed him around the ship, Magus' shifty eyes were alert to every one and their activities. Like a politician running for office, Magus made his way around the ship shaking hands and speaking in a caring voice. Even though he was not understood by most, he acted friendly toward everyone. Rumors spread through the ship about this poor, amiable, shipwrecked fisherman that everyone liked. As he was welcomed among the hundreds escaping from Babel, he received small gifts of precious food and drink. Soon he was dressed in the patched clothing of a tradesman that helped him blend with the other refugees.

Captain Okan turned his attention to piloting the boat down the river with his son at the helm. He set the throttles to "Slow Ahead" for reasons of safety and to conserve fuel. His destination was an island on his chart that he knew as "Bosrah" with a good harbor on its northern side and which he heard was inhabited. He would try to reach that destination where people might find food ashore. Okan was a captain with more loyalty toward what he now considered *his* ship than to the king or the city of Babel. In the best maritime tradition, the safety of his ship and the welfare of his crew and passengers were his primary responsibilities. His three sons shared his seafaring devotion. They spoke his language and helped him run the ship. Thinking ahead, he contemplated finding more food and fuel on Bosrah and departing one day with his family and any others who wished to join him toward the east to begin a new civilization.

Later that afternoon, Hidush reported back to his father. "You were right. That character is no fisherman. He's ingratiating himself with everyone on board like a politician. He's found a couple families who understand his language, along with Toliara. They've formed a small clan in one of the staterooms, where he speaks at length about things that I don't understand. When they saw that I was watching them, the fisherman singled me out using what I took to be angry words. He gave me such a dark, sinister look that I shivered. I don't like him and I don't want to be near him."

"I'll deal with the matter later," Okan replied. "We need to find a safe anchorage for the night. There's rain coming and I want to be double-anchored in case the wind picks up. This is the first rain since we've been underway. I hope everyone on the deck can find shelter. I'll go around and check on them once we've stopped for the night."

Into the night, Magus spread poisonous rumors among the crew and passengers. When Okan or his sons circulated to ensure shelter for passengers from the coming rain, conversations abruptly stopped and eyes glared or turned away. An insidious undercurrent of mutiny flowed through the ship. By morning, Magus had infected the ship with a manufactured hatred for Captain Okan and his three sons.

Magus claimed that as soon as they were put ashore on the island of Bosrah, a deserted island devoid of water or food, so he said, the captain intended to strand them there and escape on the *Defiant*. He and his sons were deceiving them with false kindness now so they could have the ship for themselves later. The people needed to trust "Fibbian" because he knew these waters better than the captain. He would lead them to a paradise of water and plentiful food where they could start a better life!

On the crowded upper deck, a former tower guard listened to stories attributed to the fisherman with increasing skepticism. Something about this fisherman was familiar. He thought he had seen him months ago in the tower. He had been dressed in colorful flowing robes and hurried past him with a cruel, angry scowl. Now he was dressed in rags and pretended to be everyone's friend. Was this the same man he had seen at the tower? If so, what was he doing impersonating a fisherman?

CHAPTER 53

Euphrates River, Pele's *Dolphin*

Evening, two days later

It was wise to make small repairs to the *Dolphin* before they risked more damage on the river or took on water while at sea from unseen leaks. Pele and the crew spent two days repairing minor damage to the hull and cleaning the vapor boiler. After they had picked up survivors from the *Savage*, they reunited with their families on the barge and relaxed between short repair shifts. If they worked around the clock, they could finish essential repairs by the next morning. With no more threats to worry about, they looked forward to a glorious family reunion at Bosrah!

Two cannonballs had hit the *Dolphin* while the *Savage* pursued them in the winding channels. Although most shots missed them entirely or had been deflected, two hits had gone unnoticed in the chase. One came precariously close to piercing the vapor boiler, when it tore through the pile of black rock at the stern and carved a large groove in the fuel storage bin. Valuable black rock spilled into the river before anyone noticed later. The other had fallen short, skipped along the surface of the water, and made a dent in the hull at the waterline. A crack had worked open that let water seep into the bilge. Pele ordered a tarp lashed over the spot from the outside and a rag was stuffed into the crack from the inside to stem the flow. When the bilge pump cleared the water inside it was easy to fill the crack permanently with putty. It was as good as new and able to withstand their passage in the Southern Sea. When the *Dolphin* left the scene of the *Savage's* grounding they easily repaired the black rock storage compartment and, at the suggestion of newly arrived Captain Ghamal, shifted some of the heavy fuel further to the rear, thereby lifting the bow higher so the hole was almost above the waterline, where it could be repaired.

Satisfied that repairs could be finished in the few hours of daylight remaining, Pele suggested that they celebrate that night with a feast and family fun. Everyone was recovering from the stressful ordeal of their escape from the *Savage*, and that included Captain Ghamal and Midshipman Banerjee, who displayed a more gentle spirit than anyone anticipated of military officers in Nimrod's navy. It was evident that their true allegiance was to serve their countrymen and uphold the more honorable traditions of river sailors. Pele and Ghamal, without speaking the same language, were cut from the same cloth as captains. They conversed in sign language, enjoyed dinner and laughed while the children sang their favorite songs. The young midshipman was shy and in awe of Dov and Kitt, who were only a few years older than him but much more confident of themselves. Banerjee hoped that one day he would be accepted into their group. He would probably never see his family again and this thought dampened his interest in the festivities.

Dov and Evina moved away from the noisy celebration in the barge to the front of the boat where they could speak in private. Even though this was supposed to be a time of "relaxation," Dov was anxious to reach Bosrah and find out what had happened to their friends and family there. With the singing and laughter of the feast in the background, the two sat on the railing and admired the sparkling moonlight on the river. They watched Javak and Kitt redistributing supplies on the far side of the deck in preparation for departure in the morning.

"Have you talked with your father about what we'll do when we reach Bosrah?" Evina asked.

"No, I haven't," Dov confessed. "It's obvious that we can't stay there permanently, even if most of our family speaks the same language, which is unlikely. God divided our one worldwide language into hundreds of languages for a larger purpose which we cannot ignore. He's forcing people to disperse across the globe. That was his original intention when Noah and our forefathers left the ark."

"Where will we go?"

"I don't know exactly, but I am certain of one thing—I want to be with you forever. Will you . . ."

"Can I join you two?" a voice behind them interrupted.

"You sure know how to break into a romantic moment, Sis," Dov said in mock irritation.

"Romantic? My brother? That's a joke!" his sister chided in return.

"Come sit down over here next to me," Evina motioned. "I think Dov was about to ask me to marry him." Evina's radiant smile encouraged him to speak up. "Were you?"

"Well, I *was*, actually. Apparently it doesn't come as any surprise to you or my sister. So will you?"

"Oh, yes!" Evina flung her arms around Dov and nearly knocked them both into the river. Evina and Yanis embraced.

"Now," Yanis said when she settled herself beside Evina, "if only Kitt would get the same idea. It's hard to drop casual hints using sign language."

"If we wait here maybe he'll come over and pop the question when he's finished on the *Dolphin*," Dov said.

Sure enough, soon Kitt came over and sat next to Yanis. "What's up?" he asked her innocently. By now she understood a handful of phrases in his language. "Why do Dov and Evina have silly grins on their faces?" he asked her.

I might as well try, Yanis thought. She didn't know how to say it, so began a long explanation in sign language interspersed with words that she had learned.

Gradually Kitt came around. "Congratulations to you both!" He shook Dov's hand and hugged Evina enthusiastically.

"Now comes the hard part," Yanis said to her brother. She fluttered her eyelashes at Kitt and gave him a dreamy smile. "And so . . . and so . . ." Would he get the idea?

"And so . . . I think it's a great idea," Kitt replied. The silence dragged on further while he pretended to not get it. Finally, he gave in.

"And so . . . and so . . . you and me, too?" he pantomimed.

Yanis nodded with delight and pulled Kitt with her off the railing and into the cool water. The splash and their laughter drew Pele and others to the bow thinking someone had fallen overboard by accident. "What's going on here? Are you all right?"

"Everything is *wonderful!*" Evina exclaimed as she pulled Dov's hand and the two tumbled into the water to join Kitt and Yanis. She surfaced in the shallows shaking her head and splashing water everywhere. "We'll have *two weddings* in Bosrah!" she shouted happily.

The crew and families stayed up late talking with the newly engaged couples about their plans for the future. Pele arose an hour before dawn to rekindle the boiler fire so the engine would be up to operating pressure in time for an early start. Truth was, he didn't sleep at all because of the exciting news about his twins and thinking over last minute details before the final leg of their voyage.

CHAPTER 54

Euphrates River, Pele's *Dolphin*

Next morning

When the *Dolphin* finally got underway, Captain Ghamal and Pele stood next to Kitt, who was helmsman that morning. In less than a day the former master of Nimrod's cruiser, still dressed in his tattered and faded blue uniform with missing rank insignia, had proven himself to be a valuable asset to the boat's crew. All eyes were on the bend in the river ahead, where they saw the *Savage* stranded on the bar. One fourth of the ship's forward length was firmly wedged in the mud and sand. They saw men in the shallow water with shovels. Ghamal snorted at the impossible idea that two men with shovels could extricate such a large ship. The opposite end of the long ship was underwater. The boilers and vapor engines were beyond repair. Sailors sat listlessly on the deck. There was no sign of Nimrod.

When Kitt turned the *Dolphin* to approach closer, Captain Ghamal gestured that they continue on and not offer assistance. His sentiment was reinforced when other sailors and passengers on the deck of the cruiser jeered angrily at them. The influence of Nimrod's hate reached across the narrow gulf between the two ships. Pele reluctantly agreed and motioned Kitt to steer toward the main river channel. They would leave the memory of Nimrod and his ship behind. Pele had no further obligation to the crew of the *Savage*.

Just as the *Dolphin* proceeded slowly around the last turn in the side tributary and merged into the main river, they passed behind a stand of tall cypress trees. Through the trees they saw dense black smoke. Within seconds, they came upon the *HRS Defiant,* which had slowed earlier when it saw the *Dolphin's* smoke. Pele quickly disengaged the vapor engine's drive and the two vessels drifted parallel to each other no more than one hundred yards apart.

People on both ships eyed each other in silence. Ghamal lifted a distance magnifier tube to identify who was in charge of the *Defiant.* When he had departed Babel, the *Defiant* listed mortally at its pier. He could tell from the smokestack emissions that they ran only one boiler. When Captain Okan stepped onto the bridge wing to survey the small ship across the way, he was surprised to see his friend Captain Ghamal on the deck of the *Dolphin.* He waved to the figure in the tattered uniform, and Ghamal waved back half-heartedly. The two captains were cautious when they confronted unexpected situations. They weighed what they saw against the horrific destruction of the past week in Babel and arrived at similar conclusions. Okan had last seen his counterpart on the bridge of the *Savage* where Nimrod shouted commands in the captain's face. Now he was on the bridge of a small boat, to his knowledge the only other vapor-powered craft in existence, but he was evidently not its captain. The man standing next to Ghamal was the boat's captain, who issued calm instructions to the helmsman while Ghamal looked at the naval ship that he knew well. Okan was confused by the juxtaposition of his friend on the *Dolphin;* he was unable to see the *Savage* beached and broken only a quarter of a mile away around the bend in the side channel.

Ghamal was more troubled than confused by what he saw on the *Defiant.* The ship's hull was heavily damaged as evidenced by patched planks, a buckled deck, and broken glass in the portholes. The ship barely had enough propulsion to maintain headway for steerage and it was overloaded beyond its safe capacity. This meant that Okan had left the Babel shipyard out of desperation, and that was not a good sign. When he focused on the people lining the side of the ship, his apprehension increased. The *Dolphin* passed downwind and the smell of hundreds of sweating, soiled, unwashed bodies carried across the water causing him to gag. Dirty, gaunt, despondent faces stared back in silence. They were starving, and starving people could act unpredictably.

The stench washed over those on the *Dolphin* in a revolting wave. Meanwhile, Shadow's hypersensitive nose was fast at work. Bombarded with thousands of signals, where the humans sensed only one smell, his brain catalog detected one individual's odor that triggered an instant reaction. He barked and growled with an intensity they had never heard before.

"Easy boy," Pele said. Dov and Evina restrained him from leaping into the water. He settled down to a steady, deep snarl. There was someone on that ship who he didn't like.

Pele thought he would try something since there were hundreds of people on the ship across from him. If one person aboard could understand him maybe they could find out more about the ship and its plight. He cupped his hands to his mouth.

"Ahoy, there! Does anyone understand me? If you understand me, speak out!"

A hundred voices responded instinctively to the unintelligible greeting in dozens of different dialects. No single voice could be heard amid the din from the ship beside them. Pele told Kitt to bring them closer so he could single out one person with whom he could communicate. As Kitt did so, Ghamal grumbled his objection to getting too close. Pele used his arms to quiet the crowd as their distance to the ship was cut in half. He could see each individuals clearly.

"If you understand me, wave a hat."

Over the confused buzz of men, women, and children gathered before him, a small man, dressed in the once-fine clothing of a prosperous merchant, waved his hat back.

Pele pointed to him with a laugh. The crowd turned its attention to the man in their midst, and quieted to listen to him speak. His words meant nothing to them, but it was clear that he could speak with this vessel's captain. Surely he would convince him to send them food and water.

As Pele and the refugee named Singh spoke across the gap between them, Magus watched with a scarf over his face. Donated garments had replaced his expensive though tattered clothing so that he would not be recognizable from the *Dolphin*. Of course, he recognized Pele immediately. He also picked out Jengo among those standing on the deck of the boat, along with several others still dressed in blue ascender operator uniforms.

Pele left the bridge to confer with the others while Kitt pulled away slightly and maintained their position off the larboard side of the battle cruiser. He had firm instructions to not get ahead of the *Defiant* in case someone tried to fire a bow chaser cannon at them.

"Best I can tell, they're a refugee boat from Babel," observed Pele. "They're in need of food and relief from the overcrowding."

Jengo added, "I saw some uniformed soldiers and sailors in the crowd, but I have the feeling from their demeanor that they don't have intentions to harm us."

Pele agreed. "I'm concerned that so many people could overwhelm us out of desperation if we gave them the opportunity. I'll make them the offer of following us to Bosrah, where we can give them food and shelter. I'm certain that Botwa would not deny them these necessities. Any other suggestions?" Pele looked at his immediate family gathered around him.

Jengo urged caution. "I agree about not getting too close. Also, I could tell that Captain Ghamal didn't want us to approach closer. My eyes are watering from the filth on the open deck, so I can't imagine what it's like below. There are families with young ones so I agree that they are unlikely to pose a military threat. We should help them somehow, but we can't do much for them here in the middle of the river."

"I agree," added Dov. "Maybe we could bring that man aboard so we can learn more about the mood on the ship and get some idea of what to expect when they reach Bosrah. If we arrive a day ahead of them it would give our friends there time to prepare for hundreds of refugees."

Everyone nodded. Pele summarized the situation: "So here's what we'll do to make the handover as safe as possible for us. I can't risk pulling close along the side to bring Singh aboard or others might try to jump, and there would be injuries. Nor am I willing to send our only rowboat to them in case they grabbed its crew as hostages. I'll suggest that Singh be rowed to us in one of their small boats."

"Maybe Shadow can give him a sniff before he comes aboard." Evina suggested.

"Good idea." Hearing no other comments, Pele climbed the ladder to the bridge.

Kitt had easily maintained the boat's position to the side and behind the larger ship. Thanks to the wind direction he found a spot where he could avoid the smoke and cinders from the black rock boiler and breathed welcomed puffs of fresh air from across the water. He doubted he would ever become accustomed to the smell of hundreds of bodies packed that close together.

Pele explained to Singh across the open water what they wanted to do in hopes that he would agree to come with them, so that the inhabitants of Bosrah could be ready for their arrival later. Singh's reaction was that the refugees didn't want to go to Bosrah because he was told that it was uninhabited. When Pele told him that Bosrah had plenty of food and water, more than an hour passed while frantic haggling in different languages took place on the ship. Eventually, four rowers brought Singh to the side of the *Dolphin*, and the older man climbed unsteadily up the rope ladder at the side. Shadow terrified the man when the huge dog met him as his foot touched the deck. Within seconds the dog stopped growling, turned around with apparent indifference and walked back to the forward deck.

Singh waved to his family on the *Defiant*. His wife wept openly and their five young children, also in tears, huddled around her. Singh was clearly torn by the decision to leave his family behind, but he eventually turned his back and eagerly accepted drink and food. Not wanting hundreds of starving, exiled passengers to watch him eat, he stepped behind the *Dolphin's* deckhouse, where he devoured his meal in seconds.

Pele gave the order for Kitt to set a course for Bosrah at maximum speed and retired below. Kitt watched the bow chasers as he pulled ahead of the *Defiant*. They remained unmanned as long as he kept them in sight. When the battle cruiser disappeared behind in the distance he breathed a sigh of relief.

Dov joined Pele on the bridge while others assembled to obtain as much information as possible from their new passenger. Dov looked back to see his mother hand Singh a bar of soap and a towel and motion him to the shower stall far to the rear of the *Dolphin*. Nobody wanted to be near him until he washed off the stink from the battered

Warship that had become a floating pigsty. Dov turned back to his father and expressed something that had been bothering him.

"What do you think of that man's story about Bosrah being uninhabited and without food or water? Do you think all is what it appears on that ship?"

"I have no reason to think otherwise. I admit that I don't have a good feeling about letting hundreds of starving strangers loose on the island. Shadow's violent first reaction to the ship should be a warning to us. There's no telling who is mixed in among that wretched bunch and what they would do to people on the island."

Dov tried to articulate what was nagging him. "It's one thing to want to help others who are so clearly in need of help. On the other hand, we have to balance that against self-preservation. I don't want to risk our lives to help someone who might turn around and harm or kill us." It is God's way to help those in need and show them compassion and kindness. How far should you go to help people who could easily turn around and harm, injure, or murder you or your family? That fear was compounded because they didn't understand the others' languages. It was easy to suspect the worst and avoid helping them out of fear.

"Maybe Jengo will learn something from Singh that will alleviate our concerns. I'd like to think that those hundreds of hungry and displaced people would receive our aid with appreciation, but I can't help wondering what might happen if they panicked and became violent." The two stood in silence on the bridge while Kitt steered them down the middle of the river. Those interrogating Singh in another part of the boat did not realize that the newly arrived stranger unwittingly had information that, when revealed in a casual comment two days later, would make everyone's anxiety level skyrocket.

CHAPTER 55

Euphrates River, Royal Battle Cruiser *HRS Defiant*

No sooner had the *Dolphin* disappeared from sight than Magus began the mutiny. The chief magician's trademark of deceit, lies, and intimidation were deftly employed to take over the *HRS Defiant* within an hour. With the ship under his command, he would overrun Bosrah and resume building the world of his dreams!

He gathered a half-dozen armed soldiers, whom he had bribed with promises of wealth and position when they captured Bosrah. Toliara joined him with similar enticements. Her facility with languages was what first attracted him to her. He marveled at how quickly she was drawn to him when he confided that he was no mere fisherman. She willingly helped him sow seeds of discontent among the passengers. His subversive story was simple: Captain Okan was a traitor with no intention of taking others with him on the *Defiant* when he disembarked his passengers at Bosrah. He would take the cruiser and leave them stranded on an island with no resources. Contrary to what their captain had told them, Bosrah was a deserted island with no food or water. Of course, these were lies. The captain was portrayed as a scoundrel who should be overthrown so he, Magus, could lead them to another land with abundant food and water. If they trusted him they would be safe from harm.

Before climbing up to the ship's bridge, Magus was assured by his loyal soldiers that two of Okan's sons were bound and confined in a storage room on the lower deck. When the crafty magician, Toliara, and two guards appeared suddenly on the crowded bridge, they startled Okan.

"Get off the bridge immediately!" he ordered. "This is a difficult stretch of the river and we must have free movement up here. Leave at once!"

"Not so fast, captain. You are no longer giving the orders here," Magus said through Toliara, and motioned for the guards to tie up Bharata and take him below. Toliara told the guards to send another soldier to the bridge.

"What do you mean by this? What do you think you're doing with my son?"

"I am now in command here, and you will do as I say," Magus pronounced with newfound authority. "Now all three of your sons are under armed guard to ensure that you obey my orders. If not, they will be thrown overboard, bound as they are, with a length of chain wrapped around their necks." The visage of the "fisherman" was so contorted with cruelty and malice that Okan recoiled in revulsion.

"You can't do that!"

"I can't? You fool! I've done far worse than that. I wouldn't hesitate for a minute if it advanced my ambitions. Now you listen to me." He pointed to the guard standing next to him. "You will show this man how to steer the ship safely to get us to Bosrah. You will stay here under guard until we reach our destination. If we run aground or if anything happens to this ship, your sons die one by one." Magus grabbed Okan by the throat, pressed him against the bridge console, and leaned into his face. "Do you understand?"

"Yes. I understand." The naval captain choked. He couldn't bear the thought of anything happening to his sons.

Magus stepped outside onto the bridge wing where he could look fore and aft at the mass of people gathered on the deck. He raised his arms in victory and shouted, "The ship is ours!" Cheers from the hundreds below rose in waves to feed his ego. His ambition for world domination was rekindled. He would move on to the next step and take over Bosrah. Toliara stood at his side and joined in the adulation. If she stayed by his side, she was confident that she too would share in the glory of a new world age. If she had known more about Magus she would have dispelled any notion of him sharing anything with her.

Captain Okan was a defeated man. He remained on the bridge to fulfill his duty of keeping the ship, and his sons, safe from harm. The soldier assigned as the helmsman was a quick learner in spite of the language impediment. When dusk approached, he allowed the captain to take the helm himself to anchor for the night. When he was satisfied that the anchor was secure, the boiler was put on standby, and cooking fires on deck were safely monitored, he dismissed the soldier assigned to be the helmsman but he refused to leave. Soon, Magus and Toliara entered the bridge control center with another soldier. Okan wondered to himself why he never noticed how many soldiers were on the ship. This one carried a length of chain in his hand.

"I want to see my sons," Okan demanded. "Are they being fed and cared for?"

"You still don't understand, do you?" Magus mused through his interpreter. "Your situation is hopeless unless you do what I say. You should thank me that your sons are in 'protective custody,' or else the passengers would have killed them by now. They think you and your sons will make them castaways so you can run away with *my* ship. As long as you get us to Bosrah safely they will not be harmed."

With a gesture of his hand the soldier accompanying him stepped forward and roughly clamped the chain around Okan's wrist. He pulled him across the bridge and locked the other end of the chain to a stanchion. Okan was bewildered at the treatment.

"Am I meant to stay here all night?" Okan asked indignantly.

Magus gave his answer by departing for the deck below. Toliara threw him a glare over her shoulder and the guards left him alone on the bridge for the night. Okan sat on the floor and tried to make sense out of what had happened that day. He stayed awake through most of the night thinking of ways he could release his sons and recover the ship from that madman.

While Okan sank into misery, Magus, Toliara, and a crew member named Kalani threaded their way forward on the crowded upper deck by the light of a single lantern. Men, women, and children were settling in for the night, vainly cushioning their weary bodies from the harsh wooden deck. Sleeping on the deck timbers was better than suffocating in the fetid effluvium below decks.

Kalani, the chief gunner's mate, led his new "captain" to the bow, where he removed the tarpaulins that covered the two swivel cannons.

These guns were smaller than the bow chasers on the *Savage* but could be aimed more easily and reloaded faster. The dull bronze finish of the two guns caused them to seemingly melt into the shadows, where it was difficult to distinguish their priming and aiming mechanisms. Nonetheless, after clearing people away, the gunner's mate opened the gun ports, set the guns into their firing positions, and silently demonstrated how they recoiled back when fired and were reloaded. Satisfied that he had one more advantage over the *Dolphin*, Magus instructed the mate to conduct firing practice the next day.

By the time the former chief magician settled into his private tent on the ship's fantail he had convinced himself that his strategy for overtaking Bosrah was foolproof.

CHAPTER 56

Southern Sea, Pele's *Dolphin*

Two days later

Those on the *Dolphin* were thankful that the weather allowed them to easily leave the protected river delta and enter the Southern Sea. Even the natural chop at the confluence of the muddy Euphrates and the aqua-colored ocean was minimal. Pele steered on an eastern heading along the shore and toward the island that he knew was miles away over the horizon. Unfortunately, they would not be within sight of the island until after sunset and thus not be able to enter the dangerously narrow entrance until dawn the next day. Prudence dictated that they wait safely offshore, assuming the wind and waves cooperated, for daylight to show them the channel into Bosrah's protective harbor.

After the boat was anchored in shallow water near the mainland and the barge was tied alongside for the night, Dov and Pele spoke while they secured lines about their plans for reunion with their family in the morning. They expected that the battle cruiser was at least a day behind them. Jengo called to Pele from the barge, where the evening meal was almost ready.

"Pele! Come quickly! You need to hear this right away!" Jengo's voice sounded alarmed.

When Pele and Dov stepped over the railing of the barge they were met by Jengo, who excitedly nudged Singh and said, "Tell the captain what you just told me."

"Well, sir," Singh replied haltingly, "I was just saying that a few days before you met us in the river we picked up a fisherman on a sandbar in the middle of the river. Honest, I never thought anything of it until I said something to Mr. Jengo here, casual-like. Seemed odd to the wife and me at the time that a lone fisherman would be that far from the city, but then I didn't think anything more of it until just now."

"What more? Tell me."

"Yes. Well, it seemed funny that this 'fisherman' as he called himself didn't look or talk like a fisherman at all. Of course, I didn't understand his words exactly, but his voice sounded educated-like. I mentioned to Mr. Jengo here that he wore a fancy gold ring on his right hand. He tried to hide it under his cloak, but I saw it gleam once and that made me more curious. I watched for the ring later to see if it was really made of gold and noticed that it had a bright red stone in the center. That ring must be worth a fortune! Why would somebody with a ring like that be stuck on a sandbar in the middle of nowhere and pretend to be a fisherman?"

"Magus!" Pele blurted in disgust.

"You know him?" Singh asked incredulously. "He sure made friends on the ship quick enough. By the time I joined you all he had the ship's passengers, especially the soldiers and sailors, doing his bidding. Does that mean anything?"

"It means we have a problem," Jengo replied. After sending Singh back to his dinner with the family, Pele, Dov, and Jengo stepped away to discuss what they had just learned. Dov expressed his surprise and frustration. "He watched us the whole time we were beside the ship! He knows who we are and thinks we don't know he's on the *Savage*."

"True," Pele agreed, "and I wouldn't doubt that he has something evil planned for when he arrives at Bosrah with a warship and hundreds of refugees under his control. He's probably promised them the world by now if they go along with whatever he intends. This is a most dangerous situation."

"Yes, but maybe we can blindside him when he arrives at Bosrah. He's so arrogant that he probably can't imagine that we'd find out about him. He thinks he'll be welcomed with open arms by unsuspecting islanders. I'm sure he'll pull some trick when he has a chance. So, maybe it's our turn to trick him." Dov suggested turning the crew and passengers against Magus by exposing him at the right moment as the Chief Magician of Babel who made their lives miserable by forcing them to build his One World Tower.

"We have to get to Bosrah before the *Savage* arrives. They could enter the harbor right behind us in the morning and we wouldn't be able to stop them." Pele left to notify the family that the barge should be prepared for towing as soon as possible. The *Dolphin* would have to risk entering the sheltered harbor of Bosrah through its hazardous channel—in the dark.

Southern Sea, Bosrah Island—Harbor Approach

The volcanic island of Bosrah was formed hundreds of years earlier in the catastrophic upheavals of the Great Flood. Worldwide shifts in the earth's crust uplifted tectonic plates and volcanos erupted where plates collided, separated, and shifted. A large volcano in the Southern Sea exploded, leaving a deep crater or caldera on one side of the island that was engulfed by the raging waves of the sea. The circular crater, surrounded by lava rocks, presented a small opening to the sea with vertical cliffs on the far side opposite the entrance. It was a perfectly shaped deep harbor with shelter from violent Southern Sea storms.

The safety and protection of Bosrah's harbor came at a price: the entrance was so narrow that it could only be used during daylight. Like the pincers of a lobster's claw, the arms of rock on both sides of the entrance threatened to crush anything that passed between them. Pele stood on the *Dolphin's* deck, straining his eyes. The water leading to the approach was deep, so he was not worried about running the *Dolphin* aground inside the approach. His concern for the safety of the vessel, along with his family and passengers, was that he would have no advance warning before he crashed onto the volcanic rocks. He saw a continuous dark line and the silhouette of black cliffs before him against a starlit sky. Somewhere out there was a narrow opening that led to safety. If there were a sea running that night he might have spotted the white foam of waves breaking on the rocks or heard their slapping sound, but tonight the sea was a flat calm and eerily quiet.

Dov was at the helm when his younger eyes noticed a light against the dark cliffs. "Father? Do you see that light halfway up the cliff?"

"I do now," Pele replied a few seconds later. "What is it?"

"I can't tell; it appeared only a minute ago. We're so far out that it's nothing more than a pinpoint of light, but halfway against the dark cliff it's unmistakable. Should I steer for the light?"

"Let's continue slowly forward for now and see if we can distinguish what the light is. Maybe it's a lantern or a torch. Whoever put it there may be trying to guide us in, although I can't imagine who would know that we're trying to enter the harbor tonight," Pele wondered.

After no more than ten minutes, another light appeared low on the horizon and under the upper light, but to its right. Dov became excited when it dawned on him what the lights signified. "Those lights are for us!" he shouted. "I know what they are!" He motioned for his father to come back so he could point to the lights.

"It's parallax! Whoever put those lights up has them aligned with the center of the channel. The top light is farther back from the bottom light, which means that if we move so the lights are in a vertical line, we'll be lined up perfectly with the entrance. We need to steer more westward before they're in a line for us to aim south." He turned the *Dolphin* slowly to starboard and their perspective of the bottom light moved as well. Within minutes the two lights were exactly one above the other. Dov proceeded slowly toward the bottom light while maintaining the two vertically aligned.

When they came closer they saw that the bottom light was a large bonfire whose flames reflected on the calm surface of the sea. "I can see the lower fire clearly now. There's nothing between us and the fire's reflection on the water. That means we're in the entrance channel!"

Still crawling forward at their slowest speed, it took them fifteen minutes more to reach the stone pier at the base of the cliff where the bonfire blazed. A lone man retrieved their mooring lines and tied the *Dolphin* and its barge securely.

"Welcome to Bosrah!" the voice intoned. The speaker was a silhouette against the bright light of the fire. Pele and Dov stood on the pier, while the others disembarked and stretched their legs appreciatively on dry land.

"Let me guess," their greeter began, "it was Dov who figured out the meaning of my range lights, was it not?"

"The Watcher!" Dov recognized the voice. "How . . . ? What . . . ?"

The mysterious man, clad in his usual black clothing, welcomed the crew and passengers. Javak, Kitt, and Ash stood by without speaking. They knew the man's identity but assumed that he would reveal himself to the others in due time. Shadow let out a yelp and jumped from the barge to the pier. He ran to the Watcher and contentedly rubbed against him.

Dov struggled to overcome his shock at seeing the Watcher in Bosrah and being greeted by Shadow with such familiarity. He had so many questions but was exhausted. Everyone milled about on the pier seemingly forgetting why they had made the dangerous landing in the dark. Dov interrupted the excited chatter.

"A battle cruiser will be here in the morning." His urgent warning quieted the crowd and caught the attention of their welcoming emissary. "The island is in danger!"

"What do you mean?" the Watcher asked.

"That battle cruiser loaded with refugees that you passed on the river—that was you I saw riding on the baiji that night wasn't it?—well, it'll be here soon. Magus is on that ship and we think he could be planning to assault the island. We need to prepare for him."

That was enough to spark the Watcher into action. He suggested that they climb up to Cliff Crest where they could refresh themselves and Dov could explain further. There would be no sleep between now and dawn.

CHAPTER 57

Southern Sea, Bosrah Island—Cliff Crest

After midnight

Botwa's home atop the cliff was thrown into turmoil with the arrival of so many guests in the middle of the night. Everyone would be taken care of by the island's residents. Ash rejoined his family and took Benji with him. Saris disappeared into the kitchen. Family greetings were exchanged with warm embraces that needed no translation. During a hastily prepared meal they quickly discovered that there were three languages in their small group: some in the line of Shem, represented by Pele, Jengo, and their families plus Evina, spoke one of the languages; the line of Japheth, represented by Javak's family, including Kitt, and Ash was another; Botwa and his family, although descendants of Shem, spoke something different. The mysterious Watcher moved fluently between the three languages.

Dov could stand it no longer, and voiced his curiosity so energetically that all conversation at the table stopped. "Who *are* you?"

Botwa spoke through the man in question. "You deserve an answer, young Dov. This man's identity has been kept secret from you and your friends for many reasons. You know him as 'the Watcher,' but his name is Tiras, the seventh and last son of Japheth. He is the most skillful member of our community on the island. I do not exaggerate when I say that he is a worthy descendant of Methuselah in his intellectual, creative, and medical abilities."

Botwa continued, "Tiras has a newfound capability since the miraculous fragmentation of our common language into multiple tongues and dialects. The languages at this table are only three of the many languages on the island. At last count there are over twenty different languages here since God changed us a week ago. In that time, Tiras has mastered all of them. If the universal diffusion of languages is a miracle of God, then Tiras is a gift from God to our family and possibly the world. I consider him a *savant* whose abilities are unique in all the world."

Tiras faltered in his translation and shook his head in modesty.

"No, this is true," continued Botwa. "He is an expert in all of the known sciences as well as martial arts and espionage. He is not only multilingual or polylingual, but very likely he is uniquely *omnilingual*, if there is such a thing, thanks to God's work as miraculous as the multiplication of languages itself."

"What was he doing in Babel?" asked Dov.

"I sent Tiras to Babel over a year ago when it came to my attention that the Triad's vision of the future meant permanent slavery for all in the city. My fear was that all of you would become entangled in their one world system and be held hostage to their demands. I commissioned Tiras to be my eyes and ears inside the Triad. He had all of this island's wealth and resources at his disposal. When you advised us of the approaching asteroid, his focus shifted to getting you out of the city as soon as practical. You and your friends, Dov, did not make his task any easier when you attempted to rescue your beautiful bride-to-be."

"How could you know she agreed to be my wife?" Dov sputtered. "That was only three days ago. Were you spying on us then too?" He addressed Tiras directly.

"No, I did not spy on you then," he replied calmly. "I merely made a logical deduction after seeing you jeopardize your life multiple times to save her. The fact that the two of you are from entirely different family lines but speak the same language only validates my logical conclusion." It was evident to Dov that Tiras was both smart and wise. He liked him even more now that he knew his true identity.

"Enough of this discussion about me," Tiras said. "With Botwa's permission, I believe we must discuss a way to deal with the approaching battle cruiser. If it arrives at dawn, which is in a few hours, then we must have a plan that can be implemented quickly. I can tell from his excitement that my young cousin is anxious to share his ideas with us. Will you tell us how we can stop Magus from taking over the island."

Dov gulped nervously and his eyes twitched.

"You're doing it again," his sister said.

"I can't help it. I do that when I'm excited or stressed."

"I know. Which has been a lot lately."

"I think it's cute," Evina said sweetly.

Now Dov was even more nervous with everyone staring at him. Setting his anxiety aside, he outlined something that had been on his mind ever since he found out that Magus was alive and in control of the warship. He wove into his plan the ability of Tiras to speak many languages and to learn new ones almost on the fly. To his relief, Tiras and the others readily agreed to go along with what he suggested. Although most of them had been awake for more than thirty-six hours, they dispersed to accomplish their assigned tasks while a lookout was sent to the highest point of the island to watch for the approaching ship at dawn.

Evina had been at Dov's side while he explained what he thought they should do. They walked out onto the verandah overlooking the dark harbor. "I'm proud of you," she said softly as she stood close to him. "Your plan is sensible and unifies our families to defend the island and our way of life. I'm at peace with whatever God choses to do today. I hope you are too."

"I am," Dov replied with unfamiliar confidence. He held her close in the black night. "When I think about all that's happened to us in the past week it's almost overwhelming. I believe that God's hand was in it all."

CHAPTER 58

Southern Sea, Bosrah Island—Cliff Crest

Early morning

The lookout's call came shortly after sunrise. The sighting on the horizon meant that their overnight planning would be put to the test. Women and children had been busy throughout the early morning packaging food and water for hundreds of refugees. Men worked on the cliff top, readying giant catapults capable of lofting boulders as far as the harbor entrance almost a mile away. A small vapor engine puffed in the background, ready to lower pallets of supplies from Cliff Crest's kitchen to the pier at the base of the cliff. Led by Tiras, half a dozen men descended the carved steps, where they readied a skiff at the pier to row out to the ship when it anchored. They were confident that the captain of the *Defiant* would not bring the ship directly to the pier. He would anchor in the middle of the deep, circular harbor until he knew that the water's depth near the pier could accommodate his large ship. When the depth was confirmed, he would tie to the pier and disembark his passengers.

Dov, Pele, and the rest of the family watched from the verandah of the house as the scene unfolded in the harbor below them. The *Defiant* slowly glided into the harbor in the bright morning sunlight. Unlike the *Dolphin's* harrowing experience in the dark, the battle cruiser maneuvered easily in a gentle arc to stop with its bow pointed out toward the harbor entrance. Their effortless anchorage in the center of the harbor meant that the captain of the *Defiant* was still in control of the ship's steerage. No sooner had the anchor dropped into the translucent turquois water than Tiras pulled away from the pier at the helm of the skiff. The Watcher was certain that Magus would not recognize him.

The refugees on the *Defiant* clamored to the side of the ship in order to peer at the small boat, rowed by six rough looking men and guided by a man whose bearing and clothing spoke of his authority. This time, Captain Okan said nothing when the ship listed sharply from the weight of hundreds pressed against the railings. Tiras directed his hail to the two men and one woman standing motionless on the bridge wing who observed him stoically.

"Who are you and what is your purpose here?" Tiras replied in a language that Singh told him sounded like that spoken by Toliara. On his first attempt he received confirmation that he had chosen the correct language.

"We come in peace," the woman replied while Magus whispered what to say. "We wish only to seek refuge ashore for food and water for us and our children. We have escaped from the destruction of the city of Babel. Will you help us?"

"You are an armed warship of King Nimrod's navy! How can we trust that you are here in peace? I wish to speak with your captain." Tiras wanted to determine if the man in the captain's uniform was actually in charge of the vessel or if Magus had taken over the ship. Magus stood close to the grim-faced captain. Toliara made no attempt to lower her voice as she spoke with Magus and the captain. Tiras overheard and soon made out their conversation. He made a mental note of the languages used by each.

"You can see that our people are starving," Toliara said as she motioned to those lining the side of the ship. "We cannot survive if you do not help us. Please!" There was no question that sanitation on the ship was appalling. Men, women, and children were starving and dehydrated. Their situation was desperate, but Tiras stuck to what they had agreed.

"I cannot allow you to come ashore now. I am sorry. There is obvious sickness aboard your ship. I cannot risk infecting those on our island until I have conducted a medical inspection. That will take one or two days."

The discussion between Magus and Captain Okan, with Toliara translating rapidly between them, became more animated. Magus said something to Toliara that caused her to recoil. Magus then motioned to the gun crew to turn the nearest cannon on the small boat. Now Tiras knew who was in charge.

Tiras was prepared for this, and stood immovable at the helm of the rocking skiff as if he did not notice the movement of the gun crew at the bow of the ship. He held his gaze on Toliara.

"The captain says that a storm is coming," Toliara translated. "We must stay in this safe harbor until it passes. He cannot expose families on the open deck to a storm that could kill them."

"Do I have your word that you will not attempt to come ashore until I have inspected the sick passengers and given my approval?" Tiras asked.

Toliara looked at Magus and then back at Tiras. "Of course. You have the captain's word."

Tiras suppressed a smile. The uniformed captain, obviously under duress, was someone he could probably trust; Magus could be trusted no more than a common pirate—maybe less. He moved the negotiation to the next phase. "I am satisfied with your pledge," he replied solemnly. "To prove that we are not without compassion, I will bring food and water to you now to relieve your immediate suffering. This is a good-faith gesture which I trust you will honor by remaining on the ship."

He instructed his rowers to pull away from the ship a short distance. He shouted a final warning: "You will be watched at all times, and if anyone attempts to leave the ship we will retaliate with force." Tiras pointed to the cliffs behind him and waved a white cloth over his head. Within seconds, a black speck lifted into the morning sky from behind stone ramparts to one side of Cliff Crest. The object flew high over the harbor and converged rapidly on the ship. A collective gasp rose from the passengers. A gigantic boulder hit the surface of the calm water within fifty feet of the *Defiant*. A geyser lifted into the air and drenched the deck. The destructive power and accurate aim of the catapult were obvious.

Tiras shouted louder to make himself heard by Toliara over the screams of terror. "If you do not hold to your promise, your ship will be destroyed instantly. If you attempt to hold anyone hostage when we bring food or water, we will not hesitate to reply with similar force."

The rowboat reversed its direction to return to the pier. So far everything was moving along as planned. Dov watched from above and hoped that their demonstration of the catapult's lethality was enough to deter Magus, for today anyway. Given the magician's arrogance he doubted that he cared if people were hurt or the ship was destroyed, as long as he saved his own skin.

When Tiras returned to the shore from his brief negotiation with the ship's captain he initiated the process of ferrying relief to the passengers. A vapor-powered crane lowered crates of food and barrels of water to the base of the cliff where barges convoyed supplies to the ship. A party of men boarded first to establish the orderly distribution of food and water. After pushing and shoving at first, there developed a loose semblance of order at feeding stations for the hungry and thirsty masses. The multitude of languages, the desperately filthy conditions, and the tight confines of the ship kept the well-intentioned humanitarian aid on the edge of pandemonium. Tiras led a team to identify those most in need of medical care. In the misery of packed bodies below the hot deck of the ship the smell was overwhelming. Clearly passengers had to leave the ship in the next twenty-four hours or deaths would begin multiplying. By tomorrow the distress could turn to anarchy. The islanders had done all they could for now.

Tiras was exhausted when he boarded the last boat for the island at sunset. He looked back at the naval cruiser and ached for the poor souls unwittingly misled by the most devious man on the planet. Amazingly, the linguistic savant was now sufficiently conversant in enough languages to set a trap for Magus in the morning that could free all those helpless captives on the *Defiant*.

Dov and the others met Tiras at the pier in the shadow of the cliff. "Do you think he'll try to reach the island tonight?" Dov asked.

"I'm certain of it," Tiras replied. "Magus is an opportunist and a liar. I'm sure he'll send someone ashore as soon as it's dark so he can bring the ship to the pier by morning. We'll be ready for him."

Southern Sea, Bosrah Island Harbor—Royal Battle Cruiser *HRS Defiant*

Late at night

As Tiras suspected, the wily magician had no intention of honoring the captain's so-called "promise." No sooner had the last relief worker left the ship than he gathered a half-dozen soldiers who shared his ruthless ambition. They would scout out the harbor pier area and then sabotage the giant catapults that threatened the *Defiant*.

"I've studied the pier and the catapult on the cliff top using the captain's distance glass," Magus explained through Toliara. "You must measure the depth of the water between our ship and the pier. Is it sufficient for the battle cruiser's draft, which the captain tells me is twelve feet? Also, the catapults are accurate and lethal at great distances out to the mouth of the harbor, but they cannot target us when we are tied to the pier directly under them at the base of the cliff. You must destroy their catapult firing mechanism or render it inoperable. You must also destroy the vapor engine of the crane used to lower supplies down the cliff. I will move the ship in the darkness before the moon rises and tie it to the pier. When the crew and passengers are released they will do our work for us. Their instincts for survival will take over and they will overwhelm the island defenders in their sleep. By dawn the island will be ours!"

The *Defiant's* crew silently lowered three boats into the water when the cloudless sky was completely dark except for stars that cast their light on the mirror-like surface of the harbor. The moon had not yet risen and the wind had died. Each one of the three boats was propelled slowly by oars wrapped with rags to muffle their splashes. The scouting boat, rowed by soldiers armed with axes for disabling the catapult and vapor engine, headed in the direction of the pier, while two other crews of sailors attached ropes from their boats to the bow of the cruiser and prepared to tow it slowly to shore when they saw the lantern signal that all was clear.

The lone boat of soldiers slowly took soundings along its way. The water's depth exceeded the draft of the cruiser with clearance to spare. When they drifted into the pier pilings with a mild bump, they waited for a sentry to sound an alarm. When none came, their leader motioned for a final depth measurement and was pleased to find a five-foot margin over the draft of the ship at the pier. When the tide rose in the morning they would have even more clearance. After five minutes waiting in the silence next to the pilings, one of the soldiers climbed a ladder to see if anyone was guarding the dock. When he found none, he whistled and the others joined him after tying the boat. Confident that there was no lookout, they moved quietly as a group toward the stairs that led up the face of the cliff to the ramparts high above.

After minutes of climbing the cliff stairs, the team's leader looked toward the harbor and identified their ship as only a murky smudge, slightly darker than the shoreline in the far distance. All lights had been extinguished and the two boats were ready to tow the ship. They had to disable the catapult and vapor engine quickly and give the arranged signal to move the ship before the calm harbor became bathed in moonlight. Confident that he and his men could reach the top and finish their mission in plenty of time, he continued steadily upward. He noticed indentations, at regular intervals, in the side of the cliff that added a shelf or platform a few feet wide next to the stairs. Resting spots, he thought, and paid them little attention. He never noticed the thin, almost invisible, fishing net.

When Dov dropped a net on the group's leader he became entangled to the point of being unable to retaliate with his axe, and was also thrown off balance so that his only concern became not falling off the side of the cliff. He panicked and shouted to alert the others behind him before Pele's hands clamped over his mouth and pulled him into the nearest niche in the side of the cliff.

The cry of alarm threw the five behind their leader into a frenzied retreat. Jengo, Javak, Kitt, Yanis, and Evina each released nets on them and their bundled bodies were soon carried by others to the top of the cliff. Even though some of them cried out, their voices did not carry out to the battle cruiser where Magus waited for the all clear signal that never came. Had the soldiers left a lookout at their boat tied under the dock he might have heard the alarms from above and returned to the ship with information. In the silence that shrouded the circular harbor Magus could only stomp back and forth on the ship's bridge and mutter in frustration. When the moon rose above the shoreline and he could see and be seen clearly, he called the two small boats back to the ship and fled to his tent in a rage. So they were discovered and this attempt had failed! No matter. In the morning he would explain the incursion as that of a desperate captain and overzealous soldiers. He was confident that he could talk his way onto the island tomorrow in spite of this setback.

CHAPTER 59

Southern Sea, Bosrah Island Harbor—Royal Battle Cruiser *HRS Defiant*

Next morning

Tiras was more worried about this final step in the plan because everything hinged on his ability to persuade the passengers and crew of the *Defiant* to turn on Magus before the sorcerer could retaliate against him. The linguistic savant was the only one who could make it happen. His brain ached from the many languages bouncing around inside his head. He had conversed with hundreds of people yesterday, while at the same time using his considerable medical skills to comfort them. He tossed and turned in his bed while mentally parsing the many dialects he had learned and deciding which dozen or so he would use to maximum effect. He was exhausted from the intensity of effort and lack of rest. He looked out on the ship before him in the morning light and wondered how he could be successful.

As the skiff moved slowly toward the cruiser, the six rowers choked from the smell of overnight sewage dumped into the pale blue waters of the harbor. Shadow sat in silence next to Tiras. "Get us upwind so I can clear my head and speak without retching," Tiras ordered. The rowers needed no more encouragement to put their backs into turning around to the other side of the ship. They gulped fresh air and held the bow of their skiff pointed into the wind and the rising chop. Their backs were turned toward the ship and Tiras faced the side, which was now lined with people hoping for more water and food.

He told his rowers to ease closer to the ship where he could see Magus and Toliara on the bridge and speak directly to them. The captain was not in sight. Tiras waited a full minute and then spoke in the language that Toliara could understand; he still did not want to reveal that he understood Magus' every word.

"Your attempt to come ashore last night was most unwise. I told you there would be consequences if you betrayed your promise. Today there will be no food or water."

A sharp cry went up from a few along the railing who understood him. When Toliara translated this to Magus, he expressed mock astonishment. He spoke through Toliara, "Honestly, we know nothing of this. It must have been the captain's doing on his own initiative. We do not see why these poor people should suffer for his stupidity. When will we be allowed to come ashore?"

The imposter's innocent look and contrived answer came as no surprise to Tiras. It was clear that Magus would continue to play him for a fool. He was fine with that because it meant that he suspected nothing. He still thought Tiras and the simple islanders to be naïve.

Tiras whispered a command to the rowers, and the boat drew closer to the side of the ship. He took a deep breath, looked at the people along the railing, and spoke directly to them.

"My friends, I have bad news for you," he began, using a dialect that Toliara did not know but a half-dozen of the families before him understood. "You have been betrayed by the man that you rescued from the river a week ago, and because of him we will give you no more food or water. He told you he was a poor fisherman, but he is not. He is Magus, Chief Magician of Babel, and a member of the Triad. He is lying to you and is using you as he did when he taxed you and forced you to build his foolish tower. This is the truth. Do you wish to be free on our island, or do you choose to be slaves to Magus and suffer under his tyranny?"

Those who understood his words did not know what to make of them at first. They were being pressed to choose between the smooth-talking magician and this man who asked that they trust him instead.

When Tiras proceeded to make the same speech in other languages, Magus demanded that Toliara translate, but she could not. His suspicions mounted as he puzzled over what was happening before his eyes. Why was this man speaking directly to the passengers? What was he saying?

Finally, a former tower guard, who thought he had recognized Magus when he first came aboard, spoke up. "Yes! I've seen that man before! Among the tower guards he was known as 'Magus the Maggot,' and everyone hated him. I've seen him joking and laughing in the presence of King Nimrod and the high priest. He's not a fisherman! He's an imposter!" Those who understood the guard spoke up in outrage. Others asked among the other passengers for the meaning of the commotion.

Kalani, the gunner's mate, thought back to how the "fisherman" had given him orders to prepare to fire on the *Dolphin*. He could only shake his head in disbelief at how foolish he had been to believe him. He motioned his counterpart at the other bow chaser to quench the burning wicks kept at the ready for the magician's orders to fire. They would not be discharging their guns today.

Neither Magus nor Toliara understood what was being said. However, the magician sensed from the way the passengers stared at him that Tiras was speaking about him. He saw indecision, confusion, and hatred in the movement of the crowd. He shouted to the gun crew and motioned for them to fire on the skiff from pointblank range. The gunners looked from the gunner's mate to Magus on the bridge to Tiras in the waiting skiff and remained immobile. Kalani shook his head. Toliara shouted commands at them, but they ignored her. It was clear that they and many of the crew had been persuaded. Now for the clincher, thought Tiras.

Still addressing the passengers, Tiras gave his ultimatum. "Turn Chief Magician Magus over to us and you'll be welcomed ashore now and given all that you need. You'll be free to stay on Bosrah Island or depart as you wish. If you refuse, you will be fired upon. You will not set foot on our island. *Turn him over to us now!*" He quickly gave his ultimatum in as many languages as he could recall and waited.

Two soldiers, who stood silently inside the wheelhouse guarding the captain, moved into the sunlight and clamped a burly hand on each of the magician's arms. He sputtered as they bound his hands behind his back and easily lifted him off his feet. They manhandled him down the stairs to the main deck while he struggled to no effect. When the skiff drew alongside they threw him into the boat and he landed in a heap on the skiff's oak bottom at the feet of the rowers. A cheer arose from the crowd on the deck. When the dazed magician blinked in the morning sunlight, he faced Jengo and Pele holding their oars. Shadow bared his sharp teeth in a savage snarl.

"Oh, no!" Magus moaned.

Tiras looked up at Captain Okan, who had assumed his rightful place on the bridge of the *Defiant*. The two smiled at the irony of what had just happened. "Captain, you may disembark your passengers at our pier. The water there is deep and the welcome will be hearty!" Tiras removed his wide brim hat and waved to the shore which was lined with islanders. A cheer went up that echoed off the cliff and across the harbor. Within twenty minutes black smoke poured from the stack of the *Defiant*, her anchor was raised and she moved slowly toward freedom.

By the time Jengo and Pele carried Magus up the cliff and deposited him on the grass behind Botwa's house, he was literally foaming at the mouth in rage. His cursing and threatening were starting to grate on the family.

"What should we do with him?" Dov asked. "We spent so much time planning a way to get him off the ship and into custody, that we haven't talked about that."

"I'll leave it to Jengo and Pele to come up with something appropriate," Botwa said. "You know him better than any of us and appreciate how dangerous he can be. My suggestion for now is to chain him in one of my kennels away from the house where we won't have to listen to his foul cursing. He'll have water, food, and shelter from the sun. My dogs will keep him company." Dov gave the instruction to Saris who stepped forward with a broad smile, grabbed Magus by his arms, and dragged the whimpering weasel to the dog pens.

Pele spoke up as they walked back to Botwa's house. "Although I'd just as soon push that scoundrel off the cliff, I think we should take Magus and Toliara with us when we leave the island on the *Dolphin*."

"What?" exclaimed Dov. "Take them with us?"

"I'll explain in a minute," Pele assured him.

They joined Yanis, Evina, and the others on the verandah for their first real meal since they arrived. Elsewhere in the house several families from the ship were washing in fresh water.

"It was always my intention since we left Babel to replenish here in Bosrah and then move onward in the *Dolphin* to start afresh as a family. Clearly, God is giving us a second chance to obey Him and spread over the earth as He commanded after the Great Flood. We'll gather supplies for an extended voyage that will take us to another land far from the influence of Babel." There was full agreement with what Pele had in mind.

"But why in the world would we take Magus and that woman with us?" Evina asked as they ate. She'd heard of Pele's intention and was as shocked as everyone else.

"They won't stay with us for the entire trip," Pele assured his future daughter-in-law. "We'll leave both of them far from here, and far from us, where they'll never bother anyone else again. Like I said, my feelings toward Magus are that he should die for all the evil and misery he has caused others. Toliara was a willing partner in the mutiny and shares responsibility for the harm done to Captain Okan and his sons. A fitting punishment would be to make them live with the harsh consequences of their hatred. We'll drop them off on a jungle infested island where they can't harm anyone."

"I can accept that," Evina said emphatically. She turned to Yanis with a girlish grin on her face. "Now, we have weddings to prepare!"

CHAPTER 60

Southern Sea, Bosrah Island

Two months later

Dov and Evina stood as husband and wife one evening on the stone pier beside the *Dolphin*, which had been loaded with fuel and supplies for its voyage the next morning into the Southern Sea and new, unexplored lands. To their right was Nimrod's *HRS Defiant* battle cruiser, which had been converted into a passenger vessel and renamed *Virtue*. Workers covered in black dust finished transferring fuel from rail carts where black rock was dumped down chutes into bulk storage below decks of the converted warship. The *Dolphin* and the *Virtue* would depart from Bosrah together. When the turquois sea waters met the deep indigo of open ocean a week's journey south, their vapor engines would take them in opposite directions to places that they could hardly imagine. According to Botwa, there were lush green lands in both directions where they could start new civilizations. The couple's excitement for adventure was only slightly tempered with fear of the unknown.

"Four months ago you knocked at Pele's workshop door looking for my father to build you a fancy predictor engine," Dov said. "You were a fearful young astronomer and mathematician searching for answers in the universe. I'm glad you came back that night."

Evina wrapped her arm around his waist. "Back then I was a girl afraid of death more than anything. All I saw was a horrible fate for my city, my family, and myself. God graciously made Himself known through His universe and I believed in Him, thanks to loving encouragement from you and Yanis. He's been gracious to us in countless ways, hasn't He?"

"Yes. You were a gift to me from God. He's taken care of us ever since. I must say that life has been 'exciting' since I met you," Dov mused.

"If you call being imprisoned, chased through dank corridors by attackers, climbing down a tower ascender shaft, plunging into the Euphrates River from an aerial cable, being fired at by a battle cruiser, and outwitting an evil magician, not to mention facing global annihilation by an asteroid and now being surrounded by people babbling in unknown tongues *exciting*, then I suppose so. Will we have more excitement where we're going?"

"Not the same kind of excitement, I hope, but I guarantee plenty of action and adventure. We'll eventually settle in the wilds somewhere and build a place to live. We'll have children, lots of them, and grow old watching sunrises and sunsets together. However, there may be no astronomy or advanced mathematics in your immediate future." Evina gave him a mock frown. "Then again, you never know," he added quickly. "You might persuade me to build you a telescope; you can teach our children about the planets and stars. Most of all, we'll teach them about the wonderful God who created all that exists and who cares for them. Sound like a good life to you?"

"Heavenly," Evina sighed as she drew her new husband close to her. "We'll do all of that and more—you and me—together forever."

Kitt and Yanis strolled along the top of the cliff overlooking the circle of crystal clear water below. Behind them, the giant catapult stood silent amid the weeds. A vapor engine hissed in the distance, lowering last minute supplies down to the pier. The *Dolphin* and the *Virtue* looked small against the placid seascape that extended to the far horizon. With language differences between them almost a thing of the past, the couple made plans for the new life that was ready to unfold before them. Pele had suggested that Kitt and Yanis come with him and the family on their westward journey, but they had not given him their final decision. Kitt's language was not a major factor any longer, certainly not between him and Yanis; they had been learning each other's languages since the miracle happened. An inexplicable feeling was building inside Kitt that kept him from agreeing to go with Pele.

"It's hard to describe," Kitt said as they walked together. "I feel this nagging restlessness; an urge to be on the move, either on land or sea, to explore new places. If I had to settle in one place for the rest of my life I wouldn't be able to stand it. Even now, on Bosrah Island, I can't stay much longer. I can't explain it," he lamented. "It's like an itch that I can't reach. I don't think I'd be satisfied unless I was on the move."

Yanis sympathized with him. "Whatever you decide to do, I'm with you all the way," she assured him. "When Dov and Evina find a place to their liking they'll settle there and raise their family. I think Pele feels the same way. He's getting old and hopes to die with his grandchildren around him. That's fine for them, but I want to be wherever you are."

"Imagine that," Kitt said in astonishment. "You're willing to leave your amazing family behind and come with me, even though I have no idea where I'm going. We'll be on the move all the time."

"Hannah was an adventurous sort too," Yanis observed.

"She was quite a woman," Kitt agreed. "She married Grandfather Japheth one day after she met him and she promised to be with him wherever he went. Once they settled most of the family on Bosrah, they loaded their boat with other children and grandchildren and headed off to parts unknown. We've never heard from them since. That was almost a hundred years ago. Maybe our family is destined to be nomadic," Kitt wondered.

"I have an idea! Let's ask Father if he'd be willing to give us the *Dolphin* after he, Dov, Evina, and the others find places to put down roots. If he agrees, we'll load it with fuel and supplies and see how far we can go before the old *Dolphin* finally rusts out. How does that sound?"

Kitt's answer was a lingering kiss. Silently he thanked God for a wife whose wisdom was more valuable than riches and for a spirit of adventure that matched his.

Next morning

Aided by Botwa and the other islanders, some of the refugees from the old *Defiant* had already departed Bosrah's harbor in small boats and begun their migration around the globe. For centuries before, migratory islanders had built boats, provisioned them from the island's abundant resources, and bid farewell to friends and family with no expectation of ever seeing them again. Now Botwa was doing the same, and it was his way of encouraging and helping others to obey God's command to spread around the earth. Because of work by him, and many who went before, thousands had already reached distant lands that he would never see. The largest numerical migration in history would finally begin that morning to touch the far corners of the globe. It took God's miracle of languages to make this a reality.

An air of excitement mixed with sadness was palpable among the crowd who stood on the stone pier that held the *Dolphin* and the *Virtue* with the last strands of rope connecting them to what they would think back on as the Old World. The *Dolphin's* barge was loaded to its limit with black rock fuel and supplies. Pele's family and other passengers crowded the deck of the runabout waving goodbye to their remaining family and friends and a small gathering of other islanders on the pier. A smile creased Botwa's weathered face and tears welled in his eyes. He forced a smile to give his extended family a final measure of encouragement. Pele motioned for the lines to be cast off and gave a shrill blast on the *Dolphin's* vapor whistle that caused the onlookers to jump, though everyone expected it. Laughter mixed with the whistle's echo and reverberated from the cliff and out into the harbor. Shadow stood next to Tiras and barked his final farewell. The *Virtue*, carrying more than one hundred excited passengers, released a deep blast from its horn, and the crowd cheered. Co-captains Okan and Ghamal waved from the bridge wing while Okan's son, Bharata, spun the wheel and expertly eased the giant ship away from the dock.

Islanders threw flowers and wreaths into the water as a sign of their final farewell and prayed that their family and friends would have smooth sailing, wherever their craft would take them. When the two vessels trailed slowly through the narrow harbor entrance for the last time, they sounded long farewell blasts that reached the remaining crowd and dwindled into the cloudless sky.

The Great Ocean

One week later

The two vessels steered opposite courses and sounded their vapor whistles in final farewells across the blue ocean. They watched each other until black plumes of smoke disappeared over the horizon.

"Now we're alone," lamented Dov's little brother Maasi, who had climbed up on the railing to catch the last glimpse of the *Virtue.*

"Not at all," Dov replied as he scooped the youngster in his arms before he fell overboard.

Evina rubbed the little boy's head. "What Dov means is that, no matter where we go, we'll never be alone. Just like your great-grandfather, Noah, and the others on the ark, we have the presence of God with us. We can't see Him, but we know He's always with us."

"Someday your Aunt Evina will show you the stars through the telescope I'll make for her and you'll come to appreciate how great our God is. Yet, our infinite God is never far from us. She'll tell you all about those stars and how she came to know the One who created them."

Maasi lifted his face and squinted into the clear sky. "I'd like that."

EPILOG

The fictional characters in this story represent a few of the hundreds of thousands that could have suffered in the time of Nimrod, lived in the city of Babel, and worked to build the tower whose name is forever linked to confusion and dispersion. Some of the worldwide migration prompted by the miracle of languages is listed in Genesis Chapter 10 where the emphasis is on families who moved by land to the north, east, and west. Those families grew into tribes and then nations that influenced Biblical history even to the present day.

Our characters were drawn by the sea to begin new civilizations, some of which remained isolated and undiscovered for thousands of years.

The *Dolphin* and the *Virtue* steamed their separate ways where the Persian Gulf meets the Indian Ocean. It took months for the *Dolphin* to slowly make its way along the east coast of Africa. The *Dolphin's* passengers were relieved when they put Magus and Toliara ashore on Madagascar to fend for themselves. Dov and Evina found modern day Kenya to their liking and were joined by Pele and Jengo and their families. Kitt and Yanis took the little *Dolphin* farther than anyone could have imagined. After crossing the South Atlantic Ocean, they abandoned their decaying boat somewhere on the Amazon River. Kitt and Yanis' descendants populated the southern continent to the Pacific Ocean before seafaring clans migrated westward across the Pacific.

The rugged *Virtue* deposited families from the coast of India to the continent of Australia, where the former warship ended its life on a reef. Captains Okan and Ghamal abandoned their vessel there and led their families deep into Australia's interior. They lived the rest of their lives without seeing the ocean again.

Tiras had different plans. He and his family, accompanied by Shadow, trekked back to the Plain of Shinar where he retrieved books written in the original language of Shem and Japheth. He spent the rest of his life deciphering and translating them into understandable languages. Tiras eventually settled along the Nile River where he and his descendants began a new civilization rich in agriculture, art and technology.

A descendant of Tiras (Imhotep) will be featured in a sequel to this book that takes place around Israel's exodus from Egypt.

AFTERWORD

Five or six generations after humanity scattered across the globe from the plain of Shinar, the Bible tells us that Abram (later named Abraham) . . . *believed in the LORD; and He* [God] *accounted it to him* [Abram] *for righteousness.* (Genesis 15:6) God accepted Abram because he believed (trusted) in what God said about Himself.

Faith or trust in God's revealed truth about Himself has always been the basis for individual salvation—coming into a right relationship with God. This was the case for Noah and his children before the Flood, for those who lived in the time of Babel, for Abram in Chaldea, for Christians in the first century, for us today. However, the scope and detail of God's revelation has progressed from early, observable creation, to the accumulated, preserved writings of the apostles and prophets in the Bible. (Hebrews 1:2; Ephesians 2:20, 3:5; II Peter 1:20-21)

Our completed Bible has more revelation about who God is than at any other time in history. This divinely inspired book—the Word of God—also shows us who we are and how we can be right with Him. (II Peter 1:3) It shows us how infinitely offensive our sin is to God (Romans 3:10-12, 23); He cannot allow anything sinful into His holy presence. (Isaiah 59:2; I John 1:5) As painful as it is, the Bible brings us face-to-face with the reality of our sin. We cannot "buy off" God to earn His favor, do something good, or promise to stop sinning, because all that is impossible. (Isaiah 64:6-7; Hebrews 11:6) Instead, God has a solution to our most pressing sin problem. We must believe Him and approach Him *by faith* on His terms.

The infinite offense of our sin against a holy God requires infinite compensation by a perfect person. God sent His Perfect Son, Jesus

Christ, to earth to die as a human being in our place. (Romans 5:8) The idea that God's own divine Son, the second person of the Trinity, would shed His blood on the cross of Calvary as an infinite substitute for our sin should strike us like a bolt of lightening. Jesus' death is not some long-ago, dry, abstract fact. The historical, divine Jesus of the Bible died for *me personally* so all my sins would be forgiven, so I'd be right with God and so I would be born into God's family! (John 3:3, 7; I John 2:2)

How does someone benefit from this wonderful truth? The simple answer comes straight from the Bible: *believe on the Lord Jesus Christ and you will be saved.* (Acts 16:31) Faced with the impossibility of paying for your sin or earning your way into heaven, you must come to God His way if you want to be right with Him. (John 1:12-13; 14:6) You have a wonderful opportunity that is freely offered: believe on God's Son as your sin substitute and receive Him as your Savior. As humbling as that is to do, it is what God says is your simple part in His plan. This offer of a free, perfect salvation is given to anyone who will believe God and accept the person and work of His Son *by faith.* (Acts 2:21; Romans 10:13) Will you believe God, receive Jesus Christ as your Savior and enter into God's family?

More information about how to have a relationship with Jesus Christ can be found at http://michaelvetter.net